"K. Patrick Malone, heir-apparent to the title of 'King of Horror' may aptly be labeled 'Prince of the Macabre' as his legion of readers will testify....and so will I, as I am one of the legion..." *Margaret LeNois, Author, Cremator's Revenge*

Praise for Malone's

INSIDE A HAUNTED MIND

"One may get so lost in this story that the conclusion comes as somewhat a shock. One factor that gives this story its tone— almost missed due to its subtleness—is Malone's uncanny ability to portray Chagford's downward spiral toward insanity. It is as if he himself has experienced what it is like to be 'inside a haunted mind'. The book is an excellent work, but only those able to handle graphic descriptions of depraved violence should enter Malone's world of terrifying horror."...Nelly Heitman...*ForeWord Magazine Book Review*

~

"This is a good, old-fashioned ghost story complete with an old, creepy house, spirits and flying furniture. Or is it? Could it be nothing more than the illusions of a **haunted** and disturbed mind? The reader will have to pay close attention to figure it out. At times the vividly created characters wrap readers up in their stories and eventually they are all tied to a set of long-ago murders....overall, a good read."....*Chattanooga Times Free Press*

~

"A dark story about a relentless evil force closing in on small town police chief Chagford. A suspense-laden deconstruction of a good man's mind gone terribly wrong, laced with shocking revelations and edge-of-the seat tension."....*Midwest Book Reviews*

THE DIGGER'S REST

"When people search for proof of the legendary King Author, few think to hunt down his skeleton. *THE*

DIGGER'S REST is a story of a team of archaeologists as they dig through the ruins of an ancient medieval castle for the body of Arthur. While they begin to shine a new light on one of history's mysteries, the terrifying discovery isn't the one they were looking for. Adventure blended in a large bit of horror, THE DIGGER'S REST is a solid pick for suspense readers."…..The Midwest Book Review

~

"Outstanding bit of writing, sure to keep the reader enthralled until the final unexpected twist…..A must for the readers of the Stephen King ilk…." Mid-Atlantic Review.

~

"Now and then an author comes along who tops each of his preceding work with one that is even better. Malone is already an adult in the realm of the macabre, and continues to grow with this latest chilling novel. THE DIGGER'S REST…Read it if you dare"……J. Jackson Owensby, author of Deliberate Indifference and My Sister and I: We Are Survivors.

Inside A Haunted Mind

****Honorable Mention, Hollywood Book Festival, 2007****
****Winner, USA Book News National Best Books Awards, 2008****
****Honorable Mention, Arizona Author's Association, 2008****
****Honorable Mention, San Francisco Book Festival, 2009****
****Wild Card Winner, New England Book Festival, 2009****

The Digger's Rest

****Honorable Mention, New York Book Festival, 2008****
****Honorable Mention, Hollywood Book Festival, 2008****
****Honorable Mention, New England Book Festival, 2009****

An Unfinished House

****1st Runner-up Winner, New York Book Festival 2009****

AN
UNFINISHED
HOUSE

AN UNFINISHED HOUSE

by

By K. Patrick Malone

Argus Enterprises International, Inc.
North Carolina***New Jersey

An Unfinished House

A-Argus Better Book
For information:
Argus Enterprises International, Inc.
P O Box 914
Kernersville, NC 27284
www.a-argusbooks.com

ISBN:
9780981907581
098190758X

Book Cover by Dubya

Printed in the United States of America

Dedication

Dedicated to all the contractors, workmen, carpenters and woodworkers that I have had the great privilege of knowing in my life. They make our homes warm, safe, comfortable and beautiful. However, they rarely, if ever, reveal their backaches, hardships and heartaches, seeming to the outside world to be "tough as nails," but in reality hiding fragile souls and hearts as big as the outdoors they work in through all weather. So it is with great pride that they have felt secure enough to reveal themselves to me as they truly are. I feel so honored. You've tapped into a part of my soul I didn't know was there and I will now never live without. Here's to you guys, blisters, splinters, callouses and all. *"Bang, bang! Thump, thump! Crash, bang, thump, vrrrroooommm."* KPM

"Blame it all on my roots, I showed up in boots . . .Yee haaa!"

I've got Friends in Low Places
Garth Brooks

Acknowledgments

Thanks to Trish (Goddess) Moore. It just goes to show you how a random chance meeting can prove so very creative; to Mike & Rona A., my most very special readers. Your support and encouragement has meant more than I can say and for me that's going a distance; to John and Anna Dorsey for sharing my artistic eye, and to GHE9 whose particular inspiration made *An Unfinished House* possible.

"He came to the river Jordan, Saint Peter on the other side, singing 'good ride, cowboy, good ride'."

Good Ride Cowboy
Garth Brooks

<u>BOOK ONE</u>

Sleight of Hand

I'm waking up at the start of the end of the worl,
but its feeling just like every other morning before
Now I wonder what my life is going to mean if it's gone
The cars are moving like a half a mile an hour and I started staring at the
passengers who're waving good-bye
can you tell me what was ever really special about me all this time?

But I believe the world is burning to the ground
oh well I guess we're gonna find out
let's see how far we've come
let's see how far we've come
Well I, believe, it all, is coming to an end
oh well, I guess, we're gonna pretend,
let's see how far we've come

I think it turned ten o'clock but I do't really know
then I can't remember caring for an hour or so
started crying and I couldn't stop myself
I started running but there's no where to run to
I sat down on the street, took a look at myself
said where you going man you know the world is headed for hell
say all goodbyes if you've got someone you can say goodbye to

I believe the world is burning to the ground
oh well I guess we're gonna find out
let's see how far we've come
let's see how far we've come

Well I, believe, it all, is coming to an end
oh well, I guess, we're gonna pretend,
let's see how far we've come

How Far We've Come
Rob Thomas & Matchbox 20

Chapter One

Cruel Magic

M ike Golden sat quietly on a pallet of bagged mortar in the late autumn sun, bent over with a book in his hand, his lunch half eaten by his side. He heard the sound of footsteps come up behind him. "Reverend Willis!" he said, brightly smiling as he turned his head to see the shiny black face framed with a white collar approaching slowly with the aid of a walking stick.

"I jus' came by to see how things were goin', Michael. Sorry I missed you last week. I had a holy roller convention in Newark," the old man said laughing. "So whatcha readin' *this* week, son?"

"It's called *Brideshead Revisited*, by an Englishman named Evelyn of all things," Mike replied, a little embarrassed. He'd spent most of his adult life hiding from the world the fact that he couldn't get enough English and American literature, and especially the fact that he had to wear glasses to do it. He was a contractor, after all, rough and tough, none too sensitive, and dirty most of the time. It would ruin his image if anyone knew that he was in the middle of reading the *Modern Library's List of the Top 100 Novels of the Century*. Only Jane really knew about his passion for books, and understood how he came by it. She was the only one he ever told that it was how he managed to come through the battlefield of shouts, slaps, bellows and screams that was his parents' marriage; hiding in the laundry room out of the line of fire with a book in his hand.

There he discovered a world where all he ever had to do to escape was to turn the pages, and he'd be transported to some other place, some other time, become somebody else. Otherwise, he was pretty successful at his camouflage. With his black hair shaved, rugged features, outdoor complexion and big, burly build, no one would ever have guessed just by looking at him…but the Reverend Willis was no fool. He knew the old adage about the eyes being the windows to the soul was true.

The old man reached into his jacket pocket and pulled out a small volume. "I thought about you while I was gone," the Reverend said, handing Mike the book. "I found it in a used book store when I was out one day and couldn't help but get it for you," he said smiling with satisfaction. The sun behind him made his black-clothed figure and skin seem like a silhouette. "It's called *Uncle Tom's Cabin* by Harriet Beecher Stowe."

Mike took the book and examined it closely. He put his hand out to the Reverend to shake. "Thank you, Reverend," he said smiling, genuinely touched by the old man's kindness to him in so many ways.

"You've given so much to us here at the church, I wanted to give you somethin' back so you might better understand who we are and how much your help has meant to us," Josiah Willis said, putting his hand on Mike's shoulder. The old man looked into Mike's sincere blue eyes, the windows to his soul, remembering the first time they met; this big, hulking, Aryan Nation-looking white man with a close cropped black goatee and shaved head coming up fast behind him.

The Reverend was walking to his car after interviewing builders to renovate his old 1870 church at the local Italian restaurant, Bella Angelina. He remembered how frightened he got thinking, *Oh Lord, this is it. This man is goin' to kill me*, as he tried to rush with his walking stick toward the safety of his car. But the man was too fast. A moment later the man was upon him. The Reverend turned, trapped between the man and the car, putting up his hands, instinctually defensive, almost crying out.

"Reverend Willis?" the big man asked. "I'm Mike Golden from Golden Touch Restorations and Renovations. Sorry I'm late, I almost missed you," Mike had said, seemingly oblivious to the fact that the old Reverend was obviously scared to death of him.

The minute he heard Mike's gruff voice with its gentle inflections and saw the almost childlike sincerity in his soft blue eyes, not at all understanding the effect his appearance could have on an old black man, Josiah Willis breathed a sigh of relief. Then when he saw Mike's smile, he saw what anyone with eyes could see; this big, rough man had a kindness about him, an easy friendliness and openness that couldn't help but make one take to him instantly. They talked outside of the car for awhile and Mike gave the Reverend his bid numbers and sketches for the work.

Reverend Willis hired him three weeks later. Mike had the lowest bid, the best portfolio and the Reverend just plain liked him. And his choice proved him right. The work Mike had done to restore the old church was exceptional, giving it back a life it had long lost and the fact that Mike hired some of the unemployed men from the church to help do the work and teach them a trade at the same time brought Mike close into their world. The ladies of the church were always bringing him food; Miss Ida Mae Bovee's fried chicken and biscuits her sister, Miss Gwynnie's potato salad and roast pork and especially Sister Florence's fried fish, macaroni and cheese and greens. The best Mike had ever tasted. And every Thursday as he knew he could count on, Sister Florence would pull up into the church parking lot and shout from the car with a large voice that could carry across acres. "Hi, hunee, how're you?"

As Mike and the Reverend walked through the recently completed work, they came to the back of the large, white,

one-room church, to the nave behind where the altar would
be. The back wall to the nave was covered with a multicolored, paint-stained tarp. Mike left the Reverend in the
vacant altar space and walked up to the tarp, grabbing one
end and with a swift tug, yanked the tarp from the window.
Reverend Willis gasped and took a step back. The stained
glass window he loved but couldn't afford had been installed
while he was gone. "Oh, Michael!" he sighed, covering his
mouth with his hand in awe, his eyes filling to overflowing.
"We can't afford this."

"It's already paid for, Reverend," Mike said, walking over
to the old man and standing next to him to enjoy the beauty
of the artwork. He put his hand on the Reverend's shoulder,
grinning from ear to ear with pride over his accomplishment.
"I didn't cut corners either," he said confidently. "I got the
contractor's ten percent off materials from The Home Depot
over in Fennell and twisted the arms of a few of those
starving artists over in New Hope to do the glass." Reverend
Willis just stood there, speechless before the sun-illuminated
window; John the Baptist, robed in hues of purple, sitting on
the edge of the river, radiant in hues of green and blue and
staring into the sky, his face bathed in the holy light with
yellows and oranges.

When he recovered himself, the Reverend looked at Mike
with such an expression of peace and happiness that Mike
wanted to take the old man in his big arms and hug him.
"He's your man, ain't he?" Mike asked, smiling.

"Michael, you were surely brought to us by God," the old
man said taking Mike's big, meaty hand and shaking it warmly.

"I've learned so much, gained so much. I understand so
much more for having met you and your people, Reverend.
You've fed me, cared for me and my family. Things I could
never have gotten anywhere else. Good things that've made
me a better person," Mike said solemnly and pulled the copy
of *Uncle Tom's Cabin* out of his pocket, holding it in front of
him. The old man smiled, nodding as they turned and walked
in silence back out into the sunlight.

The next time they would see each other was sooner than either of them would have expected; only six hours and, by then, the world would have come to an end for Big Mike Golden.

■

It was already dark when Mike pulled back into the church parking lot, his temples throbbing and his eyes swollen to a squint, his mind swimming with drugs and flashbacks; the police car waiting for him in his driveway when he got back to the 17th century farmhouse he and Jane had bought to "flip" the next year. People were gathered on his porch, one in a police uniform, the others, his neighbors, John and Patty Gundersen.

Hysteria ripped through him as he got out of his car and ran towards the porch. He could see out of the corner of his eye that Patty Gundersen was crying.

The policeman stepped up. "Mr. Golden?" the young officer said, a grim, pale expression on his face.

"Yes!" Mike shouted looking to pass him and get into the house. The young officer stopped him.

"Mr. Golden, I'm sorry. There's been an accident." In his panic, Mike hadn't noticed that their second car, the old VW bug the kids loved, wasn't in the drive. He stopped.

"What?"

"You're wife has been in a car accident, sir. I'm sorry," the young officer said, looking to the ground and shaking his head. The blood drained from Mike's face. He knew what that meant. Mike's mind reeled out of control, shooting in every direction. "My kids!" he cried out.

Patty Gundersen was standing next to him by then, holding him up. "The kids are fine, Mike. They're over at our house with ours," she said, tears running down her cheeks. "I'm so sorry, Mike," she said and hugged him.

Time seemed to stop for Michael Golden then. The world had just ended. For the next six hours he felt nothing and understood less. He was just a body going through the motions as he was directed by the young police officer and John Gundersen; identifying the body, signing papers he didn't read and couldn't understand. Everything seemed to be moving in slow motion. *Arrangements?* He couldn't fucking think about arrangements. "What the hell are you talking about?" he shouted through his tears as he fell apart at the hospital; a voice in his mind screaming at him in his skull, *She's dead, Michael. Jane is dead!*

She ran off the road and into a tree, he kept hearing the young officer's voice repeating in his head as he got out of the car in the church parking lot and stumbled sluggishly to the door, fumbling in his pocket for the key. *Where else could he go?* There was nowhere else to go. He went in and sat in the front pew; his head in his hands, drifting. *This can't be real, Lord. Can I please wake up now?*

It wasn't long before he felt a presence next to him and an arm come around his shoulders. He looked up to see the Reverend's saddened face. "I'm so sorry, Michael. Our Jamal Adderly is on the local EMT Squad and called me as soon as he could. I've been waiting for you, hoping you would come," the old man said quietly.

"What do I do now?" Mike asked, leaning in to cry like a baby on the old Reverend's shoulder; a big, heaving mass of muscle and flesh held gently together by only a pair of frail old arms.

"Don't you fret none, son. We'll take care of everything here at the church."

"Can I stay here tonight with you? I don't have anywhere else to go," Mike asked, sounding like a lost little boy.

"Yes, son. You sure can. You stay right here with us tonight."

■

Services were held for Jane Arnette Golden two days later at the Calvary Road Baptist Church with Reverend Willis giving the eulogy. Heartfelt, sincere, Reverend Willis spoke slowly, deliberately as he told the congregation how Michael and Jane Golden had come to the small rural town of Sayreville, Pennsylvania, only a few months ago to better the community by renovating and restoring one of its oldest standing structures, Fairfax Grange. And who, in the process, came into the hearts of the members of the Calvary Road Baptist Church with their kindnesses and generosity in rebuilding their church and becoming a part of their lives. He spoke of how close he and Michael had become over the months, and what a great loss to him it was that God had chosen to take Jane so young. Then he got rolling.

"Brothers and sisters," he started again as he came down from the pulpit and began walking among the people. "God is in this house today. If I were an outsider looking into this room, what would I see? Brother Johnson? What would I see?" he asked a middle aged, light skinned man with short cropped hair.

"A room full of Christians, Reverend," Brother Johnson answered, not bothered in the least by being called on.

"Yessir! A room full of Christians. Fine answer, Brother. But now let me ask what someone else might see; someone who is not one of us. They might answer that it's a room full of black folks and one white guy," and the Reverend gave a small laugh. "I must confess now before all of you. Before I met Michael Golden, I would have given that second answer myself," and he went on to tell in a rousing fashion the tale of how he met Michael running up on him as he rushed to his car that night, and how he was scared to death because of Michael's physical appearance. He confessed that it took his very own wife, Ella, accusing him of being a racist to make him see the light and admit he had committed a sin by judging others by their appearance, a principle he had fought against all his life.

"Amen, Reverend!" came from the pews. It was Sister Florence.

"But now that man, whom I once judged so unfairly and uncharitably sits here amongst us today alone, needing us to understand his grief and loss after he has done so much to help us," and the Reverend walked back behind the empty altar space and pointed to the new stained glass window.

Michael started to cry, saying quietly to himself. "Thank you, Reverend."

The Reverend then looked to Mike, "I do not ever want you to think that you are apart from us, Michael. Sister Florence and the Misses Bovee will feed you and your children. The men of this church will take up your work and help you through. My dear Ella will help keep your house and care for your children, and I will be your strength when you need it. You have become part of us, Michael. Part of our hearts…my heart, and we never want you to feel alone," the Reverend spoke passionately, a stage-like tenor in his voice reverberating off the high ceiling and wide walls.

"Amen!" a wiry looking man who worked with Mike stood up and called out. "We're with you, Michael." Mike just let his head hang in his hands and cried.

The Reverend started to cry, too, as he looked at the broken-hearted man he had come to care so much for, full of a world of pain. "You have our hearts, Michael, and all of our prayers for the deliverance of your beloved wife's soul into the Kingdom of Heaven. God is in the house today, for you Brother Michael, because he lives in all of us," he managed to finish before his voice gave out.

"Amen, Reverend," Miss Ida called out, waving her hands in the air in the old way. "Amen, Jesus," Miss Gwynnie called out. The Reverend went over and sat down next to Mike, his wife, Ella, on Mike's other side in the front pew, giving a signal to the dark-skinned young man with long beaded braids at the organ. A young girl with lacey black hair, full features and cocoa skin wearing a purple choir robe came to the front, walked over to the casket in front of the room and put her hand on it. The organist began to play and the girl began to sing with a voice that resonated throughout the open room, echoing off the walls that Mike, with his own two hands, had repaired and replaced. Mike fell to pieces.

"Amazing Grace, how sweet the sound…"

The Reverend and his wife each took one of Mike's hands and held them tight as the men stood up and went to the front of the room, lifting the casket to carry it out.

"I once was lost but now I'm found. Was blind but now I see…"

■

They arrived at the small, tree-hidden cemetery less than an hour later; a long black hearse and a line of four or five cars pulling up to the tall wrought-iron gates with the sign overhead, *Freedom*. Created before the Civil War as the only cemetery in the area to take the bodies of runaway slaves who'd managed to make it to the North, it was deliberately placed in a thick grove of trees, obscured from the road to avoid the desecrations common in those days. But now it was peaceful and quiet.

The small party of twenty or so mourners, all dressed in black, walked through the gates and over towards the back of the small, headstone-filled patch of grass-covered land, stopping at the freshly dug hole over in the far back corner.

The men gently laid the casket on the belted frame. Reverend Willis went to the head of the casket to say a short prayer. While he was speaking, he scanned the group, at first to see how Mike was holding up, but his always cautious eyes couldn't help but catch a glimpse of someone else; someone standing far off over on the other side of the cemetery in the shade of a big elm tree. It was strange, not only because he was white, but because he had long, straggly, dark-blonde hair wrapped in an American flag print bandana, a long shaggy beard, sunglasses and was wearing a big, black leather motorcycle jacket; very out of place at a burial in a black cemetery.

The Reverend looked back at Mike standing arm-in-arm with Ella and Sister Florence; bereft of any more emotion, drained lifeless after days of shock, confusion and grief. And when the Reverend looked back to the big elm tree, the man in the leather jacket was gone.

■

It was already early evening when Mike pulled back up to the house after the repast at the church. He and the Reverend had a few drinks and he was still taking the pills that the doctor at the hospital had given him, so when his truck crept haltingly into the driveway, he didn't at first notice the big, black Harley, covered in road dust, parked in the shadows to the side.

He walked up to the front door, his head still hanging low, heavy with loss as it had for days. A shadow stepped out from behind one of the porch columns. Mike started and stepped back.

"Who the hell are you?" he barked, angry at being jolted out of his thoughts. The man stepped out of the shadows into the glare of the porch light. Mike saw the long, shaggy, dark-blonde hair and long beard; layers of bulky shirts under his big black leather jacket coated thickly in dust, still wearing sunglasses.

"Mr. Golden?" a deep 'whiskey' sounding voice came from behind the beard.

"Yes. What can I do for you?" Mike asked, on his guard, silent warning sirens blasting in his ears.

"Well, I've come a long way ta...join yer crew if I could. A fella I met in a bar down home told me he worked fer ya once and said he thought ya might be able ta use a good hand woodworker and carpenter. I went ta yer website and saw ya had two projects goin' at the same time here and thought, well...maybe ya could use some help," the bearded man said, a drawling twang in his voice that Mike pegged for Deep South overlaid with Oklahoma or Texas, somewhere in the Southwest. Otherwise, the man sounded legit enough. Mike let his guard down a bit and went up the steps to the porch, putting out his hand.

"It's just been a very rough day for me. I'm sorry I jumped at you like that..."

"Jamie," the bearded man replied, putting out his hand for Mike to shake. Close up and in the light, Mike could see that the guy wasn't nearly as old as all the hair made him look, mid to late thirties at most. The man made another swift movement and leapt off the porch, trotting over to his bike and coming back with a large portfolio type booklet. He handed it to Mike. "My work."

Mike sat down in his old porch rocker, opened the folder and began to skim the photographs of ornately and intricately carved wood-works; wall trimmings, mantles and other types of specialized wood-working. As he flipped through, one particular photo caught his attention; a large Greek-scroll oak mantle. It stopped him in his tracks because it was just the sort of thing he had envisioned as an altar top for the new church altar.

"You did all this?" Mike asked.

"Yessir, since I was sixteen."

"Is the law after you, man?" Mike asked suspiciously. "I have two kids. The last thing I need right now is trouble with the law."

"No, sir. No warrants here. Did some time awhile back but naw, not in a long time now."

"Drugs...alcohol?"

"No, sir, I bin clean goin' on seven years now. Don't mind a few drinks ev'r now and agin, but booze was nev'r my problem. It was anythang that came in a white powder," Jamie said sheepishly, like he'd just blown the job by being too honest.

Mike didn't know what to think. He wasn't thinking clearly; his mind muddled from the last thirty-six hours. He'd just buried his wife for God's sake. But there was something about this guy. He couldn't put his finger on it, something oddly...comforting; the sound of his voice? Familiar?

"Have we met somewhere before?" Mike asked him.

"No, sir, I don't thank so," Jamie replied, sounding a little nervous.

"And how did you find me again?"

"I met a guy in a bar who said he worked fer ya once, in Florida. He gimme a card with yer website on it. He was a big guy; Buck, Bull, Bear, somethin' like 'at. I'd had a few beers. He was some kinda animal."

Mike laughed at that. "Okay well, you might be in luck. I really do have my hands full with the church job and this place, and I was thinkin' about a carved altar for the church project. Come back tomorrow when I'm feeling better and we'll talk. I can't think right now."

"Yessir!" the biker said with a sharp salute.

"Where you stayin'?"

"Well, I ain't got no place yet. I didn't want ta settle in 'til after I'd talked ta ya. I started out from Texas and my cash is runnin' low. If you'da said 'no' I'da jes' moved on. I'll go over ta the motel on the highway and git a place right now," the biker said, jumping down the porch steps in a bound.

Mike turned to go in the front door, but something inside made him stop; a feeling? Intuition? His stomach clenched and his heartbeat rose in his chest. He wasn't ready to be alone with his grief quite yet, confronting it face-to-face for the first time...alone. He turned back awkwardly.

"Wait," he said, "I'm alone here tonight. My kids are stayin' at the neighbors. You don't have any weapons on you, do you?" he asked, looking down and shaking his head.

"No, sir."

"Okay then, why don'tcha just stay here tonight? It's gettin' late and I have a few unused bedrooms and a good couch. We'll getcha a place tomorrow."

"Why, thank ya, sir. That's mighty kind of ya," Jamie said, and headed back to his bike.

Mike took a deep breath and let it out with a whistle, looking up to the sky to keep from falling apart again, then blurted out without thinking, "I just buried my wife today."

Jamie stopped in his tracks, spinning around on his heels. "I got a bottle of Cap'n Morgan in my saddle bag," he said, his voice wavering for a second, then turned and ran to the bike for his bags. Mike grabbed hold of himself and went to his truck to bring in all the food Sister Florence and the other ladies had given him, feeling somehow, strangely, not so alone anymore.

■

In the house, Mike went straight toward the back. "You can have the first floor guest room, around here," he said, pointing as he went around the stairwell toward a small hall behind the stairs, dragging his boots on the floor from fatigue. "There's a bathroom right across the hall." Jamie followed, bags in hand, as Mike disappeared around the corner. "Why don't you clean up in there and I'll warm you up something to eat," Mike said absently as he pointed to the room where he'd just turned on the light, a bathroom sink clearly visible through the partially opened door. "And you can sleep here," Mike said, flipping on another light switch in the room directly opposite the bathroom.

"Naw, ya don't hafta do that, Mr. Golden, really. You've done enough alriddy. I know how tired ya mus' be," Jamie said, setting his bags down in the dimly lit bedroom, looking back at Mike still in the hallway looking in.

"Listen, you're dusty, hungry and tired. I can see it all over you. When was the last time you slept? Lookatcha. You're dead on your feet. If you're gonna work for me, I want you well fed and strong. No benefits here, you're an independent contractor as far as that's concerned and the good ladies over at the church sent enough food for an army. Plus it'll give me something to do while I'm having that drink of the Captain you promised me," Mike said, struggling to muster a smile. Jamie reached inside his dusty black leather bag, pulled out a bottle and handed it to Mike.

"Okay, well at least ya kin have one fer me 'til I come out," Jamie said, taking off his jacket and nervously putting it on the chair next to the door, just inside the bedroom.

"And I'm not much older than you are so you can drop the 'Mr. Golden' stuff. You can call me Michael or Mike, but never Mickey," Mike said with a smile, and headed down the short hallway behind the stairs toward the kitchen; too absorbed in his thoughts to notice that Jamie hadn't taken off his sun glasses the entire time, and it was well after dark.

■

After he put a tray of macaroni and cheese in the oven next to the tray of fried chicken and turned the dial to 350 degrees, Mike grabbed a few water glasses and let himself slump into the nearest chair, lighting a cigarette. After more than six years of marriage and six years smoke free, he'd picked up a pack of his old brand, Marlboro red, the night Jane died and began lighting up again. *Why not?* he thought as he twisted the top off of the Captain Morgan bottle and poured himself a double, then another before he finished his cigarette, drifting off into his memories, losing track of time, only coming back when he heard a rattle from the bathroom door or the clunking sound that always signaled that the shower on the first floor was being used. The next thing he knew, the timer on the oven had gone off. He jumped up and grabbed Jane's gingham oven mitts off their wall hanger to rescue the food from the oven.

He'd just turned toward the cabinets, the kitchen door to his back, and grabbed silverware when he heard the shuffling sound of feet. Someone was coming in behind him. "I hope you're hungry," he said, reaching into the cabinet and pulling out two plates.

"Michael?" Jamie's voice came flatly from behind him, his name coming out sounding like *Mah-kull.* Mike turned around. Jamie was standing in the doorway with his head down, barefoot, revealing himself not to be as thick as he looked in all those clothes, nor as tall as he was in boots. He was wearing faded jeans with the knees blown out and a plain white tee-shirt, a series of Native American symbols tattooed down both his arms, the last being of a wolf's claw with scratch marks just above his right wrist. His hair was clean making it look blonder in the bright light of the kitchen; wet, combed straight and trimmed evenly to shoulder length. *The color—that color.* He knew that color. Jamie slowly raised his head to face him, clean shaven; the mask of the beard gone.

Mike's hands went weak, his mouth dropped, gaping open. Before he could think, the plates fell from his hands, crashing to the floor. His eyes went wide and his knees gave out, sliding him liquidly into the nearest chair to break his fall, staring in stark astonishment at the slim, tightly muscled figure that stood before him. Jamie had her quiet, shy, hazel eyes, and her tapered nose; her pouty lips and delicate chin with the slightest hint of a cleft. He had her face. All of it, masculine and broader, the eyebrows thicker, but it was her face.

In that moment, for the first time in his life, Michael Golden lost all touch with reality. The shock was too much for him and for a split second he splintered, looking as if he'd seen a ghost.

"Are you an angel?" Mike asked, his voice filled with childlike wonderment, tears streaming down his face.

"Naw, Michael, more like a Hell's Angel. But I am here ta help ya if I kin. If you'll let me," Jamie said, with a small, sad smile as he came closer to the table, wiping thin streams running down his own face with his hands.

Mike had to force himself to breath when he saw that smile; the overbite he'd thought was so beautiful the first time she'd smiled at him and made him fall so hopelessly in love with her.

Jamie sat down next to him at the table, more tears streaming down his face. "My name is James Arnette. Jane was my sister, my twin. The one person I loved most in the world. She loved ya so very much, Michael. She wanted me ta come. I didn't know how ta tell ya so I thought it would be best ta jes' show ya. I nev'r meant ta hurt ya. I'm so sorry," he said in-between deep breaths and muffled sobs, his head hanging down.

Mike just stared at him. He couldn't take his eyes off him. The resemblance was nothing short of remarkable; unreal, eerie...scary. Underneath the twang, even his voice had the same tenor and inflection, and his movements; masculine, but yet somehow still the same...*identical.*

"My boy is James, too," Mike said, quietly, mechanically; hearing his own voice as if it were coming from somewhere outside of himself, struggling desperately to grasp what was happening.

"I know, Michael..." Jamie said, taking hold of Mike's trembling hand, "...and Victoria."

"But I don't understand," Mike said, still sounding like a stunned child, looking up at Jamie again, back into his eyes; his own wet, swollen, red-rimmed eyes swimming in his head, two great blue spheres floating in an uncomprehending sea.

"Thar's a lot we hafta talk about, Michael," Jamie said, sounding as if he was carrying the weight of the world on his shoulders and was about to pass it on. He poured a double shot of the Captain Morgan into Mike's glass and pushed it toward him. "Important thangs."

Chapter Two

Requiem:
A Child's Guide to Shadows

M ike took the shot and downed it, still not being able to take his eyes off of that face, waiting for Jamie to say something. Jamie hesitated, having no idea about where to start. It was all so horrible and dirty. He felt dirty even letting it cross his mind, but he had to. He knew he had to. Michael had a right to know, and to know that Jane's death wasn't an accident. How could he ever bring himself to say the words? He poured himself another shot and took a deep breath, deciding to try to lead Michael into it so he wouldn't have to say it, outright, out loud.

"Didn't ya ev'r notice that Jane was a little…differ'nt, Michael?" he asked ruefully, bowing his head slowly. Mike looked at him confused, but inside knowing; reliving the night terrors he'd held her through, the dark days when she stayed in bed all day and cried, and the way she never wanted to leave the house after they were married. As if reading his mind, Jamie spoke.

"Night terrors, Michael? 'fraid of ev'r'thang and ev'r'body? How she ev'r found a way ta marry was a miracle in itself. She couldn't stand ta be touched. A man like you must've seen 'at, and the children. It all came down ta you and how much ya made her feel loved. A miracle."

Mike sat back in his chair, astonished, like he was sitting before a gypsy fortune teller who'd just read his life.

"The accident wasn't an accident, Michael," he heard Jamie say slow and low. That jolted Mike out of his haze. He grabbed Jamie's arm hard, and shook it, shouting, "What are you saying?"

Jamie just melted; liquid in Michael's huge hand, curling down to protect himself from the blow that he was sure would come next.

Michael shook him again. "What the fuck are you saying?"

"She killed herself," Jamie mumbled, turning his face away.

Mike shook him harder. "What?"

"She killed herself!" he cried out, his voice almost shrill with hysteria, and handed Mike a crumpled piece of writing paper from his back pocket, shoving it at him. Mike took the paper, straightening it out with his hands, and saw the handwriting. It was hers, but scrawled and hurried; a letter dated a few days before she died.

"*He's come back for us. He knows what we did and he's come back for us. He's trying to touch me again at night and when I'm alone. He hasn't caught me yet because of Michael, but it won't be long. I can't let him touch me again, Jamie, you know I can't. I'd rather die than let him touch me again. Please look after Michael and love my children. You've always been the strong one, please be strong for me now.*"

He looked back up at Jamie, speechless. Jamie looked down, avoiding Mike's stare; his body rigid, his hands taking on a slight tremble.

"Our father," he said in a quivering voice, a sob caught strangled in his throat.

Mike knew what that meant and jumped up out of his chair, pacing maniacally back and forth in front of the table like a caged animal. Jamie cowered away from him.

"Oh, my God! What are you telling me?" Mike bellowed at him like a bull with a knife in his back.

"Since we were five…" Jamie cried through his hands, completely bent over. "…me, too," he said, choking on the words as he turned completely away, trying to fold himself further into a ball like he wanted to disappear, ashamed beyond words.

Mike went wild, slamming his hands, pounding his fists against everything in the room, the walls, the cabinets, like a madman locked in a padded cell. Jamie just disappeared into himself; his taut, tattooed arms folded over his head, no longer able to communicate, his muscles stiffened to the point of paralysis. *Bang! Bang! Bang! Bang!* Mike's powerful hands hit the walls like thundering hammers.

As he went around the room acting out emotions he didn't recognize or knew he could feel, it all came together for him, like a puzzle with one big missing piece finally finding its place; how it had taken her so long to let him kiss her; her getting sick on their wedding night and so many nights afterward when he tried to make love to her. How she never really enjoyed their making love, seeming to just do it for him. It took months before he could get her to trust him enough to even let him see her undressed. How could he have been so blind, so innocent, not to see what was right before his eyes? He just thought she was shy, and a virgin…a nice girl after all the *not* so nice girls that he'd met in his life.

Images of a little girl terrified by what was happening to her flashed through his head. He felt like he might vomit. A sharp pain from the realization that came with it made him cry out loud like a wounded animal. All he had ever wanted to do was to love her and protect her. She was always happiest when she was home with him and the kids, and he made it happen for her as much and as often as he could. *Why hadn't he known?* Then another vision suddenly flashed before his eyes, a frightened little boy with the same face, the same terrified little face. He heard the Reverend Willis's voice play in his head, *"God is in the house today,"* and he turned toward the cowering, trembling figure in the chair.

Walking over to him slowly, Mike took him in his arms. Shaking uncontrollably, Jamie was unresponsive at first, an innocent lost somewhere safe inside himself. Then a small, little boy voice came out from under the long blonde hair shielding his face. "Owww, oww, ouch ouch. Hurts. Hurts. Owww owww. Please don't hurt me. Please, don't hurt me anymore. I'll be good. I promise, owww, oww," he cried out, clutching frantically at his crotch and rear, bouncing in the chair like he was sitting on a hot stove top, struggling to free himself from Mike's grip.

"I'm not gonna hurt you. I promise," Mike tried to soothe him, holding him tight, refusing to let him go as his own heart broke apart in chunks. More tears than Mike ever thought he could produce flooded his eyes from places inside him he didn't know he had.

Suddenly Jamie looked up, his eyes somewhere between wide-eyed innocent little boy and ruined grown man, both overflowing with unfathomable pain. "She lured him up ta the roof of our apartment house in Pittsburgh...and I pushed 'im," he said swallowing hard, then fell from the chair to his knees, holding onto Mike's legs, sobbing uncontrollably, deep gasping, choking sobs. "We killed him," he said with a deep, hitching sigh. Mike got down on the floor with him, fractured pieces of a little boy in a man's body and he heard Reverend Willis again, *"God is in the house today."*

"Shhhhhhhhh. I'm here now. Everything will be alright," Mike whispered, stroking his hair, and rocking him gently, holding the pieces together the same way he had done with Jane on her bad nights for so many years, and as was true with Jane, it worked and Jamie slowly calmed. "Come on now, let's sit up," Mike said, his head swimming with the crushing knowledge as he pulled Jamie slowly up into the chair.

Once he was sure Jamie was secure, Mike went over to the sink and turned on the cold water tap. He felt like he was on fire. He splashed the cold water on his face and held it there. It felt so good he never wanted it to stop. When his temperature seemed like it had returned to normal, he took a dishtowel and soaked it, wringing it out only slightly. He went back to the table. Jamie had his head down on his folded arms. "Come on, now, lift your head." And Jamie did. Mike put the dishtowel in his hands, then his hands to his face. "Hold it there for a while," Mike said, then reached for the bottle, poured double shots into each of their glasses; taking a good slug for himself right from the bottle before recapping it and sat down.

"Here, drink this," he said, pulling the dishtowel from Jamie's face and pushing the glass toward him. He lit a cigarette from the pack on the table. "Take this," and put the cigarette in Jamie's hand, then lit one for himself.

"Thank you, Michael," Jamie choked, taking the double in one long slug and lowered his head again. He heard Mike get up from the table and walk across the room, the whisper of a rustle of paper in the air. He heard a strange click and looked up. Mike had the letter over the flame of the stove. A flash and it was gone; ashes on the range top.

Mike looked over to him, into his eyes. "No one ever has to know," he said, his voice returning to its deep, even growl. Jamie just nodded.

On his way back to the table, Mike grabbed the tray of fried chicken and slung it on the table, the macaroni and cheese next. He picked up the forks from the counter and tossed them on the table, pulled back the tin lids from the trays then looked at Jamie. "What? Do I look like fucking Martha Stewart to you? Eat," he said, handing Jamie a fork and pointing at the trays. Jamie gave a small, sad smile and took the fork. It was like a knife in Mike's heart to see that smile again, but he held himself in, taking his own fork and jabbing it violently into the macaroni and cheese. "And I'm gonna sit here and watch ya 'til you do!"

∎

The worst of the shadows exposed, they began to talk through mouths full of fried chicken and macaroni and cheese. They talked about all the things Mike and Jane had never talked about. Jamie told Mike how he ran away at fourteen, leaving Jane to deal with their mother until she drank herself to death, two years before Jane and Mike met. He told how he took just enough money to get him far away, and about how guilty he felt about leaving Jane, but that they both knew that for him to stay would only be an unbearable reminder for both of them, of their guilt and shame; that if either of them were ever to have a chance at a normal life, it would have to be apart.

He landed in Texas with little money and no experience and was adopted by a biker chick named Roxanne who felt sorry for him because she saw him eating out of garbage cans one day, then panhandling on the street the next. He rode with her bunch, working as their gofer, boot shine and all around bike wash until he was old enough and had enough money to get one of his own. He told Michael about the old Indian man who said he had the spirit of an eagle, taught him how to carve wood and build, tattooing him with sacred symbols as signs of his accomplishment and to keep him safe. Jamie hesitated briefly. Then there were the drugs; the heroin, cocaine and bathtub meth. They filled the emptiness in his soul and the loneliness in his heart because he had nothing else…less than nothing.

All those years on the road, drifting from town to town, landing only long enough to make enough money to move on, never allowing himself to get attached to anyone for too long. His relationships with women always ended badly, mostly because of his violent night terrors. He'd always end up hitting them in his sleep, fighting his nightmares, until the women were afraid of him. Then there were the rehabs; in and out, always failing miserably whenever the shadows overtook his dreams.

But he never forgot Jane. He wrote her more and more regularly over time as their past moved farther and farther away from them, and they could pretend for a little while that none of it ever happened. He always wanted to know that she was alright and let her know that he was. Then one day a special letter came. He'd had a feeling for weeks before, an unfamiliar feeling, strange, unsettling but not unpleasant. He'd felt as whole as he'd ever felt in his life.

He was in a rehab in New Mexico when his craving for the drugs started to slip away. Then when the letter came he knew why. Jane had met a man, a very special, gentle man whom she loved very much and wanted to marry. She was happy and Jamie felt it. Her happiness filled his void, too, and the rehab took. He hadn't touched the stuff since.

Jamie thought she should have told Mike about them, and their past, but she refused. It scared her to think that Mike would think she was dirty and used. That he wouldn't love her, and she couldn't take that risk. Then when the babies came, Victoria first, then James, she'd sent him pictures. It was a miracle. She'd done it. She'd broken the curse, living a normal life, or as normal a life as she could expect, a life with love and without fear.

Mike told him how he and Jane met. How he'd gone to Valhalla, a small town just outside Pittsburgh, and bought an old Victorian house he was going to restore then resell. That's how he made his living. He stepped into a diner one day, on the very edge of the city, on his way home from the closing and sat down at the counter. It was one of those landmark diners from the fifties, like a silver train car with red, vinyl-covered booths and sheathed in chrome.

Just as he'd sat down, he heard a loud, brassy, braying voice come from a booth down the other end. "Jane, you got a guy at the counter." A minute later, the quilted stainless door that led from the kitchen swung open and a girl came through, a woman really, but with only light make-up and a quiet demeanor that made her seem younger. Dressed in a blue-and-white checked waitress outfit with a white apron, she came over to the counter with her pad and pencil out. "Can I help you, sir?" she said shyly without looking up at him. He waited deliberately until she did. And when she did it was like his eyes were opened for the very first time. She only looked at him for a second, then looked down again. "I guess the old blue plate special will be fine," he said on the verge of a stutter.

He ate there at least once every day for weeks. Whatever time he could get away from working on the house, he went to that diner. But she would never smile at him, no matter what he tried. Then one day while he was working on the house, one of his men turned too quickly with a long beam on his shoulder and caught Mike hard in the head, splitting his forehead open. He had to go to the hospital to get a few stitches; nothing much, just ugly. He'd stopped into the diner on his way back to grab a bite.

Still feeling dazed, he sat in a booth instead of at the counter. The brassy voiced waitress, a redhead called Ruby, came over. It was her table. "What'll it be, hon?" she said, her pad and pencil out, practically snapping her gum in his face. When he looked up and she saw it was Mike, she turned quickly and waddled back through the kitchen door, hips swaying.

Jane came slowly through the door and over to his booth. Mike looked up at her and she saw the egg-sized knot on his forehead covered by a large bloody band-aid. She put her hand to her mouth and rushed away. He heard the sound of loud women's voices come muffled through the door.

Another minute later, Jane came back out with a wad of crushed ice wrapped in a towel. "What happened to your head?" she asked him shyly, handing him the make-shift ice pack.

Mike looked up at her, embarrassed. "See whatcha do to me? I can't even work without running into the walls for thinking about you," he said and let out a small chuckle, blushing furiously. It was the first time he ever saw her smile, and he fell instantly and completely in love.

From there it was very slow going. They'd go for walks in the park during her lunch or window shop in the city. It took weeks before she would trust him enough to see him after dark; a movie, a carnival. She made him feel like a good man inside, not like the other women he'd known, attracted to him because he looked like he'd rough them up and smack them around. It seems they liked that sort of thing and were disappointed when they realized that he didn't.

Jane was this delicate, beautiful porcelain figure, fragile and rare, qualities that no one could see and appreciate like he could. There wasn't anything he wouldn't have done to make her happy.

They talked about his business and his travels around the country, revealing very little about herself other than in the vaguest terms. She was thirty-two, never married. He was thirty-eight, never married, lonelier than he would ever want to admit. She had two years of community college in business. He had no college but loved to read.

He knew she loved him back when they met for lunch in the park one day and she'd brought him a gift wrapped in baby blue paper with bears on it; a rare copy of George DuMaurier's *Trilby*, recounting the tale of Svengali and how he hypnotized a pretty washing girl into being an opera diva. He knew she loved him then because he'd only mentioned it in passing on one of their afternoons out and they went into an old bookstore and he'd come out disappointed when they didn't have it.

She must have searched high and low to find that book, and paid a good bit for it. It meant she knew him, understood him and wanted to make him happy, too, and to Michael Golden, that was love. It was also the first time she took his hand first, before he took hers. She held his hand, smiling quietly as he read excitedly from *Trilby*, laughing as he tried to imitate the funny foreign accents of the characters, but not at the fact that he wore glasses to read.

The next week he proposed to her in kind, with his favorite quote from *Jane Eyre*, hoping it would convey to her just how he felt. He took her on a picnic out by a lake. They took a small rowboat out and let it drift, and as he sat across from her in the late summer sun, he opened *Jane Eyre* and read:

"I sometimes have a queer feeling with regard to you—especially when you are near me, as now; it is as if I had a string somewhere under my left ribs, tightly and inextricably knotted to a similar string situated in the corresponding quarter of your little frame. And if that boisterous channel, and two hundred miles or so of land come broad between us, I am afraid that cord of communion will be snapt; and then I've a nervous notion I should take to bleeding inwardly. As for you—you'd forget me." Then added his own, *"Please marry me, Jane. I love you."*

Mike got lost in time then; a sad, pained look on his face. Jamie knew what that meant, knew what he was thinking.

"I'll understand if ya want ta leave, Michael," he said, dejected and not wanting to wait to be asked to leave. "I don't imagine ya want a drug addict and a killer 'round the children, or a constant reminder of…thangs," he said calmly, rationally, but saddened as he turned his face away; the old feeling for a fix hovering just beneath the surface. It startled Mike out of his nostalgic haze and made him angry, angry for reasons he didn't quite understand, and the knuckle-scraping caveman in him came out. His eyes got serious, his eyebrows furrowed and he pointed his finger at Jamie.

"Now you listen to me. I've already lost one Arnette this week and it almost killed me. If it weren't for the kids, it *would* have killed me. I'll be God-damned if I'm going to lose another one. Do you understand? I have two beautiful, innocent kids to raise without a mother, one she named after you. I can't do it alone and you're going to help me. It's what she wanted and it's what *I* want," he said, a low growl resonating from his throat, pointing his finger again. "Now it's late, my head is splitting and I'm so God-damn tired I can hardly get myself out of this chair. I need at least a bad night's sleep tonight because Victoria and James are coming home tomorrow, and you're going to be here to love them. Your home is here with us now, safe under my roof. Do you understand me?" he said as an unequivocal command.

"Thank you, Michael," Jamie said, his eyes filling again, but this time with relief, for being wanted in spite of all he was, all he'd done, and suddenly the ghost of his craving for a fix went away.

"Come on, let's get ya some sheets and things before I pass out," Mike replied, barely able to drag himself out of the chair and down the hall.

Too tired to lift his feet anymore, Mike left Jamie sitting on his bed and shuffled toward the door. Just as he got to the doorway, Jamie's voice came from behind him.

"Michael, thank ya fer not sendin' me away. I was so ashamed ta come here like this," he said, leaning over, elbows on knees, staring at the floor.

"Shame is for the guilty. You'll never be guilty in my house. No more than she'll ever be in my heart. We'll make you a woodworking shop this week in the dining room where the light is good and get you started working."

Chapter Three

Panwiches & Tattoons

T he next morning, Jamie woke early to the sunlight coming through the slats in the shuttered windows. Still groggy, he sat up in his new bed, not quite sure where he was. Then, he remembered the night before. *Oh my God! Michael. Whut he must thinka me,* he thought, rubbing his face anxiously with his hands, then got up slowly and went over to the bathroom across the hall, still dressed from the night before. He didn't bother to look in the mirror. He just turned on the cold water tap and soaked his face. It gave him a chill when he dried off, a draft seeming to come from somewhere he couldn't quite detect, so he went back over to his new room and threw on a green-and-blue plaid flannel shirt and some socks before venturing out into the house.

Back in the kitchen, he saw the automatic coffee maker over on the counter by the sink. Knowing Jane the way he did, how organized she always was, he knew whatever he needed to get a pot started would be close at hand and opened the cabinet directly above the coffee maker. *Bingo!* There it was, everything he needed; coffee and filters. While the coffee was brewing, he sat at the kitchen table and lit a cigarette from the pack Michael had left out, looking out of the big bay window into the back yard. It was beautiful and…peaceful, a rolling green lawn only lightly covered with newly fallen autumn leaves from the surrounding trees. It stretched back about a half an acre, stopping at the edge of a small lake tucked between the yard and a hill behind it to the right, covered by tall grass and crowned by an enormous oak tree, looking hundreds of years old.

When the coffee was done brewing, Jamie fixed himself a cup, black, and went back to his room for his leather jacket and boots. It looked so peaceful outside, he wanted to let its serenity fill him, calm his nerves and let him center himself before he had to face Michael again. He walked slowly around the yard first, smoking and sipping his coffee, absorbing his surroundings, letting the quiet work its magic on his shaky hands.

He saw a square concrete slab over to the left by the lake, a fire pit in front of it, two chairs and a small round table. As he walked past, he noticed the bottom of an old Rubbermaid tub under the table, empty beer cans filling it half way. He walked past the fire pit toward the lake where he could see the mist rising from the glassy surface, just starting to burn off in the sunlight, like spirits ascending to heaven, and he envied it; to be able to just fly away.

As he walked closer to the lake, he heard a rustling come from somewhere over in the brush at the lake's edge, to his left. A few seconds later he saw a duck swim out toward the center of the lake, a quack, then another, and a second duck followed the first out from the brush, more quacking, almost like the first one was talking to the other and it was responding. Then there were more until seven or eight of them were paddling in an inverted vee formation toward the center of the lake; their quacking reminding him of an odd laughter, taunting, mocking, like they knew his secret and were laughing at him. "Stop laughin' at me," he said under his breath as he walked around to the right, then up the hill, about two hundred paces to the top.

The view into the valley below was nothing less than breathtaking as he stood there worrying how he could ever face Michael again after what he'd told him, deciding that he shouldn't have come. He knew it then. He should have left Michael alone and in peace. Suddenly overwhelmed with guilt and feeling a chill from the rising mist on his skin, Jamie walked back to the house having decided to tell Michael that he would leave that day. He didn't want to taint him any further, or the kids. They had a right to be left alone. His troubles weren't their troubles. It wasn't fair.

Back in the house, he had just taken off his jacket and boots and refilled his coffee cup when he heard a knock at the door. He looked at the clock on the stove, nine o'clock. Another knock, rapping, then the sound of a woman's voice calling through the door. "Mike, are you awake?"

Jamie walked through the kitchen door. A woman was standing just inside, a tall blonde with a ponytail, in her early forties and dressed like a suburban housewife, mom jeans, flat shoes, and a soft looking pink sweater underneath a dark pink jacket. The minute she saw him her mouth dropped open, her hand going up to it with an expression of...shock; speechlessness.

"I'm James Arnette, Jamie. Jane's brother," he said to the stunned woman. The woman hesitated, then took a step forward with her hand out.

"I'm Patty Gundersen from next door." He took her hand. "Please forgive me," she said, "...it's just that..."

"I know," Jamie said, smiling weakly. "Please don't be sorry. I got used ta it a long time ago," he said, resigned to at least one or two more of these encounters before he left. "I got here last night, as soon as I could from Texas."

Patty nervously changed the subject, still more than a little uncomfortable with what she was seeing. "Mike said I could bring Victoria and James back this morning. I've had them with me since before...They don't know anything, only that she's gone away for awhile. They're in the car outside with my oldest, but I can take them back with me. It's no trouble," she said, sympathetically, almost apologetically.

"Michael's still asleep. He was so tired last night. But I'd like ta meet 'em before I go, if that's okay," he said sadly.

Beginning to tear herself, Patty went out the door and came back a minute later holding a little blonde boy in her arms, not three years old, and holding the hand of a little girl with big blue eyes, shoulder length black hair with bangs, like a page boy cut, about five years old.

The little boy wriggled in Patty's arms until she set him down. He ran over to Jamie, "Mommy, Mommy!" little James called out running toward him. Jamie bent down to take him up in his arms in as natural a movement as he'd ever felt, like he'd done it a thousand times before. Patty Gundersen pulled a handkerchief out of her pocket and wiped her eyes, then looked down and spoke to the little girl.

"It's alright Victoria. He's your mommy's brother, like James is your brother. He's your Uncle Jamie." The little girl took a few hesitant steps forward, her eyes not leaving the strange figure before her; studying him. Jamie knelt down to her level, James still clinging to his neck.

"He's not Mommy, James. He's a boy," she said, looking confused herself.

"Well, ain'tcha jes' the purdiest little thang? I'm Jamie," he said to her quietly, his heart thumping in his chest at the sight of the little girl. She had Michael's black hair and blue eyes, but she had Jane's features just like he remembered from their growing up, the shape of her eyes, and his, but without the fear and pain behind them. Victoria slowly took a few more steps toward him, unsure, but never taking her eyes off his face. A few steps more, then a few more until she was close enough to reach out and touch him, still looking in his eyes. Then in a burst, she leapt at him, throwing her arms around his neck and holding him tight. Jamie choked, restrained sobs forcing their way out of him, tears running down his face as he held her to him.

"Don't cry, Jamie. It'll be alright," she whispered in his ear, sounding so much like her father had the night before. "James just doesn't know the difference between boys and girls, yet."

Patty Gundersen nodded approvingly, gesturing with her hand that she was going and closed the door behind her, leaving them alone.

Still holding James on his shoulder, his heart full beyond recognition, Jamie took Victoria by the hand and went into the kitchen. "Did the nice Mrs. Gundersen give you guys breakfast?"

"Yes," Victoria replied, pulling a face. "But she's a vegan so all her food tastes like cardboard. I took a few bites but James wouldn't eat anything." Jamie laughed.

"We'll jes' hafta fix that then, won't we? Whut wouldja like?"

"Well, James likes the toasted raisin bread with butter and I like Captain Crunch and orange juice," Victoria chattered like a little adult.

"Toast an' Crunch it is then," Jamie said, putting James in his high chair. Victoria sat at the table like a big girl as Jamie went to the cabinets, taking his cue from her as to where to find everything.

The table set with breakfast, Jamie helped himself to another cup of coffee and watched them. James had finished eating his toast, having been endlessly fascinated by the cinnamon swirls. His eyes began to droop and his head nodded. "He always does that," Victoria said, an air of superiority ringing in her voice as she went about finishing her cereal. Jamie sat down next to her, not knowing what to say next, then it just came out.

"Do ya thank it would be okay if I stayed here fer awhile?"

Victoria nodded, not lifting her eyes from her cereal bowl.

"Thank you, Victoria, but if I stay, I'll need yer help, ta know thangs, how ta do thangs. Will ya help me?"

She nodded again, this time looking up from her bowl and smiling at him with her father's eyes. "I know lots of things," she said prodigiously.

"Okay, well let's see. Whut does Daddy like ta eat fer breakfast, his favorite thangs? When he's tired or doesn't feel good."

"Mommy makes panwiches for him. That's his favorite," she said, back to staring into her bowl. "You talk funny, Jamie."

Jamie chuckled. "Yes, I do, darlin'. Most folks would call me a 'redneck'."

Victoria laughed delightedly at that and Jamie saw her look at his neck to see if it really was red.

"It means that I ain't got much education and hafta work with my hands out in the sun, so my neck gits red," he said with a sad smile and a sigh. "That's why it's so important fer ya ta stay in school. I nev'r did," he said, hoping she couldn't read his embarrassment, then came out of it for her sake. "So come on, whut's a panwich?" he asked.

She giggled. "Well, Mommy makes a bunch of pancakes and bacon and Daddy puts the bacon in between with some syrup and eats it," she said, pulling another face, like she did about the vegan. "He eats them with his hands and gets all sticky and then tries to touch us. Yuck!" she said pulling another face, this time made all the more comical by her exaggerated claw hand motions, giggling loudly.

Jamie barked out a laugh, then shushed himself, putting his finger to his lips. "Daddy's sleepin'. He's real tired today, Victoria. We should be quiet and let 'im sleep."

She leaned in at that and whispered to him, "Mommy keeps the pancake powder in the cabinet over there," and she pointed to the left cabinet next to the stove, which just happened to be over the griddle pan.

"You are jes' the smartest little girl," he said, getting up and going to the cabinet. I'm real glad I have ya ta help me."

"My teacher, Mrs. Garrett, says that, too," she said proudly.

"I'm sure she does, so how 'bout we make some cookies later after I git the panwiches done." He knew Jane had to have baking things all over. She had always been very domestic and loved to bake. She baked, he carved. They both loved to work with their hands.

Victoria looked up at him, flashing him again with Michael's big blue eyes, smiling, and said, "Mommy keeps her baking things over there," and pointed to the cabinet directly above the stove. "James likes anything with raisins, I do too, but Daddy likes nuts and coconut in his."

And so the bake fest began. Victoria helped mix the batter for the pancakes while Jamie fried the bacon. Once that was done and in the oven to stay warm, they started on the cookies, little James fussing only occasionally at the clank of the pans. As Jamie was pouring a cup full of nuts into Mike's batch, Victoria ran her hand up and down his arm. "What are these?" she asked, fascinated by the tribal symbols running down his arm.

"They're called tattoos, li'l darlin'. It's art, like a paintin' or the thangs ya draw in school."

"Do they come off?" she asked innocently. Jamie chuckled at that.

"Naw, sweetheart, they'll stay thar forev'r."

"I like them. They're pretty," Victoria said, running her hand up and down his arm again. By then the house smelled like a bakery, fresh coffee, bacon, cinnamon and raisins.

Mike woke to the mix of aromas wafting under his door almost two hours later, his eyes still so swollen he could hardly open them. Hoping that somehow it had all been a bad dream, he stumbled to the kitchen, almost blind, then stopped in mid step. James was asleep peacefully in his chair. Jamie was standing behind Victoria watching her take the warm cookies off the baking sheet with a spatula and putting them on a plate. They both looked up at him at the same time. Victoria smiled but Jamie looked like a deer caught in headlights. If it hadn't been so tragic, it could have been a Norman Rockwell painting, and Mike wanted to cry again.

"Daddy!" Victoria squealed, waking James up in a fuss.

Jamie went, "Shhhhh," mouthing to her without words, "Daddy's not feelin' good."

Victoria ran to Mike whispering, "Daddddyyyyy!" Jamie picked James up and held him on his hip, just like Jane used to do. Mike wanted to turn and go back to bed; try again, but he couldn't. It was too late and wouldn't change anything anyway. "Come see what we made," Victoria said quietly, taking him by the hand and leading him to the table. Mike took a seat.

The tension in the room was stifling, suffocating, so much that should never be spoken of again; a stone maze that bound them both within its walls while at the same time creating an impenetrable barrier between them that could never be breached. Jamie put a cup of coffee in front of him, neither of them looking at the other. Mike only saw Jamie's hand put the plate of pancakes and bacon in front of him.

"Panwiches," Victoria said excitedly, still whispering.

Mike didn't look up, his heart was still too raw, still hurt him too much to see that face again.

Victoria came around and sat down next to him. "Daddy, did you know that Jamie has 'tattoons' on his arms? And that he talks funny because his neck is red?"

Mike almost choked on his coffee and he broke up, laughing out loud before he could stop himself, and kept laughing.

"Yes, sweetheart, I know all about Jamie's 'tattoons' and his red neck," he said, laughing again, finally finding the strength to look up and see the pitiable insecurity in Jamie's eyes. Memories of the night before washed over him; a shattered little boy hiding within a broken man. "My neck has gotten pretty red once or twice in my life, too, sweetheart," he said as he got up from the table and went over to the cabinet behind Jamie, brushing slightly against him as he reached over his shoulder. Jamie flinched. That hurt Mike, reminding him just how often Jane had done the same thing early on in their relationship.

Mike hesitated, then pulled back and handed Jamie a plate. "You were saying something about not being around my kids," he growled under his breath, an open acceptance in his swollen eyes betraying the gruffness in his voice. He took Jamie by the shoulders, sat him in the chair and put James to cuddle comfortably in his lap. "Take a load off, Tex. Looks like you've had a busy morning," Mike grumbled, grabbing a handful of pancakes with one meaty hand, and pointing to the platter on the table with the other, grunting, nonverbally ordering Jamie to eat.

Sitting back with his mouth full of panwich, his voice still not having recovered its normal tone, Mike growled, "You know, I always thought I might like to get a *'tattoon'* myself someday. You know where I can get a good *'tattoon'*?" he asked with a deadpan expression on his face, looking directly into Jamie's eyes and shaking his fork at him. Jamie laughed out loud himself at that, feeling grounded again inside. *"Guess I ain't goin' anywhar after all."*

"Tattoons! Tattoons!" Victoria squealed, clapping loudly and laughing, "Daddy's gonna get a tattoon!" Mike winced at the shrillness of her excitement. Jamie saw it and put his finger to his mouth to remind her, "Shhhh."

Thank you, Michael.

■

A silent understanding reached, Mike looked at his kids, completely unaware of what the previous thirty-six hours had brought. *Please! What do I do now?* he thought, grasping at whatever alternatives would be least traumatic for them all. *Just act normal…like nothing ever happened,* was his best answer to himself. *But how? Everything has happened! The world you went so comfortably to sleep in Wednesday night doesn't exist anymore,* he asked himself, quietly rubbing his head in his hands at the table while Victoria finished her Captain Crunch and James struggled to take off his shoes. Jamie helped.

Why not? he concluded with a deep breath and a sigh. It's not like he was left with a lot of choices. *Help me, Jane. I'm so lost.*

"Victoria, why don't you take James in the other room and watch TV or play, sweetheart. I need to talk to Jamie for a while," Mike said.

"Yes, Daddy," she said, knowing enough by then to realize that Daddy was not feeling well *at all*.

Jamie held his breath as he put James down on the floor; Victoria waiting in front of them to take his hand. Mike waited until he heard the TV voices to light a cigarette before he spoke.

"The yard needs work. Looks like hell. I've gotta mow, hopefully for the last time this season, and clean up before it gets too cold. I don't like the cold. It makes me feel...cold," he said struggling to sound and feel as routine as he did three days before. "I'm gonna take a shower first, to get my blood pumping again, clear the cobwebs out."

"Michael, I..." Jamie stammered.

Mike cut him off with a firm wave of his hand, his eyes drinking in every aspect of that face in the daylight, like a man dying of thirst in a desert, thinking, *"Don't you dare tell me you want to leave,"* then spoke it, "You were gonna run this morning, weren'tcha?" he asked with a soft growl so the kids couldn't hear, his hands on his hips holding his baggy flannel pajama bottoms up.

Jamie didn't answer. He just nodded his head, looking down.

"Why?"

"I was...afraid," Jamie said with a deep sigh, still not lifting his head.

"Of what?" Mike asked, not taking his eyes off of Jamie.

"I dunno," Jamie said, his voice going lower, barely audible.

"Are you afraid *now*?" Mike asked, moving back in closer to the table.

"I bin afraid all my life, Michael. Runnin' all my life," Jamie responded, looking up at Michael for the first time, desperate to be as honest as he could. Michael deserved that much from him after he'd brought such shame down on his house.

Mike moved in closer and leaned across the table, his hands propping him up, bringing him in closer to Jamie's face.

"Are you afraid now?" Mike asked again, looking into what had only days ago been Jane's eyes. "Right now…at this very minute?"

Jamie looked up at him again, into his true blue eyes and told the truth. Mike saw it before his lips moved to speak.

"No."

"And how does that feel?"

"Good," was all Jamie could get out, nodding with a small smile, his eyes filling again, forcing him to look down, ashamed, but yet somehow still not ashamed as he had been the night before.

Mike stood up. *God that smile hurts so bad*, he thought as he walked back toward the door, feeling like he'd been stabbed in the heart with a rusty spike.

"Settle in and make yourself at home then," he said without turning around. "Oh, and by the way, I like coconut and nuts in my cookies," he grumbled as he went out through the doorway.

I know.

■

Victoria Golden heard the shower turn on upstairs and clanking in the kitchen. Watching the adventures of *Dora the Explorer* on the TV in front of her, she enjoyed her ever-growing role as big sister. James was quiet, mesmerized beside her. The phone rang loudly, disturbing her viewing. She turned to see if anyone was going to come and get it. It rang again, then again. No one came. Daddy didn't like her answering the phone, just in case it was a client and he wanted everything to sound professional.

The phone kept ringing. *Doesn't anyone hear that?* Victoria thought to herself; increasingly annoyed at being disturbed in the middle of *Dora*. It rang again, loudly; insistently. *Enough is enough!"* Victoria thought, irritated by having to get up, leaving James wide-eyed before the magic box and going over to the old fashioned phone on the small table beside the stairs. It rang again and she picked up.

"Hello."

■

Mike dressed in his old Carhartts, his body stiff and sore as if he'd been in a car accident himself. He looked in the mirror. The puffiness in his eyes had gone down and they didn't seem as red. He smelled the glorious aroma of coconut baking downstairs and the comforting sound of the TV playing. *Just a little peace, God, please,* he thought, preparing to go outside and lose himself in the hum of the lawnmower and the constant repetition of going back and forth, back and forth across the lawn.

The weather was crisp and clean outside. He took a deep breath, *Ah, October!* he thought as he went around back to the tool shed over by the far back corner of the house. "Please, start. Please start," he pleaded as he pulled the hand start cord. *Vrrrrooooommm!*

"Thank you," he said out loud, looking up toward the overcastting sky. He did the front first. It didn't take long. Most of the front yard was a thicket of trees around the long driveway and the rest had been parceled into flower beds by a succession of previous owners.

He'd only just begun to sweat under his heavy coat when he headed toward the much larger back yard and took it off, leaving it on a chair over by the fire pit. Back and forth, back and forth he went, gaining force as he pushed and pushed, lost in the loud rumble of the old machine. Soon he was soaked with sweat, pushing harder and harder, faster and faster, more determined than ever to thoroughly exhaust himself.

Inside, with the coconut macadamia nut cookies in the oven, Jamie made himself a cup of coffee and rolled a cigarette out with his machine and tobacco pouch, then lit it; watching through the bay window from behind the curtain as Mike took out all of his frustrations on that length of lawn. *Poor, Michael, ya look so lonesome,* he thought shaking his head, then went to peek in the living room to make sure all was well there.

The warmth of the oven and the smell of the spices seemed to give Jamie some peace, too, as he baked, knowing how much Jane had loved it. Using her things seemed to make him feel close to her again, not as divided as he'd felt for the last few days.

He'd just taken the cookies out of the oven when he heard a knock at the door and looked at the clock. It was already close to one P.M. Another knock and he walked through the doorway into the entry hall next to the stairs; Victoria and James, now both hypnotized by some fantasy film. He saw an old, dark-black man outside and opened the door.

The old man took a step back, putting his hand to his chest. "Sweet Jesus!" the old man exclaimed, taking another step back. Jamie opened the screen door, knowing that he was about to have another one of *those* experiences.

"You must be the Reverend. I saw ya at the funeral. I'm Jamie Arnette, Jane's brother." The old man took a step forward, staring intently at Jamie's face like it was a sight gag or the result of a magic trick.

"Yes, Josiah Willis," the old man said, putting out his hand hesitantly. Jamie took it, leading him into the house. "Great day in the morning!" Reverend Willis said as he passed into the house, astonishment written all over his face, studying Jamie's.

"I came ta help Michael with the kids 'til...well...'til," Jamie said haltingly. "Please come in, Reverend. I got a fresh

batcha cookies jes' out and a pot o' coffee." Reverend Willis
followed Jamie into the kitchen. "Michael is out mowin' the
lawn, workin' off some energy," Jamie said with a small smile,
pointing out the bay window with one hand as he handed the
Reverend a cup of coffee with the other. "I'll tell 'im yer
here," Jamie said, noticing the expression on the Reverend's
face when he smiled.

"No, no, don't bother him, son. I can wait," Reverend
Willis said, sitting down at the kitchen table to sip his coffee.
"I jus' wanted to drop by and see how he was making out,
under the circumstances. See if he needed anything. Michael
is very close to us over at the church."

"Yes, I understand that and I wanted ta thank ya fer the
beautiful funeral ya gave my sister," Jamie said, his eyes
clouding over.

"But I don't remember seein' you there," Reverend Willis
said curiously. "I wouldn't have missed you...under the
circumstances."

"I was the guy with the bike under the tree. I walked
'round ta the back ta hear ya speak," Jamie said, flushing with
embarrassment.

The Reverend nodded, pointing his crooked finger at
him. "I knew there was somethin' different about that."

"It's a very long story, Reverend," Jamie said, shaking his
head, looking down.

"Don't trouble yourself, son. There's no need to explain
to me. I had a feelin' when I saw you at the cemetery. Didn't
know what it was then, but it makes sense now," he said
sympathetically. "You have my condolences, son."

"Thank you, Reverend," Jamie said, setting down a plate
of cookies on the table. The Reverend took one. They both
heard the rumbling engine outside stop suddenly and looked
out of the window to see Mike drop himself into one of the
chairs by the fire pit, the light mist of his chilled breath
coming in rapid bursts. Jamie got up and made another cup
of coffee, black, and the plate of cookies to take outside, the
Reverend opening the door for them to go out.

Mike stood up instantly, his spirit lifting the minute he saw the old man, and rushed toward them. "Reverend!" Mike called to him, hand out, then pulled the old man in and hugged him.

"How are you doin', Michael?" the Reverend asked delicately, his gentle black eyes shining with sympathy.

"Better, Reverend, better. Thank you," Mike said, relieved inside to see the old man. Jamie handed Mike the cup of coffee and plate of cookies, then walked back toward the house. "I don't want ta leave the kids alone too long," he said, backing away with his hands in his pockets, not waiting to be spoken to.

Mike and the Reverend sat down by the fire pit. Mike got up again nervously, putting new wood in the pit and lighting it. Suddenly there was a loud rush, water splashing and the sound of flight. The two men looked up to see a flock of ducks take to the sky, as if they'd been frightened, heading to the other side of the lake.

The fire caught nicely because of the over dried wood. Mike sat back down next to the Reverend to talk, not sure what he wanted to say, so he began with the obvious. "So, you met Jamie."

"Yes, Michael I did. Set me back a turn, I'll admit. I didn't know Jane had a brother, let alone a twin. Lord have mercy, Michael. It's amazing," the old man said, shaking his head; an inkling of what Michael must see when he looked at Jamie passing through his mind.

"I didn't either, until last night. She never told me," Mike said, the faucets that used to be his eyes, having taken on a life of their own, turned on again, slowly letting another stream of water run down his cheeks. "There was so much she never told me," he said, drying his eyes and then changed the subject. "He's a woodworker, very talented. I'm gonna try to get him to make the new altar for the church," then paused. "But I gotta tell ya, Reverend. It breaks my heart every time I look at him," Mike said, wiping his eyes again and poking at the fire nervously. "I don't know what to do."

"I know it may seem like cold comfort to you now, but I believe that the Lord never gives us more than we can carry, and they don't have a mother anymore, Michael."

Mike looked up to the old man, startled, like the old man had reached inside him and grabbed hold of what his own mind could not consciously conceive by itself, leaving him too stunned to speak.

The Reverend reached over and took Mike's hand, looking seriously in his eyes. "The Lord moves in mysterious ways, Michael. And this is as mysterious a touch of his hand as I've ever seen," he said, shaking his head; incredulous. "Take it as a sign, Michael; a sign from God. Accept his blessing as he has seen fit to give it to you...and your children." Mike jumped up and started pacing, rubbing the back of his neck roughly.

Jamie watched Michael's agitation through the window, wondering. He watched them walk around the house, toward the front, the old man's hand on Mike's arm. He heard a sizzle and turned. The soup he'd put on for the kid's lunch was boiling over. "Dayum!" He jumped and turned it off, then took the grilled cheese sandwiches out from the warmer, put them on the kitchen table and went toward the living room.

Victoria was just putting down the phone. She turned and saw Jamie, surprised, saying innocently before he had the chance to ask, "Wrong number," then skipped over to the couch and came around with James by the hand, singing to him, "Chick-chick-chicken noodle soup. We love chicken noodle soup!" James giggled, trying to imitate her, "Chick-chick-chick."

Chapter Four

Birds of a Feather

W hen Mike came back in through the front door after seeing the Reverend to his car, Victoria was making boats in her soup out of the bite sized pieces of grilled cheese sandwich that Jamie had cut up for her. Jamie was having less success because for every piece of sandwich he got James to eat, he ended up wearing another one. Then there was the soup splashing. Little James was just full of piss and vinegar that afternoon, giggling with glee at the noodle that had just landed in Jamie's hair as Mike walked through the kitchen door. Mike laughed out loud, then put on his firm "Daddy" voice.

"James, you stop that right now," he barked.

Startled, James stopped, turning toward the door, eyes wide, not expecting Daddy to catch him acting up. Mike raised an eyebrow at him and pointed his finger, "Right now!" and James quieted, by then covered in soup and sandwich himself. Mike looked at Jamie, wanting to burst out laughing again, but held himself in, walking over to the coffee pot to refill his cup. "You're some tough biker guy there, aren'tcha?" he said out of the side of his mouth, plucking the noodle out of Jamie's hair, then sat down next to Victoria. "C'ave'sum?" he said to her and opened his mouth wide. Victoria dipped the spoon into her bowl and came up with a boat, putting it into Mike's mouth, "Ummmmmm."

Jamie just sat there bewildered, yellow spots of chicken soup dotting his otherwise white tee shirt, cookie flower on his arms and in his hair, worn out and feeling like he'd failed some cosmic test of domestic acceptance. Mike could hear the sound of the washer and dryer running in the mud room off to the right, an old pantry. He went over and took James out of his chair, then walked over to Jamie, pointing his finger at the toddler and deepening his voice again, "You don't be a bad boy for Jamie."

"Michael, please, it's okay," Jamie pleaded. Mike ignored him.

"Now you kiss your Jamie to let him know you're sorry for giving him a hard time," Mike said, leaning James in close to Jamie's face. The little boy put his lips out lightly touching his cheek. Jamie froze. A child's kiss...he'd never felt that before. The blood drained from his face and his body went rigid until Mike pulled the boy back.

"That's a good boy," Mike said to James, tickling him. James wiggled and writhed, giggling and squealing until Mike put him down. Mike rushed after him. "We're gonna clean up. Be right back." Victoria got up and came around to Jamie's side of the table, handing him her napkin to wipe his eyes.

"You cry a lot, Jamie. Are you very sad?" she asked, kindly searching under his hair for his eyes.

"No, sweetheart, I'm very happy," he said quietly, wiping his face with the napkin she'd given him.

"Can I come and sit by you?" she asked. He nodded and she went and got her chair.

■

Mike came down a few minutes later with a newly cleaned James squirming in his arms. Victoria was sitting next to Jamie munching on a cookie. "Sweetheart, could you take James and entertain him so Jamie and I can..."

And she finished his sentence for him, "...talk for a while."

"Boy, you are my smart girl, aren't you?"

"Yes, Daddy," she answered, like she'd heard those words a million times before, and took James by the hand, leading him back to the TV.

Once she was safely out of earshot, Mike went and sat at the table. "Are you alright?" he asked, under his breath. Jamie nodded. "Did James upset you?" Jamie shook his head.

"Naw. It was...wonderful," he said, touching his cheek, the color rising up in his face.

"Yeah?"

"Yeah," Jamie affirmed, nodding his head again, then got up and took his jacket from the hook behind the door, not looking back at Mike. "Kin I go set by yer fire fer a while, git some air?" Jamie asked as he opened the door. Mike stood up.

"Yeah, sure," and he reached over to the counter for what was left of his pack of cigarettes. "You need this?"

"Naw, I roll my own," Jamie said, pulling the suede pouch out of his pocket for Mike to see.

The blaze of the fire Mike had made had faded to glowing embers by the time Jamie got out to the pit. He grabbed some kindling and threw it in, then put on a quarter log. He sat down and rolled a cigarette from the suede pouch and sat back to watch the fire build. When he looked up, the sun had started to sink below the horizon.

He touched his cheek again, trying to remember what it felt like. *Is that whut happiness is? How would I ev'n know? The only happiness I've ev'r known came in a white powder.* He watched the sunset and smoked, smiling to himself as he touched his cheek again. Michael's voice replayed itself in his mind, *You're some tough biker guy there, aren'tcha?* and he shook his head, still smiling.

As he watched the sun set even further, it seemed to be trying to pull him closer. He got up and walked towards the lake, meandering until he got to the edge. A rustling sound came from the brush again and he watched as first one duck, then another came swimming out, heading toward the middle of the lake. Then more, and quacking, singular at first, then more, until it was like a chorus, rising in pitch and frequency. They were laughing at him. He knew it; laughing because they knew…what had been done to him and what he'd done. "Stop laughin' at me!" he said quietly to himself at first, but they wouldn't listen. He pointed his finger out to the middle of the lake, pleading at first, then angry and hurt. "Stop laughin' at me!" he cried out, wrapping his arms around himself, stomping back toward the fire.

He picked up another quarter log and threw it into the lake. The ducks scattered with an alarming cry as they rose in the sky above his head. The biggest one laughed as it flew off, seemingly into the setting sun. Another one cried out, cackling with laughter as it followed the first. Then they were gone. He was alone again, his hands shaking as he tried to roll another cigarette, huddling by the fire.

The sound of a door slamming came from behind him a moment later, then Mike's voice grumbling in the distance, "Hey, what's going on?"

Jamie turned back to see Mike coming toward him, Captain Morgan bottle in hand. Mike plopped himself down in one of the chairs, putting his feet up on the wood pile with a crash. He took a quick slug out of the bottle then handed it over to Jamie who took a good slug for himself and handed it back.

"Reverend Willis wants to look at your portfolio to see about an altar," Mike said, very business like.

It went right over Jamie's head. He was too busy looking back at the house.

"Don't worry. They're quiet. The front door is locked and Victoria can be very grown up when I need her to be."

Jes' like her Daddy, Jamie thought, relieved and turned back to business. "I really could use the work, Michael. I don't have much money left, and…I cain't depend on yer kindness ferev'r," he said, flushing with embarrassment.

"What kindness?" Mike said, exasperated. "You've only been here twenty-four hours, for God's sake. Give it a chance," and he took another slug of the Captain then handed over the bottle. Mike could have kicked himself then, for being so off-handed and rough.

You've really become a certified knuckle scraping ape there, haven't you, Mike, he thought with a wince, then took a deep breath. "Okay, let's look at it this way. We've already established that you're going to stay, right?"

Jamie nodded.

"You've cooked, done laundry and watched my kids all day. That counts, too. I've got more work than I can handle going on, *paying work.* The church has to be finished by Thanksgiving and I need an altar. I promised the Reverend, and we have to get this place at least leak and draft proof before the winter, so the kids don't get sick, then we can work on the inside until the spring.

"On top of that, I have to be at the church every day to make sure that it gets done and I don't have anybody to take care of the kids. Is that enough work for you?" Mike asked, winded by his rapid delivery.

Jamie nodded smiling.

"Come on now," Mike said standing up. "I'm gettin' cold. I don't like the cold and I still need to shower off the afternoon's sweat…and I need to ask you for a little favor."

Jamie looked up, curious.

Mike's face took on a tough look in the glow of the firelight. "Come on I'll show you."

■

Inside the house, Mike gave Jamie a tour of the upstairs, the kids' room, his room, *their* room, the extra rooms, the attic door, then a small door at the end of the hall.

Mike took out a key and opened it, flipping on the light, looking back at Jamie. "No kids allowed," he whispered and walked in. Jamie followed.

It was a small library, two full walls of hastily made, unfinished pine bookshelves housing hardcover books. The rest of the room looked like a cyclone had hit it; disorganized, disheveled, completely untended. There were books everywhere; old, new, used, damaged, mostly paperbacks; an overstuffed, ratty easy chair tucked in the corner by the window, a mismatched foot stool and chair-side table filled with empty coffee cups, glasses and dishes.

"My sanctuary," Mike said with an odd mix of embarrassment and pride in his voice, shrugging his shoulders. He went and sat in his chair, pulling the volume of *Uncle Tom's Cabin* from his side table; flipping through it with his thumb and setting it back down. He looked up at Jamie, standing there and looking around, confused. "I need some down time, Jamie. I haven't had a minute to myself to think since the accident, just a little time, a few hours, please."

Jamie still didn't understand. "So whuddya want me ta do?" he asked, still taking in the books all around him, bending over to pick up a paperback copy of *Farenheit 451* from the floor near his foot and setting it on Mike's table.

"Well, I thought after we get ourselves showered up and get the kids clean and fed, maybe you could keep an eye on them so I can have a few hours by myself here, just to be alone and think. I really need it bad," Mike said, almost apologetically, cracking his knuckles nervously.

Jamie smiled, bending over to pick up another paperback from the floor by his other foot, D. H. Lawrence's *Women in Love*.

"Sure, I kin do that," Jamie said easily.

Mike let out a deep sighing breath. "Thanks, why don't you go shower first and I'll get Victoria up here to take her bath and get her ready for school tomorrow. Then we can switch…I'll shower and you can wash James. He must have shit himself at least once today. He's getting better. We just haven't gotten quite there yet."

Jamie laughed, blushing.

"Yeah, this afternoon after 'is nap. Victoria and I took care of it while ya were mowin' the lawn. I know whar ev'rthang is now," he said, putting his hand over his mouth, muffling another laugh as he remembered the smell, saying out loud, "Peee Yeeewww, Dayum," then let loose a chuckle, shaking his head.

Mike got up and went to the door, brushing past Jamie in the small room, barely touching him. Jamie flinched again. It hurt Mike and made him angry. He let it go for the moment, bellowing through the door, "Victoria! Time to come up for a bath, sweetheart." He turned back to Jamie and stopped, then made like he was going to rush him. Jamie jumped, closing his eyes, defensively covering his face like a boxer, waiting.

When nothing happened, Jamie's hands dropped and he opened his eyes, feeling foolish. Mike was still standing in the same place with his hands on his hips, his black eyebrows furrowed, his blue eyes, true blue, worried, hurt. "I'd never hurt you any more than I'd've hurt her...and I never hurt her, not once...not ever."

"I know."

"I may be big, and I may be ugly, but I don't hurt things," Mike said, his eyes filling again as he turned to leave, calling out the door angrily, "Victoria! Now, sweetheart!" The hurt look in Mike's eyes struck Jamie like a blow to the chest.

"I know," Jamie said again. He had to do something, and grabbed for what he could. "Okay, try it agin," Jamie said, making the "come on" motion with his hands. Mike hesitated; turning away then jerking his shoulder forward. Jamie felt a panicked urge to flinch but held himself and smiled. "Better?"

"Much," Mike replied, blushing himself, embarrassed at being caught acting so childishly, "Victoria!" he shouted out the door again.

"Michael, she cain't leave James alone downstairs. I'll go," Jamie said shaking his head and smiling. On his way out he brushed past Mike, giving him a good nudge with his shoulder as he went, calling downstairs, "I'ma comin'!"

leaving Michael Golden standing there feeling like a buffoon; a great big, grumbling, growling buffoon, and Mike was okay with that. It was one small battle won. He breathed a sigh of relief, satisfied with the knowledge that in a short while, he'd be losing himself in the old South of *Uncle Tom's Cabin;* another time, another place, anywhere other than where he'd been for the last four days, anyone other than who he had been for the last four days.

When Victoria heard Jamie's footsteps coming down the stairs, she hung up the phone quickly and ran to the foot of the stairs. "I'm ready," she said, as she passed him on the stairs. "James is on the couch watching the cat."

Cat? Whut cat? Jamie thought as he headed toward the couch. James was sitting there, motionless with fascination, staring blankly at the orange glow coming from the body of a...cat. It was a lamp, looked like an antique. He went over and looked closer. It was the strangest thing he'd ever seen. It had the brass head of what looked like a male cat wearing a formal bowtie. The body was amber glass molded into a cat's torso, sleek vertical striations giving it the look of hair, sitting on a brass base made to look like a fancy pillow.

"James," Jamie called to him. "Bath time."

James didn't move.

Jamie went over to him, still as a statue, staring at that cat, hypnotized, and picked him up, holding him to his shoulder. James didn't fuss. He just continued to look over Jamie's shoulder at the glowing cat lamp, waving his little hand at it until they'd turned the corner and it was out of sight.

■

With both kids bathed, Jamie showered first while Mike watched them, then Mike showered while Jamie fed them. Already in his oversized tee shirt and plaid flannel pajama bottoms, Mike peeked around the corner and saw Jamie had everything under control. James was eating macaroni and cheese with his fingers, only a few pieces flying through the air, while Jamie played airplane with bits of chicken on a fork. Victoria, as lady-like as ever, used a knife and fork on hers with a plate of cookies off to the side, so he took the opportunity to sneak away to his room.

After Victoria and James were done eating, Victoria took James to the TV to entertain him for the short time it took Jamie to clean up. He took the two small dishes and washed them in the sink, then went to put away what was left over, not much, maybe a lunch worth or two. He opened the refrigerator door, put the leftovers in and went to shut it, but stopped. Something tugged at him. He opened it back up and looked in. Something drew him to look in the cold cut drawer. He went with it and pulled it out, nothing unusual, two or three wrapped packages of sliced meat and cheese, just like in any other house.

He reached in and took the two top packages. The minute he held them in his hand he remembered the letter, could see it in his mind. *Please look after Michael...* and he knew, like a bright light going off in his head. *Michael hasn't eaten since breakfast.*

The idea grew into action as he reached back in without thinking; rye bread, Hellman's Mayonnaise, Gulden's mustard. His hands were full. He laid the things on the counter and opened the first package; red-edged Virginia baked ham. The other was sliced baby Swiss cheese. He reached back into the refrigerator; dill pickles, a gallon of milk. The next thing he knew, he had a plate and was smearing a thick layer of mayonnaise on one piece of the rye bread and the mustard on the other, then filled them thickly with the ham and cheese. He cut it crossways into triangles and put two pickles next to it.

He took the blue tray from next to the toaster, loaded it with the plate and a big glass of milk and headed toward the door. He hesitated, stopping in mid step. *Somethin's missin'.* He looked at the tray, then turned around with the tray in one hand, backed up, grabbed a handful of coconut macadamia cookies from the big plate on the table and dropped them next to the milk. He looked at the tray again, satisfied. *It's right now,* and headed back out the door and up the stairs.

Outside the room at the end of the hall, he stopped. *Whuddo I do now?* His hand went up and he knocked lightly.

"It's okay, come in," he heard from the other side of the door. Jamie turned the knob, balancing the tray tenuously with his other hand, and went in slowly. Mike was all curled up in his chair, a huge bare foot sticking out from underneath a faded patchwork afghan, an old fashioned floor lamp behind his right shoulder. Jamie did a double take. Something was different. It only took a second to put his finger on it. Michael was wearing glasses, gold, horn-rimmed glasses... and was holding the copy of *Uncle Tom's Cabin* in his hand. They made him look so...different. Nice, and not so rough. Jamie went over to the side table and set down the tray.

"I thought ya might be hungry," Jamie said shyly and turned to go, his own energies flagging and not wanting to disturb Michael's down time. Mike looked at the tray and the words stuck in his throat, "How did..." was all he got out, leaving "...you know?" to remain caught inside him, crowded by other words, not his own. It was the Reverend Willis' voice, *The Lord moves in mysterious ways, Michael...Accept his blessing as he has seen fit to give it to you...*

"Ya haven't eaten all day, Michael," Jamie said, shutting the door quietly behind him and going downstairs.

A few minutes later, Jamie collapsed comfortably in what he didn't have to be told was Jane's cushioned rocker, dead on his feet. Victoria informed him that he'd already missed the first part of the first Shrek, but was obviously pleased to fill him in using rapid kid speak, "And...and...and..."

Tired and struggling to listen attentively, he felt a small tug at his leg and saw a little blonde head pop up from the floor. James was crawling up in his lap with his night-time bottle. Jamie pulled him the rest of the way up by the seat of his pajamas. Within seconds, James was snuggling deep into a warm niche under Jamie's arm, gazing lazily at him, the shine of near sleep in his eyes like it was the most natural thing in

the world to him. It felt good, so good and so…real. Jamie
held him close and started to rock, closing his own eyes. He
felt himself riding, miles and miles, all those dark, lonely
roads alone, so long, so many; coming from nowhere, going
nowhere. The Daughtry song *Home* played in the back of his
mind. He'd heard it at every truck stop and biker bar on the
way as he rode almost non-stop from Texas to Pennsylvania.
*"I'm staring out into the night, trying to hide the pain. I'm going to the
place where love and feeling good don't ever cost a thing. And the pain
you feel's a different kind of pain…"*

He rocked the boy slowly with a soothing natural rhythm
and began to hum, then sing softly under his breath.

*"Well I'm goin' home, back ta the place whar I belong, and whar
yer love has always bin enough fer me. . ."*

As the tune played itself out in his head, Jamie drifted off
somewhere inside himself, the clean sweet baby smell making
him feel safe, secure and…loved, for the first time since he
was that age himself. *I love you, James.* Victoria had fallen
asleep, too; next to them on the couch. *I love you, Victoria,* and
he was out like a light.

When Michael came downstairs a few hours later, rubbing
his eyes and scratching his balls, he found them, all three of
them, on the couch. Jamie was snoring lightly, holding James
curled under his arm in front of him, snoring, too. Victoria
was behind his legs, wrapped in her blanket with her head
resting on his hip, and for the second time in his life, Michael
Golden felt himself splinter.

He looked down and saw his own hand reach out to
touch that face, stopping only inches away, catching himself
just in time. He shifted and reached over to Victoria instead,
gently lifting her into his arms and taking her upstairs to her
room.

He came back down a few minutes later and stood just
staring at them, rubbing his temples and shaking his head in
the dim light of the television set; his two blonde Jameses.
Not having the heart to disturb either of them, he just took

the blanket and covered them both, turned off the TV and went back to his room alone.

■

Jamie's eyes opened just as the sun was coming up over the horizon. He got up and took James to his room, then went back downstairs and put on a pot of coffee. The clock on the microwave told him it was almost six A.M. Michael would be getting up soon and he had to get ready.

When the coffee was done, he poured himself a cup, put on his boots and Michael's big Carhartt jacket from the back door hook next to his leather one, and went out back to smoke. The first of the real autumn chill was in the air, freezing his breath in small clouds as he walked close to the fire pit. The wind blew sending a palette of brightly colored leaves in his direction. Another wind brought more leaves, all seeming to land around him, swirling around his feet. He turned to head back toward the house, and they followed him. He heard that rustle again and the splash of water behind him. He looked back. They were there staring at him, three large ducks, more coming up on land to join them, staring at him.

Almost at the back door, he broke into a trot, closing the door behind him, breathless, and went to the window. They were gone. He heard Michael's alarm go off upstairs and took a deep breath, letting it out in a whistle as he took off his boots and Michael's jacket.

He heard heavy footsteps upstairs, then the shower start. Comforted again by not being alone, Jamie went to the refrigerator and took out some eggs and bread for Michael's breakfast, making his and Victoria's lunches while the eggs cooked. He heard Mike's footsteps again, this time descending the stairs, and he was ready.

When Mike walked though the kitchen door, dressed roughly for work, the swelling in his eyes now almost completely gone, the table was set and waiting for him.

Before Mike could say a word, Jamie was past him, nudging him slightly with his shoulder followed by a rushed, "I gotta git Victoria up and riddy fer school. I'll tend ta James while she's eatin'." Mike stopped and turned to see him about to rush up the stairs.

"Good morning, Michael," Mike said to himself loudly.

"Good mornin', Michael." He heard Jamie's voice come back from halfway up the stairs.

He'd just finished eating his scrambled eggs and toast with his second cup of coffee and was having a cigarette when he heard Victoria's thumping skip sounds coming down the stairs. "Good morning, Daddy," he heard from the doorway and leaned over for their morning ritual, feeling her lips on his cheek.

"G' morning, sweetheart," he rumbled as she took her seat and he poured her a bowl of Captain Crunch. "James pooped himself last night and Jamie is changing him," she said very matter of factly. "They'll be down in a minute."

Mike pulled a face thinking, *Boy, have you got a nasty eye opener comin' to you.* Then laughed to himself, shaking his head.

A few minutes later, there were more footsteps on the stairs. Jamie came in bouncing James on his hip and put him in his chair. He was back a minute later with James's tipless cup filled with apple juice and half of a blueberry muffin cut up into little chunks.

By eight, Jamie had James on his hip again and was walking Victoria to the school bus. When he got back to the house, Michael was waiting for them. Jamie passed him and went into the kitchen coming back a few seconds later juggling James from side to side as he handed Mike his old black tin workman's lunch box with one hand and his portfolio in the other. "If Reverend Willis kin pick a design from thar and ya kin git me some dimensions, I'll start callin' around fer the wood I need. I have all the hand tools I need, might need to borrow a router though, dependin' on whut he decides on," Jamie rattled, going back into the kitchen again and coming out with his coffee cup.

It all seemed so routine to Mike, so familiar as he stood by the front door, waiting, looking at Jamie with James on his hip and waiting, seeing Jane there and waiting, waiting for the good-bye kiss he'd gotten every morning for the last six years of his life. Catching himself when he realized that it wouldn't come, he took a deep breath, his shoulders slumping, and walked out the door; angry, so angry, refusing to let himself cry again, but losing the fight as he closed the door to his truck.

Chapter Five

Mike the Builder

"G' mornin', Mike," Alex Timbers said, putting his hand on Mike's shoulder. Small and dark, Alex was the oldest of Mike's crew; about fifty, and the most experienced, a carpenter of the old school.

"G'morning," Mike responded, rushing along side Alex across the parking lot, squinting at the sun in his eyes; overly energetic, almost manic. It had started when he got in the car and continued to grow the closer he got to work; a nervous energy, until he felt like he would explode with it and when he hit the site, he did explode; into a sweating grunting, hammer wielding, pale faced, blue eyed John Henry with the Inkypoo hot on his tail.

The men just went about their business; painting, sanding and roofing, and staying out of Mike's way. They knew there was nothing they could really do for him but be sensitive and caring in a guy sort of way; be there when he needed them and not grieve him over the small things. But they'd have done that anyway. They all liked Mike; the way he never talked down to them when teaching them something. He had all kinds there, a few part-time students from the Community College, a few guys who worked nights and needed the money for a new baby or a new car. They all believed it was in God's hands for him to work it all out of himself the best way he knew how.

Bursting with adrenaline and working three times faster than he normally did, Mike the builder took all of the most strenuous tasks from the other men and lost himself in them. He went from one area of work to the next, lifting bags of sand and mortar, unloading lumber and most of all using his saw and hammer like a virtuoso, his otherwise heavy tool belt seeming light as air. *Bang, bang! Thump, thump! Crash, bang, thump, vrrrroooommm,* went on ceaselessly for hours until Mike saw the Reverend coming toward him from the parking lot. He stopped and went to him, breathing hard. The old man smiled and handed him his handkerchief to wipe the layers of grime from his face.

"You alright, Michael?" he asked, concern hovering behind his otherwise placid black eyes.

"Yeah," Mike said, nodding and wiping his face. "I'm glad you're here. I have something I wanna show you," then trotted over to his truck, coming back with a black portfolio in his hand and his lunch box under his arm, completely out of breath.

The two men walked slowly into the church. Mike regained his breath as they went and handed the portfolio to the old man. "Take a look at these, Reverend, and tell me what you think," Mike said, taking a seat in the front pew and opening his lunch box. The Reverend sat next to him and flipped through the pages. Mike took out half of a bacon and cheese sandwich and took a bite, waiting anxiously for the Reverend's thoughts.

"This is his work?" the old man asked, noticing the hot wired energy behind Mike's eyes.

"Yeah, beautiful isn't it?" Mike asked excitedly, like a kid hyped up on sugar. "Which one do you like best...for an altar top."

"Michael, we can't afford this. These things cost a fortune."

"Yes, you can," Mike said, a firm conviction in his voice, taking out the now dog-eared copy of *Uncle Tom's Cabin* from his back pocket; waving it in front of the old man. "Because it's my gift to you. Remember what you said to me yesterday about God sending me a gift that I should accept. Why should it be any different for you? If God sent him to me, then why couldn't God have sent him for you, too? Look at those pictures," Mike said, turning to the page with the Greek scroll mantle. "That's real art, Reverend, and well...the guy spent practically his last dollar to come here from Texas...to help me, and God didn't give him any gas money to get here.

"Jamie's in a bad way, Reverend, worried about carrying his own weight and he won't take money from my hand. The wood'll only cost a couple of hundred, and well, you leave his pay to me. He doesn't have to know."

Reverend Willis looked into Mike's eyes and raised his finger, then hesitated, shaking his head; struck speechless by Mike having turned his own words and logic back on him, then recovered himself, "So. I guess it looks like I'm gonna have myself two white boys to pray for now, a builder and a biker. Lord have mercy. What next? Wait 'til Ella hears about this," he said laughing.

Mike laughed, too, relieved, then jumped up, pulled his tape measure out of his tool belt and stretched it across the empty altar space, then again in the other direction. "I think it should come out about six or eight inches over the existing space. Don't you?" Mike asked looking back at the old man thumbing through the book again. The Reverend looked up at him, his finger holding down a page. "I kinda like this one," he said, smiling brightly and pointing to the simplest, most dignified design.

Mike went to the door and called out, "Alex! I need ya."

Alex's small, dark wiry figure appeared in the doorway a minute later. "What can I do for ya, Mike?"

Mike quickly pulled out his wallet and handed Alex two hundred cash and his Home Depot card, lowering his voice, "I need you to go over to the mill in New Hope and get me a slab of red oak, three by seven, six inches thick, for an altar. You know what I need."

Alex nodded. "Yes, I do, Mike."

Mike rattled on in rapid-fire kid talk, like Victoria. "And...and...and while you're there, stop in one of the art shops and pick up some tracing paper, a lot, and some charcoal pencils. Then I need two saw horses and a sheet of three-quarter inch plywood from The Home Depot in Fennell, and while you're there rent me a router and a couple of heavy duty sanders, one belt, one disc, and a shop vac. Pick up a mixed bag of sandpaper packs, coarse, medium and fine, and some carpenter's pencils, too. Take any one of the other guys with you, then call your wife and tell her I need you for an extra hour today, overtime."

■

Jamie bundled James up to go outside after lunch. He had to get an idea of what needed to be done to the outside of the house before it got really cold. He did his first walk-around with James firmly attached to his hip. There were at least four loose boards in the white clapboard exterior that needed to be fixed, one hanging by only a thread. He'd fix that one first. He also noticed large gaps around some of the windows, bound to let in some wicked drafts in December and January. They would be next.

It was pleasantly chilly out, but not cold. He let James down for a minute to chase some leaves so he could poke around the black louvered shutters, paint peeling, some also hanging by only a thread. He had to get to work, and fast.

Ready to get started, he turned around to look for James. He wasn't there. Panic welled up in his guts as he scanned around, calling out, "James! James! Whar are ya, son?"

Suddenly his mind screamed at him, *The lake!* and he ran around to the back of the house. "James! James!" His eyes caught the boy in a flash, ambling as fast as his little legs could carry him toward the lake. Jamie's mind kicked into high gear, "James! No!" as the little boy got closer to the water, not listening. Then Jamie saw the ducks, three of them at the waters edge, quacking; laughing at him again.

A burst of energy shot through his legs; turbo-charged fuel injection. He ran up on the boy just before he reached the waterline, and snatched him up, out of breath, heaving and clutching him close to his chest. "Oh my God! Oh my God!" Startled, James shrieked, "Mommmmmmmy!" Jamie shushed him, holding him tightly and rocking him as they headed back toward the house, looking over his shoulder at the ducks swimming away.

Back in the house, Jamie put James in his chair; still working to catch his breath, then went to the refrigerator to get the boy some milk and cookies to quiet him. Once James was quiet again, Jamie sat down to roll himself a smoke, still shaking, and kicked himself in the ass, over and over. *Whut were ya thankin'? Fuckin' idiot! How close? How close?* He held his head in his hands, his heart almost beating out of his chest. *How close?* Across from him, James sat contentedly shoving a cookie in his mouth. "Duckies," he chirped loudly, giggling with his mouth full and pointing out through the bay window.

After he calmed down, Jamie collected his thoughts to get back to work. He still had to earn his keep. He went downstairs to the basement to look for a ladder. It was dark, the only light being from the few small windows high up by the rafters.

He saw a string in the middle of the room and pulled it. A dim yellow light came on and he saw the walls, shallow red brick arches lining the foundation covered with the neon painted bubble-like graffiti lettering of the seventies, slogans; *Make Love Not War, Peace, Love & Hope, Flower Power*, hot pink, lemon yellow, cobalt blue and bright vivid green; and there were pictures; a smiley face, peace symbols, pot leaves, and names with dates, *Bobby loves Trish 1971, Adrian lives here, Angel Baby, George Washington slept here, LSD*, and *Helter Skelter*. Jamie slowly spun around in a circle, taking it all in. It was creepy…but somehow fascinating. *This place musta bin one helluva trip room*, he thought, grabbing the five-foot ladder from over in the far corner and turning to go back up the stairs.

He pulled the light cord and was back in the dark, the only other light coming from the open door at the top of the stairs and the basement windows. *Jamey James,* he heard whispered almost imperceptively in his ear. He jerked his head around, *Nothin',* then ran back up the stairs, clanking the ladder loudly against the narrow walls of the stairwell as he went, his heart raging in his throat, and slammed the door behind him. *It's jes' yer 'magination.* Only his father ever called him *Jamey James.*

He took the ladder outside and leaned it against the porch, then grabbed his tool belt and a long length of nylon cord from his bike bag. A minute later he had James back on his hip and they were outside in the sunlight again.

When Mike pulled up the driveway at five with another truck behind him, he saw Jamie on the ladder on the far left side of the house wearing a rolled-up straw cowboy hat and a big bulky tool belt hanging off his waist. Before he went around to Jamie, he walked back to the other truck. Three men got out and started unloading from the rear. Mike took Alex up to the door with him and went in. They went into the old dining room to the left of the stairs where Mike explained to Alex what he needed him to do, telling Alex he could have the old dining room set if he wanted, if not just to leave it by the road for the trash, then went back outside to keep Jamie occupied for the time it took to make the switch. He'd just gotten off the porch and was almost around the corner when he heard Jamie's whiskey twanging voice singing from the other side, and he stopped.

"Brang me two piña coladas, one fer each hand," he drawled out. Mike stood still and listened. "We'll set sail with Capt'n Morgan and nev'r leave dry land..." Mike couldn't help but smile, then turned the corner. ". . .troubles, I fergot 'em. I buried 'em in the sand, so brang me two piña coladas and say good bye ta yer good timin' man. Yee Haa!"

"What are you doin'?" Mike asked with a chuckle, caked in his own work dirt as he walked up to the ladder. Jamie looked down.

"Hey, Michael, I'm fixin' yer loose shutters. And givin' James my big country heart," Jamie said, tipping his hat with his free hand and smiling that smile. Mike's heart skipped a beat and his eyes got wet.

That's alright then. We'll take it.

Jamie just rattled on. "I alriddy dun the loose boards. Oh and Patty Gundersen called and asked if Victoria could git off the bus at her house ta spend some time with her Anna. I didn't thank you'd mind, so I said 'Okay'," Jamie continued, putting a bunch of nails between his lips. Mike looked around making like he'd gotten something in his eye.

"Where's James?" Jamie looked down and lifted a white nylon cord tied to his thigh, then tugged. Mike followed the vibrating cord to the other end next to a nearby tree; tied to James' waist as he snoozed away in his stroller, his little face almost completely covered in a blue knit scarf. Mike laughed out loud, his hands on his hips, shaking his head. *My two Jameses,* he thought, then went over to the tree and untied the knot around James's waist, picking him up. "Okay, it's almost dark out and it's getting cold, Tex. Let's get you guys in the house."

Alex was waiting for them on the porch when they came around, the other men having already gone back to the truck. "Jamie, this is Alex, one of my best men. He just came by to drop something off for me," Mike said, winking at Alex who shied away down the porch steps, looking like he'd seen a ghost. Hearing about it was one thing, but seeing it was something else completely.

"I'll see ya tomorrow, Mike," Alex said hurriedly.

"Wait!" Mike shouted down the drive, rushing toward Alex's truck. He took out his wallet and handed him three ten dollar bills. "A twelve pack for each of ya," he said. "Thanks, guys."

"Mike you don't have to…" Alex said, trying to give it back. Mike stopped him.

"I want to," he said, walking backwards with a smile and a salute. "Have one for me."

When he turned back towards the house, his two Jameses were waiting for him on the porch.

"Whut was 'at all about?" Jamie asked.

"Ah, nothing, just a little side project I have going," Mike replied, opening the front door and taking James from Jamie's hip. The first thing Jamie saw was the kitchen and he stopped. *Dinner! How could I've fergotten! Michael'll be so angry.*

"Michael, I'm so sorry. I got so involved outside, I fergot ta make any dinner. You gotta be starvin'. I'm so sorry. I'll see whut I kin rustle up real quick," Jamie said, almost stuttering, his shoulders rounded like he was waiting to be scolded.

"Whoa, whoa, whoa," Mike said, bouncing James on his hip and tickling him. "Lemme see your hands," Mike asked, holding James up close to his head so they were both looking at Jamie from the same level.

"Whut?"

"Lemme see your hands," Mike said again, this time with some firmness. Jamie held out his hands, palms down. Hard worked and scarred, they had fresh nicks, scrapes and scratches on their backs. Mike went to the stair side table and opened the drawer, then dialed a number. "Hello? Bella Angelina? Michael Golden here. Can I get two large pies delivered? Yeah, one plain the other with meatballs, peppers, onions and…anchovies?" he asked, waiting for Jamie to answer but already knowing what it would be, testing him to see if they had the same tastes. Mike loved anchovies but Jane hated them. She always wanted mushrooms.

Jamie made a face, wrinkling his nose comically. "Naw, mushrooms," and he smiled that smile, feeling awkward and embarrassed for thinking Michael would be angry.

The nose wrinkling at the mention of anchovies sent a load of buck shot into Mike's chest and that smile got him every time, and not a small one as he had before but a full one; showing the full effect of the overbite. The force of it almost pushed Mike's back against the door jamb. He took it with a deep sigh, "Make that with mushrooms instead of anchovies," he said into the phone and hung up, then looked at James. "What's tonight gonna be, oh son of mine?" he asked the little boy with histrionics. James looked back at him, not understanding. "It's gonna be Jamie's night, no cooking, no cleaning and NO ASS WIPING!" he answered himself, tickling the boy again until he squealed, "Jeeme night!"

Mike went into the kitchen to put James in his chair, shouting back out into the hallway, "Oh, and by the way, I have a jar of Beaver Grease on the dining room table for those hands. Works like a charm...overnight."

When Jamie walked into the dining room and switched on the light, the entire room was changed. No longer a dining room, it had been transformed into a woodworking room. *His* woodworking room, with three windows overlooking the work area to give him the proper light; a huge slab of dressed red oak plank with tracing paper and pencils on it, laid out on a piece of ply wood supported by two saw horses; and tools, a router and two sanders lined up on the floor along the wall. He saw an envelope with his name on it in the center of the slab and opened it; a note with three one hundred dollar bills folded in it, Mike's handwriting. *Deposit for one carved altar, ten breakfasts, lunches and dinners, five nasty ass wipings, and for staying with us. Love, Victoria and James Golden.*

Jamie came back into the kitchen and stopped. James was already close to nodding again in his chair. All the fresh air from the day had really worn him out. Mike was having a beer at the table and making faces at James trying to keep him awake long enough to eat. Unable to speak, Jamie paced in short struts behind Mike's back, struggling so hard for something to say but coming up empty. Instead, he rushed past and went for the coat hooks. He took Mike's big coat and put it on. Mike stood up and turned to him, waiting for a reaction. "Well?"

Jamie didn't know how to behave. He wanted to do something, say something, but he didn't know how. It was all locked up deep inside him, in a tiny little lead box encased in concrete, the lid of the box airtight and marked with bold red print, *Danger. Contents Unknown.* Jamie hurried back past Mike toward the front door, managing only to nudge him with his shoulder as he rushed by, hoping that would be enough, and it was.

The next thing Mike heard was the sound of the front door opening and Victoria's voice calling out, "Daddy, the pizza man is here." Turning to get up, he saw Jamie pass quickly behind her and into the dining room; the sound of the door shutting behind him. Mike went to the front door and met the pizza man, handed him the cash and took the boxes. The sound of Garth Brooks's voice began rolling out from under the dining room doors.

Back in the kitchen, Mike grabbed a big plastic plate, threw on three slices and gave it to Victoria on a tray with two boxes of Ssips. He looked at her, into her eyes that were his, a reflection of everything he ever thought was good about himself.

"Can you do Daddy a big favor, sweetheart? Can you take this in to Jamie...in the dining room? Go slow and be careful." Victoria nodded, taking the tray from his hands, holding it tightly like a big girl, and headed toward the door. Mike stopped her. "Oh, and sweetheart? Can you stay with him for a few minutes, talk to him for a little while." Victoria turned back, looking back at Mike, a flash of an expression making her look just like her mother.

"I know what to do, Daddy."

When Victoria came back James was already fed, pizza sauce all over his face and shirt, snoring in his chair. She pulled her chair close to Mike and sat down. He put a slice of the combo pizza on a plate and gave it to her. She looked back at him, that same expression on her face and, whispering as if she was telling him a secret, said, "Daddy, Jamie cries a lot," then went about eating her pizza.

"Yes, sweetheart, I know. Jamie is a very special person and we have to treat him very specially," he said, pulling her to him and kissing her forehead, thinking how much he'd cried himself in the last week but not feeling particularly special himself at all. Victoria nodded her agreement as she picked a piece of that nasty old onion off her pizza. "I know, Daddy."

■

The next morning seemed like any other morning before. Jamie was up early and getting Victoria ready for school; James, particularly full of piss and vinegar again, was redecorating the kitchen with Fruit Loops and milk. Mike got up before his alarm and showered again, even though he'd showered before he went to bed to get the day's muck off of him. His muscles and joints hurt him from his combination Hercules and Thor impressions at the church the day before and a hot shower would at least get him out the door. *You're forty-four fucking years old. What the hell are you doing?*

Dressed again for work, he passed Victoria and James's room and saw the plaque on the door that wasn't there the day before and stopped. "Victoria & James," it read in intricately carved letters surrounded by the same Native American symbols that were on Jamie's arms with leaves and vines around the edges; beautiful, so delicate. It must have taken him all night. Then not knowing why, he looked behind him, at his library door; another plaque, big bold square letters carved deeply, rustic and roughly hewn, "Micheal's Room." He was so struck by the thought that went into the carving, it didn't even occur to him until he was on his way down the stairs again that Jamie had spelled his name wrong. Then found that he liked it all the more because of it, seeming to make it personal, to him and him alone. Yes, strangely enough, he liked it very much. It was his.

When Mike got down into the kitchen, James was just about to launch a spoonful of Fruit Loops into orbit. He snapped his fingers loudly, barking, "Yo! Boy!" and James put the spoon back in the bowl looking at Mike sheepishly. Jamie was at the counter just having finished packing their lunches and jumped when he heard Mike's voice.

Rushed to get Victoria to the bus on time, Jamie slid a plate of fried eggs and link sausage with toast in front of Mike followed by a cup of coffee, then grabbed Victoria's lunch box. Mike leaned his cheek down to her level. She kissed it and ran to meet Jamie by the front door, snatching up her book bag along the way.

Mike was already at the door with his coat on and his lunch box in his hand when Jamie came back in, one hand over the other up to his mouth, blowing warm breath into them. "Dayum, it's gettin' cold out thar. Not used ta that."

Mike couldn't help but notice that the knuckles of both of Jamie's hands were scraped and swollen, a few more scratches and red nicks on his fingers, one thumb and index finger wrapped in band-aids. *Blisters.* Jamie saw him looking and hurriedly shoved his hands in his pockets, embarrassed, and looked away. "They're beautiful," Mike growled softly under his breath, then spoke to him in their own silent language, nudging him with his shoulder as he passed him on his way out the door. *Thank you.*

■

Back at the church and fueled to urgency not only by the increasingly cold weather but also the return of his own internal power station from the day before, "Big Mike," as his crew liked to call him, went at it with a vengeance...again. *Bang, bang! Thump, thump! Crash, bang, thump, vrrrrooooommm! Bang, bang! Thump, thump! Crash, bang, thump, vrrrroooommm.*

By noon the temperature had risen close to sixty-five and Mike was sweating so hard he had to take off his jacket, then his shirt, working in only his tee shirt. He stopped only long enough to shove his lunch in his face and pour some water on his head, then it was back to work again. *Bang, bang! Thump, thump! Crash, bang, thump, vrrrrooommmm.*

The blood felt good pumping in his veins again. He would pay for it tomorrow, for sure, but for the moment he was living it, it felt damn good. He felt alive again for the first time in days; being a builder, building things, strong things, lasting things, things people valued and thought were beautiful. He was Mike the Builder, and he was going to leave his mark, no matter what, even if it killed him.

Late that afternoon, when Mike pulled back up into his driveway from work, Jamie was sitting against a column on the porch, his face held high to catch the last of the rays of the late-day sun. As Mike walked up to the porch, he sensed something was wrong. He could see Jamie's hands shaking from twenty feet away. Something was definitely wrong. He looked over to the side of the yard and saw the white nylon cord just off to the left, James at the end of it playing contentedly with a pile of toys in front of him. Mike had to concentrate to keep his voice down as he sat down next to Jamie on the porch. "You okay?" he asked quietly, calmly.

"Yeah, sure," Jamie replied in short bursts, almost a squeak at the end of each word, his hands trembling. He was definitely not okay.

Mike searched for his eyes, questioning the statement silently.

"It's nothin'. I jes' had a bad dream. That's all. James was nappin', I put my head down on the table and fell asleep," he mumbled, trying to avoid Mike's glance, pulling out a cigarette and fumbling in his jacket for a match. Out of the corner of his eye, Mike could see Victoria watching them through the window.

"Tell me."

"It's stupid, Michael. It's nothin', really," Jamie said shaking his head, the trembling in his hand making the cigarette vibrate as he checked another pocket for a match. Mike reached into his own pocket and took out a lighter.

Jamie leaned in while Mike cupped his hands against the wind. Just as Jamie touched the cigarette to the flame, Mike touched his hand and said quietly, "Stop shaking. Everything's alright now," as he had done so many times before when Jane woke up from one of her nightmares inconsolable. Jamie looked up; his eyes glassy and wet, and his hands slowly stopped shaking. It had worked for Jamie as much as it did for Jane.

"Thar's a…monster…in my dreams. It's bin years since I had one, but I did today."

"Tell me," Mike said again, quietly insisting.

"I cain't see his face, but he's big like you and…my father; a big, dark shadow tryin' to kill me. I keep fightin' 'im, goin' after 'im, knowin' I hafta kill 'im before he kills me. I keep runnin' at 'im and runnin' at 'im, hittin' 'im with anythang I kin find, but nothin' stops 'im and I git so tired, too tired to fight anymore, knowin' that whin I stop, he's gonna kill me. Then I wake up," Jamie said, wiping his eyes with his hands. "I didn't want ta be in the house alone, so I came out here with James 'til Victoria got home, then stayed out ta wait fer ya."

Mike thought for a minute, wondering if Jane had had the same monster in her dreams. She would never tell him. She'd only say that she'd had a nightmare and make him sleep with his arms around her.

"Well, I'm here now, and I'm not gonna let any monster getcha," Mike said, then, trying to make light of it, pointed to his chest and said, "I'm the biggest monster in this house," and nudged Jamie's shoulder. "Come on. Let's go in. It's gettin' cold again," he said, instinctively putting out his hand to pull Jamie to standing; wincing and gritting his teeth when Jamie gripped it.

"But I didn't fergit dinner. Thar's a chicken pot pie topped with mashed taters in the oven," Jamie said, coming back to himself.

"Good, because I'm fucking starving," Mike growled laughing, the rumble in his stomach making him feel like his knuckles were about to scrape the ground again and thinking he really could use another dose of *Uncle Tom's Cabin* tonight.

Chapter Six

Jamie's Room

S itting around the chicken pot pie that night was the first semblance of normalcy any of them had had since the accident. The swelling around Mike's eyes had stayed away. Now he just wept quietly, silently when he was alone; the passenger side floor of his truck littered with old damp paper napkins.

After the shock of it all, the finality of it, and acceptance had sunk in, there was still the grief, like half his body had been torn away violently. He could still feel the physical pain of it, and then there was the emptiness and the fact that fate, or God, maybe, had made him break his promise to himself to do whatever he had to do to provide a normal, healthy life for his family; one completely different from his own upbringing. No selfishness, no fighting, no fear or anxiety when they walked through the door from school like he'd known as a young boy, never knowing what he would find. The bitterness of the divorce, and the hate.

He'd heard someone on TV once say something about divorced parents that, *You've got to love your children more than you hate each other.* But that wasn't the case with Joe and Rose Golden. They didn't love their child more than they hated each other. He was only an object of contention between them when they weren't ignoring him completely during the marriage, and he'd become only a pawn in their ongoing tug-of-war to hurt each other after the divorce.

When Michael Golden grew up to be a man, he'd promised himself that come hell or high water, he would never let that happen to any family he might have, and up until a few days before, he believed he'd accomplished that. That was why he had waited so late to marry, to meet a good-hearted woman that he could love and build a life with, who could love him back with all his flaws. Then after years of looking and giving up hope, he'd found her; a pretty blonde girl named Jane Arnette with quiet eyes and an overbite smile, who took care of him, loved their children…and suffered terribly inside, not trusting him enough to tell him how badly she hurt. *Oh, sweetheart. I'd never have left you, no matter what.*

But that was all gone now. His world had been turned upside down, ripped to shreds and thrown back in his face until he didn't know which way was up anymore; then Jamie coming and their secret. *Oh, dear God, my Jane!* he wept alone in his room at night. Then when he got hold of himself again and took stock of what was left, he knew he had to focus on making sure the kids didn't feel what he felt.

He worried about when they grew up. Would they resent him for lying to them? *Mommy had to go away to work in a far off place and she sent Jamie to look after us,* he'd told Victoria, breaking apart into little pieces inside with each word he spoke, trying desperately not to let her see it. Victoria didn't question him. She never did, and James was too young to question anything at all. It all lived inside him; how he'd failed her…and them, failed to protect them from the world like he'd promised himself he'd do.

Little droplets of water began to fill his eyes as he slowly put forkfuls of chicken pot pie in his mouth, his head down, remembering everything he'd ever loved about her, feeling it drifting further and further from his grasp.

A voice brought him back to the table, "Michael, are you alright?" he heard Jamie say quietly from next to him at the table.

Mike just shook his head, and said softly, "I'm not alright." He felt a nudge at his hand, a paper napkin. He took it and dabbed his face trying to make it look like he was wiping his mouth for the kid's sake, then looked up at Jamie, into those eyes that he'd loved so much, and the hair that he'd touched a million times in his seven years with her; all of it, all of it, *identical.* He heard Reverend Willis's voice in his head again, *The Lord works in mysterious ways, Michael.*

But why me? he asked himself. *Why did the Lord pick on me? I'm just a regular guy who works hard, loves his family. Why her? We never hurt anybody.*

Jamie saw it coming and took the kids into the living room telling them that they wanted to, "…talk." Victoria finished his sentence. When he came back into the kitchen, he could see the tears falling from Michael's face into his plate, his big chest heaving and his hands trembling on the table, fists clenched, rocking back and forth.

Seeing this poor man in so much pain made Jamie's insides rattle like a water tower in an earthquake. Everything she'd ever written to him about Michael came to life right before his very eyes. Something erupted in the little lead box wrapped in concrete that had lain sealed tightly inside him for so long, cracking it from the force, just a small breach, just enough to let him feel, *What?* Feel this poor man's pain, and he acted. He couldn't do anything else. He took a chair and sat by him, putting his arm around him, feeling his big frame shaken to its core with grief, silent.

In the living room, Victoria took James and sat him on the couch in front of the cat, then walked over and flipped on the switch making it glow in the dim evening light. James looked up at it and was gone wherever it was he went when the cat was lit. Victoria sat next to James and waited patiently. She didn't have to wait long before she heard it, the telephone. She could tell by the ring that it was for her, her special ring. She got up quickly and answered before anyone else could come for it.

"Hello," she whispered into the receiver so no one else could hear. "Yes," she said looking around to see if anyone could see her, then crouched down behind the far side of the table from the kitchen door. "It's okay."

After the river raging through the kitchen had run its course, Mike got up and washed his face in the kitchen sink. A stinging, burning pain shot through his fingers, into his wrists. He looked down at the broken blisters covering his palms, beginning to look infected. "I'm sorry," he said, his back to the table, hearing the clatter of plates as Jamie cleared the dishes. The next thing he knew he felt a slight nudge as the plates slid into the sink from behind him, then heard a deep sigh.

"Jesus, Michael. Whut've ya dun ta yerself?"

"I need it. I need the pain to feel alive," Mike said, his eyes closed, his gravelly voice wavering.

Jamie knew what that was about, all too well, from the days when he used to cut himself before he discovered drugs. The next thing Mike knew, Jamie was guiding him back to the table, a clean white towel laid out on the top. "Wait here. Don't move."

A minute later, Jamie was back with the can of Bactine from the bathroom cabinet Jane had bought to use on the kids' scrapes and cuts. He sat down next to Mike and began to spray. Mike winced, growling and tried to pull away. "Shhhh," Jamie whispered, holding tightly onto his arm. "It'll be alright. I'll take care of it."

As soon as the Bactine had a chance to numb Mike's hands, Jamie opened the tube of antibiotic cream he had in his bag from the fresh tattoo he'd had done just before he left Texas, after he got the letter. He dabbed the cream on the blisters slowly, lightly, then opened the box of band-aids and dumped it out on the table. "Shhh," Jamie said again, like he was soothing a wild animal caught in a trap when Michael went to pull away again. "It'll be alright now, big guy."

Three large, two medium and six small band-aids later, Jamie sat back to take a look at his handiwork. All the blisters were cleaned and covered. Mike just sat there, his head hanging in shame at his own lack of self-control and pulled back into himself, non-verbal. Jamie got up and went over to a corner of the kitchen counter, to a lump-covered with a dish towel. He took the towel off, turning around, a sad small smile.

"I made yer favorite pie today. It was supposed ta be a surprise. Victoria gave me the recipe…blueberry."

It brought Mike back to himself and he smiled, weakly with a sigh.

When they went into the living room with the pie cut into slices and small plates on a tray, Victoria was already entranced by the movie on the TV, *Jungle Book* on Turner Classic Movies. James was silent as a church mouse gazing almost comically at the glowing cat lamp, his mouth open like he was catching flies. Halfway through her second piece of pie, Victoria took Mike's arm and pulled, "Come upstairs, Daddy, I wanna show you something," she said, tugging insistently. He went with her, groaning, his muscles and joints running riot as he labored to get up off the couch.

Upstairs, Victoria took him into her room and shut the door, then went over to her little desk and opened the drawer. "Look, Daddy," she said, sounding pleased with herself as she examined the piece of paper in her hand. Mike looked over her shoulder. It was a sign, crooked, misshapen, multicolored letters surrounded by lots and lots of little red hearts and blue flowers, *Jamie's Room*.

"Do you think he'll like it?" she asked, hoping that Mike would like it, too. "I made it in school today, in art class."

"I think he'll love it, sweetheart," Mike answered, shaking his head and thinking, *How did such a remarkable little girl ever come out of a big lump like me I'll never know.*

They went back downstairs, both of them calling out at the same time, "Close your eyes, Jamie." At the bottom of the stairs, Victoria peeked around the corner. "Are they closed?" she asked loudly.

"Yeah, they're closed," Jamie's voice came back around from the couch.

They tiptoed across the hall over to the dining-room door, Mike with a roll of Scotch tape held with two fingers.

"Kin I open 'em now?" Jamie asked, curious.

"Just a minute," Mike said, fumbling with only his fingertips to tape the sign on the door well over Victoria's head, then pointed to her to go over and get him.

"Keep your eyes closed." Jamie heard from right next to him as Victoria took his hand. He got up and let her lead him the few steps to the door. "Okay, you can open them now," Victoria said excitedly. Jamie opened his eyes. "Do you like it? Do you like it?" Victoria squealed jumping up and down.

The crack in his lead box widened a little further and he picked her up and hugged her tightly, looking at Mike over her shoulder.

"I love it! I love it! I love it," he shouted loudly, swinging her around. A minute later, James was at his feet making the "up" motion with his hands. Jamie picked him up, too, so they could all swing around together. "I love it, I love it, I love it," he chanted, the two kids giggling and getting dizzy.

When they stopped twirling, James looked at Mike, his eyes swirling in his head from spinning. Mike put his finger to his own cheek, tapping and nodding toward Jamie. James leaned his head in close to Jamie's cheek and kissed it. His body didn't go rigid this time. He just smiled that glorious overbite smile, flushed with color. Then James pointed at Mike's band-aid covered hands. "Daddy, boo boo."

Outside in the back yard, the ducks were standing between the water's edge and the fire pit, the largest of them moving out to the front, staring blackly at the back of the house. More swam rapidly toward shore, flattening reeds and grass as they went, crying out wildly, shrill laughter; flapping their wings in a frenzy of splashing, piercing the quiet darkness of the night.

■

Mike got up earlier than usual the next morning. His body ached; his muscles and joints rebelled against his efforts to raise himself out of the bed, then the pain in his hands kept him from hoisting himself with their aid. *What the hell have you done to yourself, Mike?*'he asked himself, groaning as he worked with his elbows to get himself sitting over the side of the bed.

He put his head in his hands, waiting for his second wind to get him to his feet. Even the hot shower didn't help much. He resorted to taking two Advil as he got dressed; very unlike Michael Golden. He hated taking pills and resorted to them only when absolutely necessary, like in the last week.

Having come to his senses, at least on one issue, he wrapped his hands with sterile gauze and put on a pair of loose fitting gloves to cover his…embarrassment. His head was clear and he had to go back to the church and face his men. *What must they have been thinking?* And poor Alex, not only his best worker but his friend, watching for two days as he seemed to try and destroy himself. *Show them you're alright, Mike. Stop falling apart like a child. You're a grown man, for God's sake. Act like one.*

He got dressed quietly, not wanting to wake the others, and went downstairs. He made a pot of coffee, and while he waited for it to finish, gazed out of the bay window on the yard; *his* yard, *his* lawn, *his* fire pit, *his* lake, *his* hill and oak tree topper. It never occurred to him to think of it that way before that moment.

When they bought the house, it was to have some fun restoring it, modernizing for living and then reselling it. But all that had changed last week and he never even knew it, never occurred to him until that moment. Even in death, he could never, *would never*, leave Jane. She was buried here. He had to stay, so he could be close to her, and when the time was right, years down the road, try and explain it to the kids.

It was home, the last home she'd known, and now his. There was no decision to be made. He would stay and raise his children there, near their mother, and at least for him, the Reverend would be close. He'd come to depend so much on the Reverend's soothing voice and sincere eyes, the way he could make Mike feel peaceful inside for a little while. Before he left, he wrote a note to let Jamie know he'd gone, then headed out.

On the drive over, he stopped in town. Nothing says, *I'm better,* than a couple dozen donuts, so he went into the coffee shop with the frilly curtains, Fay's. Dressed in his usual worn Carhartts, he looked like any of the other workmen who came in there every morning on their way to their respective jobs. There were a few scattered here and there, at the counter, a few in a booth, others standing around waiting for their orders to take out.

When it was his turn in the take-out line, he ordered two dozen assorted doughnuts. While he was waiting, he noticed out of the corner of his eye another workman, dressed very much like he was, about his age; light brown hair in a ponytail and a soul patch under his lower lip. What made him different though was that he seemed to be talking with his hands, in sign language, to a short, thick, brunette waitress down at the other end of the counter. She looked at Mike and talked back to the other man in sign. The man looked at Mike. Mike turned his face forward to avoid their stare. They were talking about him, probably about the accident. When Mike looked back, the waitress was signing and pointing through the window at his truck, then at him, and nodding.

By the time his order was ready for pick up, the brunette waitress was standing across from him with the two boxes of doughnuts. "The guy over there," she said and tilted her head towards the deaf man, "says he heard you were the guy who bought the Grange." Mike looked at her curiously, then at the deaf man. The deaf man made some signs to the waitress. "He says, could you come over and talk to him."

"Is he looking for a job?" Mike asked, feeling a little weird about what was going on, remembering the last time a stranger came to him looking for a job.

The waitress signed the question back to the man, and they laughed. "No, he's not looking for a job, Mister. He has his own tile business over in Fennell. He's my husband," she said smiling. "It's just that he used to work with the guy who owned the Grange a bunch of years ago." She tilted her head to Mike again, "Come on, come talk to him. His name is Tommy…Lorello. I'm Alice."

Mike walked over by the man with his hand out to shake. Tommy Lorello motioned with his hand for Mike to sit on the stool next to him. Alice brought over a cup of coffee. Then Tommy started to talk to Mike, through Alice.

"He used to work with a man named Graham Stanhope, another builder, general carpenter and cabinet maker, in the early nineties," Tommy said with his hands, while looking into Mike's eyes. He bought the place to restore and live in with his wife and kids, long before it was fashionable to "flip" houses for a living. He was a local guy. They'd grown up together and had worked together for years in the area, so Tommy knew Mike's house well, had even done some work on it. He was wondering how Mike was making out, the shape of the house.

Tommy went on with Mike forming his own words carefully, so Tommy could read his lips while Alice filled in the blanks in sign. Tommy had helped Graham put in the bay window that overlooked the back yard. Mike complimented him on his work. That bay window was a real gem.

Talking through sign and lips was easier than Mike would have thought and it wasn't long before he was using his own hands, sore as they were, to form rudimentary symbols of his own; house, window, lake. Just when the conversation seemed to fall into a rhythm of understanding, Mike asked why more work wasn't done, the bay window and the appliances seeming to be the only newer items in the house when he did his first walk-through.

Tommy looked at Alice with a blank expression on his face. Alice shrugged. Tommy made a few gestures to her. "You don't know?" Alice asked Mike.

"Know what?"

"The realtor didn't tell you?" Alice asked, frowning.

"Tell me what?" Mike insisted, getting agitated by the turn this seemed to be taking and looking straight at Tommy. "What?" Tommy shrugged to Alice and made a few signs. Alice hesitated then spoke, plainly.

"Graham committed suicide in that house," Alice said, stopping to refill a coffee cup for the guy two seats down from Tommy, then came back. The color had drained from Mike's face. Alice kept talking. "His wife left him and took his kids a few weeks after they moved in." Tommy looked away while Alice kept talking. Mike was already on his feet, feeling like he was going to throw up. "Tommy and the other guys went to pick him up for work on that Monday and found him; blew his heart out with a gun in the pantry," Alice said, her eyes taking on a sad glaze as she looked at her husband, his face still turned away so he couldn't read her lips. She tilted her head toward her husband. "Tommy took it really hard. They were pretty close," she said, taking a plate of bacon and eggs from the other waitress and setting it in front of the man next to Mike.

Mike's mind spun out of control. Just the words alone, "committed suicide," set all his alarms off screaming at the same time. He turned to rush out, feeling a tightness in his chest, like he couldn't breathe.

Alice stopped him. "They shoulda told ya," she said coming around the counter and putting the boxes of doughnuts in his arms. He had to get outside. Air, he needed air.

Outside, he rushed to the safety of his truck and sat with the motor running. *What? A suicide's house?* He could hardly grasp the concept. He'd bought a suicide's house and no one had told him. He brought his Jane and their kids to live in a fucking suicide's house...in the pantry...a room Jane walked in ten, fifteen times a day; a man dead in the pantry.

His mind scattered in a dozen directions, none of them taking much shape, a cloud of confusion. He got lost in it, the enormity of it. He heard a knocking on the driver's side window and looked over. It was Alice with a heavy sweater wrapped around her. He rolled down the window.

"I'm real sorry, Mister. We didn't mean to upset you," she said sincerely, shivering in the early morning cold. He looked up to the shop window in front of him. Tommy Lorello was standing there making signs with his hands, a worried look in his eyes. The blast of chilly air in his face brought Mike back to himself.

"It's okay. I'm alright, really," he said, trying to convince himself as much as Alice. "You better go back in before you catch your death," Mike said flatly, trying to think of his next move. *The realtor, that fuckin' realtor!* flew through his mind as he put the truck in gear. Alice turned to go with another, "We're really sorry, Mister," then went back into the coffee shop.

Mike pulled away, checking his watch; eight-thirty A.M. He was over at the realtor's office in five minutes. The lights weren't on yet, not open. He waited. He'd wait as long as he had to, hot anger growing inside him with every second. There he was, getting out of his car, walking up to the door, putting in his key and turning it. Mike was behind the man before he knew it, closing the door behind them.

The skinny young realtor who sold him the house turned around and saw Mike, and what he saw made him start stepping backward.

Mountain Mike was on him, matching him every step until he was pinned against his desk. "I...I don't keep any...money here, so it's no use trying to...rob me," the realtor whined and stuttered, squirming against the desk.

Mike brought his face close, his eyes crazed with pent up anger at being...duped? Lied to? ROBBED?

"Rob you? Rob you? You sold me a suicide's house, you mother-fucker!" Mike growled, his face so close that the man had to turn his face away from Mike's hot breath. The realtor's eyes got wide, almost relieved.

"Wha...?" he squawked.

"You sold me a mother fucking suicide's house and didn't tell me?" Mike seethed through his teeth in the man's face. The realtor's eyes rolled in his head like marbles, looking like a little white mouse about to be eaten.

'I...I...I didn't know. I s-w-w-w-wear. I didn't know." He peddled as fast as he could. "I...I only came back to take over the business a f-f-f-few years ago, when m-m-m-my father died. I didn't know. All I kn-kn-know is that it was built in 1679 by the people who settled this place, and that it can't be torn down without an ordinance declaring it unsafe because it's a historical landmark. I told you that," the guy squirmed around to the other side of his desk, feeling much more secure having a big wooden desk between them.

Given the fact that Mike could have snapped this dweeb's neck with little more than a deep breath and the dweeb knew it, Mike forced himself to believe him and turned away, remembering that he wouldn't be doing his family any good if he got himself thrown in jail. He stomped back toward the door and slammed it, the pictures on the wall shaking with the force.

■

"Did you know, Reverend?" Mike asked the old man, sitting next to him in the same front pew he had that night; neither of them hearing the door open and close quietly behind them.

"No, Michael, I didn't," Reverend Willis said, shaking his head with disbelief. "I didn't come here until nineteen ninety-five after the old pastor retired, because Ella's people are from here. She grew up here. "

"I did," a voice came from the back of the church. They turned. It was Alex. "I didn't mean to eavesdrop, Mike, Reverend. I jus' came in for a box o' nails," he said approaching slowly.

"Why didn't you say anything to me, Alex?" Mike asked, dumbfounded.

"We all thought you knew. They have to tell new buyers these things. Don't they?" Alex said, standing next to them by then.

"Come sit with us, Brother Alex," the Reverend said, patting an empty space in the pew next to him.

"Mike, I'm sorry. If I knew you didn't know, I'd'a tol' ya," Alex said, his head down, feeling sad and guilty for his friend. "It was jus' an ol' house. Things happen in ol' houses. We didn't think nothin' of it."

"It's not your fault, Alex," Mike said, his own head down, rubbing his temples.

"Anybody who's lived here for a while knows about it, and about the hippies, too," Alex said with a voice of common knowledge.

"Hippies?" Mike and the Reverend said in unison. Then Mike remembered the graffiti in his basement, not having made anything of it at the time.

"Before the man who…died in there, I think ninety-two or ninety-three, the Grange was empty for a long time. Before that it was some kinda hippy commune or art colony or somthin'. I was only a young man then, but I remember it was the only time '*the man*' wasn't on *us*. He was on *them*; always roustin' 'em, looking for drugs. It got really hot for 'em around here after the whole Charles Manson thing out in California happened, so they packed up an' lef'. Hell, none of the shops in town would sell to 'em. It got so that the shopkeepers was glad to see *us*," Alex said, looking at the Reverend so he got his meaning. The Reverend looked sternly at Alex for using the 'H' word so casually in the house of God, when it didn't come from the Bible for the pulpit. Alex knew what the Reverend meant without him having to say it.

"Pardon me, Reverend," Alex said, contritely, wordlessly scolded. The Reverend nodded his forgiveness.

Chapter Seven

Autumn Leaves

W hen Mike pulled back into his driveway that evening, he didn't go straight into the house. He went out back, built a fire in his fire pit and sat down to think. It was all too much, too crazy, suicides; the word stuck in his throat like a splintered board; and *hippies? What the hell was that all about?* He kept hearing Alex's voice in his head. *It was jus' an ol' house. Things happen in ol' houses.* He lit a smoke and stared deep into the fire. *They don't know about Jane,* he remembered. Only he and Jamie knew. And then there was her letter. *He's come back for us. He knows what we did and he's come back for us.*

What the fuck is going on? he thought, rubbing his temples about to get up and go in the house.

Inside the house, Jamie opened the door to the mud room to change over the laundry and stopped short. His breath caught in his chest, a scream caught sideways in his throat. Mike's big frame was crumpled in the corner, a big brown spot leaking through his chest, decomposing flesh, an evacuation puddle under him, his true blue eyes cold and dead, open and gazing toward the ceiling. Jamie put his hand over his mouth, his eyes bulging, the muffled scream still strangling itself in his throat. He turned to run but hit a wall, but it wasn't a wall, it was Mike standing behind him.

"What's wrong?" Mike had him by the arms. Jamie was covered in a cold, clammy sweat, breathing heavily through his mouth and nose; unable to speak, falling against Mike's chest, his hands trembling.

A cool rag to the head and a half a cup of tea laced with Captain Morgan brought Jamie back to lucid. "I'm alright. It was jes' an anxiety attack. I git 'em ev'r now an' agin," he said, trying to sound rational and working to avoid looking Mike in the eye. He couldn't let Mike see him fall apart again; losing touch with reality again. He had to straighten up or Mike wouldn't let him stay around the kids. He had to be strong for the kids. He couldn't stand it if Mike asked him to leave, worried about his stability and not wanting him around Victoria and James. He loved them so much, more every day, every hour, every minute. He couldn't live if that happened; to lose them all now after he'd just found them and be all alone again, after he's felt so…loved, to be so empty again. He couldn't live with the loss.

He saw the bandages on Mike's hands, colored with leakage and needing to be cleaned and changed. Seeing his opportunity to be useful again, Jamie got up and got the Bactine, antibiotic cream and band-aids from the counter and put them on the table, then unwrapped Mike's hands and tended them, all the while not looking him in the eyes, afraid of what he would see there; disgust, contempt, revulsion, *Dirty, filthy boy! Drug addict! Killer!* rang in Jamie's head. *Please don't take 'em away from me, Michael! Please don't make me leave! I'll be a good boy, I promise. Run, Jamie, run away, now, before he…makes ya go.*

As he watched Jamie's own well-worn, scarred hands tend nervously to his blisters, so careful not to hurt him, Mike decided he couldn't tell him what he'd learned about the house that day. The anxiety attack didn't bother him. He'd been through it all before, but he didn't want to risk another one, because as much as he told himself he was used to it, it didn't mean that it didn't hurt him to see them that way, Jamie and Jane, both of them; *identical*, but something was wrong.

"Why won't you look at me?" Mike asked, needing to see their eyes. Jamie stopped moving, sat down and put his hands in his lap, like he did that first night. He hesitated for a moment, fumbling with his fingers nervously. "Jamie?" Mike said, like he was talking to one of the kids, "Tell me."

"I'm afraid," Jamie said, letting his hair fall in his face from behind his ears, his hands taking on a slight tremble again.

"Of what? Is it the monster?" Mike asked, lowering his voice to try and smooth it out. Jamie's shoulders started to shake. "Jamie, please?" Mike pleaded, the way he should have with Jane instead of just letting it be; guilty for not pushing harder with her, trying harder to save her. *It scared her ta thank that ya would thank she was dirty and used. That ya wouldn't love her and she couldn't take that risk. That's one way we were different. She had ever'thang to lose. I got nothin' left ta lose,* Jamie's words came back to him from that first night, haunting him.

"Please don't make me leave 'em, Michael, Victoria and James. Please, Michael, don't make me leave! I'll git better, I will," Jamie begged, muttering, stumbling.

"What the hell are you talking about? Look at me. Why would I do that?"

"Because...ya know...whut I am, and I'll nev'r be norm'l," Jamie said, defeated, looking away, ashamed again.

"Yes, I *do* know, but I don't think you know who *I* am," Mike said in a firm, steady voice; intentionally smooth and comforting. He nudged Jamie's shoulder with his fingertips. "Hey, look at me!"

Jamie looked up slowly, his eyes only just showing from underneath his hair.

It upset Mike so much inside to see him that way. The color came up in Mike's face and he pointed to his own chest, looking Jamie in the eyes. "*I* am Mike *the builder.* Old houses are my specialty; broken, damaged, abandoned and forgotten. I make them beautiful again, strong and lasting...valued. Do you understand me?"

Jamie nodded, finding the strength he needed in Mike's true blues, kind but firm, stable and real, not the disgust, contempt or revulsion he'd feared so much.

Jamie let himself get lost in those eyes, his and Victoria's, taking a deep sighing breath and letting it out, his fears going with it and leaving him feeling whole again.

"I would never, *not ever*, try to keep them from you or you from them, and don't you ever forget that," Mike said, putting his blistered hands out, palms up for Jamie to see again, somehow feeling like he was being given another chance.

The Lord moves in mysterious ways, Michael.

■

While Daddy and Jamie were talking grown up talk in the kitchen, Victoria was just getting up from the couch to answer the phone. "Hello…yes, I understand. Yes, I will. No, I won't. Okay, Bye."

James was quiet on the couch watching the cat, the orange glow growing with each second as the sun went down, casting a cat-shaped corona of light in the colors of autumn leaves against the wall behind it. "Oooooooohhhhhh," James cooed, hearing a hum in his ears as the glowing cat figure on the wall grew bigger and the sun continued to set.

■

In the back yard, the sun was also setting slowly into darkness over the Grange and the ducks began to gather at the edge of the lake, wading through the mist forming on the water's surface. The very last sliver of color from the sunset washed over the back bay window before disappearing behind the horizon, blood red, as Mike and Jamie sat at the kitchen table, visible to the outside; dozens of shiny black eyes staring at the back of the house, watching them through the encroaching mist; whispers, faint, hushed, accusing, *Sodomite!*

Blasphemer! A form rose from the mist behind the flock, curls of fog creating an image; a faceless, shapeless figure, changing with the breeze, dispersing into the night air as the ducks lined the edge of the lake.

■

Feeling a sense of peace come back over the kitchen, Mike headed upstairs to change into his comfortable pajamas while Jamie started dinner. He was all out today, as tired on the inside as the out. Victoria was in front of the tube as he expected with James's head lying quietly in her lap. *Peace and quiet, thank God!* and he headed up the stairs.

As soon as Victoria heard Mike close the door to his room, she was up, carefully putting a pillow under James' head while he sucked his thumb, and on her way into the kitchen. Jamie was chopping something on the cutting board on the counter. She sat down in her chair. "Whatcha makin?" she asked, her thoughts somewhere else completely. Jamie turned around, his hands continuing to chop.

"Well, I thought I'd make somethin' I learned ta do out west, kinda TexMex."

"You mean tacos?" Victoria asked, showing she at least knew what he was talking about.

"Hmmmm kinda, but not really. Do ya like tacos?"

"Oh yes, we used to make them all the time, with sliced chicken."

Jamie pushed the chopped onions, garlic and peppers into the hot frying pan and gave it a stir, then turned around.

"Well then I thank you'll like this. Think of it as tacos with rice instead of a shell." Jamie gave the pan another stir and covered it with a lid, then grabbed a box of Ssips for each of them from the refrigerator and sat down with her.

"Anna Gundersen says they have a Pumpkin Festival here with a giant pumpkin weigh-in contest for Halloween. Can we go?" It never occurred to Jamie, it was the end of October.

"Well, we'll hafta talk ta yer Dad, but I thank it'll be alright."

Victoria deliberately took a long sip from her box and pointed behind her head to the calendar on the wall, tacked to the corkboard. Jamie got up to look at it closer, zooming in on the last little square of the month circled in red. He went closer. Scrawled in Jane's handwriting was a note *M. B-Day*.

Jamie turned back to Victoria. "Yer father's birthday is on Halloween?" he asked scratching his head curiously.

Victoria nodded, her mouth full of juice again. Jamie went over and kissed her on her forehead. She smiled.

"Thank you, Victoria," he said, his mind scrambling for a plan, a cake, some presents, something to make Michael feel special, not forgotten or lost in all that had gone on.

Victoria smiled again. She liked it when Jamie kissed her on the head. She liked Jamie a lot, pretty like Mommy, but with big hands.

Jamie went back to the pan and stirred it again, adding something from a plate next to the stove. He spoke without turning. "Victoria, darlin', whut kinda cake would Daddy like fer his birthday?"

"Chocolate…with cherries," she replied on her way to the door.

"Oh and, darlin', this is jes' between us, right?" Jamie asked still stirring the pan.

"Uh huh," she said, stopping to point at the little black box marked *Recipes* next to the toaster oven on the counter so Jamie could see her, then was gone through the doorway, bouncing past Mike with a quick, "Hello, Daddy," as he came back down the stairs in his bedtime tee shirt and baggy, flannel pajama bottoms.

"Wow, what do I smell?" Jamie heard come from the doorway.

"Chicken fajitas, sorta," he replied with a chuckle, "Home style." Mike sat down at the table. Jamie went over to the fridge and took out a beer, flipped the cap and set it down in front of Mike, then went to fluff the rice in the other pot with a fork. Next he was at the plate cabinet and then the flatware drawer, setting the table.

"Victoria'd like ta know if we kin go ta the Punkin Festival and giant punkin weigh-in tomorra night. Kin we, huh? Kin we? Please, Daddy, Pleeeaaassse," Jamie whined, pumping up and down in a variation of the 'potty dance'.

Mike laughed out loud, shaking his head and rolling his eyes. "Yes, of course."

Jamie called out into the other room, "Victoria! James! Dinner!"

■

The next morning, exhausted and wearied, the weight on his mind, body and soul finally crashing in on him, Michael Golden did something he'd done only a very few times in his life before. He called the Reverend and begged off going in to work. It was Friday and Alex could supervise.

"No, nothing's wrong, Reverend. I'm just over tired and could use spending some time with my family this weekend. I'll tell ya what. Why don't you and the missus come over for dinner Sunday night? The weather's supposed to be nice. We can have a drink by the fire pit. Yeah, come early. Four P.M. is fine, spend some time with us," Mike said into the phone, his eyes still barely opened, nodding the question to Jamie as he zoomed another piece of cheese omlette airplane into James' mouth. Jamie nodded back, mouthing silently, "Yes."

Mike breathed a sigh of relief after he hung up the phone. His hands had stiffened, his body forced him to take more Advil and he just wanted to be with his kids for awhile. It seemed like he'd been so apart from them since...He'd spent no time with Victoria teaching her to read and hadn't really held James in what seemed like days. He shuffled into the kitchen, filled his coffee cup and sat down, unshaven and unwashed as Jamie handed James a piece of toast to munch on.

"The lawn needs to be raked before it gets too bad. I'll make a start on it today," he grumbled to Jamie across the table.

Jamie kept quiet. *If it looks like a bear, growls like a bear and shits like a bear, it's a bear,* Jamie thought as he slid a plate with a cheese omelette and toast in front of Mike. *If he wants ta rake the leaves, let 'im rake the dang leaves. Ya jes' gotta be ready ta redress his hands whin he's done.*

By the time Jamie had put Victoria on the bus and got back to the house, the food was gone, the coffee done and Mike had transformed from grizzly bear back to teddy bear. "So what's this you were saying about some Giant Pumpkin Festival tonight?"

"Well, I figur'd I could find out the details whin I go out today. I thought since yer home, maybe ya could watch James while I go out and blow some carbon off my pipes, maybe pick up a few thangs…for Sunday dinner, a roast or somethin'," he said facing the counter, his back toward Mike as he opened the little black box, flipping through the cards until he came to a recipe with a big 'M' in red and the heading, *Black Forest Cake,* thinking *Chocolate and cherries. That's it!* and slid the card into his pocket.

"You're going out?" Mike asked, like it was an unusual occurrence, feeling what? Danger? Insecurity? Loss? He rebounded. "Why don't you take the truck…you can carry more if you need to and…it's safer," Mike said, knowing it was just a lame excuse to cover his own anxiety.

"Thanks but I'd really like to ride, the weather is nice enough," Jamie replied, then like he'd read Mike's mind said, "I'll be alright, Michael," nudging his shoulder on his way through the door to get his gear.

Mike's head throbbed with tension as he and James watched from the front door, Jamie starting his bike for the first time since he got there. *He's not coming back,* raced through Mike's mind. *He's gonna run.*

Jamie revved the bike a few times looking back at James, smiling from under his helmet and waving to the excited little boy. *Vrooom, Vroooom*, Mike went, bouncing James on his hip, revving his own imaginary throttle for him while in the back of his mind saying, *Please be careful... and come home safe.*

■

Bundled against the chilly wind under his big leather jacket, geared up full in his boots, chaps and sunglasses, when he walked in the Read 'em and Weep Bookstore, he could almost sense the dowdy sales girl's finger on the security alarm button. "I'd like ta talk ta somebody 'bout somethin' in 'merican lit-rah-chur, somethin' that has ta do with buildin' thangs," he said to the nervous sales girl, the gravel unintentionally coming back into his voice. The sales girl breathed a silent sigh of relief.

"Why yes, of course, American lit, did you say? With a theme of building? Hmmmmm," she said and came around the counter.

"Yes, ya see, I have this...friend...It's his birthday..." He followed the girl over to a section over by the front window.

"I think I may have just the thing for your friend," she said pulling a thick volume from a middle shelf. "It's about a man, a builder, an architect and his struggle to maintain his artistic integrity when all everyone wants him to do it sell out," the girl said proudly, reading from Jamie's expression at her description that she'd hit the nail right on the head. Ten minutes later he walked out of that bookstore with a copy of Ayn Rand's *The Fountainhead* wrapped in '*Happy Birthday*' paper with a big bow.

Down the road at the end of Main Street he saw a sign, Sayreville Sportsman, with a Harley shop next to it and a bunch of bikes parked out front; his brothers hanging around outside. He pulled in slowly. They waved him over. Among his own for the first time in what seemed like ages, they all shook hands and he stayed and talked with them. "Where ya goin? Where ya been?" They were on their way to a rally down south, somewhere in North Carolina from Michigan. He could ride with them if he wanted.

For a split second he had a knee jerk reaction and *Run, Jamie, run!* came across his mind, but never for a second, split or otherwise, would he have ever acted on it. *No more runnin'.*

Instead, he found his eyes drawn to the small model version of a big bike made for toddlers in the shop window. "I got people now, not far from here and they...need me. I'd love ta guys, thanks but no thanks," and he went in the shop, coming out with the small Harley for his James and strapping it to the back of his bike. "Keep an eye on this fer me, guys. Will ya?" Then it was off to the Sayreville Sportsman and a small bag, then the art supply store next to that, another bag. *Geez, Michael was right.* He should have taken the truck. He was already loaded down and he hadn't even been to the grocery store yet.

■

Mike had just finished showering and dressing, feeling more like his old self for the first time since...worn jeans, soft, old flannel shirt. Victoria heard his steps on the stairs and put down the phone. "Who was that, sweetheart?"

"Nobody, Daddy, wrong number," she said a little nervously. Mike looked over to the couch, the cat lamp was on; its glow not so noticeable in the daytime with the light from the window not far off to the side. He looked over the top.

"Victoria, where's James?"

"He's right there, Daddy, on the couch." Mike panicked and went to the front door. It was locked. "Victoria, I need you to look for James with me, sweetheart," he said, trying to contain himself and walking fast to the back door, calling out to the air around him.

"James! James! Where are you? Come to Daddy! Come out, come out wherever you are!" The bolt on the back door was pulled. Locked. He heard Victoria's voice call out from the hallway, "Daaaddddeeee!" He flew to her. She was standing outside the basement door, pointing. The door was open, over a foot, and the light was on. Mike ran down the stairs stubbing his toe on the stringer. "Oh fuck!" he cried out, a sharp shooting pain jolting up his leg as he clutched at the handrail, struggling to keep from falling down the remaining few steps.

He landed hard but on his feet and let out an enormous sigh of relief. James turned and looked up at him, not bothered, putting his hands out in the "up" motion. He was sitting next to one of the wall arches playing in the dirt, his face and hands covered with it. Mike went to him and bent down to pick him up. He'd been digging a hole in the dirt floor at the foot of one of the arches with an old screw driver. *Whew!* Mike picked him up and limped back toward the stairs. "Victoria, it's alright, honey," he called out, taking the light pull and giving it a good tug.

Victoria was waiting when they got back to the top of the stairs, a worried look on her face, "I'm sorry, Daddy."

"It's okay, sweetheart," he said, putting his hand on the top of her head. "We just have to make sure that *that* door stays locked, too," and they all went into Jamie's bathroom to clean James up.

Mike had just given James and Victoria their lunch when he heard the sound of a motorcycle pull up to the house, his heart jumped and he stood up, putting his hand to his temples and rubbing hard, *Whew!* The front door opened and Jamie called out from the hall, "I'm baaccckk!" then the sound of him going into his wood room and sliding the door shut.

He came out into the kitchen a few seconds later, set down his grocery carrier bags on the counter and immediately started taking things in hand. "Well, well, whut do we have here?" he said as he wiped the strawberry jam off of James' face. He refilled Mike's coffee cup next, winking and nodding at Victoria from behind Mike's back. She smiled back, then went about finishing her grilled cheese and tomato soup.

When he bent down to pick up a piece of runaway peanut butter and strawberry jam sandwich off the floor, Jamie saw Mike's bare foot, the skin of his big toe split deep; swollen, covered in dried blood. Jamie picked up the sandwich and stood up looking at Victoria, then to Mike. "Whut am I ev'r gonna do with ya?" he asked, shaking his head and went to the counter, making a warm, damp dish towel and grabbing the Bactine and cream. "Come on now," Jamie said and pulled up a chair, sitting across from Mike, pointing his finger at his lap. Mike put his foot up with a wince and a groan. He looked up into Jamie's eyes. It was there, the same look he got from Jane when he went into the diner with his head split. Mike looked into those eyes and he heard his own Daughtry song play in his head, the guy was everywhere. *"When it's all said and done. I can't believe you were the one to build me up then tear me down like an old abandoned house."*

Victoria piped up and saved the day for him, averting another flood hiding behind his eyes. "Daddy stubbed his toe looking for James," she said.

"Whar?"

"In the basement," Mike grumbled. "He was just digging in the dirt. It was nothing. We just have to make sure the basement door is locked from now on."

Jamie finished cleaning Mike's foot; spraying and creaming the toe. Mike growled.

"Easy thar, big guy," Jamie said in a voice he'd learned to use during a short stint as a horse groomer in Wyoming, when one or another of them got caught on a barb in the corral wire, which, apparently, was now going to have another use. He wrapped the toe gently with a gauze roll and tied it off. "Victoria, could ya run upstairs and git Daddy a pair of his white socks from his sock drawer, darlin'?" Jamie asked.

Mike growled again, but by then Jamie well knew how to handle him. He looked up, for the first time intentionally using the secret weapon nature had given him. "So do ya have an ol' sneaker we kin cut the toe out of?"

"Grrrryeeaaahhhgrrrr," Mike growled. Jamie smiled and suddenly Mike felt *all better.*

After Jamie had fed him his lunch, Mike went upstairs to cut himself out a hole in his old Converse All Stars; fuckin' pissed him off. He loved those things. He came downstairs feeling like a clown and put on his coat from the back door hook. Jamie was just finishing the kitchen.

"When're ya gonna stop hurtin' yerself, Michael?" he asked, turning to look at him before he went out the door.

"When you do," Mike grumbled and shut the door behind him. The second the door slammed behind him Mike stopped. *Pick your big fuckin' knuckles up off the ground already, Michael. What the hell is wrong with you, saying something like that to him? Do you want him to leave?*

"No!" he answered himself out loud. Inside Jamie leaned against the kitchen counter, set back a pace but unharmed.

Is 'at whut it's gonna take?

■

The leaves had piled up pretty good in the last few days, mounds and spotted blankets of reds and oranges, yellows and browns; the glorious colors of fall. The air smelled crisp and clear, a hint of the acrid twinge in the air that comes along with the season. Mike got his hand rake from the small lean-to on the side of the house, limping slightly, the throb in his foot reminding him to take it slow. Steady and slow, he began in the front and worked his way around the side to the back, leaving small piles along the way to be picked up later.

Out back, he stopped to take in the view; beautiful; small ripples in the lake made by the gusts of wind, the trees behind the lake creating a backdrop any painter would envy. *A suicide's house.* He put down his rake and walked slowly toward the hill, then up it.

At the top he gazed over the landscape view into the small valley behind it, suddenly feeling sad, lonely, but it was different from before; melancholy, longing, *for what?*

He heard the wind blow through the old oak next to him, almost sounding like a song. Leaves came down around him, landing on his shoulder, touching him; a sad song, like the tinkle of piano keys as the leaves fell around him, and his eyes filled. "Stop it! You stop it right now!" he commanded himself loudly, then walked slowly back down the hill to his rake, in a huff; angry, so angry.

Lost in his thoughts as he raked up a big pile, he heard the back door slam and heard Victoria's voice. "Daaadddeee," she came running toward him. "Jamie says it's okay if we come out and play in the leaves if it's okay with you," she squealed, then threw herself in the pile he was raking before he had a chance to answer. *Whhhooooossssshhh!*

He laughed out loud and bent down to pick her up, his sadness and anger washing away as he held her close to him, hugging her tight. "I love you, Victoria, very much" he said, not wanting to let her go.

"I know, Daddy. I love you, too," she said tightening her arms around his neck. The back door slammed again and they looked over. Jamie was walking over with James on his hip, all bundled up and ready for a leaf fight.

"Daaaaddddeeee!" James called out with his arms open. Mike put Victoria down and swung James up. Jamie handed Mike his big ring of wound nylon cord, nodding to him to watch the lake, then walked down to the water by himself. *No ducks.*

He wandered slowly off to the left, kicking at the leaves as he went, hugging the water's edge as he got farther away from the house. In the distance he saw an old decaying dock half sunken in the water. He took a deep breath and lit a cigarette, still kicking at the leaves as he walked over to it.

The wind blew behind his back and he heard a rustle in the brush. The hair stood up on his arms. Someone was watching him; eyes staring at him. He turned around, no one. He looked out over the lake and saw the ripples coming from his left. Then he heard them, laughing, *Jamie...Jamey James.* He turned, walking hurriedly away, back toward the yard. They followed him, two, three, five, eight, coming from every direction; laughing. He looked down towards his feet, the leaves. They were swirling around them again. More laughing, loud, cackling, bitter, hateful, laughter, mocking him.

"Stop laughin' at me," he yelled back at them.

We know what you did, Jamie, a deep stern voice accused him. *Incest! Unclean!* it spat, making him feel lower than dirt. The big one was in front of the rest, swimming toward him, black eyes shining, cold, dead black eyes, coming after him. His heart pounded in his chest as he turned to look back, afraid to see how close they'd come.

He looked over towards the yard. He could see it. He could see Michael raking, Victoria and James running around in circles throwing leaves at each other. His feet felt heavy. He looked down. They were caught in the mud. Sucking sounds as he took each step, slowing him down. He looked back again, they were behind him, laughing. *Jamey, James,* echoed in his ears. "Stop laughin' at me!" he cried out, his feet struggling to pull themselves out of the mud; but the mud seemed to be trying to hold him.

In his panic to get away, he fell hard on his chest, knocking the wind out of him. "Stop laughin' at me. Please stop laughin' at me," he whimpered, feeling the cold damp ground on his face as he breathlessly tried to scramble back to his feet. *Michael help!* he tried to call out, but the words stuck in his throat, paralyzed with fear. He looked behind him again, still unable to get his legs to move him to standing. They were on land, coming closer to him.

Just as he was about to make a dash, he heard Mike's voice, close, "Jamie! Hey, you out there?" When Jamie looked back the ducks were gone, off swimming in the opposite direction. He struggled to get back on his feet, winded, terrified, the laughter still ringing in his ears, and that word, accusing him out loud for the world to hear, *Incest!*

Once up, he wiped himself off. He couldn't let Michael see him that way. He just couldn't. He washed the mud off his hands at the water's edge, then wiped his face with his shirt. He heard Mike calling to him again. "Jamie!" then saw him come limping around the corner. They met at the edge of the lawn. "James got so excited he just shit himself again," Mike laughed. "Can ya help me out?"

■

"Okay, let's take a head count. James?" Mike called out and bent over checking the little boy's scarf and hat, then stood him by the front door. "Victoria?" and he made sure her jacket was zippered up properly and stood her next to James. "Jamie?" and he went over and zipped up Jamie's leather jacket, tucking in his scarf, then took him by the arm and stood him next to James for a full troop inspection. "Okay, let's go," Mike said, satisfied that all was in order and opening the front door, expecting them to file out.

"Wait!" Victoria said, holding Jamie's hand. "What about you, Daddy?"

Mike looked at her...puzzled.

Victoria waved him down to her level. When he was sufficiently low, she pulled up his collar and pulled up the zipper on his jacket. "Okay, now we can go."

They all piled into the front seat of Mike's truck; he in the driver's seat, Jamie in the passenger seat with James in his lap, buckling the seat belt over both of them and Victoria scrunched in the middle. "Off to the giant pumpkins we go," Mike said, giving Victoria a nudge with his elbow. She looked over at Jamie expectantly. He winked at her. She smiled and turned back to Mike.

"Can we get our own pumpkin there?"

"Hmmmm, yeah, I think we can work that out."

The entrance to the Pumpkin Festival was a huge, bright orange pumpkin made out of plywood with lanterns glowing behind the eyes and nose holes, propped up only by a weak nailing of two-by-four braces. Mike and Jamie looked at each other and laughed, reading each others minds as they walked through the gaping jagged mouth of the giant pumpkin.

Either or both of them could have done better without breaking a sweat.

The fairway was a row of ordinary peddler's booths done up in orange and black crepe paper streamers and balloons housing a variety of activities and goods; pies, drinks and, of course, pumpkins of every size, color and variety up on step-like display platforms, the larger ones lazing on beds of hay surrounded by cornstalks. Then there were the games: people throwing balls at targets made up like monsters and ghosts; the barkers waving the passers-by in and, calling out, "Three for a dollar, here. Three for a dollar!"

Mike saw Patty Gundersen dressed in orange and black with a witch's hat and a cape in a booth ahead of them, apparently selling something. He waved to her. She waved back, smiling and pointing down under the counter and mouthing, "Anna."

Mike nudged Victoria and pointed over to where Patty was waving something in her hand; raffle tickets. "Can I, Daddy?" Mike nodded, waving to Patty again and pointing to Victoria already walking in her direction. She nodded, waving at Victoria to join them. Mike motioned with his hand to Patty again, pointing and making like he was shoving food into his mouth indicating that they were going over to the hot sausage stand. Patty nodded that she understood just as Victoria got to her booth, Anna popping up just in time to say "boo!" to the delighted squeals of both girls.

Mike pushed the stroller but Jamie had James, where else, on his hip, as they walked up to the food counter. "I'll have one half hot, half sweet with everything," Mike said to the red-headed teenager working over the grill, then looked to Jamie. "Same…" Jamie said, then asked the teenager, "and ya got any burgers or dogs back thar, some fries maybe with cheese?"

"I got dogs and fries, no cheese," the red-head replied, concentrating on keeping his grill from burning.

"Okay, two dogs and some fries, please, and kin I git a plastic knife and fork. Oh, yeah, and plenty of napkins, please," Jamie told the red-headed kid, smiling and pointing at James.

They took the food over to a picnic table and sat down. Jamie set his sausage aside, cutting up the hot dog first and squeezing a packet of ketchup on the fries. He put James in the stroller while Mike ate, holding the plate and letting James take what he wanted, but still keeping the fork handy just in case he had to do the airplane thing, or maybe the train.

He heard Mike chewing behind him, then silence. "I shouldn't have said what I did to you today. I had no right," Mike's voice came softly growling from behind him as Jamie leaned over to the stroller for James to take fries off the plate.

Jamie stopped; silence, then, "I ride inta yer life from oblivion, takin' away whut little ya may have left. Ya take me inta yer home, patch me together, trust me ta care fer yer children. Ya got ev'er right, and more, Michael," Jamie said without turning from the stroller in front of him.

"I thought...when you went out today..." Mike said from behind him.

"I know," Jamie said softly, finding it was time he resorted to the hot dog airplane express. The fries didn't need any transportation.

"Yeah?" Jamie heard Mike's voice ask like he was surprised, then felt a nudge from behind and saw Mike's big, band-aided hand reach out and take the plate from him.

"Yeah," Jamie said without hesitating, nodding. Mike nudged him again.

"Come on, scoot over. Your sausage is getting cold." Jamie shifted himself over on the bench to eat, letting Mike take his place.

"Come on, boy. Take a bite for your dear ol' Dad."

A few bites later, Mike heard the familiar sound of little girls clamoring and squawking. He looked up to find Victoria and Anna Gundersen running up to him, orange cotton candies bigger than their heads in their hands.

"Daddy, they're having a hayride. Can I go?"

Anna Gundersen chimed in. "My dad is driving the horse cart, Mr. Golden. Please can Victoria go, pleeeeaaasssee?" she whined with desperation the way only little girls can do at that age.

Mike was just about to agree when Jamie's voice came from behind him.

"Hold on, that!" and he held the other hot dog out to Victoria and took the cotton candy. "Eat this first, okay?"

Victoria took the hot dog and bit in. Mike gave her a sip of his soda, the back and forth of it going on until the hot dog had disappeared. Jamie handed the cotton candy back to her.

"Okay, ladies, you're off," Mike said, taking out his wallet and handing each girl three single dollar bills. "Don't spend it all in one place," and stuck his cheek out to Victoria, tapping it.

"Thanks, Daddy," Victoria said and kissed him.

"Thank you, Mr. Golden," Anna giggled, thrilled with some extra spending money and they ran off back to the raffle booth across the small fairway.

"Yo! And tell your father I'll meet you at the pumpkin contest after the hay ride," Mike called out after them as they ran away.

"Okay, Mr. Golden!" echoed back.

They worked their way down the rest of the fairway towards the end, following the odd sign that read: *"Giant Pumpkin Contest THIS WAY!"* James was fed and quiet, fascinated by all the colors and movements going on around him, craning his neck every now and again when something particularly spectacular caught his eye; the funny scarecrow clown on stilts, pumpkin balloons floating around everywhere.

"Three for a buck, try your luck," a barker in a corny flat top straw hat called out as they started to pass one of the game booths. Jamie stopped, nodding his head to Mike with a strange gleam in his eye, mischievous, devilish. Mike shrugged and they went over. "Three for a buck!" the barker with the straw hat brayed at them. "Three for a buck, try your luck!" Jamie went up to the counter.

"Tin for three?" he asked the barker.

"Sure."

Jamie handed the barker the money and he came back with ten balls in a wire basket. Jamie looked at the row of Halloween-themed rag doll targets; a witch, a sheet ghost, a scarecrow and a pumpkin, then behind at the wall of prizes. A big stuffed brown pony with a saddle caught his eye. Jamie turned to Mike and winked, then took off his jacket and handed it to him. Mike stood back to watch.

Jamie picked up the first ball. Instantly his face became serious. He screwed up his mouth, scrunched his nose and squinted his eyes, then in a blink of an eye turned into a rapid fire machine gun with fingers. *Bam! Bam! Bam! Bam! Bam! Bam! Bam! Bam! Bam! Bam!* One after another, the targets flew back and stayed down. Mike stepped back, his mouth hanging open. The barker's eyes went wide.

When the echo had faded and the dust cleared, the barker went to the wall of prizes and came back with a little blue teddy bear. That pissed Jamie off. His voice seethed through his teeth sounding like Clint Eastwood's *"Ya feelin' lucky, punk,"* voice in Dirty Harry, but instead came out, "I took 'em all down and my boy wants the poh-nee."

The barker started to back peddle, "But, but…"

Mike, quick on the uptake, stepped up to the counter, his big shoulders arched, staring the barker in the face, his thick black eyebrows furrowed into almost a uni-brow, his blue eyes blazing, his nostrils flaring. Mike growled, "Uuuuurrrrr," like something out of One Million B.C.

The barker looked back at Jamie as if to say, *"Call him off, call him off."* Jamie sneered, his upper lip curling up at one end, "I say-ed…my…boy…wants…the…poh-nee."

The barker was back in a flash, the big, brown saddled pony in hand, "Okay! Okay!" He pushed it at them.

As they walked away barely able to keep from busting up, Mike turned to Jamie. "Where did you…"

"Misspent youth," Jamie finished for him, smiling that smile again, proudly, and taking a bow just as they were passing a shooting gallery. Jamie stopped again. "Whuddaya thank Victoria would like?" he asked, arching his right eyebrow and winking at Mike again. They walked up to the range. Jamie stopped short. The targets were…ducks…and he saw red.

The next thing Mike knew his ears were being assaulted by a series of loud popping sounds. A gun was jerking in Jamie's hand and his lips were moving like he was mumbling something under his breath. *Pow! Pow! Pow! Pow! Pow! Pow! Pow! Pow! Pow! Pow!* Each duck fell back in order all the way across the line until they were all down. Jamie stepped back and looked at Mike, blowing imaginary smoke off the tip of the BB gun like he was Wild Bill Hickock or somebody, then set it down on the counter.

Stunned for a second, then a quick recovery, Mike took his cue and stepped up to the counter, dwarfing the much smaller barker in his shadow, and growled, "My little girl wants 'at big ol' panda o'er thar."

The barker looked at Jamie; eyes squinted, lips pursed, the right side curled up in another sneer.

"Yessir," the barker said, holding up his hands in surrender, backing up quickly and coming back with the panda. Jamie took his jacket back from Mike and put it on; the leather snapping with proud flourish as he jerked it over his shoulders.

"You're a hustler,' Mike said laughing. Jamie shrugged.

"Only ta eat whin work was slow, or ta teach some asshole a lesson," he said, laughing and snapping his leather again. Then it was on to the next stop, the Giant Pumpkin Contest.

When Jamie saw Victoria and Anna Gundersen coming toward them with a middle-aged, balding, soccer dad looking man behind them, he knew he was in for another one of *those* experiences. Not in the mood, he kept his head down.

"Mike!" John Gundersen called to them, smiling and waving. "Hey, John, thanks for keeping an eye on Victoria for me," Mike said loudly as they approached. Jamie turned away while Mike shook John's hand.

"How ya makin' out, Mike. I've been thinkin' about ya."

"Thanks, man," Mike said, "…'preciate it."

"Anytime. You can count on us anytime," John said sincerely, but doing the 'men not looking at each other' thing when something hits too close to home. There was a pause and Mike remembered himself.

"Oh, I'm sorry, John. This is my brother-in-law, Jamie Arnette." John pushed out his hand toward Jamie. Jamie took it but kept his head low and his hair down, doing his best to look sideways.

"Yes, the motorcycle man with the red neck," John smiled. "Victoria talks about you all the time, and don't worry, my wife already filled me in. I'm ready."

Jamie lifted his head slowly and looked directly at him. John Gundersen was not as ready as he thought. They all heard him gasp. "Oh, my!" he said, his eyes big as marbles.

Jamie looked back down again. Mike nudged him gently, then turned his attention back to John.

"So John, how's the pumpkin weigh-in going?" Mike changed the subject nervously. Quick on the upswing, John rattled on about the winner being a six hundred and eighty pound whopper, a record for the county. Mike was glad he'd missed the excitement of the actual weigh-in. His toe was starting to throb badly, James was looking ready for sleep too early and Victoria's eyes had the look of one too many bites of sugar for one day. *Home, Sweet, Home! Here we come.*

On the way out, they passed the pumpkin carving competition; blue ribbons, red ribbons and yellow ribbons. Rows and rows of both artfully carved and *not* so artfully carved Jack O' Lanterns, all lit up with candles; an eerie pageant. Mike carried Victoria. Jamie carried James and pushed the stroller holding the pony, the panda and their own pumpkin with his other hand as they walked among the glowing gourds.

With each row they passed, Jamie got the feeling that he was being watched…again. The Jack O' Lanterns were watching him, staring at him, like the ducks, whispering, *Jamey James*. Snarling, jeering, knowing smirks of ridicule, dozens of them, glowing, laughing, taunting him, tormenting him. *Weeeee knooooowwww*. His heart started pounding, tightness in his chest, sweat building on his forehead. He hurried past Mike, making sure Mike had his back until they were through the jagged mouth of the exit and safely at the truck where they couldn't get him. *Unclean!*

A short drive later they were back at the house and in their kitchen. Victoria couldn't wait any longer. "Now? Now?" she danced at Jamie's elbow like she had ants in her pants.

"Yes, now," he whispered back and she ran upstairs, coming back down a few minutes later with two packages wrapped in bright colors.

"Happy Birthday, Daddy," she squealed excitedly, handing Mike the packages. Jamie was right next to him holding James to Mike's cheek and saying, "Happy Birthday, Daddy!" James kissed it. Mike took a deep breath and held it. He'd forgotten all about it. He'd had so much on his mind.

"Jaammmiiee!" Victoria whined, reminding him that he'd forgotten something.

Jamie went to the counter and came back with a cake plate covered with a lid. He sat the plate down on the table, then hesitated.

"Come on!" Victoria cried impatiently.

Jamie slowly lifted the lid. Victoria went quiet. Mike pushed a tear out of his eye with the butt of his hand, the only part other than his fingertips that wasn't blistered, then laughed out loud, a deep, bellowing guffaw. Jamie just shrugged and blushed. The cake looked like a half flattened tire, lolling to one side, the cherry filling having made the top layer slide half way off.

"I love it. I do. I love it, really Jamie. Thank you," he said sincerely but still laughing.

"Open your presents, Daddy. James is falling asleep."

Mike opened the first card, *From Victoria*, and ripped open the package. It was a pair of green khaki-colored, fingerless knit gloves. "To keep your hands warm so you can still use your fingers," Victoria said, looking at him with his own eyes.

He grabbed her and kissed her hard on the head. "Thank you, sweetheart. I love them," he said to her, looking at Jamie out of the corner of his eye.

"Now James'," she said pushing the other package toward him, *From James*. Mike looked at Jamie across the table putting candles on his lopsided cake as he opened the package. It was a camouflage ball cap with a John Deere label on the front and a navy wool cap with his favorite Carhartt tag on the front. "To keep your head warm outside," Victoria explained. Mike put the cap on, brim to the front. Jamie shook his head, sighed and rolled his eyes. "Not like 'at, Michael," then took the cap off and turned it around, brim to the back for him the way the kids did it, "Like 'at."

Victoria looked at Jamie, waiting. "Jamie! What about your present?"

Mike frowned. "Victoria, that's not very polite. Jamie doesn't have to get me anything. Adults are different, sweetheart," Mike said patiently while Jamie maneuvered himself behind him, mouthing silently to Victoria and pointing his finger in the air, "It's upstairs." Victoria giggled.

"Okay, how about some cake, ev'r'body?" Jamie asked, moving back to the cake quickly before Mike could turn around and see him. "But I do have an idea," Jamie said as he searched his pants pockets for a pack of matches, found one and began lighting the candles. "Why don't we let Daddy have a "Daddy's Night" and spend some quiet time in his special room upstairs. Would ya like 'at fer yer birthday, Daddy?" Jamie asked.

Victoria nodded.

Mike nodded, too, saying quietly, "Yes, I'd like that."

Then with all the candles lit, Jamie brought Mike's lopsided cake over and set it down in front of him singing, "Happy Birthday ta yoooouuuu," with well more than a hint of a Country Western twang. "Happy Birthday to Yoooouuuu!" Victoria joined him, jumping up and down. "Happy Birthday dear…Daddy…Michael! Happy Birthday to Yooooouuuuuu!" and they all clapped, waking James up from his half nod just in time to clap with them as Mike blew out the candles with one big, *Wheeeewwoooooofff!*

After the cake was eaten and Jamie got Victoria and James settled on the couch with the TV and the cat lamp glowing in the dark, he went back into the kitchen to clean up. Mike was still sitting at the table. Jamie nudged him with his hip on his way over to the sink with his hands full of dirty cake plates and milk glasses. Mike got up and stood behind him, so close Jamie could feel his breath. "I spent my twenties learning about life, my thirties thinking I knew about life, but now at forty-five, I finally realize I know nothing at all," then he turned and went upstairs.

Jamie counted the number of footfalls it took for Mike to get to his library door. In front of his door was a small package wrapped in 'Happy Birthday' paper and a big blue bow.

Mike opened the door to his "quiet place" and walked in, opening the card as he went, *For Mike, the Builder,* then the package; *The Fountainhead* by Ayn Rand. Mike turned it over and read the back cover; *The Fountainhead examines the life of an individualistic young architect, Howard Roark, who chooses to struggle in obscurity rather than compromise his artistic and personal vision by pandering to the prevailing taste in building design.*

He remembered when Jane had brought him the copy of *Trilby* he wanted so badly that day in the park and how much it meant to him to know that she understood him, now Jamie with *The Fountainhead.* He sat down in his chair and cried his forty-five-year-old heart out into his tired, blistered hands. He'd had *The Fountainhead* highlighted on his Modern Library's Top 100 Novels of the Century Reader's List for months, and for the third time in his life, Michael Golden splintered, but for the first time wondered why he just didn't go with it; let it take him away. Any place had to be better than where he was, alone in *a suicide's house.*

Downstairs, Victoria was settled in on the couch in front of the TV with *Harry Potter and the Sorcerer's Stone* on the Family Channel while James was somewhere in that half sleep where small children go, asleep with their eyes open, content just to be staring at the glowing orange cat with the bowtie. It gave Jamie a moment to breathe and he decided it was probably a good time to get started with the sketches for tracing the Reverend's altar top.

He went into his woodworking room, sliding only one of the doors closed, leaving the other open, just in case the kids needed him. He turned on his portable CD player and put Garth Brooks in again, setting it at *Much Too Young To Feel This Damn Old.*

As the lonesome fiddle opened the song, Garth began to sing in the otherwise quiet house, *"This ol' highway's getting longer. It seems there ain't no end in sight. To sleep would be best, but I can't afford to rest. I gotta ride in Denver tomorra night,"* Jamie thought of Michael and *The Fountainhead.* He was *his* Michael now, and he had to do his best for 'im and his babies, just as she would have done, like she wanted him to do. He set the thin white tracing paper out over the plank and began to draw with one of the charcoal pencils.

"And the white line's getting longer and the saddle's getting cold, I'm much too young to feel this damn old." His hand moved like satin over the filmy paper, his thoughts ceasing to be actual thoughts, just his hand moving, gliding across, black lines across the white paper, then swirls and arches as Garth's voice rang in the background, *"All my cards are on the table with no ace left in the hole. I'm much too young to feel this damn old."*

Before he knew it, leaves and curling vines took shape around the edges of the paper-covered plank. He thought about Ol' Pa and how he used to guide his hand when he was just starting out, telling him to open himself up to the old spirits that guided their lives, the owl and the jaguar, the eagle and the cougar. The ancestors would be with him wherever he went

I miss you, Ol' Pa, he thought as he let his hand drift over the paper. *So kind ta me whin I was in trouble. I'll nev'r fergit ya,* and he closed his eyes, remembering what it was like to feel the old man's gnarled, sun weathered hand on his, teaching Jamie how to let himself go. *Yes, yes 'at's it. Jes' let 'er go.*

And he did, he let himself go. "*Lord, I'm much too young to feel this damn old.*" He opened his eyes and watched as his hand swept across the surface, long strokes, curves, texture, life. The crack in the little lead box inside him widened; grief overwhelmed him. His hand scrawled and scratched; abandoned, dark, so dark and lonely. *Oh, Michael.* Sadness, anger, fear...lost. *Where am I?*

Jamie's eyes began to dim as his hand worked in long stokes up and down the paper; light being blocked out, smaller and smaller, so dark. *I'm afraid.* Another pencil, quick. *Don't leave me.* He wiped his face to see. Loss cleaved his heart in half, his breath came faster and faster, choking in his throat as Garth sang.

His hands were covered with charcoal. He could see drops falling on the paper, smearing the lines, but he couldn't stop. His hand continued to move effortlessly, guided by the outpouring from his little box out onto the paper. *It's dark and I'm afraid. Where am I?* He thought he would explode with it. The light went out and he heard a scream, a horrible, gut-wrenching, terrified scream coming from somewhere inside him then fading, fading. It took his breath away. Blackness. *I'm dead.*

The CD ended. Stillness. Silence. Nothing but the sound of his own breath heaving in his chest, he pulled himself away from the plank, backing up, wiping his face, his white tee shirt smudged with charcoal, soaking wet. It was gone. He was quiet again inside. He stepped back up to the plank, staring at it.

A tree had taken shape in the center of the paper, a wide, weathered trunk trailing up into thick branches, reaching like hands to the heavens, higher and wider, some gnarled and bent, others winding, reaching like outstretched arms. *Where are you?* It was the most magnificent thing he'd ever done, staggering in its power and depth. He wiped his hands and face on his tee shirt, settling back into himself as he looked at the drawing, then at the clock, an hour had passed. It was late. *The children!* He ran to the couch. Victoria was sleeping; her head on a pillow, James nestled behind her legs.

He went into the kitchen to get a cold drink and a clean tee shirt from the dryer. The door to the mud room was open, only a crack, but not closed with the latch hooked like he'd left it. He thought of the Michael he saw there, heart blown out, the look in his eyes as they stared up into nowhere, the gun hanging from his fingers. Jamie's own words came back to him. *When're ya goin' ta stop hurtin' yerself, Michael?* The door hinge squeaked, and the door opened further. *Oh God! Please no! Not Michael!* He wrenched the door the rest of the way open; nothing, just the washer and dryer. He took a deep breath and let it out, *Oh, Thank God!*

He grabbed a clean tee shirt nervously from the dryer and changed quickly; throwing the dirty one in the basket, then went to the sink and washed his face and hands. His feet took him over to the refrigerator as if he'd done it every night of his life. He took out two eggs, some bread and the fajita leftovers, a frying pan from the cabinet and some butter, then set to work.

Ten minutes later he was standing outside Mike's library door, afraid to knock. His hand went up and tapped softly. "It's okay. Come on in," Mike's voice came back. Jamie opened the door, balancing the tray as he'd done the other night.

Mike was sitting in his chair, all curled up in his flannels again, his glasses propped on the end of his nose and holding his finger in the pages of *The Fountainhead*. He had his huge foot sticking out from underneath the afghan again, too, his big toe still bandaged. Jamie went in slowly, silently, and put the tray down next to Mike on his table. Mike watched the light reflecting off of Jamie's hair as it fell carelessly from behind his ear.

"It's bin a long day. I thought ya might like a snack. Leftover Fajita Frittata and toast," Jamie said with a small smile, grateful to find Michael the way he was, then turned to go.

Mike splintered again. He heard his heart cry out, *Don't go. I'm so lonely*, but his lips didn't move. He just stared at that face, the kindness in the hands that thought enough of him to bring him something; the hands that held his children. Jamie looked back, into his living true blue eyes, the image from the mud room flashing through his mind. *Whut kin I do, Michael?* the crack in the little lead box inside him called out as he closed the door.

He stopped outside Mike's door, waiting. He wanted to go back in, to comfort him somehow, but he didn't know how. He walked slowly to the stairs, red faced by his frustration at being so...inadequate. He'd just taken the first stair when he was pulled out of his thoughts by a sound downstairs. He listened intently, something metallic rattling, getting louder. He took two more stairs slowly, the old wood giving way slightly and creaking under his weight.

He listened carefully; more rattling, coming from behind the stairs. *Whut the hell is 'at?* He tiptoed, down the rest of the stairs. The rattling got louder, metal on wood, almost like chains being jerked across the floor.

Back on the first floor, he walked softly around to the back of the stairs, holding his breath as he turned the corner to face the sound. "Whew!" he let out with a whistle when he saw what it was. James was sitting at the foot of the door, pulling at the bottom corner, trying to shake the lock to make it open. The rattling was the loose latch hook well above his head. "Whut're ya up to, my little man?" Jamie whispered to the boy, shaking his head as he bent down to pick him up.

High in Jamie's arms, James pointed down to the door, "Azzzze-an."

∎

Jamie woke up late Saturday morning. Michael must have come in and shut off his alarm to let him sleep. Still barefoot, he went upstairs to check on the kids; the smell of fresh coffee passing under his nose as he went. James had crawled into Victoria's bed with her, his little snore telling Jamie that he still had a few minutes to get dressed, make himself a cup of coffee and have a quiet smoke for himself before he had to start...housewife-ing? He had to get his baking done that day, too, so he could use the oven for his pot roast for the next day's Sunday dinner with the Reverend and his wife.

Just as he was pulling on his jeans, he heard sounds not far outside his window. He pulled back the curtain slightly to look. Mike was already bundled up outside, wearing his new navy Carhartt hat and strolling around the back yard, picking up dead and broken tree limbs that had come off in the strong November winds the night before; his brow furrowed and a look on his face that signaled that he was concentrating on something important, something very important.

In the kitchen, Jamie made himself a cup of coffee and rolled a smoke, looking out of the bay window from the right side so Mike wouldn't see him watching. Clouds were forming in the distance, gray but darkening as they collected far off behind the lake and the tree-covered hills. He watched Mike collect his arms full of branches, twigs and limbs; his face grimacing each time he bent over for a handful, then dropping them in a growing pile on a spot over where the yard met the woods, so lonesome against the cold gray sky.

As the pile grew higher, Mike's grimacing expressions grew more severe and the time it took him to stand back up from a bend got longer, laboring. Jamie couldn't stand it any more. He got up and made Michael a fresh cup of coffee and took it out to him, handing it to him silently. Mike just grunted without lifting his head, "Thanks."

When Jamie got back to the door, James was watching, his eyes barely high enough to see over the solid wood panel at the bottom of the old fashioned wooden screen door. Jamie shoo'd him back in loudly. "It's cold out thar. We don't need no sniffles 'round here," he said pinching James on the bottom, sending him running and giggling into the living room. Jamie turned on the cat to keep James occupied until he had breakfast made and went back into the kitchen. "So what'll it be, this mornin'," he asked, thinking Victoria must be close by, then not seeing her within eye shot called out, "Victoria! Whatcha want fer breakfast?" No response.

He walked back to the doorway. Victoria was just turning around, standing by the telephone table, rubbing her eyes and looking sleepy.

"Hungry, darlin'?"

She nodded, her eyes still not yet fully open. He went over to her and picked her up. She laid her head on his shoulder and closed her eyes. She was a big girl so he didn't get to hold her much. It was nice, made him feel...complete.

He stroked her hair and sat her in her chair. She put her head down on the table. Something about it bothered him, something not right. He leaned over and kissed her forehead to feel for a fever. Nothing. He sat down next to her, "Ya okay, darlin'?" Victoria nodded, her head still on the table, looking at him sideways. "So whut kin I make ya?" She shrugged her shoulders. "Panwiches?" he asked, trying to get her to talk to him. Nothing. "Please, sweetheart, tell me whut's wrong?" He stroked her hair again.

"You won't let Daddy leave us will you?" she asked him, looking about to cry.

"Naw! Yer Daddy would nev'r, ev'r leave you and James. He loves ya more than anythin' in the world," Jamie said and pulled his chair close to her, putting his arm around her. "Why would ya ev'n thank such a thang?"

Victoria shrugged again, little diamond-like tears just about to drop. "I had a dream Daddy was on a train, waving to us, James and me and you, going far away, and he was sad. Don't let Daddy go away, Jamie, please," she put her arms around his neck.

"Oh, baby." He could feel her warm tears against his skin. Jamie picked her up and put her in his lap, holding her head to his shoulder. "Yer Daddy is not goin' anywhar. I won't let 'im. I promise," he said, wiping her tears with the tail of his tee shirt.

"Really?"

"I promise, sweetheart. Daddy'll be happy agin. He's jes' real tired. Daddies git that way sometimes," he said rocking her back and forth, keeping an eye on the locked mud room door. "How 'bout some...French Toast now?" Victoria nodded against his chest.

Jamie got up and went to his cabinets; cinnamon, sugar, then the fridge, eggs, milk, bread...*James!*" James was awfully quiet in the other room, so quiet Jamie'd forgotten all about him. Jamie went to the doorway. "James!" The cat with the bowtie was still glowing. He walked over to the couch. James was sitting there staring with his mouth open, his eyes glazed over in a trance at the orange light dancing on the wall. Jamie went around and picked him up. "Come on my little man. Let's git you fed and dressed."

"Azzzze-an," James said quietly over Jamie's shoulder as he carried him into the kitchen and put him in his chair.

"Ummm, that smells goooood!" Victoria said when Jamie got to cooking.

"You betcha!" he said, smiling over his shoulder at them, then turned around with the frying pan in his hand so they could see him flip it.

"Yaaaayyyy!" Victoria shouted with each skillful flip, James clapping every time she did. Once the serving plate was full of cut up French toast slices, Jamie set them both up with small plates and forks, James' tipless filled with juice and Victoria's glass with milk. He was just about to sit down, deciding which mode of transportation he might need for James when he heard an engine, small, grinding and humming; a chainsaw. *"Michael!"*

His ass never reached the seat. He was out the door, barefoot and coatless; only his thin tee shirt out in the cold November morning wind. Mike was standing above the pile of branches and limbs.

"Michael!"

Mike turned and saw Jamie coming towards him.

"Michael, come on now. Give yer poor hands a rest. Will ya?" Jamie said but was thinking, *"I kin wrap blisters and I kin bandage a toe, but I cain't reattach a finger or a hand or..."*

"I gotta keep the yard in order. We got people coming. I can't let the neighbors think I can't keep my house in order," Mike said flatly, not looking at him. Jamie went in closer, slowly reaching his hand out for the saw.

"Okay, then...I'll do it. Jes' gimme a few minutes ta git my coat and boots on and git the kids dressed," he said searching for Mike's eyes, feeling resistance when he went to take the saw. Mike finally looked at him. Jamie was shivering with cold.

"Fine!" He growled and let go of the saw, stomping off. Jamie shut the saw off and set it down on the far side of the wood pile. Mike grabbed the rake from against the tree behind the pile. "I can still rake can't I?" he grumbled and started walking toward the hill.

"Jes' take it easy and go slow..." Jamie yelled at Mike's back as he walked away in a lumbering sulk, "...and wear some gloves!"

Mike pulled his new pair of fingerless gloves from his pocket and waved them over his head without turning around, his shoulders slumped, his big frame pounding up the hill with the rake over his shoulder. Jamie ran back in the house to find Victoria watching out the window. "Ya see, he was wearin' yer hat and gloves," Jamie said, blowing on his numb hands and doing a little dance to get his feet warm.

Victoria nodded, satisfied. James laughed at the cold feet dance.

Jamie put on a pair of socks then poured himself a cup of hot coffee. He watched through the bay window as Mike raked on the hill and Victoria and James finished eating, finding himself momentarily relieved that their food wasn't flying or that any mass transit was required.

"More! More! More!" both kids called, bringing Jamie off the hill and back to the room. He refilled both their plates, cutting James's up into little bite-sized pieces again. When he looked back out of the window, Mike was standing on the hill under the very edges of the almost leaf barren branches rising from the old tree. He was looking over the lake and valley; just standing, the rake still in his hands, staring out over the horizon, looking like he was all alone in the world.

When the kids were done eating, Jamie hurried to change and dress James who was, thankfully, only a little wet. Victoria, being the big girl that she was, dressed herself in the warm clothes he'd laid out for her. He bundled them both up, then threw on his boots and jacket. When he looked out of the bay window, Mike was still on the hill, not standing but sitting, still staring out over the landscape.

As a last minute thought, he told the children to wait there, then ran upstairs to their room and started grabbing handfuls of their toys, anything that was close and seemed like it would be of current interest, and threw them all in a pillow case. Back in the kitchen his two little angels were waiting patiently by the door.

Just as Jamie was almost out the door he backed up. "*Not ready.*" He grabbed some of the leftover French toast, soaked it in syrup, threw it into an old Tupperware tub and tossed it into the pillowcase, then poured a hot cup of coffee into Mike's thermal cup and closed it tight; into the toy bag. *Maybe I should git me a diaper bag,*" he thought, smiling to himself. They were ready now.

Outside, Jamie headed toward the wood pile. "Jes' stay thar…" he told Victoria, "…hold James's hand and watch.

I'll be done in a second." He picked up the saw and started it rumbling and vibrating in his hand. He looked over to see that Mike was looking and held the grinding saw high in the air so that Mike could see that he was doing it.

It took Jamie all of five minutes to cut up the branches, none of them being really more than four or five inches thick. James loved the sound, imitating it as little boys will do, blowing air through his lips and making a *brrbrrbrrr* sound. Jamie dusted off his hands as if to say, *Done!* then grabbed the pillow case, pulled James up on his hip, took Victoria by the other hand and started walking toward the hill, looking suspiciously back over his shoulder at the lake to make sure there were no...ducks. *Whew.*

"Daddy!" Jamie called out breathlessly as they were almost at the top. Mike looked over. Victoria was waving at him. She ran and jumped in his arms. "Daddy!" Mike looked at Jamie, still working his way to the top, the addition of his namesake to his hip making him have to work a little harder, move a little slower. When he reached the top, he was breathing heavily, puffs of chilled breath making him look like the magic dragon.

He put James down who immediately ran to Mike with his usual "up" motion. Mike picked him up; a kid in each arm. Jamie put his hands in his pockets trying to think about how to work around Mike's mood and started kicking at the ground. "Victoria, darlin', kin ya take this bag over thar by the tree fer me?" he asked.

Victoria nodded and Mike put her down. Jamie opened the pillowcase and took out the Tupperware and thermal cup, then handed the bag to Victoria. She took the bag obediently and walked over to the tree. Jamie tried to hand the container to Mike. He frowned. "I'm not hungry," he said shaking his head.

Do whut ya hafta, Jamie thought to himself, not above a little emotional blackmail to get his way anymore. He remembered when he and Jane were children, about Victoria's age, and could wear the same play clothes, how crazy it made everyone in the neighborhood and at school, and decided to use his secret weapon again, *Shameless.* He looked up at Mike with that thought in his mind and mouthed silently, "Please...fer me," and took the lid off, holding it out for him again.

"Oh, alright," Mike growled, the emotion of what he saw making him as pliable as the kids' Play-Doh. He took a piece and shoved it in his mouth, chomping loudly and looking exasperated, then another and another until the container was empty. Jamie handed him the thermal coffee cup. Mike opened it and took a long slug. "Happy now?" he growled. Jamie nodded, pleased with himself for being able to get Michael to do what was best for him, but hesitated before saying anything.

"Yeah, I am...but, I still hafta go out and git some thangs fer tomorra's dinner." It was as good an excuse as any to force Mike to pull himself back, to be with his children, especially Victoria.

Before he'd even finished his sentence, he saw Mike's eyes change; tense, dark, hurt, afraid. Jamie recognized it as the same look he had when Jamie had gone out the day before. It didn't take a brain surgeon to know what Mike was thinking. Jamie took a deep breath and held out his hand, moving his fingers in the "gimme" motion. The clouds in Mike's eyes disappeared and the questioning crease in his forehead eased itself from his brow. He reached into his pocket, pulled out his big clunky key ring on a chain and put it in Jamie's hand.

"I'll even go ya one better," Jamie said smiling. "I'll take James with me, too, okay?" Mike smiled for the first time that day as he leaned in to give James over. Jamie held out his finger, curling it in the 'come here' motion, and leaned into Mike again. Mike met him, putting his cheek out then caught himself. "She needs ya today, Michael," Jamie whispered, looking into his eyes to make sure he got his meaning. They were open and accepting again, *True blue Michael.*

Mike nodded that he understood, his cheeks flushing with embarrassment that he hadn't realized it himself. He looked over to Victoria digging in the bag, remembering when she was so small and cutting her first teeth. How she would give Jane the worst time all day until he came home from work. The minute he walked in the door Jane would hand her to him and within seconds Victoria would stop crying, every time, until she had all her teeth. Frazzled but still smiling that smile, Jane would say, *She's her daddy's girl,* and kiss him on the cheek before going upstairs to wash off the day. "Still your Daddy's girl?" Mike said as he walked over to the tree and grabbed Victoria, tickling her sides. Victoria giggled and squirmed.

"Yes, Daddy," she squealed loudly.

"Forever and ever and ever?"

"Yes, Daddy."

Jamie bounced James on his hip as they galloped down the hill, *Bub bump, bub bump, bub bump,* but stopped half way down, breathless again and turned back to look at them on the hill. Something nagged at him, something familiar. He couldn't put his finger on it. He turned galloping down the hill again, *Bub bump, bub bump, bub bump,* and stopped to look back again. Mike was sitting on the ground with Victoria between his knees going through the bag then dumping it out on the ground. *What is it? What the hell is it?* Then it came to him, struck him right between the eyes like a bull's eye; against the backdrop of the clouding sky, the tree. It was the tree, the tree on the altar. The tree on the hill was the same tree he drew the night before; strange and beautiful, but somehow sad, like it was reaching out for something. *Where are you?*

The next thing he knew, James was pulling on his nose and laughing and Jamie knew he had to hurry. The clouds were rolling in and he wanted to get back before it rained. He called back to Mike, "I won't be long, Michael. Maybe half an hour. You be a good boy for Victoria, Daddy." Both Mike and Victoria waved, smiling.

"Yes, Jamie. I will," Mike yelled back.

Chapter Eight

No Rest For The Wicked

W | hen the two Jameses got back from the grocery
store, Jamie dumped the bags on the table, put
James in his chair with a cup of juice and looked out the bay
window. Mike and Victoria were still up on the hill. *So much
fer rakin'.* He was on a roll today, no saw, no rakin', got him
to eat *and* spend time alone with Victoria. If Jamie could have
reached behind and patted himself on the back he would
have.

As he watched them on the hill, he was suddenly struck
by his own image reflected in the window glass. There was a
knock at the front door. "Who could that be, I wonder?" he
asked little James comically pulling a face, thinking it was one
of the Gundersens. He tickled James under the chin before
he went to answer it; another knock.

The first thing that caught his eye was the black leather,
then a face, a woman; cheap dyed-blonde hair with dark
roots, teased high and heavy make-up, like an old mannequin
that had been painted over and over to look young. He knew
that look and stepped back. "Jamieboy!" he heard the shrill
voice come through the door. "It's me, let me in." More
knocking, louder, banging. He looked back to make sure
Michael wasn't coming through the back door. Could he hear
the banging from the back yard? "Let me in Jamieboy. It's
me, Roxanne."

Afraid Michael might hear or walk in on them, he decided it was best just to see what she wanted, then get rid of her as quickly as possible. He opened the door. "Jamieboy!" she shrieked again, her pupils dilated, high as a kite as she came through the door and threw her arms around him, kissing him on the cheek with a loud smack. He cringed, stiffening. She smelled bad. "Whut're ya doin' here? How'd ya find me?" he asked flatly. "Everybody knows where *you* are, Jamieboy. I was just the closest one to come on by and see ya." She pushed passed him. "Nice digs ya got here," she said as she strolled into the hallway, looking around admiringly. "Real nice, and cozy too, real cozy."

"What th' hell do ya want, Roxanne? Ya cain't be here. This is not my house," he said, embarrassed to even have her anywhere near him, reminding him of a past he was trying to forget, especially in Michael's house, around the kids. "Well, I was just in the neighborhood and I thought I might bring ya a present, bein' as we used to be so close," she laughed and slapped him on the ass.

"Keep yer voice down! I got kids here. Whuddaya want? Money? I ain't got none."

"I know all about 'em, Jamieboy! Not *your* kids, your sister's, your sister's house, your sister's husband. Nice set up," she said, wandering around the living room. "What was once hers is now yers," she rhymed, looking at Jane's knickknacks and picking up a picture of Michael in a silver frame from the phone table, running her fingers over it. "Some hunk, ain't he? Real manly. Bet he's hung, too. Grrrr," she growled with a smooch. Jamie snatched the picture from her and put it back on the table.

"Don't ya touch 'im!" he spat angrily through his teeth in a whispered shout.

"Oh, I din't come here for that, or to take nothin' neither. I came here to bring ya somethin'."

"I don't want anythang from ya. Now please go."

"Ya sure?" she asked and reached into the pocket of her leather jacket, pulling out a handful of little white square

packets. As much as he tried to deny it, the minute Jamie saw
it he felt the craving. The hollowness inside him came back as
she waved the packets in front of his face. He fought it. She
saw it in his eyes and tried to put them in his hand. "Ya know
ya want it. Once a junkie always a junkie," she said, her thick-
caked make-up starting to crack as she spoke. He fought
it...hard. Holding onto everything he had to fight it. *I love you,
James. I love you Victoria.*

"Whut the hell're ya doin'? Are ya crazy? I have kids here.
Get out. Get out now!" he shouted, grabbing her by the arm
and pushing her toward the door. Halfway to the door he felt
the pain in his guts making him want to double over; a cold
sweat breaking on his forehead. She pulled away.

"Not so fast, Jamieboy," she said and walked over to the
small, oval mirror over the phone table to primp her hair. "I
came to do ya a favor, boy."

"I don't want any favors from ya. Didn't ya do enough?
Payin' me in smack instead of cash fer all the work I did fer
ya and yer ol' man," he shouted, forgetting for the moment
where he was. His hands started to shake; his veins pulsing
under his skin. She turned to him from the mirror, the make-
up on her face cracking wider as she smiled. Then he
remembered. She saw the look of recognition in his eyes. He
backed away horrified. His eyes bulged with a knowledge that
couldn't be real. "Yer d-d-d-dead. You took a hot shot five
years ago. Yer dead." She smiled at him, her make-up
cracking further from the tension, long fissures running up
her face from her mouth to her eyes, her smile widening.

"And so will you be too, soon, Jamieboy." Make-up
started falling from her face in chunks, wads of hair dropping
from her head onto the floor as she sidled up close to him. "I
always say if ya gotta go, its better to go feelin' good than
feelin' bad and ya got a whole lotta feelin' bad comin' to ya.
Take the shot, Jamieboy. Go feelin' good."

By then more than half the thick make-up on her face
was gone revealing the rotted, decomposing flesh of a corpse
underneath as she backed him against the wall, holding the

little white packets up to his face with blackened fingers. He wanted to take them. He hurt so bad, *Oh, God!* His stomach lurched.

"God ain't gonna help you none. You been bad all your life, bad from the cradle," she said, her teeth decaying before his eyes. "Your asshole still hurt, Jamey James?" she snickered.

He opened his mouth to scream. She grabbed him by the throat. "Ya made him do it, ya know, temptin' the old man every day with that pretty face and that tight little boy's ass. It was all your own fault."

Jamie started to slide down the wall. She held him up, forcing him to look into her eyes. He could see his father's face reflected in her oversized pupils. "You and that little slut bitch sister of yours. She got hers, now you're gonna get yours. You think a house in the country and your sister's family is gonna clean the shit offa ya? A filthy, dirty, disgusting Daddy's boy like you?" she sneered at him, her rotted teeth falling out one by one as she spoke, poked out by her blackened tongue. "Ya think I don't know? We all know. Everybody knows. I'm doin' ya a favor here. Take the shot. It's a whole lot better than what ya got comin' to ya. Trust me, Jamieboy."

He heard the back door open. "Michael," he tried to call out, but it only came out as a whisper. Her hand was so tight on his throat, choking him, his eyes going gray.

"Michael?" she said with a whining jeer. "He's already dead. He just doesn't know it yet," she laughed. "I'll be fuckin' him in hell before long, don't you worry," she said, letting go of his throat and blowing at the thick yellow fingernails of her rotting fingers like she'd just had a manicure.

"Jamie?" He heard Mike call out, his heavy footsteps coming from the kitchen. *Quack, quack,* Jamie heard in his ear, then a loud *Whoosh* and *Bang* as the wind blew the screen door open, slamming it against the outside of the house. Out of the corner of his eye he saw Mike standing in the doorway, coming toward him in slow motion, then blackness.

He woke up on the couch, Mike sitting close beside him holding a cold cloth to his head, terrified true blue eyes. "What happened?" Mike asked, his voice as quiet and gentle as Jamie'd ever heard it.

Jamie bolted upright, his eyes bloodshot, insane with fear, and slid under Mike's arm and away like greased lightning. Running, he grabbed his jacket and flew out the front door. Mike ran after him. Jamie leapt onto his bike. One kick start and the engine roared to life. He kicked it into gear and started to roll. Mike ran and stood in front of it, blocking it, holding on to the handle bars. "Where are you going? What the hell are you doing?" he yelled over the roar of the engine, trying to push the bike back, throwing his full weight against it.

Drawn by the loudness and confusion, Victoria was watching through the window. Panicked, Jamie let the clutch slip. The bike bucked forward hitting Mike hard between the legs. "*AARRRGGGhhhhh,*" he cried out in pain, grabbing himself and falling over on the ground. Victoria screamed from the window, "Daddy!" as Mike rolled back and forth on the ground, curling himself into a ball, holding himself.

Seeing the startled look in Mike's eyes when the front of the bike hit him, then watching him hit the ground like that brought Jamie back to himself. *Ya hurt Michael. How could ya hurt Michael?* His fear slid away, drowned in a wave of guilt so intense it ran a new fissure in his little lead box. Jamie dropped the bike and went to him. "Michael, I'm so sorry. Please. I'm so sorry," he pleaded, taking Mike around his big shoulders and helping him sit up in the drive.

"It's okay. I'm alright," Mike said, gritting his teeth, short shallow breaths forcing their way out of his chest as the excruciating pain between his legs finally began to recede into a dull ache and he could sit up.

"Michael, please. I...I...I," Jamie stammered, searching for Mike's eyes.

"Help me up," Mike groaned. "The kid's are watching," he said without even having to look, knowing his Victoria well enough to know she was in the window. Jamie held Mike by his arm, helping him to his feet, still bent over struggling to get his full breath back. "Help me walk it off," Mike gasped, working to straighten up, a ball of fire still burning in his belly. Jamie held him up as he ambled to take a few small steps toward the porch.

Mike looked and saw Victoria in the window, bouncing up and down, crying, "Daddy!"

He put his hand up, mouthing to her, "It's alright, sweetheart," as he took the first step up the porch, groaning, still needing Jamie's support to keep from falling over.

Victoria met them at the door and like the big girl she was becoming, took Mike's other hand to help him into the kitchen and a chair where his breath slowly returned to normal. When he could raise his head again, the first thing he saw was James sitting quietly in his chair, his little hazel eyes, their eyes, wide and staring at him. Half of a big cookie in his hand, the other half smeared across his face, James held out the uneaten half to him, "Sum?"

Victoria heard Mike get up from the table and open the fridge. She had to hurry. "I don't know," she whispered into the phone, looking around to see if anyone was watching her. "Yes...I can do that," she whispered softly. She heard the snap of Mike's beer can and Jamie moving in the woodworking room. "I have to go now," she said into the phone and hung up quickly, then went into the kitchen and stood next to Mike, waiting for his attention.

"Come sit in my lap, sweetheart," he said and lifted her up, working to not let his face show how much pain he was having in his groin. She laid her head on his shoulder.

"Are you okay now, Daddy?"

"Yeah, I'm fine," he said holding her head close. "Let's talk about this, okay?" Victoria nodded. Mike thought for a moment on how best to handle the thing. He took a deep breath and let it out with a sigh. "Well, do you remember when Jamie first came and you told me that Jamie cries a lot?" Victoria nodded against his shoulder.

"Yes."

"Do you remember what I said about Jamie being a very special person? And that we should treat him specially?" Victoria nodded again.

"Yes."

"Well, Jamie has bad spells sometimes, sweetheart...his head hurts and he gets upset." Mike pulled her forward then, so he could see her eyes and wanting her to see his. "What happened today was an accident, sweetheart. Jamie didn't mean to hurt me. The motorcycle just got away from him and hit me. He didn't do it. It's like when I stubbed my toe, or when you fell off your bike last summer, an accident. Do you understand what I mean?" he asked her.

"Yes, I know," she nodded, her eyes like crystal pools of childhood innocence forced into a wisdom beyond her years.

"Good. So will ya promise your old dad something?" She nodded.

"Don't ever get on a motorcycle when you grow up," he said and pulled her back close to him, hugging her tight.

"I won't, Daddy. I promise."

"...or better yet, just don't ever grow up at all." He looked at James then, watching the whole scene intently. "And don't you even think of getting on a motorcycle, boy! Not ever," Mike said shaking his finger exaggeratedly at the wide-eyed little boy with cookie all over his face. James laughed and gave him the raspberries.

Mike couldn't help but think of Jamie when he looked at his own boy, remembering the first night Jamie had come to them. So much pain in his eyes, and fear, and shame. It seemed so long ago, like he'd always been there, or that Jane had never left. He'd lost his own innocence that night, too, then just now and that crazy fear in Jamie's eyes, like he was running for his life. *But from what? From us? From me?* Mike leaned in, sniffed James and kissed him on the head. *Whew!* He was clean.

"Where's Jamie now?" he asked Victoria.

"He went in the wood room." Mike got up and went to the cabinet and took out a coffee cup, filled it half with water and shot it into the microwave. When the timer went off he took the cup and filled it the rest of the way up with Captain Morgan, a tea bag sugar and milk. "Entertain James for a little while for me will ya, sweetheart. Jamie and I have to…"

"…talk." Victoria finished his sentence for him.

"Yes."

Mike went to the wood room and put his ear to the door, nothing, then knocked lightly. "Jamie it's me. Can I come in?" Silence, then a muffled voice.

"Please don't, Michael. I'm sorry."

Fuck that, the caveman in Mike appeared as he slowly pulled back the sliding door. Jamie was sitting with his back to the door; short jerky movements and muffled whimpers. Mike walked up behind him, trying not to make a sound, then around to his side, and Mike splintered.

Jamie had one of his carving tools in his hand, pulling the sharp blade across his inner forearm; a third straight red line. He was cutting himself, and shaking, his eyes closed, grinding his teeth and whimpering. Suddenly Mike wasn't in the wood room anymore; he was walking with Jane in nice weather in the park on her lunch break. She was wearing a pretty pink and white blouse. It was the first time he had seen the lines on her arm; three long thin lines, very straight. He took her arm gently and touched them. *What's this?* he'd asked her.

She pulled away. *Oh it's nothing,* she said shyly, turning away from him. *I got my arm caught in the lettuce slicer at the diner when I first started.* Then there were the others on her upper thigh. She'd told him they were from a bad cat scratch when she was a young girl, and he'd bought it hook line and sinker. Mike almost swooned from the realization. *Why not, they were identical, weren't they?*

Mike reached down slowly, taking the hand with the tool. Jamie looked up, his eyes vacant. "Let me have it, Jamie," Mike said softly. Jamie let his head hang and let go of the tool. Mike grabbed a tee shirt from the table and covered the cuts, holding it tight to stop the bleeding.

"Please don't look at me, Michael," Jamie said, his body going limp as a rag.

Mike caught him and sat down next to him, letting Jamie lean his weight on his shoulder.

Jamie started heaving, great abandoned sobs. "I...would nev'r...hurt...ya...fer anythang in the...world, Michael," he cried, leaning over still shaking, hiding his face.

Mike just held him tight, pushing the cup of Captain tea into Jamie's hands, thinking, *Oh, my two poor beautiful Arnettes,* but saying, "You didn't hurt me, Jamie. I'm okay, really. I'm fine, a little dirty maybe, but I'm fine. It was an accident. I'm more worried about you. What happened? Was it the monster again?" Jamie nodded then downed the tea. "Is it gone now?"

"Yes," Jamie said, nodding his head again; the shaking having come down to little more than trembling.

"See, I'm still the biggest monster in this house," Mike said with a chuckle, trying to get Jamie to look at him. "And I really didn't want any more kids anyway," Mike smiled giving him a good ol' boy nudge. Jamie gave in and looked up at Mike, his eyes still glassy and wet, but not afraid, and he smiled that smile again. It made Mike weak. He took a deep breath and stood up.

"Come on, now. Let's go get you fixed up in the kitchen. Victoria is worried sick about you. That's not right for such a little girl. Come make nice with her."

Jamie stood up with him and followed him to the door. When he opened it, Victoria was standing there waiting, her eyes wide and worried. "It's okay, sweetheart. Jamie just scraped his arm on the bike. We're gonna get it all cleaned up and then I'll make you some lunch. How's James?"

"He's napping in his chair," she said pointing over her shoulder.

Mike took Jamie to the kitchen sink and turned on the tap, running warm water over his arm. It stung. Jamie winced and jerked his arm. "Michael, ya don't hafta..." he said wanting to crawl inside himself to a safer place, mortified that Mike had caught him cutting. Mike gave him the brow, holding fast to his arm.

"Listen, you wrapped my fucking toe the other day for God's sake. Let me do this. Will ya?" Jamie nodded and relaxed his arm. Mike dried it off lightly, sprayed it with the Bactine, then smeared it with cream, wrapping it with gauze after he was done. Victoria didn't leave their side for a second, watching quietly and listening closely.

"All better now?" Mike said. Jamie took a deep breath, nodding. The next thing Jamie knew, Victoria had him by the fingers and was leading him over to the table. When he sat down, she climbed up in his lap. Mike winked at her and nodded. "Okay, so what'll it be?" he said smiling wearily but still trying, his groin throbbing, and took out the frying pan. "Grilled cheese boats and soup?"

■

As Mike fried up the sandwiches and made the soup, Jamie sat at the table sipping another Captain tea and telling Victoria and James stories about his travels in the West; cactuses, buffalo, Indians and cowboys. He told them how he'd been to rodeos in Arizona, shoed horses in Wyoming and seen bullfights in Mexico. Victoria was fascinated, looking up at him adoringly as he spoke. James was entertained by Jamie's impressions and dramatics. "Giddy up, giddy up," he said holding his hands up with imaginary reins and bouncing up and down in his chair with Victoria still in his lap. Bouncing her from side to side she giggled loudly. "Whoa, Nelly!" he pulled back on the reins.

Every now and again, Mike would turn around for a moment to watch them. He couldn't help but notice the difference in Jamie whenever he was around the kids. The worry lines around his eyes and mouth seemed to soften, his eyes themselves shining, and his smile, so genuine and loving, happy, like there was no one else in the world but them; unrecognizable compared to the terrified, shaking man-child he'd become on that first night, or in the wood room just a short time before.

There was a sense of peace, a naturalness about him as he told them about the old Indian man, Ol' Pa Running River, a real Comanche elder who taught him to have pride in himself and a real sense of accomplishment in the artistry of his wood carving, and how Ol' Pa gave him a new 'tattoo' every time he reached a new level of carving. "This one means *'brave son'*," he said pointing to the one on the top of his shoulder, "and this one means *'soaring eagle'*," he said pointing to the next one down. James listened quietly, laughing and clapping when Jamie did his fire dance impression in a way they could understand, "Hey-ya-hey-ya-hey-ya-hey-ya," and showed him with his hands what a bow and arrow was, making sounds, *Whoooosh, thunk, thump.*

Mike found himself turning around from the stove to look at them more and more, finding his own sense of peace seeing the worried look had disappeared from Victoria's face, hearing James laugh and seeing Jamie smile that broad beautiful overbite smile. He could almost convince himself that nothing had happened, that nothing had changed. This was the way it was and always had been, that Jane was right there with him, still loved him and their children. He didn't hurt so bad, didn't feel like crying. *Build, Mike, build,* came wordlessly from inside him as he turned around for the last time with his hands full of sandwiches and soup.

After the plates and bowls were set out, Mike took James out of his chair and put him in Jamie's lap, taking Victoria to sit in his own. He saw the bandage he'd wrapped around Jamie's arm, then looked at James with Jamie's arm around him making an airplane out of a piece of sandwich. James saw Mike point to his own cheek, nodding toward Jamie. James leaned in and kissed Jamie's cheek. The look on Jamie's face was so different from the first time, unmistakable, pure and…healing? It was love, the cure. Their love could fix Jamie, making up for all he never had as a child himself.

Sufficiently fed and entertained for the afternoon, Mike sent the kids into the living room for some TV and cat time, leaving him and Jamie alone. He cleaned the kitchen in silence, looking over to Jamie as much as he could, thinking, *Why won't you look at me? Why?*

Jamie kept avoiding Mike's glance, staring out of the bay window as he rolled a cigarette from his pouch and papers, then lit up. He watched the tree; its branches blowing in the wind of the coming storm and thinking, *I'm so embarrassed, Michael, so ashamed. I brought so many ugly thangs inta yer life, inta yer house, the ugliest thangs in the world, dirty, sick, unspeakable thangs, hurt ya and fer ya ta see me like 'at. Not worthy, not worthy.*

Jamie got up and went to the window, looking out over the yard, small raindrops splashing here and there. He saw the pillowcase from earlier that morning blow by in a gust. He looked over to the hill, toys were scattering in the wind, blowing down the hill. Mike had forgotten to bring them in.

Jamie grabbed Mike's jacket from the hook and ran out the door. "What are you..." Mike called out after him. He saw Jamie grab the pillowcase before it blew completely away, then run up the hill.

Jamie felt the drops of rain get bigger, splattering against his face as he hurried to gather the toys one by one; one book, two books, a box of crayons, a truck, a train, and a drawing pad. *One more, jes' one more,* he thought as he was about to bend over to pick up what looked like the newest incarnation of the old fashioned Etch-A-Sketch. Drops of rain splattered the surface. He saw the magnetized particles start to move, slowly taking shape. He stopped. The particles seemed to be raising to the surface, forming letters, cursive, one by one. The letters came and went so fast, he could hardly put them together;

F...i...n...d   A......d......r......i......a......n

A clap of thunder assaulted his ears from behind, a bolt of lightning blinded him for an instant as the sky opened up and a driving rain came pouring down on him, the wind whipping a sheet of water into his eyes. When he opened his eyes again, the letters were gone, if they were ever really even there. He couldn't be sure. So much had happened that day to make him unsure of things he saw.

He heard Mike call out from the back door, "What the hell are ya doin'? Hurry up, you're gonna get soaked."

Jamie picked up the toy, threw it in the bag and ran back to the house, stopping only for a second to look back over his shoulder at the tree; the wind and rain making it whip back and forth violently as if it were reaching out for him.

Where are you?

He was in such a hurry to get out of the rain he didn't see the ducks hiding in the brush watching him, gathering behind the largest one with the shiny, dead black eyes.

The sins of the father shall be visited upon the son. You shall not worship them or serve them; for I, the Lord your God, am a jealous God, visiting the iniquity of the fathers on the children, on the third and the fourth generations of those who hate Me.

■

"Here," Mike threw him a towel.

"Thanks," Jamie said, dropping the wet pillowcase on the floor, hanging Mike's jacket back on the hook behind the door and sitting back down at the table.

"Here," Mike grumbled again and pushed another Captain's tea in front of him.

"Whut're ya tryin' ta do, git me drunk?" Jamie asked, still without looking directly at him.

"So, what if I am?" Mike growled. "The only time you talk to me is when you've had a few. You won't even look at me. Why won't you look at me? Have I done something?"

"Ya thank I'm prouda whut ya saw in thar? That I hurt ya after ya've been so good ta me?" Jamie asked, his body tensing as he spoke.

Mike took a slug from the Captain Morgan bottle on the counter, swallowing hard, and walked over to the table. He put his dry, cracked, blistered hands out where Jamie could see them. Jamie looked up at him, his eyes looking more like Jane's than ever.

"Michael. I'm ashamed. Is 'at whut ya want ta hear?...fer bein' used, and dirty and...sick," Jamie whispered so the children wouldn't hear.

"That's not how you feel with them," Mike whispered, pointing to the living room.

"No, it's how I feel with *you*," Jamie said and got up to go, to hide anywhere he could, his bedroom, the wood room, anywhere Michael couldn't see him, away from those eyes that knew.

"Sit down!" Mike ordered. Jamie stopped, then slowly sat back down.

"You wanna talk about shame? Let me tell you something about shame. *I* am ashamed," Mike said, sitting down at the table with the bottle in his hand and pointing at his own chest. "For loving someone so much I thought my heart would explode and not *knowing*. For being innocent and ignorant of the signs; for not asking, not finding out.

"*I* am ashamed for failing the one person in the world who understood me and could still love me for who I am, who loved me enough to do that for me," he said pointing to the living room again, to the children "...because she knew how important having a family was to me. *I* am ashamed for going to work that day...just like any other day, but it wasn't any other day for her. How can I look at them and not be ashamed, knowing that if I'd been more sensitive, more in touch with her, loved her more... been a better husband, a better man, I could have done something.

"Your shame comes from crimes against you. My shame comes from inside *me, my* failure to save what I loved most.

It's *my* crime. *I* own it," Mike said taking another long slug from the bottle. "And it owns *me*." His face had turned almost crimson as he pointed to his own chest again before getting up angrily with the bottle still in his hand and grabbing his coat from the hook, slamming the backdoor behind him.

Rain pelted his face as he stomped across the yard towards the hill. He was soaked and chilled by the time he reached the top, going for the protection of the tree, taking another good slug as he leaned against the back of it, facing the valley. Mike hung his head sadly, feeling the raindrops trickle their way through the leaves and landing on his shoulders. He felt the sadness come back, creeping over him, through him, so deep, so lonely. He heard Alice Lorello's voice, ...*wife took his kids and left him...blew his heart out with a gun in the pantry.*

He took another drink; overwhelming sadness. *Don't leave me.* He closed his eyes, hypnotized by the sound of the wind blowing through the trees, tears running down his face, mixing with the raindrops falling on his head, dripping from his brow, his nose, his lips. *A suicide's house.*

He opened his eyes and looked up, watching the dark clouds rolling overhead. *Nothing to live for...Victoria...still your Daddy's girl...Forever and ever and ever?* The wind picked up making the rain sting his face...*wife took his kids and left him.* He took another long drink. ...*blew his heart out with a gun in the pantry.* Sadness, endless sadness, melancholy longing; pain in his heart, physically aching...breaking. *Where are you?*

■

Jamie paced back and forth in the kitchen, stopping every round to look out the window. He heard the mud room door hinge creak behind him. *Don't look.* The image flashed in his mind, Michael, a hole in his chest, his heart blown out, his true blue eyes staring up to the ceiling. Then the startled look on his face when the bike bucked, hitting him hard, hurting him and the sound of Mike's voice when he was wrapping his arm, *Let me do this.*

Jamie grabbed Mike's coat off the hook and went out, letting the door slam behind him. When he got to the top of the hill, Mike was gone. The bottle of Captain Morgan was cradled between two roots at the base of the tree, empty. He heard the truck engine start and tires tear out of the driveway.

■

Fifteen minutes later Mike pulled up into the parking space in front of the closest liquor store, Sayreville Bottle and Tap, and went in. He grabbed another bottle of the Captain off the shelf and stomped to the cashier, then out. Back in his truck, Mike looked up into his rearview mirror and saw the store behind him, The Sayreville Sportsman. There were guns in the window, rifles, shot guns, handguns and a sign, *Immediate approval with valid ID*. Mike opened the new bottle and took a long drink, then got back out of his truck and walked over.

■

It was dark when Jamie heard the sound of Mike's truck pull into the driveway. Beside himself with worry, he paced as he waited by the door for it to open. When it did and Mike came through, he looked like he'd been through a war; soaked and sad, slumped and dragging. Everything Jamie did to try and help him just made him growl, "Just lemme alone."

"Michael, please let me help ya."

"You mean the way you let me help you? Like the way Jane let me help her?" he said bitterly, then took two fingers and his thumb, held it to his heart like a pistol and pulled the trigger. "*Pow!* You're a good shot, why don'tcha just fucking do it for me?" he said and stomped up the stairs.

Jamie stood stunned in the hallway, scared, not knowing what to do, the little lead box inside him not telling him what to do like it did with Victoria and James. *Help me!*

Upstairs, Mike took one of the pills the doctor at the hospital had given him, stripped and got into the shower. He turned the water on hot, very hot and got in, letting it run over his shaved head, and just stood there waiting. *For what? You're big, ugly, forty-five years old with a dead wife, a broken down old house and two small kids you don't know how to raise. Was she ever happy? Were you ever happy or was it all just make believe? An illusion you created for yourself because you were so pathetic and lonely. What do you do now? You don't even have the illusion to hold on to now.*

Downstairs Jamie resumed his pacing, waiting for his little box to tell him what to do. He heard the shower turn on upstairs and stared at the mud room door, remembering Mike with his two fingers and thumb to heart like a pistol. *Pow! You're a good shot, why don'tcha just fucking do it for me?* He looked at the kitchen clock. It was getting close to dinner time. He had to feed the kids. He went to the refrigerator and opened the door. He closed his eyes and it was there again, the answer, the letter. *...Please look after Michael...*

I don't know how!

He took out the fixings for the burgers and cheese fries he'd promised the kids to make a rainy day picnic. With the burgers done and the fries in the oven, he jumped in the shower himself, scrubbing down, shaving close and dressing in his '*angel*' clothes; white tee, ripped jeans and no shoes.

When Mike came back down twenty minutes later in his pajamas, Jamie was ready. Victoria was eating her burger very ladylike with a napkin tucked in her collar and James was in his chair with his mouth open, waiting for the cheesy fry express. Jamie was at the stove with his back turned. Mike sat down silently.

"Michael," Jamie said quietly, turning around with a full plate ready for him in his hand. Mike looked up at him and his true blues came back, Jamie's face and clothes having the effect he'd planned, reminding Mike of the first time he saw Jamie, in that doorway, *Are you an angel?*

"That's not fair," Mike growled like a lion with a thorn caught in his paw.

"I don't care," Jamie said, his eyes intent, serious, then whacked him hard with the smile as he set the plate down in front of him, giving him a good nudge with his hip. Mike nudged back.

"I'm sorry," Mike said, a slight tremble in his lower lip, looking down at his plate.

"Me, too."

James wailed and whined impatiently from across the table, rocking his chair back and forth with his hands out. "Jeeme! Choo choo!"

That evening Mike spent with his kids on the couch watching TV, the third *Harry Potter* on the Family Channel Marathon. Jamie stayed in the kitchen baking. He had to get ready for Sunday dinner with the Reverend and his wife and he was way behind. He felt safe in the warmth of the kitchen, the heat radiating off the oven, puttering around, combing the recipe box and the cabinets for whatever he could use and hadn't thought of buying. Had he ever felt so safe before? He couldn't remember.

He stirred peanut butter and chocolate chips into the mixing bowl as per Jane's recipe card, a note in her handwriting at the bottom of the card reading, *Cold rainy days.* The room began to smell wonderful from his first attempt at a batch of brownies as the peanut butter cookies waited for their turn in the oven.

He made himself a cup of tea, without the Captain, and looked through the cards for a simpler cake recipe, then found it, *Pound cake,* with another note at the bottom of the card, *Foolproof.* Jamie couldn't help but smile to himself. *God love ya, Jane. Ya know I'm a fool,* he thought, remembering when they were kids and tried to stay together as much as possible. The old man never came after them when they were together, only when he could get them apart and their mother was out of the house, or too drunk to notice, or care.

He tried to remember what was good about their lives then, and thought again of the note. *You were always the strong one, be strong for me now.* But that wasn't true. He wasn't the strong one, she was. How she stayed with him and held his hand when he bled and thought he was going to die. He thought of when they would stand in front of the bathroom mirror together, looking at each other's faces, not really understanding how they could be so alike, *identical.*

He was the one who ran away, not her. He was the one who took to drugs while she struggled to care for their mother and go to school to try and better herself. She was the one who found a wonderful man to love and love her, had children, while he...never sought any real intimacy with another human being, and never liked sex very much, never feeling the connection other people seemed to get from it.

He took the brownies out of the oven and put the cookies in, then began with the dry ingredients for the cake, remembering the first time he could recall that *it* happened. They were old enough by then to have developed their own interests. She loved Home Ec at school while he started getting involved in sports, sixth grade, just before puberty. She burned her hand on the hot stove at school, not badly, just a small red cigar shaped welt on her wrist.

Later that day when he got home from baseball practice and was showering, he noticed the small red cigar shaped mark on his wrist, wondering how that happened, then at dinner saw the same mark on her wrist.

The next time was a few weeks later and he'd slid into home base at a game and skinned his knee. The next day when Jane came out of her room to go to school, she had a bruise on the same knee, and then there was the worst of it, how each knew when their father was touching the other, that horrible trapped feeling; the fear and the pain, reaching out to each other for help. It only stopped after they had killed him, but that was when the cutting started.

His scars became hers and her scars became his. They never talked about it, never had to, until the letters came. It seemed to lessen after he ran away with only the most intense experiences traveling over the distance; his craving for the drugs going away then getting the letter telling him about Michael, the terrible cramps he got making him think he was going to die from withdrawals in that dirty, cheap motel outside Mesa until he got the letter a few weeks later telling him that Victoria had been born. Then when James came, he knew before the letter arrived. Then there was that last time when he felt ripped apart inside, torn in half.

He put his hand to his chest as he remembered it, feeling the bruise of the steering wheel still sore and aching on his chest, wiping his eyes with the dishtowel. *I was nev'r strong, it was always you,* and he mixed the bowl of cake batter as he remembered her doing. The kitchen was her place, now his, the smells, the comfort, like a nesting bird, making a home for their young, *...and this one means soaring eagle.*

The next thing he knew, the cookies were out of the oven and the cake was in. He heard a shuffling sound by the doorway bringing him out of the private little world of his thoughts. Mike was standing there sleepy eyed, like an overgrown kid in his flannel pajamas, his cracked, blistered hand out, "Sum?"

Chapter Nine

The Reverend & Mrs. Willis Come to Dinner

"R everend Willis," Jamie said, opening the door to the old man. "So good ta see ya agin," Jamie smiled, genuinely pleased and somewhat relieved to see him. The Reverend had such an effect on Michael's mood. Jamie had done his best to dress better for Michael's guests; his least worn flannel shirt, black and white buffalo plaid tucked in his least faded jeans. He deliberately went to the door in only his white socks so as not to have to wear his old beat up boots. They were all he had.

The Reverend Willis stepped aside to reveal a striking older woman, stylish in a quiet, elegant sort of way; gray hair swept up behind her head, medium cocoa skin with full red lips and features that reminded Jamie almost of an ancient statue or a good queen from a storybook. "And you must be Mizzuz Willis," Jamie said politely, waiting for the usual reaction.

"And you must be Mr. Arnette. My husband has told me so much about you," she said, a smooth, even toned, comforting voice, her dark amber eyes twinkling with interest but nothing more. It caught Jamie off guard. It was the first time in his memory that someone who had known Jane, then met him, hadn't displayed any of the usual array of expressions; surprise, shock, disbelief.

Suddenly a cold wind blew and Jamie remembered himself, casting his eyes down with a blush. "Oh, forgive me. Please come in," he said to the woman, embarrassed. Mrs. Willis walked through the door followed by her husband. "Please, let me take yer coats."

The Reverend and Mrs. Willis removed their coats and handed them to Jamie. Jamie excused himself and took their coats into the wood room. While he was gone, Ella Willis turned to her husband, the look on her face expressing everything she had held back when she first saw Jamie. Her eyes widened with amazement as she mouthed to her husband, "What is going on here?" Josiah Willis just shrugged his shoulders, shook his head and leaned in to whisper to her quietly.

"The Lord works in mysterious ways, my wife."

By the time Jamie returned, the Willises were waiting patiently, very self-composed. "Michael is still upstairs gettin' dressed. He was out in the yard all day playin' with the kids and got a late start. Please sit down," Jamie said, motioning with his hand to the couch. Josiah and Ella Willis sat down as Jamie went to the stairs. "Michael, Reverend Willis and his wife are here!" he called into the stairwell.

"I'll be right down," Mike's voice came back down the stairwell. A minute later, Victoria came slowly down the stairs, holding James by the hand as he labored with each step. Jamie had dressed her himself in a beautiful little blue velvet dress with a sailor's collar edged in lace and a little blue bow under her chin, white tights and little black patent leather Mary Janes. James was dressed like Jamie, almost like a little lumber jack, green and blue-plaid flannel shirt, blue jeans and little work boots.

"Oh, how sweet," Ella Willis exclaimed, standing up and going over to them at the bottom of the stairs.

"You remember Mrs. Willis, don'tcha, Victoria?" Jamie asked. That was her cue to greet the guest like he'd taught her.

"Good afternoon, Mrs. Willis," Victoria said bashfully.

"And you remember my...nephew, James, Mrs. Willis?" Jamie asked her.

"Oh, yes!" she said, then looked up at Jamie, the resemblance between the little James and the bigger one not at all lost on her. "He's so adorable I could just eat him up," she said and tickled James' belly. He laughed. Jamie took the children by the hand to the couch and sat them down.

"Now, ya jes' stay here and talk ta Reverend and Mizzuz Willis while I run ta the kitchen fer a minute, okay?" Jamie asked Victoria. She nodded and sat down. Ella Willis picked James up and sat him on her lap talking baby talk to him. A minute later Jamie was back with a large tray of finger foods, cheese and crackers, sliced salami, pepperonchinos and olives. "Please help yerselves," Jamie said, setting the tray down with one hand and a set of small plates with napkins with the other. "Kin I git ya somethin' ta drank?" he asked his guests, running through the list of what he'd gotten the other day; "wine, beer, coffee, tea, soda, juice, you name it, I got it," he said smiling brightly and feeling closer to normal than he had since he arrived.

"I'll take care of the drinks," Mike's voice came from the bottom of the stairs. Dressed in a new pair of blue jeans and a light blue V-neck sweater over white tee shirt, white socks, too, no shoes, he walked over to his company. The minute Jamie saw him, he knew. Jane had bought him that sweater to mirror the color of his eyes. "No, please don't get up, Mrs. Willis. So good to see you again. Thank you for coming," Mike said, working to take the normally rough edge off his voice.

"Michael, you look so handsome," Ella Willis said, her eyes awash with sincerity and sympathy. Mike blushed like a teenager.

"Nah, it's just the sweater," he said, remembering when Jane had brought the sweater home and made him try it on. She'd said the same thing. He had to remind himself to keep a firm grip. He shook the Reverend's hand. "So what'll it be, Reverend?"

"Well, something soft would be nice," Josiah Willis replied then continued, "but you know Michael, I'd sure like to take a look around the grounds before it starts to get too dark, if I could. The weather is good and I've been cooped up in church all day. Could sure use the fresh air," and he winked at Mike, "and it'll give Ella and Mr. Arnette a chance to get acquainted. You'd like that wouldn't you, my wife?"

"Yes, I'd like that very much, Josiah," she replied smiling. He was up before she finished her sentence and taking Mike by the arm.

After she heard the back door shut, Ella Willis looked at Jamie and smiled, shaking her head. "You know, Mr. Arnette, I've been married to that man for forty years and he still doesn't think I know he has a pint of something in his upper pocket," and she laughed.

Jamie laughed too, flashing her the full breadth of that overbite smile. Ella Willis had to use all her training to keep from gasping, thinking to herself, *Sweet Jesus*, then rebounded. "Why don't we take this in the kitchen, Mr. Arnette and be casual with each other," she asked as she picked up the tray of food and stood.

"Yes, I'd like that very much," Jamie said, letting out a sigh of relief. He was so unskilled in polite company and he really wanted the Willises to like him, for Michael's sake as well as his own. He pointed to the TV so Victoria could see him, and then the cat, so James would stay occupied for awhile as he led Ella Willis into the kitchen.

■

"So tell me a little about yourself, Mr. Arnette," Ella asked as Jamie put down a glass of white wine for her, then his beer.

"Please call me Jamie," he said smiling shyly.

"Okay, Jamie," she said searching his eyes, and reading him like a book. She'd spent forty years in the church and knew how to read people. She could tell he was hurt inside, real bad, afraid. His eyes told her and she felt the rest in her heart; just like she had with Jane. With Jane it made her understand why whenever she and Mike were together that he always stayed so close to her, protective. Jamie nodded.

"Well, I came from Western Texas whin I got the...news. I knew Michael would need me. So I came," Jamie said, turning to the stove and opening the door to check on the roast. "But kin I ask ya a question?" he asked with his back still turned.

"Yes, of course, son. Ask away."

"You didn't react whin ya saw me. Ev'r'body else does. I'm not sure whatcha expected."

Ella took a sip of her wine before she spoke. "Well, when Josiah came home and told me that he had a white biker to pray for, too, I knew you must be a good person. Josiah is nobody's fool and he likes you. He also told me that you and Jane were twins and that the resemblance was remarkable. So when we came here today, the last thing I wanted was to make you feel uncomfortable, son, so I drew on my training. I was studying to be an actress when I met Josiah in college, used to be pretty good, too," she said proudly.

Jamie laughed as he turned and sat down at the table with her, glad for the opportunity to take the subject away from himself.

"So that explains it," he nodded, smiling and refilling her glass, then took a slug of his beer. Ella Willis took another long sip of her wine and leaned in.

"Yes, I wanted to be the next Ruby Dee or Diahann Carroll. I trained in college and then in New York during the summers. I was going to help break the color line just like they did, but then something happened."

Jamie was rapt as he listened.

Her voice took on a professional tenor, smooth as silk, evenly measured but tinged with nostalgia. "I met Josiah in my last year of school. He was a little older and had come up north to meet my roommate. It was a set up date between their mothers.

"While my roommate was getting ready, I sat and talked to him. He was so sincere about everything, doing God's work, his passion for the Civil Rights movement, and I found that to be so attractive. I've never found anything more attractive in a man than sincerity, more than looks, money or anything else. I couldn't help but fall in love with him." She stopped and took another sip, then laughed shaking her head. "I remember when I took him home to meet my mother and she saw how dark he was, she pitched such a fit," and she laughed again, the glow of remembrance shining in her eyes,

"Now, remember, my generation was raised to respect our parents. They worked so hard and struggled so much to give us a better life and I never once defied her, but when she forbid me to marry him, I looked her in the eye and said, 'Now Mama, I don't care if he's black, blue, green or red. He's the finest man I ever met and I'm gonna marry him!' And I did, and we've been happy now for forty years. Sincerity, Jamie, it's all that matters. Michael is like that, too. That's why he and Josiah get on so well and why we all love him so much at the church. Broke all our hearts to see him in so much pain when..." she said tapping his hand.

He nodded that he understood.

Ella Willis looked deep into his eyes then, "And since we're talking here, I want you to know, Jane was in good hands with Michael, loved her like crazy. Anyone that ever saw them together could see it. The way he would hold her hand when they were out in public, just like sweethearts. I just wanted you to know that."

She felt the muscles in Jamie's hand go rigid and saw his body follow suit. He stood up and went to the stove again, not wanting her to see his face. She got up and went to him, watching him fumble nervously to put on the oven mitts, his hands shaking.

"What's wrong, son?" she asked quietly, putting her hand on his back, searching for his eyes. Jamie looked up at her, his eyes telling her he wanted to speak but didn't know how. He looked back down.

"I'm a drifter, Mizzuz Willis; a wanderer on the edge o' yer world. I'm the kinda guy a lady like you would cross the street ta git away from. I nev'r ev'n once set down at a table with as fine a lady as you…bein' so kind ta me an' all whin here I am cain't hardly read or write, jes' enough ta git by," Jamie said and looked back up to her, waiting.

The minute she saw his eyes Ella Willis's heart opened wide like the first rosebud of spring and love came flooding out. She took him into her arms, holding him close. "I saw your motorcycle out there when we drove up. Are you runnin' from something, son, or is there something you're runnin' to?"

She felt his body stiffen again, but she didn't let go. "You've had an awful lot on your shoulders lately, too, haven't you? You know, I have a son about your age." Jamie nodded against her shoulder.

"I bin trying' so hard."

"And you're doing just fine, son, real fine. Now you just sit down and have a beer for yourself, relax a bit and let Mama Willis take care of the rest of this," she said taking the oven mitts from him.

■

Reverend Willis walked toward the lake to watch the sun set as Mike went about making a fire in the pit. A few ducks swam by from right to left, gathering in the reeds close to a tree at the water's edge. The evening sky colors were so bright, an autumn sunset, so beautiful. A few more ducks swam past joining the others in the reeds, then started moving onto land, seeming to gather behind the tree.

Reverend Willis took out his pint and took a sip, then lit a small black cigar.

When he looked again, more ducks had gathered behind the tree, almost in order of size, the largest at the front with shiny, cold, dead, black eyes. They seemed to be staring at him. It made him uneasy, like they had intelligence.

He started to move away, back toward where Mike stood at the fire pit. He heard a rustling in the brush behind him and looked back. For a split second he thought he caught an image out of the corner of his eye, misty, not solid, a man, standing behind the largest duck, a long black frock coat, ruffled collar, long white hair and large flat black hat, vaguely familiar for some reason, but the eyes, shiny, cold, black dead looking eyes. *"Nigger slave!"*

He blinked and it was gone; nothing but mist and ducks. He turned to head back up the yard, then stopped and turned again. The ducks were gone too, swimming off across the lake into the sunset. *Somethin' wrong with you ol' man?* Josiah Willis thought to himself as he approached the concrete slab with the fire pit where Mike was waiting for him. The Reverend greeted him with the pint out in his hand. Mike took it and had a nice long slug, then handed it back. "Thanks, Reverend, just what I needed."

"Me, too," the Reverend smiled. "Even I can get enough of holiness and need some time to be just plain ol' Josiah," he said and laughed. "So, how ya making out, Michael?"

"Okay, I guess," Mike shrugged and sat down in his chair. The Reverend sat down next to him and took another slug. "But I guess you've figured out that you're gonna have me on your hands for good now," Mike said, shuffling his feet and staring into the fire. The Reverend looked at him curiously. "It only came to me the other day myself. I can't sell this house and leave now that she's buried here."

"Well, if that's the case, I can't think of anyone I'd rather have on my hands, Michael," the old Reverend said, smiling and reaching over to give Mike's knee a nudge.

"I lied before, Reverend. I haven't been feeling so well," Mike blurted out. "I just feel so...hopeless. When I'm alone nothing seems to matter anymore. I feel okay now, here with you, or with the kids or Jamie. But at night, when I'm all alone, I feel like my insides are caving in on themselves and I could just...die," Mike said, wiping his face with the back of his hand.

The Reverend had a more than a simple pang of anxiety at Mike's confession and handed Mike the bottle again. He'd heard those words so many times before in his career and it worried him.

"It takes time, Michael. Take it one day at a time, son."

Mike took a slug and wiped his mouth again, his mood sinking lower, an echo in the back of his mind seeming to call to him, *Come to the tree, Michael.* He stood up and started to walk slowly toward the tree. The Reverend followed him, his walking stick punching holes in the damp ground as he went.

At the top of the hill, Mike just stood silently looking out over the valley, the Reverend beside him. The sun had almost set, vibrant reds, oranges and yellows lining the sky; a thin slivering line between the darkening night and the horizon. A wave of sadness came over him. He sighed loudly, letting his shoulders slump like he was a deflating balloon. The Reverend watched him, seeming to be able to feel what Mike was feeling. He felt the sadness and the loneliness, too, like a wave of it had just washed over him.

The wind blew and leaves swirled around their feet. The Reverend sought out Mike's eyes and knew what he was thinking. "Think about your children, Michael. What would become of them if anything were to happen to you? Think about the people who love you. We will shoulder your pain with you."

Mike nodded, a thin stream of tears running from his eyes. The Reverend took out a handkerchief and gave it to him.

"I don't know what to do," Mike said, shaking his head and wiping his eyes.

"Then do nothing. When you don't know what to do, the best course is always to do nothing. Promise me, Michael, you'll do nothing," the Reverend said, forcing Michael to look into his shiny black eyes so full of concern. "I am always here for you, day or night," he said and put his arm around Mike's waist.

The wind blew again and a chill ran up the Reverend's spine. He took another slug of whiskey, suddenly feeling the need to look behind him over to the left of the lake. He couldn't see anything in the dark, but he got the feeling that they were being watched, reminding him of those filthy words in the back of his mind, *Nigger slave.*

■

"So, my husband tells me you're a woodworker," Ella Willis said, trying to draw Jamie out of himself as she stirred the Miracle Whip into the bowl with the cabbage and carrots Jamie had shredded earlier for coleslaw.

"Yes, ma'am, since I was sixteen," Jamie said nodding proudly, now on his third beer, smiling and feeling better.

"He tells me that you're going to carve us an altar for the church. Something out of your book of pictures," she hinted. Jamie snapped to at the suggestion.

"Oh yes, would ya like ta see 'em?" he asked getting up from the table, anxious to show her that he had a worthy talent he could share.

"Well, I thought you'd never ask," she said, smiling brightly as she put his freshly baked biscuits into a basket and covered them with a napkin.

"I'll be back in a minute," Jamie said, and rushed through the doorway towards the stairs. He took the steps two at a time until he got to the top, then stopped suddenly. The door to the attic was swung in, opened slightly, and the light was on. '*at's not right*, he thought and called out quietly, "Victoria? Are ya in thar, darlin'?" No response.

He went closer, slowly reaching his head through the doorway. *"Jamey, James."* His mouth opened but the scream never left his throat as he felt himself pulled violently in by the hair, a whisper in his ear, *"The devil hath power t'assume a pleasing shape, James."* The light went out as he was dragged further into the darkness, kicking and struggling, just then able to scream as the door slammed forcefully behind him with a thundering slam. *Bang!*

Victoria heard the scream, then door slam, and ran up the stairs. Ella Willis ran to the foot of the stairs when she heard it. Mike and the Reverend Willis heard the next series of screams all the way up on the hill and ran, Mike bounding across the yard like a bull at the gate, throwing the back door open and dashing up the stairs.

Victoria was standing outside the attic door, jumping up and down and pointing, tears running down her face. Mike didn't stop to think he just slammed his mass against the old wooden door, blasting it into pieces as he rushed into the darkness.

He heard a strange sound before each scream as it came from the blinding black of the far corner; a whirring noise, then, *Thwak! Thwak!* He scrambled for the light cord and pulled on the light. Jamie was crumpled in the corner against the far wall, his body shaking; frenzied jerking, one arm over his head and the other trying to reach his back, seeming to try and crawl away from...what? There was nothing there. Mike ran to Jamie and the sounds stopped.

Driven by an enormous rush of adrenaline, Mike scooped Jamie up in his arms and bolted out of the room, standing in the hallway, not knowing what to do next. The Reverend and Mrs. Willis were waiting there, panic and fear all over their faces, Mrs. Willis holding Victoria tightly to her leg.

Mike took Jamie to the closest bedroom, the kids', and laid him down on Victoria's bed. Jamie was shaking terribly, so pale he was almost blue, twitching and quaking from the core of his being. He looked up into Mike's eyes, his own otherwise shy hazel eyes crazed and bulging with fear.

"Don't let 'im git me, Michael, please don't let 'im git me!" he cried out in the little boy voice Mike heard the first night Jamie came, clinging to Mike's arm.

Before Mike could respond, the Reverend and Mrs. Willis were standing next to him. Mike looked to them. "What the hell happened?" Victoria was off to the side in the corner.

"The attic! The attic!" she cried, seeming to try and hide in the corner, her own eyes radiating a fear that Mike would never have wanted her to know. He looked back at Jamie cowering on the bed. Ella Willis sat down next to him, putting her hand on his forehead. Jamie's eyes went blank and rolled up in his head, his movements stopped and his body went limp. Ella Willis called to her husband.

"He's in shock, Josiah. Gimme the bottle."

The old man handed her the bottle from his jacket pocket. She poured some over Jamie's lips. He sputtered and came around, but instead of limp his body went rigid, taut like a tight wire, and his eyes were still blank. He was trying to speak but couldn't seem to form words. Ella Willis saw the marks first, welts coming up on his side where his shirt hiked up. She motioned with her head to her husband. He came close. She whispered to him, "Take Michael out." The old man went to Mike pacing behind them.

"Michael," he said, nodding to the corner where Victoria was still trying to hide. Mike got the hint and went to her, picking her up and taking her out of the room with him. The Reverend followed him far enough to see him take Victoria down the stairs, then went back to his wife.

By the time he got back to the room, Ella had Jamie lying on his stomach and had pulled up his flannel shirt and tee shirt. Dozens of long, thin red welts were rising up, covering Jamie's back, criss-crossing themselves from the place where his belt ended, looking like they went all the way up to cover his shoulders. She looked at her husband, her eyes burning with anger. "You know what this is, Josiah. You've seen it before, lash marks! This boy has been beaten!" Josiah Willis' mouth fell open. They heard movement behind them and turned their heads to look. Mike was standing there, his eyes large and round, glazed with horror. They both looked at him at the same time.

"I...I...I didn't do that," he said haltingly.

"Who did this to you, boy?" Josiah Willis asked Jamie, quietly leaning into him, looking into Jamie's one eye as it stared blankly at the ceiling.

"I didn't do that," Mike said again, backing away from the bed. "Tell them, Jamie. Tell them I didn't do that to you," he cried out, turning in a circle, feeling trapped with no where to go. When he heard Mike's voice, life came back into Jamie's eyes, then tears.

"No...not Michael..." he said, the little boy voice having turned back into his whiskey rasp. "Not Michael...my father."

Ella Willis turned to her husband, then to Mike with some relief. "I need a bowl of cool water, some towels, and some cream, any kind. Now, Josiah!" she said raising her voice, then lowering it as she turned back to Jamie. "Come on now, son, let's get your shirt off," she said, gently helping Jamie roll back over so she could unbutton his shirt, wincing when he did as if she could feel the pain when he did. Jamie held his tee shirt closely to his chest so she wouldn't see the bruising and rolled quickly back over on his stomach.

Josiah Willis moved to leave the room. Mike followed him to help get the supplies. "Their father is dead, Reverend," Mike whispered to the old man, his eyes filling from the knowledge that only he and Jamie shared, the words from the letter appearing before his eyes, *He's come back for us. He knows what we did and he's come back for us.*

When the men came back into the room, Jamie was lying shirtless on his chest, his raw back exposed. Ella Willis took a small towel, soaked it in the pot of cool water and laid it on Jamie's back. He whimpered at its touch, but quieted with Ella's soothing voice and gentle touch, smoothing his hair.

"It's alright now, son."

■

Ella Willis came downstairs sometime later and had started the turn at the corner toward the kitchen when she heard a sound, a rattling sound coming from the other side of the stairs. She turned in the direction of the sound and saw James sitting by the basement door, tugging at the bottom corner making the latch rattle. She went over to him and picked him up. "Azzze-an," James said pointing to the basement door.

"Asian?" Ella Willis said to the little blonde boy in her arms. "I ain't no Asian, child. I'm a black woman. Can you say, *'black woman'?*" she said, struggling with a nervous laugh after the harrowing experience she'd just had upstairs.

Taking James back around the front of the stairs, she heard Mike and Josiah's voices coming through the kitchen door, but there was another voice, too, a little girl's voice, whispering. When she turned the corner around the stairwell, Victoria had just said *"Good-bye"* and was putting down the phone. Ella took her by the hand and said with a sigh, "You babies must be starved by now. Let's see if we can get you some dinner."

In the kitchen, Ella put James in his chair. Mike brought Victoria's chair next to him, but she didn't stay there. She climbed in his lap and laid her head on his shoulder.

"Daddy, I'm scared."

Mike stroked her hair and held her close. "There's nothing to be scared of, sweetheart. Daddy's here. Remember when we talked about Jamie being special?"

Victoria nodded, but the reference wasn't lost on the Reverend Willis, or his wife. Both of them looked at Mike curiously. Mike just mouthed to the Reverend. *"We'll talk later."*

"He's quiet now. I gave him what was left of your bottle," Ella said to Josiah. "He'll be down in a little while. He's worried that his dinner is ruined," she said and held up her wine glass to Mike. Josiah got up instead and went to the refrigerator, came back and filled her glass. She downed it in one gulp and held out the glass again. Mike pointed him over to the bottle of Captain Morgan on the counter. He came back with the bottle and a water glass, filled it, drank half and gave the other half to Mike. He downed it and handed it back to the old man. Filled again, they did the same thing, then again when they heard Jamie's footsteps coming down the creaking stairs.

■

No one spoke of it as they ate. Victoria ate from Mike's plate until she was full, then he ate; just picked really, dipping his biscuits in the gravy. Jamie fed James to keep him from throwing food at the guests, all the while knowing what everyone was thinking, that he'd done it to himself.

Whenever he glanced at Mike, Mike looked like he just wanted to cry. Mike knew. He knew everything, could think about it, imagine it, visualize it in his mind. Jamie fought to keep from crawling inside himself to hide from Michael's sight, thinking, "*Please don't make me leave, Michael. I know whut I am. I'll leave on my own. I'll leave tomorra.*"

After dinner, James started nodding out in his chair and Victoria on Mike's lap. He took them and put them on the couch, then left Jamie and Mrs. Willis to clean up while he and the Reverend took another walk out to the fire pit.

As soon as they were alone, Ella Willis took Jamie by the hand and they sat down at the table. He kept his head down, couldn't look at her. She put her hand under his chin and lifted it up, her dark amber eyes translating such heart and soul, searching Jamie's for some sign of what she could do for him to ease his pain, her own heart breaking with the torment she saw there. "What are you so afraid of, son?"

"That I'm damned."

■

Out at the fire pit, the Reverend spoke first. "Jamie said it was a long story about him showin' up at the funeral. Then you tellin' me about not knowing Jane had a brother. Was he in a hospital? Is that why she didn't tell you, Michael?" Mike just shook his head, took a deep breath, then looking deep into the Reverend's dark eyes, aglow with concern in the firelight said, "They were…when they were young…by their father." Mike took a good long slug of Captain Morgan and passed the bottle.

"Oh, Lord, you mean…" the Reverend asked, not able to verbalize what he was thinking. Mike nodded, wiping his eyes.

"Both of them," Mike said turning away, feeling the shame of it weighing so unbearably heavy on his soul. "Please pray for them, Reverend, their souls, both of them," Mike said then broke down, sliding down into his chair and crying into his hands. The Reverend handed the bottle back to Mike.

"I will, son. Believe me I will, powerful prayers for God's mercy, and for you, too, Michael Golden."

Mike took a long slug of the Captain and wiped his mouth on his sleeve as was his habit.

"You told me the other day that the Lord doesn't give us more than we can carry. Well, I don't know how much more I can carry, Reverend, or for how long."

■

Mike saw the Reverend and his wife out to their car. As they pulled down the drive, Ella Willis looked at her husband and he at her. "You don't even have to say it. I already know. I got a feeling when I met Jane, but hoped to God I was wrong. Now I know for sure. You take the big one and I'll take the blonde one. We have our work cut out for us, my husband," she said and reached over to take his arm.

"Yes, we do, my wife," Josiah Willis said back. "It's hurtin' Michael so bad. We gotta keep our eye on him, and we gotta work fast…and may the Lord have mercy on their souls."

■

When Mike got back to the house, James was nodding on the couch in front of the glowing cat and Victoria was half asleep watching some nature show on public television, her eyes drooping low. Other than for strains of a mournful guitar strum coming through the opening in the sliding door to the wood room, the house was quiet; then Garth's voice, smooth and low. *"So I turn out the lights and lay there in the dark and the thought crosses my mind, if I never wake up in the morning would she ever doubt the way I feel about her in my heart."*

He went back up to the kids' room and got what was left of the cream, then came back down and grabbed two beers. When he got back to the wood room, the slider was shut. He knocked but got no answer. He knocked again, still no answer. He pulled the slider back slowly, holding his breath, not knowing what to expect.

Jamie was standing at the oak plank, staring at it blankly. Mike could see faint thin lines of blood seeping through his white tee shirt. *"And if my time on earth were through and she must face the world without me, is the love I gave her in the past gonna be enough to last…if tomorrow never comes,"* Garth crooned into the calm autumn night air as Mike walked over to the plank, flipped a beer top and sat it in front of Jamie. The image of the tree sketched on the plank caught him in the guts, filling him with such loss and loneliness he wanted to crawl back out like a whipped dog with his tail between his legs. Jamie looked up at him, his eyes dark and distant. "Come on, pull up your shirt," Mike grumbled, holding up the tube of cream. Jamie knew enough not to challenge him, especially when he knew what was to come, and he pulled the tee shirt over his head as Garth sang on, *"'Cause I've lost loved ones in my life who never knew how much I loved them. Now I live with the regret that my true feelings for them never were revealed…."*

The marks had swelled to an angry shade of red, rimmed in purple, dozens of them like some sick, bizarre checkerboard. Mike squeezed a long stream of cream on his finger tips and started slowly, gently at Jamie's shoulders. Jamie flinched at first from the cold of the cream on his burning skin, then went rigid, stiff as a board.

"I know whut yer thankin'. Ya thank I did it ta myself. I'll leave," Jamie said, dejected, defeated, almost mumbling. Mike could feel Jamie's heart thumping through his back, small heaves choking in his chest.

"What the hell are you talking about?" Mike's voice came from behind him. "Why?"

"If I hafta go, I'd rather it be on my own steam than fer ya ta tell me ta leave. That would hurt me more than dyin'."

Mike stopped and carefully pulled down Jamie's shirt, blind anger rising up inside him. Like Lon Chaney, Jr., in the *Wolfman* films from the forties, Michael Golden could almost feel coarse hair starting to grow out of his arms and hands, his arms stretching lower and lower as the knuckle scraper in him came to the surface, the thin tether between man and animal unraveling as he stood there. "*So tell that someone that you love, just what you're thinking of, if tomorrow never comes.*"

"That's it! I've had enough of this fuckin' shit for one day," Mike barked, his voice taking on the firmness he used when he corrected James, "Yo! Boy!" and he strong-armed Jamie out of the room. "Come with me...now," and he led Jamie to his bedroom. "Get in there and put on something to sleep in," he ordered and shut the door, waiting out in the hall for his word to be done.

When Jamie opened the door again, he was dressed for bed in old sweats and a faded old Harley tee shirt with the sleeves cut off. Mike took him by the arm again and led him into the living room, facing the couch. "Pick your kid," Mike barked under his breath. His back was so sore Jamie chose the lighter of the two, went to James and picked him up. Mike took Victoria in his arms and pointed to Jamie. "Upstairs," Mike ordered. Jamie obeyed.

Upstairs, Mike stopped in front of his bedroom, reached in and flipped on the light, then pointed to the bed. "Get in the bed." Jamie had never been in Mike's room before, not even to clean it. *Jane's bed,* he thought and hesitated. "Did you not hear me? Take James and get in the goddamn bed before I put you there. You might think you're some tough biker guy, but I guarantee you I'm bigger and a whole lot stronger," Mike growled, his true blues glaring angrily at Jamie and pointing commandingly at the bed. Jamie did as he was told, laying James next to him in the middle.

Satisfied for the moment that he was back in control, Mike laid Victoria on his side of the bed. She rolled comfortably to James and cuddled. Mike looked at Jamie, his true blues blazing with intent, his brow furrowed into almost a uni-brow again telling Jamie he meant business. "You do not move until I get back!" Jamie nodded silently. Mike growled and left the room. "Grrrrr."

Downstairs Jamie could hear Mike's heavy footsteps and the clatter of dishes. A few minutes later he heard the bell on the microwave and Mike's heavy footsteps on the stairs again, then the door to his library opening and closing. When he looked up, Mike was back in the doorway standing with a tray in his hands. He came in and set the tray on the bedside table table next to Jamie, turning around with a big mug of Captain tea and handing it to him. "Take this and drink it," he ordered. Jamie took it, having decided from the very beginning that Michael was not a man to be fucked with lightly. "Eat this," Mike growled handing Jamie a pot roast sandwich on crusty bread with a side of his own coleslaw.

Jamie finally screwed up the courage to speak with only a simple, "Yes, Michael."

Mike went into his own bathroom and shut the door. When he came out he was dressed in his own big, plaid flannel pajamas. Looking at them so comfortable in the bed, Mike sighed deeply, then went over to the small TV on the night stand by the window on Jane's side of the bed and turned it on, handing Jamie the remote. Another deep sigh and he was over by his side of the bed turning on the lamp on his bedside table. He switched off the big light and went and sat in his own bedside arm chair. He opened *The Fountainhead* and put his feet up on the bed, his split toe still wrapped.

Mike put on his glasses and looked at Jamie, then pointed to his toe. "You see that?" Jamie nodded, taking a sip of his tea. Mike held out his hands. "And these?" Jamie nodded again. Then Mike pointed to Victoria and James sleeping peacefully next to him. "It's meant the world that you should do that for me," he grumbled lightly, trying not to wake the kids. "I told you once already and I'm not gonna say it again. We've already lost one Arnette and I'll be goddamned if we're gonna lose another one, not without one helluva fight. If you wanna leave because you don't like me or you don't love them, that's one thing," he growled, pointing at Victoria and James again. "Do you not love them?" Mike asked, his true blues wide and staring at him, waiting for an answer. Jamie nodded and whispered quietly.

"I do, more than anythang, Michael. I do."

"Alright then, don't ever try to lay that shit at my doorstep again. You're our family now. All we have is each other. We'll deal with the monster together, so don't ever cross me with that 'I'm gonna leave' shit again. Do you understand me? *I am* the biggest fucking monster in this goddamn house tonight. You hear me?" Mike huffed. Jamie nodded again.

"Yes, Michael."

"Now drink your tea, all of it…and let me see that smile, just a little one. I need it tonight. Tomorrow we'll talk about what happened tonight and figure the rest out then."

Jamie smiled a faint, uncertain smile for him with another simple, "Yes, Michael."

Mike wanted to cry when he saw that smile but held himself in, looking down and opening *The Fountainhead*, knowing that the two pills from the hospital he'd slipped in

Jamie's tea would take care of the rest. "And eat that sandwich," Mike growled without looking up from his book.

"Yes, Michael."

■

Outside in the back yard, the ducks gathered, laughing in the darkness, gaining in numbers, chattering to each other as they followed the large one closer to the house, staring up at the dim light coming from Mike's bedroom window.

■

Mike woke up a few hours later feeling a weight on his lap. When he opened his eyes, Victoria was laying with her head on his chest. "You alright, sweetheart?" he asked her, still half asleep himself.

"I'm scared, Daddy," she said, snuggling closer to him.

"What are you scared of, baby? I'm right here."

"The bad man," Victoria said in her very little girl voice.

"What bad man?"

"The one that hurt Jamie in the attic." Mike's eyes jolted open. He was up.

"How do you know there was a bad man in the attic with Jamie, sweetheart?"

"I heard him."

"You heard him?" Mike repeated not knowing what to think. Victoria nodded. "What did he say?"

"He called Jamie a '*feemer*' and a '*soda-man*.' What's a *feemer*, Daddy?"

"I don't know, baby, but we can ask the doctor we're gonna get for Jamie, a very good doctor," Mike said, taking off his glasses. He took Victoria back over to the bed and laid her down gently, then got in next to her. James was snuggled in close to Jamie's chest, both of them out like a light, snoring in a humming unison, one a miniature version of the other. His two blonde Jameses and Daddy's girl all together.

Michael Golden closed his eyes, splintering again and following it, taking what little peace that it offered him, even if only until morning. *I would protect you all to the end of the world...please tell me you still love me, Jane.*

■

The next morning the Reverend Josiah Willis came down late to breakfast. Before he even had the chance to sip his coffee, Ella was chattering at him. "Michael called to let us know everything was alright, but he wants to know if we can help him find a doctor for Jamie. He didn't say psychiatrist, but I'm sure that's what he meant. I'll take that job. He also said he needs a few days off, but said that he would call Alex and take care of things with him. In the meantime, my husband, we have Mama coming tomorrow for our turn with her for the holidays. Please be patient with her, Josiah. I know it's hard for you, but she *is* my mama and I love her," then she put down a big bowl of heart healthy oatmeal in front of him and a glass of orange juice. Josiah just sighed and took his medicine. He had hated oatmeal ever since he was a poor boy back in Chicago and that was all they could afford, now at sixty-five years old they find out it's the best way to keep his blasted cholesterol down and the worst part of it was, it worked so well he had to keep eating it.

The door bell rang and Ella went to answer it. Just as she moved away from the countertop he saw it and his heart leapt in his chest; the box of oatmeal, *Quaker Oats*, with the picture of the old-fashioned Quaker man on the front. Josiah Willis blinked his eyes and looked again. It was the image of the man from the lake behind Mike's house, but not smiling, gray eyed and friendly like the oat man; the same clothes, hair and hat but with shiny, dead, cold, black eyes, glaring at him from the mist among the ducks. *Nigger slave.*

Ol' man, you mus' be losin' yo' mind, he thought to himself, but then a worse thought came to him. It was his doctor's voice, *A little Alzheimer's to go with your clogged arteries, Reverend?*

And with Ella's dang Mama comin'...ol' scarecrow. After six weeks of her caterwallin', a stroke might very well be in order, and he shoved a spoonful of oatmeal into his mouth, frowning and pulling a face like it was poison. Even after forty years, Josiah Willis was still not exactly Bethea Walton's favorite son-in-law.

Chapter Ten

Damage Control

A fter Mike spoke to Mrs. Willis about finding a doctor for Jamie, he called Alex and told him he needed a few more days off. "No, really, Alex. I'm alright. Both my kids have colds that's all," he lied. "I just need to get them through it and I'll be back. Yeah. You know what to do. We're almost done anyway. Just get the guys to finish the spackling and painting. Yeah, call me if you need me. I won't be going too far."

With that done, it was time to make breakfast. Jamie and the kids were still sound asleep, but the smell of bacon frying and coffee perking would get them up for sure.

Jamie came down first. "Let me jes' grab a cup o' coffee fer now. I hafta git Victoria up and set her clothes out fer school. I'll be back down in a minute." He came down a few minutes later carrying Victoria in his arms and put her in her chair.

Mike leaned over for their usual morning ritual. Victoria kissed his cheek. "Good morning, Daddy," she yawned. Mike set a plate of scrambled eggs, bacon and toast in front of her, then a small glass of orange juice.

"Hungry, sweetheart?"

Victoria nodded, a worried look in her eyes. Jamie disappeared back up the stairs, coming down a few minutes later with his bundle on his hip. He put James in his chair then went to refill his coffee cup, nudging Mike with his shoulder along the way. Mike nudged him back, handing him a plate of cinnamon toast with bacon and James's tipless filled with apple juice. Jamie sat down next to James and started the locomotive.

Behind Jamie's back Mike mouthed silently to Victoria, "Everything is alright." She smiled, recognizing the strength in Daddy's eyes and nodded back at him that she understood. A minute later Mike pushed a plate at Jamie's elbow, "Bacon, egg and cheese on toast," he grumbled. Jamie took the hint and picked up half the sandwich and bit into it.

With breakfast done, Jamie got Victoria ready for school and waited with her for the bus. Before he said good-bye, he looked at her, waiting for her to look back. When she did he saw the worried look in her eyes, "Will you be here when I get home?" she asked him with her very little girl voice instead of her usual 'I'm a big girl' one, little tears forming in her true blues.

He picked her up and hugged her tightly. "Yes, yes, yes, I promise, sweetheart. I'll be here. Waitin' right here fer ya. Right here in this very spot," and put her back down. The bus driver was getting impatient.

As the bus drove off, she waved a small wave to him, trusting him to keep his word. He waved back, pointing to the ground where he was standing, "Right here!" and watched as the bus pulled away, the little lead box inside him starting to rumble again, small cracks rippling off the main fissure, a warm light radiating through him. *Please love my children*, flashed through his head from the letter.

"I do, I swear I do," he mumbled to himself as he walked slowly back up the drive to the house, trembling inside at what he faced when he and Mike were alone again, trying to explain what he thought had happened in the attic.

∎

"Off," Mike said, tugging lightly at the shoulder of Jamie's flannel shirt. Jamie did as he was told, then leaned over and laid his head on his arms folded on the table. Mike took the tube of cream and pushed a long white worm shape onto his fingertips. The angry red color and swelling of the welts had gone down some, only pink now, light scratches and some scabbing over the deeper marks. Mike sighed with relief. Jamie gritted his teeth rather than flinch at the cold of the cream as Mike touched his back. It was time for Mike the Builder's own brand of therapy.

He thought of Jane and how afraid of him she had been at first, never looking at him, never smiling. He learned then how to take the rough edge off his voice so that it sounded smooth, like dark honey, and how gentle he had to be whenever he touched her; no sudden movements, only smooth, slow gestures. He remembered how he'd rubbed her shoulders and back so many nights when she was pregnant and had such awful backaches because the kids were so heavy on her little frame, and he was ready.

"Tell me," Mike said softly as he smoothed the cream over Jamie's torn shoulders. Jamie closed his eyes and let it happen, lulled into a sense of security by the sound of Mike's voice and the rhythmic movement of Mike's hands over his sore back, the cool of the cream warming to body temperture, almost hypnotizing him.

"I went upstairs ta git my picture book ta show Mizzuz Willis. She wanted ta see 'em. Whin I got ta the top of the stairs, the attic door was open and the light was on. I thought that maybe Victoria might've gone in thar ta find somethin'. I called out ta her...but...but she didn't answer."

He took a long swallow, thinking about how to say what happened next, Mike's big hands working around to the sore spots along the outside of his ribs. "I pushed the door open and stuck my head in ta jes' peek 'round and see if she was thar." He took a deep breath. Mike could feel his heart pounding through his back again, the beat increasing as Jamie struggled to get the words out.

"It's alright. Go on, tell me," Mike said, his voice little more than a vibrating hum. Jamie started to stammer, his body tensing. Mike kept smoothing him, working the cream into welts across the broad of his back.

"I...I...I felt somebody...I heard...he called my name, *Jamey James*. Nobody ev'r called me 'at but 'im...my father...whin 'e was a comin' after me ta...Nobody else knows but Jane. She was Janie Jane and I was Jamey James...when 'e was..." Then he broke off, "I know ya thank I did this ta myself, and after the other day and the cuttin,' ya have ev'r right ta thank that. But, Michael, I didn't. I swear, I didn't," Jamie said, a hitching in his voice.

"Shhhh," Mike said, in a low hum, "just tell me what did happen."

"He grabbed me by the hair and pulled me in, then...then...then the lights went out and I felt myself bein' thrown across the room. I...I landed hard against the far wall. It knocked the wind outta me. I couldn't breath, I couldn't yell. I could hear footsteps a comin' at me outta the dark and a whirrin' sound, like bees above me, then I felt it stingin' across my back. I yelled. It was like...like hot wires, more whirrin' and that awful sound *Thwack, thwack*, each time it caught me." Jamie's body started to jerk and twist each time he said the words, *Thwack, thwack*.

It was Mike's turn to stop and go stiff then. He thought he'd heard those same sounds when he broke into the room.

"And he was callin' me names...names I didn't understand, *blass-fee-mer, sod-a-mite* and *forn-a-cator*," Jamie said, sounding them out phonetically. Jamie's back was heaving by then. Mike stood behind him, his hands still on his back but not moving. He heard Victoria's voice replay in his head, "*He called Jamie a 'feemer' and a 'soda-man.' What's a feemer, Daddy?*"

Jamie's body went into full blown shakes then. Mike held him by the shoulders, Jamie's head still down in his arms, sobbing. "I don't know whut happened, but it's happenin' ta me, too. Whutev'r happened ta Jane is happenin' ta me, too. He was in that room with me, Michael. I swear he was.

Nobody but 'im ev'r called me *Jamey James'*. He's come back fer us, jes' like she said in the letter. Maybe it's all in my head, but whar ev'r it is, he's thar and he's gonna kill me."

Mike's head began to spin, his eyes narrowed. *Come to the tree, Michael,* he heard echo in the back of his mind. He looked out the bay window at the wind blowing through the tree at the top of the hill, but this time he knew what it was. It was a female voice, girlish but flat, *Jane?* He felt drawn to it, compelled to go, but instead he looked down at Jamie, his head still down on the table, shivering with cold. Mike grabbed Jamie's shirt and put it down over his back.

"We'll getcha a doctor...this week, the best I can find." Jamie put his arms back in his shirt, wiping his eyes on his sleeve.

"I cain't afford no doctor, Michael."

"I'll pay. I'll work as hard as I have to and I'll pay," Mike said, his desperation coming through the rapidness of his words. "I already have two big jobs lined up for the spring. We'll manage," Mike said, an inkling of where this might be going stirring in the back of his mind.

"I came here ta help ya, Michael, but all I've done is hurt ya, and the kids," Jamie said sadly, his heart breaking apart inside him, the little cracks in his lead box starting to seal themselves up again. "I cain't keep fallin' apart in front of Victoria and James...and you. It ain't right. Whutev'r I got comin' ta me, I deserve it, but they don't and you don't."

Mike went around to face him, forcing Jamie to look into his true blues.

"What did I tell you last night?" Mike growled. Jamie nodded, trying to avoid Mike's gaze. Mike's eyes followed him, not letting him go. "Look at me and say it! You fucking say it to me! Say it goddamn it!" Mike said on the verge of shouting.

"We're family now. All...we have...is each other," Jamie stammered, then finished. "And yer the biggest fuckin' monster in this goddamn house," and he smiled the same sad, scared smile Jane did that first time in the diner when his

head was split open. Mike thought his heart would stop on
the spot.

BOOK TWO

Willow's Weep

I would hold you in my arms, I would take the pain away
Thank you for all you've done
Forgive all your mistakes
There's nothing I wouldn't do to hear your voice again
Sometimes I want to call you
But I know you won't be there

Ohh, I'm sorry for blaming you for everything I just
couldn't do
And I've hurt myself by hurting you
Some days I feel broke inside but I won't admit,
Sometimes I just want to hide 'cause it" you I miss
And it's so hard to say goodbye when it comes to this, oooh

Would you tell me I was wrong? Would you help me
understand?
Are you looking down upon me? Are you proud of who I
am?

There's nothing I wouldn't do To have just one more chance
To look into your eyes and see you looking back

Ohh I'm sorry for blaming you for everything I just couldn't
do
And I've hurt myself, ohh
If I had just one more day
I would tell you how much that I've missed you since you've
been away
Ooh, it's dangerous, it's so out of line
To try and turn back time

I'm sorry for blaming you for everything I just couldn't do
And I've hurt myself by hurting you

Hurt, Christina Aguilara

You took my hand, you showed me how
You promised me you'd be around
Uh huh
That's right
I took your words and I believed in everything you said to
me
Yeah huh
That's right
If someone said three years from now you'd be long gone
I'd stand up and punch them out 'cause they're all wrong
I know better cause you said forever and ever
Who knew?
Remember when we were such fools and so convinced and
just too cool
Oh no
No no
I wish I could touch you again. I wish I could still call you
friend
I'd give anything
When someone said count your blessings now 'fore they're
long gone
I guess I just didn't know how. I was all wrong
They knew better. Still you said forever and ever
Who knew?
Yeah yeah
I'll keep you locked in my head until we meet again
Until we, until we meet again and I won't forget you my
friend
What happened?
If someone said three years from now you'd be long gone
I'd stand up and punch them out cause they're all wrong
And that last kiss I'll cherish until we meet again
And time makes it harder
I wish I could remember
But I keep your memory
You visit me in my sleep
My darling, who knew

Who Knew, Pink
(From the CD, *I'm Not Dead*)

Chapter Eleven

Radical Cognitive Bonding

T he next day they had an appointment with a Dr. William Walsh, a psychiatrist over in Scranton. Mike had gotten the appointment quickly because Mrs. Willis pulled a few strings with some people she knew and had set the appointment up for them. It was over an hour's drive so they had to leave right after Jamie put Victoria on the bus and they dropped James off with Patty Gundersen.

Jamie scrubbed up nice, wearing one of Mike's smallest jackets to avoid having to wear his own big leather one. He didn't want to give the doctor the wrong impression, but then thought that after he told the doctor about his life, what other impression could there be? They didn't talk for the whole hour of the ride. Mike tried everything he knew, but Jamie kept it to one word answers, trying to concentrate on what he would and wouldn't tell the doctor.

When they pulled up in the parking lot, Mike looked at Jamie. "You're gonna have to tell him the truth if he's gonna help you," Mike said, trying to get Jamie to look at him. Jamie refused to look back, keeping his head down, his hands folded in his lap, trembling.

"I cain't, Michael."

"I'll be there with you the whole time. Every minute if you want, but you have to be honest with him about…what happened…when you were kids," Mike said, smoothing his voice out. Jamie nodded, then looked up at Mike.

"Ev'r'thang but the murder, Michael," Jamie said, the pitch of his voice rising in panic. "I cain't do that. Thar's no statute of limitations on murder. I cain't go ta jail agin. It would kill me. I know I could defend myself, but ev'n the trial would kill me, havin' ta tell 'em ev'r'thang."

Mike hadn't thought about that part, never would he let that happen, and he agreed, then had a thought about their *other* common secret.

"Okay, that'll be our secret and ours alone…and that the…accident wasn't…an accident. We take those to the grave with us, no matter what. I swear," Mike said and put out his hand. They shook on it. "But everything else, Jamie. Okay?"

Jamie nodded his agreement.

"Michael, I'm so scared," he said, a look in his eyes that made Big Mike's heart crumble.

"I…I…I'll be with you every minute. I promise. You believe me?"

Jamie nodded and they went in, feet dragging slowly.

■

The office was one of several in the larger building, pastel colored walls lined with quiet, calming, pastoral pitcures; flowers, landscapes. They walked down the hall to the door with a sign reading, "Dr. William J. Walsh, M. D., Psychiatry. Child Trauma Specialist."

They stopped outside the door. Jamie looked at Mike, into his true blues, his own shy, hazel eyes glassy with fear, a slight tremble running through his body, petrified. Mike put his hand on Jamie's shoulder. "I will be there with you every minute." Jamie nodded and Mike opened the door, preparing himself to become a shield in front of Jamie no matter what was to happen next.

The inner office was painted white. Mike looked around and noticed that the walls were lined with reproductions of old pictures of doctors through the decades treating children of all ages ranging from infant to teenager; caring, concerned looks on the doctors' faces as they thumped a knee with a mallet, looked down a throat with a wooden tongue depressor or wrapped a sprained ankle. Mike liked those pictures, very much. They were personal, not put there by a decorator to create a bland environment like was done in the hallway. *Thank you, Mrs. Willis,* he thought to himself as he walked up to the glass-enclosed receptionist area. A middle-aged woman with dark auburn hair, large green eyes with thick, long lashes and bow-like lips looked up at him. Her name tag read, *Carol Arbach, RN.*

"I'm Michael Golden," he said simply, Jamie's smaller body hiding behind his much larger one. The woman got up and came out from behind the glass enclosure with a clipboard in her hand. She saw Jamie and she knew, too.

"Please make yourselves comfortable, Mr. Golden, Mr. Arnette," she said with a light, lilting voice, pointing to a set of chairs to their right. She handed Mike the clipboard, following them as they took seats. Mike looked back up at her.

"I'd like to talk to the doctor alone first, if I may. Mr. Arnette is my brother-in-law and I'm his only living relative. I want to make certain things clear to the doctor before we begin," Mike said, smoothing his voice out completely, trying to sound like some of the more sophisticated characters he'd read about.

"I don't think that'll be a problem, Mr. Golden," she said with a voice that resonated with compassion. She looked at Jamie, who had by then drawn completely into himself. "Just fill out the forms. I'll tell the doctor that you're here and we can get started."

A few minutes later, the nurse came back out. Mike handed her the completed forms. "You can come in now, Mr. Golden," she said. Mike looked at her and cast a worried side glance at Jamie whose hands were trembling badly. Carol nodded that she understood.

She must have seen these things who knows, dozens maybe hundreds of times in her career. "I was just going to make myself a cup of tea and take a break," she said. "It gets so stuffy back in my booth. I'll stay out here and Mr. Arnette can keep me company."

She walked Mike to the doctor's office door and knocked, then opened the door. "Mr. Golden, doctor," she said, then shut the door behind her. A man in a white doctor's coat came from behind the desk toward Mike; in his early forties, average height, a little thin with light brown hair, straight Anglo-American features and the palest green eyes.

"Mr. Golden, I'm Doctor Walsh. Please sit down," the doctor said in a youthful voice, quiet and soothing, smooth as glass.

Mike sat down in front of the desk. Before he could speak, his eyes started to fill. There was a pause as the doctor looked at the papers on the clipboard, then spoke. "From this it appears that Mr. Arnette is almost thirty-nine. I normally don't treat adults so I take it we have an unusual situation here, Mr. Golden. Why don't you tell me why you're here."

Mike hesitated, wringing his hands in his lap, not knowing where to begin. He had to wipe his eye with the butt of his hand, looking down.

"My wife...was...killed in a car accident a little over a week ago, doctor. Jamie is her brother, her twin. He came to us, me and my children, after the funeral." Mike looked up, wanting to trust those pale green eyes, looking for the compassion he saw in the faces of the doctors in the pictures outside, needing to believe that this man had put them there for a reason. "I didn't even know she had a brother. She never told me," he said holding his hands out.

The doctor looked at him, pale green eyes intent, making small notes as Mike spoke.

"When he got here, to us..." Mike stopped and took a deep breath, "he had sort of a...melt down. He told me that when they were children both he and Jane, my wife, were..." and he held his fingers up to his lips. He couldn't even bring himself to say the word. "...their father," and Mike just broke down and cried, his big shoulders rising and falling like great ships on a stormy sea.

The doctor stayed silent and waited, then said quietly, patiently, "It's okay. I know what you mean." The major storm passed, the sea calmed and Mike wiped his eyes on his sleeve.

"He came to help me, help me get through it and help with the kids," Mike's voice got gentle at the thought of how good Jamie was with Victoria and James. "He loves my kids very much, Victoria is five and James will be three in January, and they love him. But...but...things have been happening to him. He's been having anxiety attacks and nightmares of a monster trying to kill him.

"Then...then...the other night, I had my Reverend and his wife over for dinner and somehow Jamie got locked in the attic. We all heard him screaming. I broke through the door and found him...oh, I don't know...having some kind of a fit in the corner of the attic. His body was...jerking and jumping like...like he was being...beaten." Mike stopped to wipe his eyes again. "Then when I got him out and onto a bed, my Reverend's wife, Mrs. Willis, was tending to him and found...strap marks all over his back." Mike stopped then, looking directly into the doctor's eyes. "And my daughter said she heard a voice through the door, calling him names. He says their father did it...but doctor...their father is dead."

As hard as he might have tried not to show a reaction, Dr. Walsh's eyebrows went up and a look of real concern came over his otherwise placid face. Mike saw but didn't know what to make of it.

Mike jumped defensively. "I'm not putting him in a hospital," he barked quickly, wiping his eyes again and feeling the knucklescraper in him ready to defend its cave from attack. "And I don't want him drugged out of his mind. He needs help, doctor. More than I can give him by myself. He's been carrying such a weight on him, more than anyone should have to bear, and now with Jane gone, we're all he has, my kids and me, and he's all we have. I saw your pictures outside, those doctors. Tell me that's who you are, that you'll be that for him and not hurt him." Mike pleaded, looking deeply into Dr. Walsh's eyes, more tears streaming down his rugged face, then looking down again, wiped his eyes, afraid of what the doctor might have to say.

■

When Mike came out of Dr. Walsh's office, his eyes were dry and clear again. He walked over to Jamie who was sitting next to Carol, Dr. Walsh behind him. Jamie looked up, such fear in his eyes, searching Mike's for any sign of trouble, looking for his strength. Mike struggled but kept himself solid.

The doctor came around to Jamie with his hand out, then stopped. He had dealt with abused and neglected children for over fifteen years and was now about to take on the result in its adult form. He looked into Jamie's eyes and could see, at least partially, why Michael Golden felt the way he did. Being the healer he always sought to be, he could see in his mind's eye the young boy Jamie had once been now seeming so unreachable before him, and in that moment, Dr. William J. Walsh knew he was going to fight this monster and do his damnedest to win.

"I'm William Walsh, Jamie," he said in his smooth-as-glass voice. "Why don't you come in and we'll see what we can do here." Jamie hestitated, looking at Carol, then at Mike. They both nodded.

Sensing that Carol had done what she does best in her work with children, comforting the wounded and creating a bond of trust, the doctor turned to his nurse. "Carol, why don't you come in with us to the examination room. I think we'll need to do some tests."

■

In the examination room, Carol helped the doctor take Jamie's vitals and chart them, blood pressure, heart rate, a brief eye, ear and nose exam. Doctor Walsh asked Jamie to take off his shirt to listen to his heart. Jamie hesitated, then did as he was asked, drawing further into himself as if he wasn't really there, degraded by having to expose himself to strangers, like the first time he went to jail for possession. They'd searched him and the minute they put their hands on him, he disappeared, only coming back to himself when he woke up in the infirmary. Jamie's body went rigid the second the doctor touched him, his mind thinking only about Michael, Victoria and James, being safe at home with them again in their quiet little house, the smell of baking in the kitchen.

Standing behind, Carol had to clench her teeth to keep from gasping when she saw the marks on Jamie's back. She looked at the the doctor opposite her, caught in his own thoughts looking at the large round bruise, now turning yellow and green across the front of Jamie's chest, a wheel. William Walsh heard Michael Golden's voice in the back of his mind, *My wife...was...killed in a car accident a little over a week ago, doctor. Jamie is her brother, her twin,* and knew instantly that this was going to be no ordinary case.

When he looked back up at Carol, she nodded to him to come around. Clicking back into his most professional demeanor, he spoke to her, "Carol, let's take some blood and run it..." then silently mouthed to her, "for everything."

"Yes, doctor," she said, having long come to understand her boss's knowing looks and signals and going to a stainless table, prepping the intruments. Jamie didn't move or flinch when she drew his blood. He had long left himself, gone somewhere safe behind his eyes. He wasn't in a doctor's office. He was at home in his kitchen with the kids waiting for Michael to come home.

With the blood drawn, the doctor went slowly about a general physical exam. He felt all around Jamie's neck for swollen glands, then raised Jamie's arms one at a time, looking under them and around them, feeling for tumors, nodes, then in-between his fingers, finding only very old track marks on the insides of his arms.

He moved Jamie to standing and asked him to undo his belt buckle. Jamie did so silently, mechanically, robotically, thinking about the letter, *You were always the strong one, please be strong for me now,* and dropped his jeans to his knees. Carol turned and pulled the screen between them. Jamie's body went stiff as a board, deep shivers running through the length his body. *Help! Help!* his little boy voice cried out in his mind. Dr. Walsh knew that reaction all too well and leaned into Jamie.

"I promise I won't hurt you. I swear. I have to do this to make sure you're alright down there," he whispered quietly, a gentleness in his voice he usually reserved for the little ones. Jamie felt the cold touch of a gloved hand on him; his balls, pulling his penis from side to side and pressing around his groin, again feeling for swollen nodes, glands, tumors. *Help! Help! Michael!* his little boy voice called out again, then he went blank. Gone. He wasn't even aware that the doctor had pulled his pants up for him and redid his belt.

When the doctor looked back up into Jamie's face, Jamie was stark white, bloodless, thin lines of tears streaming quietly down his face, his eyes vacant. "It's okay, now. We're all done," Dr. Walsh said quietly, putting a tissue in Jamie's hand, then his tee shirt and shirt. "Carol, can you run the samples next door and tell Andrea I need the results as soon as possible," then leaned into her out of Jamie's earshot, "Tell her to drop everything. I need them now!" Carol nodded her assent. She was on with him. From the first time she was alone with Jamie, she had been on with him and went to make sure the tests got done, stat!

■

"Please don't tell Michael 'bout this," Jamie asked Dr. Walsh, speaking to him for the first time when they were alone back in the consultation office and putting his hand up to the wheel mark on his chest. "Tell 'im anythang else ya want about me. He alriddy knows," he said sadly, shaking his head. "I give ya permission fer that, jes' not this. He doesn't know and I don't want 'im ta. It would jes' hurt 'im."

Dr. Walsh nodded his agreement, then asked, "Tell me about your life, Jamie."

Slowly, haltingly and as far as William Walsh was concerned, hauntingly, Jamie recounted his life, his and Jane's, the years of fear, abuse, the hopelessness of their lives, then skipped to the drugs, the loneliness, the emptiness, the rehabs, the bikes, the endlessly long roads of his life. He described what the doctor knew was his "failure to attach," when he told him about all of his failed relationships, his inability to allow himself to become emotionally attached to anyone and his need to always be on the run.

Jamie told him about his nightmares and the "monster." All of this he told without tears, devoid of any sign of emotion other than for stiff, rigid posture as he sat in the chair, avoiding eye contact, only a trembling in his hands when he talked about anything that had to do with the past. But once the past was done and he moved into the present, everything changed, like magic before the doctor's eyes. He was coming back to life. From where? The dead?"

As soon as he started to talk about Michael, his breathing increased and the paleness in his face vanished, replaced by living human color, wringing his hands as he talked about his shame and guilt in coming to Michael's house, telling him about Jane's life and his. But then when he started to talk about Michael personally, his breathing evened and his face smoothed out.

Michael was this and Michael was that, hardworking, honest, clean and strong, all the things he himself wanted to be but could never…because…and how afraid he was that Michael would think him unfit to be around Victoria and James and make him leave. "Michael is all good thangs," Jamie said and smiled shyly for the doctor for the first time.

"How do you know Michael is good, Jamie? You've only known him a short time," the doctor fished.

"I jes' do,"

"But how?" Dr. Walsh pressed.

Jamie looked up at him defiantly, directly into the doctor's pale green eyes.

"'Cause…she loved 'im enough ta make children fer 'im. Ta make 'im happy." Jamie said, then looked back down, avoiding the doctor's glance. It wasn't the answer the doctor expected. It caught him off guard and he shifted gears.

"Tell me about the children," the doctor asked. That was when the water came. Flooding tears as he told the doctor how much he loved them and that it would break his heart if he had to leave them. How there wasn't anything he wouldn't sacrifice to protect them and make sure they had good clean lives. That was why he was there in that office, why he had agreed to come, to prove to Michael that he was worthy of them all and wanted to get better for them. Otherwise, he would be just as happy to ride off into the woods and die there, where there would be no one to know or care.

Having gotten Jamie to come back to life through his feelings for the Goldens, Dr. Walsh thought he would give a try to go deeper, to the round bruise on his chest. "Tell me about Jane, Jamie."

"Ya alriddy know, doctor," Jamie said, wiping his eyes and looking back up.

"What do I know?"

Jamie instinctively put his hand back up to his chest, but said nothing.

"Okay, then, you got me. Yes, I do know. Is that how you know that 'Michael is all good things'?" He saw the look in Jamie's eyes change, defensive, protective, shutting down on him, so he switched gears again.

"Okay, we can leave that alone for now. So why don't you tell me about what happened in the attic?"

And Jamie told the truth as he knew it, the same truth he had told Michael the day before; his father had come back to 'git 'im'. Called him *Jamey James* and wanted to 'git 'im' agin'. He told the doctor how his father *beat* him when he tried to 'git' away. Called him a *blas-feemer* and a *sod-a-mite*, told 'im somethin' about bein' the devil in a pleasing shape. The doctor was just finishing up some notes when there was a knock on the door.

"I have the test results back, doctor," Carol's voice came through the closed door.

■

Dr. Walsh led Jamie back to the waiting room. Mike was waiting, pacing frantically, wiping the beads of sweat covering his brow from his shaved head with his handkerchief, worried sick. The minute they saw each other, Mike rushed to him, his arms open. Jamie fell into them, holding onto Mike for dear life, scared senseless and shivering. "I'm cold, Michael. I'm so cold," he cried as Mike engulfed him in his big arms.

Carol had to turn away to pull a tissue from her pocket.

Mike took Jamie over to a chair and put his coat around his shoulders, rubbing his hands up and down Jamie's arms to take the chill off. "It's okay now, we're all done."

"Mr. Golden, can I see you in my office now, please?"

Mike reluctantly let Jamie go, sitting him in the chair to wait.

"Carol," Dr. Walsh said to his nurse. She nodded, knowing what he wanted her to do…stay with Jamie until Mike came back out.

Behind the office door, Dr. Walsh retook his seat and held up his hand, signaling to Mike that he wanted to look at the folder in his other hand. Mike sat back down in front of him, holding his breath. The doctor took a deep breath and let it out slowly, a sigh of relief, then put down the folder, giving Mike his full attention, allowing his pale green eyes to telegraph the news he was about to deliver.

"I have good news, Mr. Golden, a lot of good news," and he smiled.

Mike choked and put his hand up to his mouth in relief.

"Jamie is definitely not *crazy* in any appreciable way. He does not need a hospital. He does not need to be medicated. He is, however severely damaged, but I don't need to tell you about that, do I?"

Mike just sighed and took a deep breath.

"These are his test results," and the doctor held up the folder. "He's pefectly healthy, slightly anemic but no disease, no evidence of any recent drug use with the exception of some small traces of a mild tranquilizer in the last forty-eight hours." Mike raised his hand to that.

"I did that. I slipped him two of mine the night of the…beating. He doesn't even know. I put them in his tea to make him sleep."

"That's alright," the doctor smiled. "But Michael…I can call you Michael, can't I?"

Mike nodded, "Yes, of course."

"We have a great deal to talk about." Mike nodded again, steeling himself for the upshot.

"I'm ready."

"Jamie has been living with an enormous, crushing amount of guilt and shame from *the activity,* so deeply rooted that men like you and I can never truly understand…violated, no longer a person but an object."

Mike nodded his head. He understood more than the doctor realized. He'd actually seen Jamie become that terrified child again, heard his voice change and admit to…murder. The doctor continued.

"So much so that it very often leads to self-hatred, the need to punish one's self for one's perceived guilt of...events. Do I believe that he consciously did this to himself as some sort of neurotic attention-getting device? Absolutely not.

"Do I think that there may be a part of his mind that he may not have control over that is determined to punish him? Very likely and he'll need a great deal of therapy to deal with that.

"But I think we can handle it. It's not too late. The best way I can explain this to you is by example. Try this. There are women who are infertile and desire a child so badly that they've been known to exhibit all the symptoms of pregnancy. Another extreme example is the multiple personality."

Mike broke in, "You mean like *Sybil.*" The doctor nodded appreciatively.

"Yes, Michael, exactly like *Sybil.* Then there are cases of what in some circles is called demonic possession."

Mike broke in again. *The Exorcist.*

"I see that you're very well read, Michael."

Not as dumb as I look is what you mean, Mike thought sarcastically to himself.

"Yes, something like that, but the good news for Jamie is that I haven't seen any signs of the severity of those types of illnesses in him. He doesn't claim someone else is inside him making him do things, but I wouldn't be surprised if there are times when he lives in a world of flashbacks as real to him as you and I sitting here right now. I also don't want to mislead you. The appearance of those marks is a very serious event. Jamie is in an extremely fragile state. Actually, I've never personally seen anything like it. I've read about them in case studies but," then Dr. Walsh put his hand to his temples and started to rub. "I don't know how to say this to you, Michael, so I'm just going to say it. It's about what may have triggered this. It's very likely that had he not come to be with you and your children, these events probably would not have occurred."

Mike's mouth dropped open, the color came up in his face and he felt his knuckes hit the ground. The doctor saw it in his face, the anger and the hurt.

"Hold on. Hold on. I'm not saying you caused this. But try and understand what I'm about to say. Jamie has never known what most people would call happiness in his life. Everything about him, his life and experiences, tells me that he's only just...suffered.

"Then he comes to you and your children and for the first time finds himself feeling secure, valued, loved and he doesn't know how to handle it. Deep inside, because of what's happened to him he feels he doesn't deserve it. Layer on top of that his feelings of guilt and grief over the loss of his sister, and not just any sister, his twin, which has its own attendant issues.

"It's just too much for him and it's triggered a reaction so intense that his subconscious is trying to destroy it. Given his history of cutting, which isn't all that unusual in and of itself, the fact that it manifested itself as a *beating* is very telling. A beating represents punishment along with the name-calling your daughter heard. Try this. There are documented histories of various religions where the practioners do beat themselves, inflict pain on themselves as a way of showing both submission and devotion to their god; self-flaggelation, extreme repentence for their sins. Try to think of it that way. Jamie is punishing himself because you and your children, living under the protection, safety and security your house provides is making him...happy, and his 'monster' is trying to take it away because he doesn't deserve it."

Mike took a tissue out of his pocket and wiped his forehead, swallowed hard, then took another deep breath and another long sigh. "Okay. So, what do we do? I'm not giving him up!" Mike growled, the coarse hairs on the backs of his hands sprouting, unintenionally revealing himself again to the doctor what an Alpha male ape he was. Dr. Walsh held out his hand in the 'slow down' motion.

"I'm not saying that. But what you have to understand, Michael, is that Jamie has been victimized almost his enitre life in one way or another and the only way he's survived this long was to develop a hard outer shell, like a turtle, if you will, the tattoos, the bikers, living on the edge of the world where no one can get to him. He's had to create a tough guy image, a mask or façade, as a means of keeping predators away, a skin so thick, even if something good were to come along, he wouldn't be able to let it in. That's where you come in. He comes to you, the trauma of your wife's death forcing him to remove his mask, ripping his shell off, exposing himself to you, like the underside of that turtle, susceptible to attack by birds of prey. It's a very slippery edge for humans to place themselves, Michael. Particularly someone like Jamie because your wife, his twin, had already established a strong trust/love emotion with you and with she and Jamie being so…close, he has an almost built-in pre-disposition to you and your children.

"He thinks the world of you, Michael. He looks up to you as his model of strength and virtue, something he's rarely, if ever, had in his life before; your wife, the old Indian man, now you and your children. When I asked him about you he said, 'Michael is all good things'." Mike's heart leapt excitedly in his chest at those words as the doctor went on, "and from what I've seen here of you today, he wasn't wrong and neither was your wife. Anyone else faced with your situation would have slammed the door in Jamie's face, rejected him outright."

"But that creates its own set of internal conflicts for him. He's worried that he won't live up to your standards because of what's happened to him and you'll eventually reject him and send him away. Therein lies the rub. He wants to be happy but can't let himself."

Mike stopped him there. "Doctor, I've told him more than once and in no uncertain terms that I'd never do that, and I meant it. I promised him. My kids love him, ya gotta see them together to understand," Mike said, holding his hands out abjectly, bewildered as to what more he can do to make Jamie understand that.

"I know you have, Michael, but you have to understand, people like Jamie have no frame of reference for trust. He'll need as much positive reinforcement as you can give him."

Mike nodded, wiping his eyes again. "I can do that. I can."

"I know you can, but that leads me to another point I'd like to discuss with you. I'd like to talk about you for a while, Michael. You come in here looking like a big, tough man mountain but you're as human as the rest of us. Even the hardest granite rock can crack if you hit it in the right place with the right chisel, and I'm as concerned about you as I am about him.

"You've had one shock after another in rapid succession. You haven't even had the chance to deal with your own grief over your wife's death much less shoulder the...knowledge, and all that's happened since. What about you, Michael? What are you feeling?"

Mike's true blues went wide like a child who's been punched in the stomach and filled to overflowing again.

"Did the chisel find that place, Michael?"

Mike stuttered and stammered. *Trust the doctors in the pictures, Mike.* He nodded, then finally said it.

"Yes," he sobbed, pointing to his heart.

"Do you have a picture of your wife, Michael?" Mike nodded and reached for his wallet, flipping it open and handing it across the desk top.

Well practiced at keeping a stoic doctor's poker face and having some advance notice as to what he could expect, Dr. William Walsh looked at the picture. The image of the wheel bruise flashed through his mind and Jamie's voice replayed in his head, *Ya alriddy know, Doctor.* He looked back up at Mike, his pale green eyes conveying what his human heart wanted to say, *You poor man. What you must be going through.*

But his doctor's training held him back, and instead he gently said, "How are we going to heal you, Michael?"

Mike looked down at his hands, still cracked with dried blisters, then looked up into the doctor's pale green eyes, *Trust the doctors in the pictures, Mike.*

"He heals me, Doctor," Mike said nervously. That got the doctor where he lived. Stunned speechless by the raw emotional honesty behind Mike's answer, Dr. Walsh shifted nervously in his chair, feeling the need to remind himself of the first rule of practicing medicine about not allowing one's self to become emotionally involved with one's patients, acknowledging to himself that this one would test his mettle like none before. He handed Mike's wallet back over the desk to him. Mike waited for a response, then when none came, he asked, "Is that wrong?" and lowered his eyes to look at his wringing hands. William Walsh's voice came softly back across the desk.

"The healing of someone in pain is never wrong, Michael."

■

Mike turned the key in the ignition and the truck engine rolled over to a low rumble. They sat in the cab waiting silently for it to warm up before they drove off. Twenty minutes later they were heading down Route 537 toward Sayreville. Mike saw a big blue sign on the left, Workman's Outfitters, and sharply cut the wheel, pulling into the front lot, not being able to stand the silence anymore. He'd decided almost from that first night that, no matter what else was to happen, he would not, could not make the same mistakes he'd made with Jane. He would make it up to her through Jamie; how he'd failed her, how he loved her and was grateful to her for loving him.

The lid was already blown off his life. *Where else was there to go?* He looked at Jamie, and could hear his voice again. *I'm cold, Michael. I'm so cold.* He found himself thinking how he'd wished he could have had the same chance again with Jane, remembering how much she suffered carrying Victoria, how afraid she was but brave for him. He had no idea how brave then, but as he sat in that truck, he did. He could understand how much she'd sacrificed of herself for him to have his children.

"I want you to know how very brave I think you were today," Mike said, a low growl in his voice. Jamie turned to him, his hazel eyes like a frightened forest creature, searching Mike's like he didn't understand, but said nothing.

"And how very proud of you I am, very proud. I never want you to be cold again. Let's go in and get you a real winter coat, my treat. You can have anything you want." Jamie looked away, back out of his passenger window.

"Anythang?" Jamie asked, still staring away out of his window.

"Yes, anything," Mike replied. Jamie took a deep breath before he spoke.

"Kin I have this one, Michael?" he asked quietly, wrapping his arms around himself, one flap of Mike's old coat over the other.

Mike took a deep breath. He should've known. He really hadn't even needed to ask. It was the smallest of his coats and the one Jane would put on whenever she had to run to the mailbox or go out in the yard, even when hers was on the very next hook. She liked wearing his coat, and his old flannel shirts around the house. He always thought it was kind of cute and funny, the way the bottom of even his smallest coat would come almost down to her knees, the sleeves so long they more than covered her hands.

"You can have anything you want and I've just declared today another *Jamie's day*," Mike said and threw the truck into gear thinking, *Anything for you, both of you, either of you. It doesn't matter to me anymore*, and finding himself not quite sure who he was talking to.

"I jes' want ta go home," Jamie said, wrapping Mike's coat tighter around him like a security blanket.

Mike's heartbeat ripped through his chest. It was the first time Jamie had called his house *home* and he knew if he had to say one more word the waterworks would start again, so he didn't, and down the highway they went toward *home*.

■

Back at the house, Mike took control again, volunteering to go pick up James from the Gundersens and meet Victoria at the bus while Jamie showered and had a chance to get himself comfortable before the kids got home. He had no sooner put his coat back on and was halfway to the door when he heard the clunking sound of the pipes telling him the downstairs shower was running.

It stopped him in his tracks and he turned, went up the stairs to his room and pulled open his shirt drawers; a green and gray plaid flannel, *too small*, and he threw it in the bed; then another, dark green corduroy, *too small*, on the bed; a worn out red, black and white plaid, *too small*, on the bed; a faded red and black buffalo plaid, *too small*, on the bed with the others; and then he came to one of his old favorites, an odd pink, gray and black check, worn almost threadbare and long ago, *too small*.

He picked them all up off the bed and headed downstairs. The shower was still running in the bathroom across the hall so he went in the opposite direction, dropping the shirts on Jamie's bed in a pile, then headed back out the door.

After he picked up James from next door, he parked at the end of his drive to wait for Victoria's bus. He watched as the bus pulled up a few minutes later and could see the panic in her eyes when she stepped off and saw it wasn't Jamie. Mike got out and met her, picking her up in one swift movement into his big arms. He spoke before she asked. "Jamie is fine, sweetheart. He's taking a shower. He's had a long day so were gonna make tonight a Jamie's night. How would that be?" Victoria pulled back, her eyes relieved, then changed, concerned.

"Is he very sick, Daddy?" she asked, becoming such a big, grown up girl seemingly right before his eyes.

"You love our Jamie, don'tcha baby?" he asked, weighing his true blues against hers.

"Yes, Daddy and James does, too. I can tell. Can you?"

"Yep, I sure can, sweetheart and the doctor said that was the best medicine Jamie could have, and that if we all love him very much, and are patient with him, he'll get better, and…stay with us. But I don't want you to worry, and you know why?" Mike said, wanting desperately to believe his own words. "Because I happen to know for a fact that Jamie loves you and James very much, too. So do your old Dad a big favor when you go in. Give Jamie a good dose of medicine; kiss him and hug him really tight and tell him you love him. He's had a long day. Will you do that for your old man?" Victoria nodded and smiled at him.

"That's easy," she said shrugging.

Mike laughed and hugged her tight, kissing her on her little pink cheek, thinking, *the day your mother gave me you, little girl, was the day I became a man.*

"Yes, baby doll, for you I'm sure it is."

Mike opened the front door with James in one arm and Victoria's book bag in the other. She went in first. When he closed the door behind them, he heard Garth Brooks and Jamie doing a duet in the kitchen, "*Well, I've got friends in low places where the whiskey drowns and the beer chases my blues away, I'll be okay.*" Victoria looked up at Mike and asked, "Now?"

Mike nodded, shooing her with his hand. "Yeah, now," and she ran toward the kitchen.

"Jamie! Jamie! We're home!" Victoria called out as she ran toward the kitchen. Jamie came to the doorway just in time to bend down and catch her as she flung herself at him, wrapping her arms around his neck and kissing him with a loud *Smack* on the cheek as he scooped her up in his arms. "We love you Jamie," she said quietly in his ear. Jamie looked up to Mike, still standing by the front door with James in his arms, not wanting to be left out and yapping loudly, "Jeeme! Jemme!"

The look in Jamie's eyes was one Mike hadn't seen since he'd arrived, pure Arnette, not muddled with fear, shame or guilt, but still one he'd seen before. Almost four years before when they were working on an old house in Ohio.

He had just walked in from work and Jane was waiting for him. Her eyes were so different, clear and confident, shining with accomplishment. "*I did it!*" she'd said proudly, standing before him, looking like she was ready to explode. It was also different because she always kissed him first thing when he walked through the door, but on that day she had her hands behind her back.

"*Did what?*" he smiled, loving what he was seeing in her face because whatever it was he knew it was good.

"*The doctor says he's a boy!*" she squealed, practically jumping up and down; taking her hand from behind her back and holding a small picture of a black-and-white swirl in front of his face. Struck dumb, he just picked her up and twirled her around the room. "*I know how much you wanted a boy this time, Michael and I did it. I really did it! Are you happy?*"

"*I am the happiest man in the world,*" he'd said to her then felt big and stupid for twirling her around like that in her delicate condition and put her back down. Her eyes changed again, still happy, but mixed with something else. She came closer to him, put her arms around his waist and her head on his chest. He pulled her gently close to him and kissed her on the forehead. "*Everything else is okay isn't it?*" he asked, knowing her well enough to know she wasn't finished. She nodded against his chest. "*So what is it?*" She hesitated for a moment.

"*I'd like to call him James. James Michael Golden.*"

"*Is that all? Oh mother-of-my-soon-to-be-born son, you can call him Rumplestilskin if you want. Whatever makes you happy,*" he said, just grateful that everything was alright. He was so happy it never even occurred to him to ask her why she picked it. Then he was back standing by the front door to Fairfax Grange, looking at Jamie still holding Victoria in the doorway, giving him a small wave and…wearing Mike's ragged old pink, black and white flannel shirt.

Mike waved back, a deep sigh involuntarily forcing itself out of his chest, then he headed for the stairs. "Come on my little Rumplestilskin," he said to James as he mounted the stairs. "Let's get you ready for bed early and save Jamie some work tonight." It took all of three steps before Mike felt James' little hand wiping the wetness from his face, finding it hard to pull himself back from that day when he'd been *the happiest man in the world,* clinging to that look in their eyes. She was happy. He was happy. Something he'd done had made them happy.

Chapter Twelve

Night Falls on a House Divided:
Part 1 (The Wind)

I t had been a long day for Mike, too, and he couldn't wait to get into his own pajamas a little early. His toe had started throbbing as soon as they left the doctor's office from spending all day in his boot, so he decided to let it breathe for awhile. As he came out of the kids' room, he heard the whiskey-voiced twang again; the sound wafting up the stairwell combined with a glorious aroma he hadn't smelled in so long, months and months it seemed, his favorite, a curry.

When they were dating, he always tried to take Jane someplace nice, to try new things. It was fun, like they were teenagers but with a better budget. They both loved anything Italian, but when given the choice, which was often, she always chose Mexican or Tex-Mex, which made perfect sense now.

She wrinkled her nose at Thai when the fish came to the table with its head still on and only ate the rice and vegtables. He still smiled when he remembered how he'd covered the fish's head with his napkin so she could eat, but the real experiment was Indian. He'd ordered chicken Tika Masala. She seemed to like it as much as he did and seemed to love seeing how much he enjoyed it. Then one day when they had only been married a few months, he came home from work and smelled it coming from their kitchen.

She'd gone so far out of her way to learn to make it and it was so much trouble. "*I love you, Michael Golden,*" she said, then took his hand in one of the few times when *she* had led *him* upstairs. Victoria Jane Golden was born almost nine months later to the week. "*Did you plan that?*"

"*Curry means 'I love you',*" he always thought after that when he walked through the door at night, so tired from a long day of strenuous work, and smelled it coming from the kitchen. But then the sound of that crazy mad guitar and Garth Brooks singing about how *Papa Loved Mama* brought him back to the present, and Fairfax Grange. "*Mama's in the graveyard, Papa's in the pen. . .*"

He crept down the stairs quietly, James attached to his hip. They stopped just outside the kitchen doorway. Garth had just changed songs. Mike put his finger up to his lips so James would be quiet as they peeked around the doorway into the kitchen.

Jamie and Victoria were standing in the middle of the floor with their backs to them. Steam was coming out of the pot on the stove, Jamie was singing and moving his bare feet, holding Victoria by the hand as she copied his movements. He was teaching her how to do a two step.

In his mind, Mike could have stood there forever, just watching. From behind and in that minute, he could almost convince himself that nothing had changed, the hair was the same, length and all, and he was wearing Mike's shirt just like she did, sleeves rolled up above the elbow so they wouldn't get messed up while he cooked.

As he watched, he let himself drift back to that day again, when he first found out James was going to be...James. Garth's hillbilly twang came through the kitchen doorway, ringing in his ears; raising Jamie's own twang up a notch, "*Well she's my lady luck and I'm her wildcard man. Together we're buildin' up a real hot hand. We live out in the country and she's my*"

little queen of the South. We're two of a kind, workin' on a full house."
He was out with the guys he was working with at the time
celebrating the news. He'd been so proud. *"It's a boy!"* the
guys called out, each of them buying Mike a drink and lining
them up on the bar in front of him. *"It's a boy!"* He could
hear George Aaron's voice again, like it was yesterday,
bellowing drunkenly in his ear, slapping him on the back and
laughing, *"Like 'em barefoot and pregnant, don'tcha there, Big
Mike?"*

"Barefoot and…pregnant," Mike thought smiling and felt the
veins in the back of his hands pulse as he held James so close
to his chest. Quietly he watched, hypnotized as Jamie and
Victoria moved across the floor, seeming so natural, so
effortless, their feet gliding together like a well oiled machine,
Garth crooning in the background. *"She wakes me every mornin'
with a smile and a kiss. Her strong country loving is hard to resist.
She's my easy lovin' woman, I'm her hard workin' man, no doubt.
We're two of a kind workin' on a full house."*

The pulsing in his hands gave way to shooting up his
arms, rocketing into his chest. *"This time I found a keeper. I've
made up my mind. The perfect combination is her heart and mine. The
sky's the limit, no hill is too steep, we're playin' for fun but we're playing
for keeps. Lord, I need that little woman like the crops need the rain.
She's my honey comb and I'm her sugar cane…"* The blood shot up
into his neck like a sudden dam burst, throbbing in his
temples from the released force as he watched the two of
them move together, so perfect, racing into his head,
collecting behind his eyes, ready to explode from it. *"I'm hers
and she's mine, and that's what it's all about. We're two of a kind,
workin' on a full house."*

For a second Mike thought he'd lost his mind, splintering
off without even knowing it, only pulling himself back when
he heard Dr. Walsh's voice come from somehwere out of the
background of his consciousness. *"How are we going to heal you,
Michael?"* And his own response. *"He heals me…Is that wrong?"*
James coughed and they turned around. The game was up.

"Daddy!" Victoria called out when she saw them. Jamie
came over to him, reaching out to take James from his arms.
"Jamie is teaching me how to do cowboy dancing," she said
excitedly, looking into Mike's eyes with a special look asking,
"*Did I do alright, Daddy?*" that let him know she remembered
what he'd said to her when she got off the bus. He picked her
up and hugged her tight, thinking, *You are so smart, my little
angel. If it weren't for your hair and eyes, I'd swear they switched you at
the hospital.*

Mike put her back down and went to the refrigerator and
grabbed two beers, flipped the lids and set one down next to
the pot Jamie was stirring and whispered, "You didn't have to
work so hard tonight."

"It's alright. I want ta and I got my little helper o'er thar,"
he said smiling and pointing his head over to where Victoria
was looking out of the bay window. "So why don't ya jes'
have a set down o'er thar an' re-lax."

Mike sat down at the table with his beer while Jamie
turned the volume on the CD player down. By then James
had joined Victoria in the window seat. Jamie called out to
him, "James let's show yer Daddy how smart y'are," he said.
James turned around and saw Jamie pointing at the CD
player. "Who's 'at James? Who's 'at?" A a spark of light came
on in the little boy's eyes.

"Garfbruks!" he piped up excitedly. Jamie looked at Mike
proudly. "Huh? Huh?"

Mike just shook his head. "What am I gonna do with you
two? What next, ya gonna get him a roll up hat and
bandana?"

"I'd sure like ta if I could. Would that be alright,
Michael?" Jamie asked smiling quietly, remembering what
Mike had said in the truck on the way home, "*Anything*," but
still feeling a little awkward, hoping he hadn't overstepped
himself by exerting so much influence over another man's
child. But then he wasn't just any man, he was Mike the
Builder.

"Well that depends..." Mike said, averting his eyes so Jamie wouldn't see what he really felt. "...do I get one, too?"

The smile that came across Jamie's face almost blinded Mike. "Yeehaa," Jamie said and went back to stirring his pots.

"Well, don't get too excited over there, Tex. I gotta draw the line at calling him '*Tater*' or anything like that," Mike said, not being able to resist the joke. Jamie turned around with such a look in his eyes, lightness, brightness, full of it, bursting with it, and he laughed right out loud, full and natural, surprising not only Mike but himself with the feeling, like it was totally new to him, or long ago forgotten. It felt like...freedom.

The wind blew, rattling the glass in the big bay window as if it wanted Mike's attention, insisting on it, demanding it. A storm was coming. It was calling to him. He saw the splatter of rain on the glass, watching it get stronger, more splatter, tapping roughly against the glass, a dark cloud rolling over his thoughts.

Mike looked at James, sitting so innocently in the window box watching the rain with his sister. His heart started to pound, more rapidly as the rain increased, whipping him into the storm, enveloping his thoughts. *"He looks just like them,"* he thought to himself, then began to wander to a time in the future, a day when James would be eighteen or twenty with a cowboy hat, looking so much like his Arnettes, telling him that he wanted to go away to college or the military. He felt his heart start to chip away. *"I would love so much for you to be like them, but what am I ever gonna do when you grow up and go away, my only son. I'll be so lonely,"* and his eyes started to fill again, hovering just behind his lids. *"Do ya love your Daddy, James?"*

"They're going to leave you, Michael," the wind whispered back in his ear, reaching through the glass to answer his unspoken question. He watched as the rain got heavier, listening as the wind gained strength. *"They're all going to leave you. She never loved you because you're ugly,"* it whispered, beating at the panes of glass, like it was trying to get at him.

"She did love me. She does love me. My kids love me," Mike tried to convince himself, letting his head hang low.

"You're ugly, Michael. That's why they run away from you. This one'll leave you, too. He'll run away, too. That's why he can't look at you...because you're ugly. Come to the tree, Michael, it's where you belong...with me...with them. You are like us, Michael...ugly. No one will ever love us. We're all you have. Come be with us." Mike felt a hand on his shoulder and he looked up, his face twisted with anquish.

"Michael?" It was Jamie.

"She never loved me because I'm ugly."

Jamie stepped back, stunned by the strike of Mike's words. "Whut?"

"You'll leave me, too, because I'm ugly. And you can't look at me," Mike said and stood up suddenly, almost knocking his chair over. Jamie caught it as Mike rushed through the doorway and up the stairs.

Jamie followed him, running up the stairs behind him. "Michael!" Mike reached his bedroom door first and slammed the door hard behind him, shaking the walls around it. Jamie heard the lock click, his mind shooting off in every direction, banging on the door, "Michael!" Nothing. Silence. "Michael, please, let me in," Jamie called through the closed door.

On the other side of the door, Mike was standing by the window looking out over the yard, listening to the wind, watching as the force of it made the long branches of the tree move, calling to him, waving to him to come to it. It reminded him of the gun, hidden under the chair in his library. *"Come to the tree, Michael. It's where you belong...with us,"* the wind moaned.

On the other side of the door, Jamie paced back and forth wracking his brain, his mind racing. Then his own inner voice took over. *"You did it. Ya hurt Michael agin. Jane ran away and left 'im and yer always tryin' ta run away from 'im, too. Don't be so ignurant. That hurts 'im. Ya've bin so fuckin' caught up with yer own shit ya forgot about Michael. And after he stood by ya taday like a real hero. Remember how much he's lost, how lonely he's bin. Don't jes' fuckin' stand thar, boy! Do somethin'. Fix it now!"*

Jamie paced back and forth in front of the door, rubbing his head for what to do, then it came to him from the back of his mind, his memories, and he ran back downstairs, to his room. He flew to his dresser and ripped open the top drawer, digging underneath his tee shirts until he came to what he wanted; a stack of papers, letters, tied with string. He pulled the knot and rifled through them until he came to the one he wanted. He took it, then tore off a scrap from one of the other envelopes, picked up a pencil from the bureau top and began to write.

Outside Michael's door again, Jamie knocked. "Michael, it's me. Please let me in, Michael!" Nothing. Frantic with worry and feeling helpless at not even being able to use his secret weapon to make Mike feel...what? *"As special as ya know he is, as you've always known...since she met 'im."* Jamie took the envelope and shoved it under the door. "Michael, please, look at this," and he sat down with his back next to the door and waited.

On the other side of the door, Mike turned and saw the envelope come sliding in. The wind told him to leave it there, but he couldn't. Something drew him to it, something stronger than the wind. He walked over to the door and picked up the envelope, turning it over to read the front. The postmark date was six years earlier and addressed in Jane's handwriting to Mr. James Arnette at a P.O. Box in Plano, Texas. Mike took the enveope and went to his bed, sat down and opened it. There were two pages.

■

Jamie, the most amazing thing has happened. You won't believe it. Sometimes, I can't believe it, but it's true. I met a man, Scout. His name is Michael Golden and he's a builder. He buys run-down old houses and repairs them. He loves me, but not because

I do things with him, not those things. He loves me for me. He thinks I'm pretty and he wants to marry me, but I'm afraid of so many things. I'm afraid because...you know...but then I'm afraid not to. He's my chance to be happy and not be alone. I don't want to miss it. I've been so lonely all these years since you left and even more now that Mama's gone. I'm all by myself all the time now.

He's really a wonderful man. He's kind and gentle and generous, but you'd never know it to look at him because he's so big, about six three I think, and all rough looking and muscley from his work. I think he's beautiful. He's got these big, big blue eyes, true blue I call them, and when he smiles at me, he's like a big, bashful teenager (he's thirty-eight) and I just want to kiss him. I've never felt that before, and when he sits next to me and holds my hand, I feel so safe, safer than I've ever felt before in my life.

I think he's lonely too and he needs me. I don't want him to be lonely, Scout. Is that love? I think it is. My heart tells me I have to do this. I love him, very much, and I know if I'm ever going to have a chance to be happy, it's with my true blue Michael. But even more than that, he makes me feel like I can make him happy back. I'm sure that's what love means. Don't you think?

By the time you get this letter, we will most likely already be married. Your last letter worried me and it's been so long since I've heard from you. I think about you everyday. Please be happy for me and let me share it with you, Scout, for all you've done for me so I could have this chance. I love you. Your other half.

PS: Sometimes I lay in bed at night and my heart starts to pound and I feel afraid like we used to, but I know I shouldn't be. Is that you? I feel it is and I close my eyes and try to help you, send you my heart filled with the good kind of love that I've learned from Michael. Do you feel better when I do that? Please let me know you're okay.

■

You are not ugly Micheal. You are everthang she said you was. And my hero. Thank you fer standin bye me taday. Jamie

■

Outside the door, Jamie heard Victoria's voice call up the stairs. "Jamie, we're hungry."

Dayum! he thought, got up and rushed back downstairs to feed them. Victoria was waiting at the bottom of the stairs.

"Is Daddy coming down to eat?" she asked.

"He'll be down in a little while, darlin.' He jes' needs ta rest. He's been very tired. I'll feed 'im whin he's riddy. Let's jes' git you and James fed first," he said, picking her up and taking her back in the kitchen, but his mind didn't follow. His mind stayed outside Michael's door.

After the kids were fed, Jamie got them all comfortable in front of the television, then went back to the kitchen to clean up, his mind still waiting outside Michael's door. Distracted with worry, Jamie did the only thing he could do to help him think. He went to the stove to warm Michael's dinner, pacing back and forth between the stove and the living room to check on the kids, looking over his shoulder whenever his back was facing the mud room. "*Look after Michael,*" kept repeating in his head. "*Help me, Jane! Help me!*"

He'd just gotten the kids' dishes done and set plates out for Michael and himself when he heard the sound of Mike's heavy foot hit the stairs. He was coming down. Jamie searched himself for what else he could do to make Michael feel better. There was only one thing, so he got ready.

A few minutes later, Mike was standing in the kitchen doorway, his head tilted down, only his eyes looking up. In that second, everything about him softened. He was Michael Golden back at the diner again, pathetic, lonely, unloved in any way that really mattered, and hopelessly in love with a shy little blonde girl named Jane with quiet hazel eyes and an overbite smile. Jamie smiled, relieved to see him.

"You're doing this on purpose," Mike said, looking down at the ground and putting his hands in his pajama pockets, then went in and sat down at the table. "*Touch 'im.*" Jamie's mind told him, and he went over and gave Mike a good nudge with his hip. Jamie looked down and saw that the bandage on Mike's toe was all dirty with dried blood. He hadn't changed it. Jamie grabbed his little first aid kit and sat across from Mike, tapping his lap for Mike to put his foot up. "Com'on, now."

Mike resisted so Jamie reached down and took it himself, propping it up between his knees and took off the old bandage, then looked up at Mike, waiting until he looked back, his eyes red and puffy. Then Jamie whacked him as hard as he knew how with that smile and Mike caved.

"*I'm so lonely,*" Mike's eyes said and let his head hang, big crocodile tears dropping into his lap.

"It's alright, Michael. I'm here now," Jamie said, gently undoing the bandage and cleaning the split. "I'll take care of it."

The toe rebandaged, Jamie went to the stove and dished up a big plate of curried chicken and rice and set it down on the table. The smell of it made Mike's head swim. "*Curry means I love you!*" And he heard Jamie's low whiskey voice come from behind his ear, "You are the best thang that ev'r happnened ta us, Michael Golden, and don't ya ev'r fergit that. Do ya hear me?" Mike nodded, his shaved head still hanging down. Jamie went back to the stove just as Mike took a huge forkful and put it in his mouth.

"Oh fuuuccckkk that's good!"

Jamie turned around sharply. "Michael! Language. The children," he smiled and pointed to the living room with his right hand, his left finger to his lips. "Ssshhhh!"

"Sorry," Mike shrugged, blushing, and Jamie saw what Jane had seen; a big, bashful teenager, and he was…beautiful.

■

Mike seemed to come slowly back to himself while he ate. Just watching him shovel large bites into his mouth was enough to let Jamie know that he'd done good. He'd started the curry on his own when he saw the powder in the cabinet. It was funny because other than for the basics and his Tex-Mex, he never counted himself as much of a cook. But then halfway through, he found himself drawn back to the recipe box. He thumbed through it, stopping when he came to the card marked *Curry* and pulled it out. *M. Indigestion. Peppermints*, then stopped. *Dayum!* He went seaching through the cupboard and cabinets, finally finding what he wanted in a red and white striped tin in back of her baking supplies and slipped some in his pocket. *Whew!*

That night they all settled in for a quiet evening at home with the first *Pirates of the Carribean*. The cat was glowing. Mike was on one end of the couch with Jamie on the other; their feet up on the coffee table, a strong Captain tea in their hands. Victoria and James were nestled between them when Jamie saw Mike start shifting his position, not seeming able to get comfortable. Jamie reached into his pocket and handed over the peppermints.

"Here ya go, Daddy."

Chapter Thirteen

Night Falls on a House Divided:
Part 2 (The Whip)

A s the closing credits rolled on *Pirates of the Carribean*, Jamie was the only one still awake. Watching Michael sleep gave him a strange sense of peace, comfort and...safety; big, strong Michael, true blue Michael, so close. *My hero. Stands by us no matter whut. No matter how much it hurts 'im, he don't run. They sure 'nough broke the mold whin they made ya, Michael Golden."*

He picked James up first, took him upstairs and sniffed him, 'sweet baby clean' and put him in his bed, a good-night kiss on his little blonde forehead, then back downstairs for Victoria. "Good night, angel," he said as he covered her with the blanket, a second kiss before going downstairs. *"Is this whut 'home' means, Jane? I like it. I...love it."*

Freed up on the couch, Mike had stretched out by the time Jamie got downstairs again, one foot sticking out from under the afghan. "Ya jes' cain't keep 'at big ol' foot a yers covered up, kin ya, Michael?" Jamie whispered quietly, shaking his head and smiling to himself as he covered it up again before heading to the wood room. *Time's a wastin',* he thought as he looked at the stencil of the tree on the plank. It

was a beauty. The day had given him so much to think about
and work out for himself, everything actually.

Jamie went to his tool bag and dumped his hand tools out
on the plank. *Somethin's missin'.* He tip toed back out to the
kitchen and came back with his CD player, closing the sliding
door behind him. He set the player on repeat and mumbled
to himself low and slow under his breath, "Ladies and
Gentlemen, Mr. Garth Brooks," then hit the button.

He stood before the plank, rubbing his hands over the
wood. He picked up his wood chisel and made his first mark
as Garth sang, *"Blame it all on my roots, I showed up in boots and
ruined your black tie affair…"*

The old feeling came back to him and he thought about
what Ol' Pa used to say about giving himself over to it, let the
spirits of the ancestors guide his hands. He'd been afraid that
with all that had gone on, he might have lost his touch, but
the minute the first slivers of wood gave way to the power of
his hands, he knew he still had it. The tool seemed to glide
through the oak as he worked the outline, using his chisel and
mallet on the areas he wanted to be shadowed and deeper.

Soon his mind started to wander, away from his troubles,
and he closed his eyes, his hands seeming to find their mark
without his seeing them. *"I've got friends in low places where the
whiskey drowns and the beer chases my blues away, I'll be okay."* His
head started to sway, lost in the blackness before his eyes.

Strange sounds came out of the darkness, like twigs
snapping, and he had the feeling of walking. He *was* walking.
He opened his eyes. He was in a forest, looking down at
muddy boots. It was cold and he had something on his back.
He reached back and felt it. It was a bundle, like a knapsack.
His feet started moving faster. He had to hurry. *I'm coming,* he
thought to himself as he worked his way down the muddy
path through the forest, only slowing down when he saw the
house.

When he looked up, he was standing outside the house in
the moonlight as his hands worked the wood, like the kind of
lover he'd never been, staring up at the candlelight coming

from one room upstairs and another one downstairs. *"I'm here,"* he heard someone say as he focussed on the light upstairs.

He felt himself bend over and could see a hand reach out for some pebbles. But it wasn't his hand, still hard worked but smaller. It picked up the pebbles and he felt himself tossing them lightly at the upstairs window. *"I'm here."*

His head swam as he swayed back and forth before the plank, his hands moving furiously over the surface, feeling each curve and crevice with his finger tips to know where to go, what to do and how hard to push. Chips started to fly in the air, sweat dripping down the sides of his face. Then that awful sound, the whirring followed by that sickening *Thwack*. A scream caught in his throat as he fell forward, landing hard on his chest, the wind knocked out of him. More strikes, again and again and again, ripping pain, shredding his back. *Thwak! Thwack! Thwack!* A weight on the back of his neck, a boot, holding him down, crushing his neck. *"Well, I'm not big on social graces, think I'll head on down to the Oasis, where I've got friends, in low places."*

He tried to scream but someone had him by the hair, pulling his head back, shoving something in his mouth. A sharp pain at the back of his head and spinning, spinning down a tunnel into darkness, his last thought making his lips move around the gag in his mouth. *"I love you."*

"Faster! Faster!" Jamie's hands urged him, limbs, leaves, roots, reaching. *"I can't find you. Don't leave me. I love you."*

When he opened his eyes again he was on his back, a dull wrenching tug, then shooting pain like needles and tension around his head. His hands were tied, and his feet. But he was moving across the floor. A sharp jerk and more ripping pain in his head. He was being dragged, pulled by his hair along the ground toward the house. *"I've got friends in low places where the whiskey drowns and the beer chases my blues away..."*

He could see the stars and the moon disappear, thumping pain in his back from being dragged over steps, then another sharp pain to his head, and the smell of leather; kicked in the head. His eyes went gray, slowly dimming to black. "*I'm sorry. Forgive me.*"

When he opened his eyes again he was in the house. He could see the ceiling moving, but his eyes stung, "*Blood in my eyes.*" He tried to wriggle himself free, struggling against the ropes that bound him, but they were too tight; another kick to the head, more shooting pain and stars swirling before his eyes, but he held on, feeling himself being dragged further into the house.

Jamie's hands moved rhythmically as Garth's voice wailed; one tool for depth, another for width, another for ridging, swiftly, smoothly, the tree had taken on life under them. The muscles in his arms started to ache but he couldn't stop. His body jerked with each blow, his ribs shattering. Sharp pains like knives stabbed his back, another kick and he was being dragged downstairs into darkness, only the dim glow from a candle in the corner. "*Help! Help!*"

He opened his eyes again, but it was dark, only a small dim light from the candle moving farther and farther away. "*I can't breathe.*"

He dropped the tools as he felt his arms being pulled up over his head, pain ripping through his whole body. "*Help, Mother. I'm afraid. He's hurting me!*" Tightness around his wrists, a quick jerk and shooting pains under his arms, he felt himself being hoisted up in the air. "*Where am I?*" A hole, a sliver of light; scraping and clanking of metal against stone. "*I can't breathe.*" His chest ached, struggling for air. "*The light! The light is going away. I can't see. I can't breathe! Help! I love you. Where am I? I can't see!*"

The light dimmed more and more, then a face, pale, bloated, and eyes, shiny, black, cold eyes. Then the pain stopped. A scream, muffled, sadness. Alone. "*I'm dead.*"

Mike heard the muffled scream and leapt off the couch, running. *The wood room.* He threw open the slider door and saw Jamie standing before the plank, soaked to the skin, his arms held high in the air above his head, crossed at the wrists, wood chips eveywhere. Jamie's eyes were open but he wasn't moving. His head was tilted to one side like a broken doll.

Mike flew to Jamie and grabbed him. He didn't respond, just blank staring eyes, his lips moving slightly; his little boy voice mumbling, "I'm dead. I'm dead." Mike shook him.

"Jamie!"

No response, just mumbling, "I'm dead."

Mike panicked and struck him, a sharp slap. Jamie blinked, life coming back into his eyes, wide and childlike, the same as when he first came, on the floor that first night.

"I'm dead, Michael. I'm dead," he said, the whiskey back in his voice.

"No, no. You're not dead," Mike shouted and pulled him roughly into his arms, his own huge body mass trembling. "I won't let you go. Not ever again."

Feeling the life come from Mike's arms, Jamie took a deep heaving breath, finally sighing, "I'm not dead." His eyes rolled up in his head and he collapsed, only Mikes's quick reflexes and strong lumber-carrying arms kept Jamie from hitting the floor.

Out of his depth for what to do, out of any depth he could have ever imagined, Mike did what his knuckle-scraping nature demanded. He carried Jamie upstairs to his room, his cave, and laid him in his bed, wringing his hands and pacing at the foot of the bed, watching helplessly as Jamie's body twitched, his muscles involuntarily contracting and relaxing.

From the back of his mind Reverend Willis's voice came to him, *"God is in the house today."* Mike went to his chair and closed his eyes, his head slumped deeply into his hands. *"God? Are you there? Can you hear me? It's Michael. Please don't hurt him anymore. Hasn't he had enough? Haven't they both had enough? I'll do whatever you want, just don't hurt 'em anymore, please. I'll do whatever it takes, just don't hurt 'em anymore,"* he sobbed into his hands. A few minutes later, sluggish and crestfallen, he got up, feet dragging, and went out of his room and into the next.

"It's alright sweetheart, Jamie needs us," he whispered as he gently picked Victoria up and carried her to his room, lying her quietly down next to Jamie. Back a few minutes later with James, Mike laid him next to Victoria then got in himself. *"God, it's Michael. What do I do now?"*

■

Mike woke the next morning to the smell of coffee brewing and bacon frying coming from downstairs. Alone in his bed, he looked at the clock. It was almost nine A.M. *"What day is it? Wednesday? Holy shit!"* He jumped out of bed, not knowing which direction to run in first, downstairs to see them or the shower to get to his appointment for the new job. They needed that job. The doctor was going to be expensive and would take a long time. But he had to see them first. He had to know that they were alright.

Working nervously at the stove, Jamie panicked when he heard Mike's heavy, rapid footfall on the stairs. Victoria was already gone and James was entertaining himself quietly in his chair with his cinnamon toast, *"Whut kin I ev'r say ta ya?"* Then answered himself. *"Say nothin'. He'd nev'r understand. Jes' run, Jamie, run away from it all, from ev'r'thang."*

When Jamie turned around, Mike was standing in the kitchen doorway, staring at him. He wanted to run away from that stare, the one that knew everything about him, could see into him making him feel so naked and exposed. Mike walked in and passed behind him. Jamie heard the cabinet door open and the clank of a coffee cup as Mike poured from the pot, then his presence next to him, close.

"Thank you for being so good to me last night," Mike said quietly, not quite able to work the morning growl out of his voice, *"Curry means I love you,"* still hovering around in the back of his mind. "How are ya?" Mike asked. Jamie looked up to him, he couldn't help it. He had to see what was in those true blues. When he did, he had to turn away and grab the dish towel from the counter to wipe his face.

"Michael, I'm so sorry," he said, his voice hitching, barely able to get the words out. Mike nudged him from behind.

"Don't, Jamie, please don't. Just tell me what I can do, anything. I'll do anything." Jamie could feel Mike's breath on the back of his neck, and his shoulders started to shake.

"Don't let 'em put me in a hospital, Michael," Jamie's voice hitched as he worked the bacon nervously in the sizzling pan to give his hands something to do other than shake.

"I will never let that happen. We'll face this together. All of us," Mike grumbled, doubtless conviction in his voice, then went and sat down at the table. A minute later, Jamie turned from the stove, a big plate in his hand, and set it down in front of Mike; panwiches. Mike looked up at Jamie, his eyes red and so afraid. *Medicine time*, Mike thought and looked over at James, cinnamon toast all over his face and one eye open. "Yo! Boy!" Mike barked quietly. James popped out of his snooze. Mike tilted his head, nodding towards Jamie. James put his hands out, "Up Jeeme."

Chapter Fourteen

Edge of the World

"**M**ama!" Ella Willis called out from the front steps as she walked down the path, her sister Dinah opening the door of the long black town car and helping the old woman out.

"Ella, my baby!" Bethea Walton called out in a high pitched voice as she gingerly got out of the car, leaning for support on Dinah's arm. Ella hugged her mother tightly, then kissed her sister on the cheek. Older by two years and more elegantly dressed, Dinah Patchford and Ella Willis were almost carbon copies of each other. But Dinah had married better, a lawyer, Dean Patchford, a man much lighter skinned than Josiah.

"How's she been?" Ella whispered to her sister.

"Ornery as ever," Dinah whispered back with a small chuckle, smiling and shaking her head.

"I heard that!" Bethea squawked. Both daughters laughed out loud.

"Nothin' wrong with your hearing is there, Mama?" Ella asked, taking her by the other arm and walking her back towards the front door.

"How's Josiah been, Ella?" Dinah asked from the other side of the old woman.

Bethea Walton frowned at the mention of his name. "Hrrrummmppff!"

"Oh he's just fine. Saving souls and working hard," Ella said loudly to make sure there was no question that her mother heard her.

At eighty-six years old, Bethea Walton had seen the hard times of the Great Depression and the death of her first husband from tuberculosis, leaving her a mother with three children to raise by herself. It made her as tough as old boots, working two jobs most of her life to support her children until she shocked her family by remarrying, a rather well-to-do Civil Rights activist she met at a march in Philly when she was in her late forties and her children were grown.

Notwithstanding her genteel manners and delicate health, Bethea Walton got more demanding in her old age and bounced back and forth between her children, Dinah, Ella and her only son, Anthony, to exercise the privilege. Now it was Ella's turn for six weeks, Ella's and Josiah's, and Josiah was, as always, less than thrilled. Bethea always made him the Judas Goat. Nothing was ever good enough, big enough or expensive enough for her daughter, and she remined him of it every chance she got.

When the three women got to the door, Josiah was there waiting for them. Dinah kissed Josiah on the cheek quickly then turned to Ella. "Love ya, baby," she said, kissing her sister on the cheek then made a hasty retreat, smiling and winking to Ella as she went. "Good luck," she laughed.

"Mama!" Josiah said, trying to sound cheerful at her arrival and kissing her on the cheek while inside feeling like he was about to be harnessed to a plow. Bethea just accepted the kiss coldly and grumbled.

"Hello, Josiah. Nice to see you again," she said without looking directly at him. Ella jerked her mother's arm lightly.

"We've been looking forward to your visit so much, Mama," Ella said through her teeth, letting the old woman know she was on to her and she wasn't having it. Bethea looked up and smiled at Josiah, not wanting to evoke Ella's ire so early on in her visit, and let him take her arm to lead her into their living room.

"I have tea made here, Mama, if you'd like some or would you rather go to your room for a rest after such a long drive," Josiah asked, trying to make the best of it.

"Yes, Mama, whatever would make you comfortable," Ella said, taking the old woman's coat and hat.

"A cup of tea would be nice," Bethea said to Ella, ignoring Josiah. Ella just looked at Josiah as he went about fixing her tea.

"So how was your trip, Mama?" Ella asked while they waited for their tea.

"Oh, my dear, it was long and bumpy, but Dinah's big, comfortable car made it bearable," she said as a slight dig. The Willises couldn't afford a big town car like the Patchfords. The race seemed to be on again, no matter what Ella did. She'd just have to grin and bear it for both her mother's sake and Josiah's, acting as a buffer between the two of them.

After tea, Bethea decided that she would like to go to her room and lie down for a bit after all. She wanted to be well rested for her first evening with her youngest daughter and her...husband.

Knowing that Bethea always liked an early dinner, Ella and Josiah worked feverishly downstairs to make the dining room as nice and cheerful as possible with fresh flowers, brightly colored table linens and their best china and flatware while Bethea rested. After the table was set, both Josiah and Ella took to the kitchen to prepare a meal Mama would like. Ella had gone way out of her way to stock up on all the things she knew her mother liked, the kind of good down home cooking she wouldn't have gotten at Dinah's, with her maids and her full time cook.

For her first night, Ella had planned a dinner of roast chicken with stuffing and gravy, roast potatoes, mashed turnips, fresh biscuits and a freshly baked sweet potato pie with vanilla ice cream for dessert. Her mother surely could find no flaw in her menu.

■

The phone rang at a little after ten A.M. It was Patty
Gundersen telling Jamie that she was taking her youngest out
for the day, and asking if he'd like it if she took James off his
hands for a few hours while Victoria was in school so he
could have a break to do some shopping. Of all people, she
knew how hard it could be to juggle kids and run a house,
especially for a newbie. Jamie accepted her offer gratefully.
He was so tired and achy from the night before, had so much
to think about and he really did need to get out and pick up
some things. He was running out of baking supplies and was
going to have to start planning dinners on his own. He was
running out of things for Mike's lunches, too, and there was a
visit he needed to pay.

Patty came and got James a little after noon, Jamie waving
and smiling from the porch as they drove off. After they were
gone, he went back into the house with a sigh of relief.
Whatever else was happening, he absolutely could not let
things at the house, Michael's house, get out of control. He
knew that Michael needed his domestic stability to function
and he was going to make sure that he had it. *Patty, you're a
godsend,* he thought as he made his list of all the things he
thought he needed.

He got dressed in his warmest flannels and leathers and
took his duffel bag to make his shopping strappable to the
back of his bike. It was only just after one when he left so he
figured he'd be back long before Victoria got home from
school, but there was one thing he hadn't counted on. That
Mike's meeting would be short and the work at the church
would be finished that day, all except for the altar top.

■

Mike was relieved twice that morning, first when he was one
of only three bidders on the old shool house job, then when
he got to the church to find that the men had completed

everything that was left but the clean up while he was out. He wasn't surprised because he knew everything would be fine in Alex's more than capable hands, but in the end, the responsibility was his so he had to make sure everything was as he would want it, especially because it was his Reverend's church.

He spent the rest of the morning mostly inspecting the work with Alex, then helping with the clean up. The inside clean up was done by one, so he thought he would leave early and let the men finish the outside over the rest of that day and the next. By then, he could admit it to himself, all he really wanted to do was to get home and look after Jamie.

On the way home, all Mike could think of was Jamie standing in front of the plank, the sound of his voice, *"I'm dead, Michael. I'm dead,"* and what it would feel like if anything ever happened to him. *"What can I do? What can I do?"* he beat himself up trying to think of something to try and make Jamie feel better, more valued, more at home, more…loved. He was just passing the road to Fennell when he thought of Jane.

He would have never let Jane go without anything she needed or wanted, which was never really very much. He remembered how thrilled she was whenever he came home with something for her, nonstick this or that, some kitchen gadget he'd come across that looked interesting, anything that might make her life more comfortable, cleaner, quieter and more secure within the four walls of his house. *Why should it be any different for Jamie?*

Jamie'd dropped everything in his life to be with them, left everything he couldn't carry to rush to them, just a backpack and duffel bag to his name when he showed up to take care of them with hardly a dollar to his name, and he was suffering so badly, to stay with them. *I can't let that stand,* Mike thought as he pulled into the parking lot at the Home Depot. *I'm Mike the Builder. I can take care of you, too,* he thought and smiled to himself proudly.

On his way in he grabbed a cart and headed to the hardware department. He found a dark-haired, olive-skinned kid with a baby face and eager eyes standing in the main aisle in his new orange apron with the name "Vito" at the top. "Okay, Vito," Mike said smiling brightly, "let's shop."

They hit the tool belt area first. That ratty, dirty old one of Jamie's would have to go, a new, clean, chamois-suede one would do. Then it was on to the tool box area, a big, new, lightweight Husky nylon carrier would do the trick, and into the cart it went. "Nineteen ninety-five. Can't beat that. Okay, Vito, now let's fill 'em," Mike said, feeling himself becoming more and more pleased with what he was doing, pointing to the things he wanted while Vito pulled the items from the shelf and put them in the cart; hammers, tape measures, more carpenter's pencils and sharpeners, a combo screwdriver set, a combo wrench set, new knee pads for the flooring and roofing parts of the jobs he had lined up; utility knives, blades. Mike's heart soared, filling itself as they filled the cart, hoping Jamie would be as happy as Jane had been when he walked through the door with his arms full, maybe smile at him like Jane used to, glad to see him.

He went to the service desk next to check out. While he was there, he had another idea. He asked the pretty service desk girl with a head full of very curly amber-colored hair, feline eyes, a pixie nose and the name "Jen" on her apron to call the home office and have Jamie put on his charge card as an additional authorized user so Jamie could get whatever he needed when he needed it.

■

The rumbling vibration of his old bike's engine between his legs felt strange, almost foreign after so much had happened. It wasn't the same, almost like an old girlfriend he hadn't seen in a while then ran into at a bar. It just wasn't there any more, filling him with a sense of sadness and a twinge of regret. But then while he did his shopping, a new-found feeling of domesticity replaced the regret giving him a sense of stability he'd never really felt before; a purpose to keep him going, things like *b-o-l-o g-n-a* and little pudding cups for Victoria's lunches and toddler diaper pants for James. He was going to have to stop pooping his pants soon. Then he went to Wal-Mart; some new white socks for Michael and a nice new pair of Converse All Stars to replace the ones with the toe cut out. The prize of the day was two roll up straw hats, one for James and one for Michael. That should make him smile, *yeehaa*, a nice new reading book for Victoria and…a bouquet of red roses from the flower shop next door.

Back on his bike and thinking of home, Jamie found himself at the tree, almost without conscious thought, the bark still freshly skinned from where the front of the VW had hit it; shards of windshield glass still around its roots. He parked his bike and got off, went over and touched the tree. "*Are ya here?*" Nothing, just the cold wind stinging his face, making the water falling from his eyes feel like it would freeze to his skin. "*You're not here.*"

He got a haunted feeling as he pulled up to the old wrought-iron gates, *Freedom*. He parked the bike just within, got off and walked in the cold wind across the dying grass; a bleak, cold horizon above the tree tops. His breath froze to his lips with each step he took, slowly finding his way to the back, to the fresh grave with the little tin marker, Jane Arnette Golden, 1969-2007.

He dropped to his knees, not feeling the chill of the dampness as it soaked into him, and gently placed the roses by the marker, crying out loud in pain and rubbing his chest as the cold wind blew around him and he relived her terror. He could hear the sound of smashing metal and shattering glass, a list of regrets racing through his mind without the use of words. "*I'm sorry fer, not bein' there whin ya needed me; fer not bein' able ta protect ya; fer runnin' away; fer stayin' away. I'm sorry fer not writin' more, callin' more, seein' ya more, huggin' and kissin' ya more, fer puttin' ya though so much worryin' 'bout me, makin' ya feel thangs that ya nev'r should've whin all ya ev'r sint me was love, life and hope. You were the strong one. I love you.*"

He looked up to the cold gray sky, the wind beating at his face, waiting. "*Are ya here? I cain't feel ya.*" Nothing but the sound of the wind as he cried into his hands for all he hadn't done to help make her life better. He had just run away and left her to suffer alone.

He got up, dejected, empty, his shoulders slumped under the weight of all his regrets, his feet dragging, so heavy he could hardly lift them, and went back to his bike. *Whut didja expect? It's too late. She's gone ferev'r and thar's nothin' ya kin do 'bout it.*

He barely had the energy or heart left to drive home, the bike practically crawling down the road into town. He had just crossed the village line, when he was startled out of his thoughts; a bird crying, calling out and he looked up to the sky. A crow or raven crossed the sky of his path, large and black, a much larger wingspan than usual, "*Jamie,*" it seemed to call and then it was gone, into the tall trees.

He drove on into Main Street and saw a bunch of bikes in front of the Harley shop, ten or fifteen. They waved to him and he stopped. "Yo, man." a big, bearded *ZZ Top* looking guy called out to him as he shut down and got off.

Jamie went over and shook hands with them. Like the other bunch, they were on their way to the rally in North Carolina, except that this bunch had gathered from around the Dakotas. More guys and a few chicks came forward to meet him. "It's fuckin' cold here. Head South, man. Come with us. We're headin' out now," a smaller, red-headed guy with the same type of long hair and shaggy beard Jamie had had when he arrived at Michael's shouted from behind the bigger one.

From the far back, Jamie saw a tall figure with long, straight, black hair and his back to him; the only one who didn't come over to shake his hand or say hello. *A red man?* This time he didn't hear the voice in his head telling him to run, but gave them the same answer.

"Naw, guys. I got people here who need me. I cain't be runnin' off on 'em." He shook his head. "I jes' figger'd I'd stop and say howdy and pick myself up a nice big bottle of Cap'n Morgan ta keep me warm fer a while," and he headed across the street to the Sayreville Bottle and Tap.

He was just checking out when he heard the roar of their motors rev, creating a vibration so loud it rattled the plate glass windows of the store front as he saw them ride by. *No regrets?* he asked himself. He thought of the two straw hats in his bag and Victoria's *b-o-l-o-g-n-a*. He thought about what it would be like to never see his little man again, "*Up, Jeeme, up*," and that sweet baby smell or even his not so sweet shitty smell or Victoria, *Can I come and sit by you?* looking at him with her father's eyes, Michael's true blues, so sincere. *Naw*, and he walked back outside. The bikers were all gone, all except one, the one with the long, straight, black hair who hadn't come around to greet him.

Jamie walked back to his bike, head down against the wind as he passed the other biker leaning against his bike; legs crossed, his long black hair blowing in the wind, eyes covered with slick black sunglasses. "Where ya headed, Goldilocks?" the biker asked smiling, the whiteness of his teeth contrasting starkly against his tawny skin and black hair. The sound of his deep voice made the hair on the back of Jamie's neck stand up.

"I'm jes' goin' home, brother, not lookin' fer any trouble."

"You mean to your little fawn, your nestling and their daddy bear, the grizzly?" the biker asked with almost a snicker, "If it looks like a bear, growls like a bear and shits like a bear, it's a bear," the biker laughed imitating Jamie's voice. Jamie stopped in his tracks, the thick, steel walls of his badass shell slamming up around him. *Boom! Boom! Boom! Boom!* He turned, fighting stance.

"Do I know you, buddy?" Jamie asked, the gruff, gravelly whiskey growl coming up in his voice as he took a step toward him, ready to scrap it out if he had to, wouldn't be the first time, or even the second. The biker laughed again.

"No, but I know you, Soaring Eagle," the biker smiled at him.

Soaring Eagle, it took Jamie's breath away, like a hand had snatched it right out of his chest. The biker put up his hands in a "slow down" motion.

"Whoa, whoa, whoa, cowboy. I'm not here to hurt ya, my Comanche brother. I'm here to help, to make sure our little bird finds his way backta his nest...just in case. Keep ya from gettin' lost, if ya follow me. Come closer," he commanded, his deep voice reverberating in the air around Jamie's head. Jamie stepped forward, closer, then closer still until they were almost toe to toe.

The biker grabbed Jamie roughly by the collar of his jacket and pulled him in. "You asked for help, actually he did, your daddy bear. You both did and I'm here, so let's not fuck around with each other, tough guy," he whispered gruffly in Jamie's ear. "I'm here to give you a message, Soaring Eagle. You're only as good as those who love you, and as good as the ones you love. Always remember that.

"Second, you have a job to do. I don't know what it is and I don't really care. I'm just doin' the old man a favor. All I know is that you're close, real close, and it's gonna hurt, real bad, but that's nothin' new to you is it? But only you can decide if it's worth it to you," then he laughed.

"And third, don't listen to that crazy ass blonde bitch. We're not all alike. She doesn't know what the fuck she's doin'. Now fly away home to your brood and don't make me have to come back. It's cold and I don't like the cold. It makes me feel...cold. Now fly, Soaring Eagle, fly NOW!" He let Jamie go, pushing him back with a shove, looking him in the face, his black sunglasses reflecting Ol' Pa's face in each of the lenses, then he got on his bike, singing, "*I've got friends in low places where the whiskey drowns and the beer chases my blues away...*Garfbruks, huh? I like that, real cute," and snapped his fingers.

Jamie blinked and the biker was gone, only a raven taking flight, gliding high into the sky, the biker's gruff whispering voice lingering in his ear, *And it wasn't your fault.* Jamie jumped on his bike and he flew, his heart pounding wildly in his chest, *My fawn, my nestlin', and their daddy bear.*

■

On the way home Mike found himself driving faster, wanting to get there and see that smile. He was so eager that when he pulled up in the driveway, he rushed to park and grab the bags, not bothering to notice that the Harley wasn't there.

With his arms full of bags, he opened the door and called in loudly like he always did. "I'm hooommme!" Silence. No response. "Jamie?" he called out towards the kitchen. No answer. Then upstairs, "Jamie!" Nothing. His gut wrenched, a voice in the back of his mind telling him, *He's gone.*

Shrill panic grew inside him as he dropped the bags on the couch and started hurriedly walking around the house, calling out "Jamie!" Nothing. The bottom dropped out of his stomach, his life…again. He went to Jamie's bedroom. His leathers were gone, then back out to the front door. The bike was gone. He picked up the phone and called Patty Gundersen, struggling to keep some semblance of control in his voice.

"Yes, Mike, I have James. I volunteered to take him so Jamie could go out while Victoria was in school. Is that alright?"

"Yes, that's fine. I got home early and was just wondering. Thanks, Patty," and he hung up, not knowing how much longer he could keep his control going. *He's gone, Michael. He's left you. Just like she did. You made him unhappy and he's gone. They're both gone. You made them both unhappy. You did it.*

His eyes filled to overflowing as he roamed around the empty house, still calling out but knowing he wouldn't get an answer. *You scared him away, chased him away, failed him just like you failed her. Not special enough to keep them, not special at all. Big, ugly, stupid man. Empty house! You're an empty house, Michael Golden, four walls with nothing in it, nothing anyone would value or love. You were a fool to think they would.* He sat on the stairs, his head in his hands and cried, "Don't leave me!"

The silence in the house echoed though his head, *Unloved, Michael. They didn't love you. No one loves you. Empty, useless, unlovable, big, stupid, ugly. No one will ever love you.*

Then the voice changed. It wasn't his own anymore, *Come to the tree, Michael, you know what you have to do*, the girlish voice said, and he did. He knew what he had to do. He got up slowly and started up the stairs, his feet so heavy he could hardly lift them, scraping the floor with the soles of his boots. The voice was right. He stopped outside the door to his library and fumbled in his pocket for the key but it wasn't there or he couldn't find it.

He heard the lock click and the door swung open. He walked in and went to his chair, then bent down, reaching underneath and pulling out a box. He sat down in his chair and opened it. He took out the gun and held it for a minute, then the bullets, loading it slowly, tears streaming with such force he could hardly see through the river raging down his craggy, forty-five-year-old unloved, ugly face. *They never loved you, Michael. No one will ever love you, come to the tree*, the voice insisted. He finished loading the gun and stood up, his big, heavy feet dragging as he scuffed to the stairs.

■

When Jamie got back, he saw the truck in the driveway and his spirit soared, *Michael's home.* The house was quiet. He saw all of the Home Depot bags on the couch and called out for him. "Michael!" No response. He went to the kitchen to hang up his jacket and looked out the bay window. Mike was up on the hill, wrapped in his coat against the cold wind. Jamie looked at his watch, it was only three o'clock. Michael was home early.

The front door opened and he heard Victoria call out, "I'm home," just like her father. "My little fawn," he said to himself, thinking how very appropriate the name was and what a beautiful young lady she'd be when she started growing up. He'd have to be sure to keep a big ol' can of *whoop-ass* handy for when the boys started noticing.

He had no sooner turned to go meet her when he saw Patty Gundersen at the door about to knock. She saw him, too, and waved. He waved back. She came in carrying James, his head on her shoulder, sleepy without his nap. "I thought I'd wait and meet Victoria at the bus. She ran ahead to see you. I hope you don't mind."

"Naw, Patty, 'ppreciate it. I jes' got in myself and was jes' goin' down ta meet her," Jamie said, working not to sound as rushed as he was. He hadn't expected to meet the bikers or be held up by the...dream.

"How'd everything go?" she asked him smiling cheerfully as she handed James over.

"Good, I got it all done. Thanks Patty. Ya really did save me today. I was runnin' out of ev'r'thang'."

"No problem," she said back, smiling and heading out towards the door, then stopped. "Listen, Jamie. You can always call me if things get a little too much for you. I have years more experience at this than you do and I really don't mind at all. I miss her, too, you know. She was my friend. Very easy to love. Let me help, okay?" Patty said, her eyes getting misty. Jamie nodded, remembering how women, girls, always seemed to take to Jane because she was so shy, felt maybe a little protective because she was so non-threatening.

Once Patty was gone, Jamie took Victoria and James into the kitchen to give them a snack. "What'll it be, darlin'?" he asked Victoria as she took her seat at the table.

"Cheese and crackers and a....grape Ssips."

"Comin' right up," Jamie said, beginning to worry about Michael. He must have heard him pull up the driveway, the bike was loud enough. He looked out the window again. Michael was still on the hill, his back toward the house.

Seeing him like that gave Jamie an odd feeling, undefinable but troubling. He looked back to James in his chair. "And whut would ya like, my little man, *my nestlin?*" he asked, stroking his little blonde head, James's eyes drooping, only one eye really open. "Oh, alright," Jamie said, seeing James would rather nap than eat and took the boy out of his chair and headed toward the living room.

When he got to the doorway he saw the cat was on, glowing, vibrant, wavy rays of orange dancing on the wall behind it. "Look James, yer friend is waitin' fer ya," he said as he laid the boy down on the couch, putting his pillow in front of him so he wouldn't roll off, then went back to the kitchen to put his groceries away and be with his little...*fawn.* He looked out the window again. *Why doesn't he come in?*

He opened the bags as Victoria concentrated on making sure her crackers and cheese were all lined up in a nice, neat row. He put the cold stuff away first, then the dry goods. A creaking sound came from behind him. He knew it immediately; the mud room door. The hair stood up on his arms. *Please, not another one.* He heard the light rattle of metal as the latch lifted out of the eye hook and swung down. He took a deep breath and started to turn around, secured only by the fact that he knew *his* Michael, the *real* Michael, was up on the hill.

Turned all the way around, he saw the door was only opened a crack but still moving. He backed up as far as he could against the counter. Victoria was still arranging her crackers, this time in a circle, and eating them one at a time.

He looked back to the door. Fingers were curled around the edge, pushing it open from the inside, *Michael's fingers. That cain't be.* The air got so thick his breath seized in his chest. He wanted to scream. Victoria looked up, smiling, and saw how pale he was. She got out of her chair and went over to him, taking his big fingers in her little hand. "Jamie, are you sick?" He looked down and saw her worried little face looking up at him. He grabbed her up and held her close to his chest, not taking his eyes off the door.

The door opened wider, his breath stopped in his chest, terrified. Holding Victoria close to him, he closed his eyes. *Go away!*

"Jamie, does your head hurt?" she asked, whispering in his ear. He saw the door open yet wider, pushing fully open, Michael standing there, his live true blue eyes sad, hopeless, like they were the night before, *I'm so lonely.*

Jamie held Victoria's head close to his shoulder, facing behind them, then he saw the gun in Michael's hand. Jamie's heart rate jumped, beating wildly in his chest, torn between rushing Michael for the gun and protecting Victoria from seeing any of it. "I love you," Michael said, tears streaming down his face as he pulled the trigger. The shot rang out and his body jumped, jerking violently as he fell back into the mud room. Crashing sounds filled the room. Jamie screamed, "Michael!" and ran to the door, clutching Victoria to his chest.

When they got to the door, Jamie looked down, Michael's true blues, staring dead at the ceiling. Jamie closed his eyes and fell to his knees, holding Victoria's head tightly against his shoulder. *No, Michael, no. Not our Michael!* When he opened his eyes again, Jamie backed away on his knees, scrambling. The face he saw wasn't Michael. It was another man, a man he'd never seen; short brown hair, graying at the sides with a full reddish beard, in work overalls. The man lifted his head, dead brown eyes, sad and lonely like…Michael's, staring at Jamie. Blood spurted from his lips, *Hurry!* Jamie screamed and fell back, clinging to Victoria with all his might.

He felt a tug on his fingers, his big fingers in a little hand. He opened his eyes, looked down and saw Victoria's true blues, innocent, loving and so worried looked back. "Jamie, does your head hurt?"

His eyes darted back to the mud room door; closed, locked. He grabbed her up and held her close to his chest again, rushing over to the window. Michael was still on the hill; his head hanging down, his big figure almost a silhouette against the autumn sky, *Ya hafta git Michael off that hill.* The strange voice from the mud room echoed from the back of his mind, *Hurry!*

"Jes' a little," Jamie said, working to keep his emotions in check so as not to scare Victoria. He picked up a dishtowel to wipe his face. "I was out ridin' today and got too much wind in my face." He touched her worried little face and kissed her forehead. "But I need ya ta be a big girl fer me fer a while," he said, walking through the kitchen doorway toward the stairs. "I need ya ta come upstairs with me and do me a really big favor. I need ya ta stay in yer room while I go out back and have a talk with yer daddy. He's not feelin' too good today and I want ta go out thar and make 'im feel better. Kin ya do that fer yer Jamie?" he asked, sitting her down in her little desk chair, "Please, darlin'."

Victoria nodded, the worry in her face only partially relieved.

He had just closed the door to her room behind him when he heard a metallic rattle come from downstairs. He stopped and wiped his face on his shirt sleeve. He thought back to what the biker in the dream had said, "*You're only as good as those who love you, and as good as the ones you love. Always remember that…All I know is that you're close, so close, and it's gonna hurt, real bad, but that's nothin' new to you is it? And only you can decide if it's worth it to you.*" Then Jane's letter, "*He's got these big big blue eyes, true blue I call them, and when he smiles at me, he's like a big, bashful teenager (he's thirty-eight) and I just want to kiss him. I've never felt that before, and when he sits next to me and holds my hand, I feel so safe, safer than I've ever felt before in my life. I think he's lonely too and he needs me. I don't want him to be lonely, Scout. Is that love? I think it is.*"

In his mind's eye, Jamie was back in the doctor's office seeing the worry in Michael's face when he came out, waiting for him, just like he promised, arms open, safe, after all he'd done, all he'd been, *Michael don't run away*, and again in the mud room, his true blue eyes, cold and dead, open and gazing toward the ceiling. He heard the rattle come from downstairs again and that voice, the dead man's voice, *Hurry!* More rattling and he ran down the stairs, *James!*

At the bottom of the stairs, he saw the door to the basement was open and heard the sound of the old wooden steps creaking. *Oh my God! James!* and he flew through the basement door. The door closed behind him, the latch lifiting itself back into its eye hook. It was dark, only the dim light from the small basement windows making the stairs visible. "James!" he called out, "Are ya down thar?" Nothing, just more creaking at the bottom of the stairs. He started down, "James?" Halfway down he heard James giggle and went down further. "James, darlin'? Whar are ya?"

When he got to the bottom of the stairs he saw James over by the wall, in one of the arches, touching it. He pulled the light cord. James was standing in the arch. He looked back at Jamie, wide eyed, rubbing the wall, then lost his balance and landed on his rear. "Azze-an!" he said, pointing to the wall, "Azze-an, Jeeme!" he said again insistently.

"Whut is it, angel?" Jamie asked, feeling drawn to the arch where the boy was sitting and pointing.

"Azze-an! Azze-an!" James yelped, frustrated by not being understood. Jamie bent to pick him up. James struggled against him, very unusual, very unlike him, and started to cry, bouncing up and down in a temper. The closer Jamie got to the wall, he thought he could hear a light hum come from somewhere behind it, a lulling, soft, hypnotizing buzz, and something touched his face, like cobbwebs at first, then more solid like hands, seeming to try and make him turn his head.

Out of the corner of his eye, he saw the graffiti on the wall. It struck him like a lead pipe to the head. "Adrian Lives Here!" and it dawned on him, *Azze-an, Adrian.* He remembered what he thought he saw on the Etch-A-Sketch but decided he'd imagined.

F...i...n...d......A...d...r...i...a...n.

"Whut the...?" He felt himself drawn closer to the wall and put his head against the brick. The hum got louder. James started laughing and clapping, "Who is Adrian, James?"

"Azze-an! Kitty! Azze-an! Kitty!" James started bouncing up and down again, pointing up the stairs, then pointing to the arched wall. "Meow!"

Jamie put his head against the wall again, the hum got louder, then seemed to turn into words. James started nodding and clapping. *Please help me*, Jamie thought he heard lightly whispered from behind the brick, almost like air, like wind. His eyes got wide, unbelieving. He pressed his head closer. *Please, I'm here*, the whisper pleaded.

Jamie looked down at James who had gotten himself up by then and was standing next to him, holding onto his leg. Jamie's head jerked forward and he felt a blinding pain at the back of his head, throbbing, eyes dimming and a sticky wetness running down the back of his neck, blackness, then a small light only a few feet from his face, but the perspective was wrong. He wasn't outside the wall looking in. He was inside the wall looking out. It was dark, all but for that little bit of light coming from a square hole in front of his face; a scraping sound, gritty. It made his teeth hurt, then a muddy plopping sound and the light got smaller.

He heard it again, a whispering voice and breathing, long labored breaths. He felt his whole body pulled against the wall. It was vibrating. *Please help me*, he heard the plaintive whisper again, stronger this time, a masculine voice, but not a man, a young man? A boy? Urgency ran up Jamie's spine, *Where am I?* The light got smaller, a smaller square and more sounds, scraping, something sandy, a thick, hard plop and the light went out, and the scream. His chest seized. He couldn't breath. *I'm dead.*

All logic and reason left him, his eyes cleared but he could still hear that sad, lonesome voice ringing in his ears, filling his heart, driving him to act. He looked down at James again.

He was digging at the foot of the arch with his hands, looking up at Jamie, seeming to want him to help.

Oh my God! Oh my God! Jamie's mind raced as he looked around the room for something to use, a shovel, a hammer, something to get behind that wall. He saw a rusty old sledge hammer over in the far corner behind the garden tools and ran to it. James clapped.

Jamie grabbed the sledge and went back to the wall, then stopped. He picked up James and sat him on the stairs, out of the way, then went back to the arch. *Oh, my God!* He took the sledge and swung it hard. The old red brick crumbled, dust flying everywhere, in his eyes, his mouth, his nose. James cheered from the stairs. Jamie swung it again and again with all his might, driven by a feeling that he somehow knew wasn't his, freedom. He swung again, then again. Three more swings and he broke through, a cloud of dust blew out, then silence.

■

When Bethea got up and came downstairs, she was freshly energized and redressed in evening clothes; a floor-length black dress with beaded cocktail jacket, her favorite strand of pearls and pearl earrings. *Show off,* Josiah thought, knowing that his own mother would have come down early in her best housedress and tried to help Ella in the kitchen, *Bless her soul.* But of course he bit his tongue.

In the dining room, Josiah held the chair out for the old woman and received a chilly, "Thank you, Josiah," for his trouble. From there Ella took up the converstation, telling her mother about all the work that had been done at the church and how much Josiah had done to restore the historic *freed man's* church for future generations to remember. As much as Bethea didn't care for Josiah personally, she was never one to turn a cold shoulder to her God or her church and found enough there to take up the conversation with interest.

Seeing that this was a way to ease the tension for later in the visit, Josiah joined in telling Bethea about how he'd found this wonderful builder who really cared about the work he was doing on the church and how he went out of his way to get them a beautiful stained glass window of John the Baptist to shine over their altar.

"The colors are just brilliant, Mama, and Mike has worked so hard. The whole building has been fully restored. They're just about finished. We can take you over to see the results in a day or so if you like," Josiah spoke enthusiastically. Then Josiah's mood couldn't help but change when he thought about Mike's tragedy. Ella saw it and took up the conversation from there telling her mother about how the builder, Mike Golden, had come to Sayreville with his wife and bought an historic, old house, Fairfax Grange, to restore but that his wife had just died in a car accident not long ago. After expressing her sympathies, Bethea looked deep in thought, like she was reaching for something; a memory.

"Fairfax Grange, that sounds so familiar." Then she got a look of realization in her eyes. "I know that place. The one with the lake and the hill behind it, and the big tree? They used to call it Willow's Weep in my day. Had a tragedy there back then, too. A man shot himself in the lake. A soldier if I remember correctly. Parker, Baker, Barker. I can't remember now. Came back from the war in Germany and found that his wife had left him. Walked out into the lake and put a gun to his chest. I remember them talking about it when I was a girl, finding him face down floatin' in the lake."

Josiah looked up, grabbed by a feeling in his belly, remembering when Michael had come to the church and asked him if he knew that he was living in *a suicide's house*. But he wasn't referring to any soldier, and the death wasn't after the war, it was recent. Josiah's guts wound tightly inside him making it hard for him to finish eating. He thought about the last time he had seen Michael, "*I don't know how much more I can carry, Reverend, or for how long.*"

"Seems like nothing good ever came out of that place," Bethea said, shaking her head. "...and then there was the old legend..." Bethea went on. That did it for Josiah. He lifted his head from his plate and looked at his mother-in-law.

"What legend, Mama?" he asked pointedly.

"Oh, some old legend about the people who built the house way back when the land was settled. An old folk tale. That's how the place got its name, Willow's Weep," Bethea said as if it were unimportant and she was ready to change the subject, but Josiah couldn't let go. He looked at Ella who got his drift, then back to the old woman, stern conviction in his eyes. Forming his words slowly, deliberately, he asked her again firmly,

"What...legend, Mama?"

■

Jamie went close to the hole and tapped out a few more bricks. A rush of stale, dusty air hit him in the face and he stepped back. James went "oooooooohhhhhhh!" from the stairs, his eyes wide with wonderment.

Inside the hole Jamie could see a space, almost a small chamber, light dimly shining on it from overhead, a rope hanging from an iron ring, then a form, a dingy, dark shape, hidden in shadows, a skull, hanging forward, and a skeleton, rags hanging from the form, arm bones held over head by the rope fixed to the ring in the wall. Jamie's eyes bulged and he couldn't move, but the shadow in the hole did, slowly beginning to take shape, misty at first, becoming more solid as Jamie stood paralyzed, motionless in front of the hole in the arch.

A figure emerged slowly from the darkness into the dim light, a young man, barely more than a boy, eighteen or nineteen years old; long hair, blonde and wavy but dirtied and matted, lonesome brown almond-shaped eyes set deeply in a heart-shaped face with thick lips and a squat, crooked nose that seemed to lean to the right, smudged and dirty, too.

He was not handsome or pretty, almost homely but for his eyes. The boy's eyes made him seem...so...lovable, needy and wanting. He had the kind of face and eyes that would make anyone want to take him in their arms and hold him. He was slim, too slim. His hands and feet were too big for his small frame, underfed. His ragged clothes filled out as Jamie watched, recognizing, knowing in his heart that he was a farmer's boy. He'd seen that look before with the poor dirt farmers in the South; hard times.

As the boy leaned forward, his form fell through the rope. His arms came down and he stood up, holding his hands out to Jamie; pleading, beckoning. Jamie backed up as the boy stepped through the hole and came toward him. James, still on the steps, called out excitedly, "Azze-an! Azze-an!" and held his arms out to the figure in his "up" motion. The boy walked towards Jamie, backing him up until he was against the opposite wall, more awestruck than afraid.

He reached his dirty, too big hand up to Jamie's face, touching it. *"I'm Adrian,"* the boy said shyly through his sad brown eyes, communicating without words. *"Don't be afraid. I am like you."*

Tears started to flow then, a stream running down Jamie's face, a trickle, a ripple, a flood. The boy's touch translated such awful loneliness and sorrow into Jamie's being, forcing Jamie to relive how badly he'd been beaten, unable to cry out, kicked like a dog then dragged down, the light going out, his suffocated cries, that terrible scream. *"I'm dead."*

Once touched, recognizing those feelings, Jamie gave himself over, no resistance, and the boy walked into his body. Jamie gasped; two hearts, two souls. He was no longer alone within the confines of his own physical body. Still unafraid, Jamie completely surrendered himself, letting the sad, lonely boy come inside him. *"I am like you."*

Their souls fused in Jamie's body, they turned to James on the steps and walked over to him. "Up," James said. They picked him up in their arms like a fragile package. *"Thank you, my little friend,"* Adrian said with Jamie's lips and kissed James on the forehead, stroking his hair as they slowly mounted the stairs. James just laid his head on their shoulder, cooing lovingly, "Azze-an," and sucking his thumb.

■

Upstairs, Victoria heard the phone ringing. She'd never once disobeyed an adult in her short little life, but that ring. It was her special ring. It rang again and again, insistently. She got up and went to the door. The ringing got louder; faster, insistent, urgent. She had to answer it. She went downstairs, looking around to see if anyone could see her before she picked up the receiver. "Hello. Yes. Yes, somewhere. I'm okay. I don't know. Okay, hold on," she said quietly so no one would hear her then put the receiver down on its side, not hanging it up.

She went to the kitchen, over to the bay window and saw her daddy on the hill, standing and looking out over the lake. She went back to the phone and picked up the receiver. "Yes, he's out back, on the hill," and she listened. Suddenly her face changed and her pretty pink skin flushed. "Yes, I know what that is," she said, her voice squeaking with emotion. "I don't know," she said and started to cry. "Yes, I will," she said then jumped, dropping the receiver to the floor and running to the stairs, yelling out "Jamie!" then she ran up the stairs.

When he didn't answer she got frantic, hysterical, running back downstairs and around to his room screaming and crying, "Jamie, where are you? Jamie!" No response. She ran back to the wood room and banged on the door. "Jamie where are you, please. Daddy needs you. He's in trouble," she cried, sitting down in front of the wood room door and sobbing.

■

Before they got to the top of the stairs, the Jamie heard Victoria running around the first floor, frantically looking for him, crying hysterically and calling out breathlessly, "Jamie! Jamie!" He wanted to run but his body wouldn't let him, it wasn't his own anymore. When they reached the top, the latch to the door unlocked and the door swung open.

Victoria heard the basement door open and close. She jumped up and ran towards the sound, right into their legs and looked up, her face wet and flushed, her eyes glazed with fear and confusion. "Oh, Jamie, Daddy's got a gun!" she sobbed breathlesly winded.

Michael!

Jamie tried to separate himself and make his body run but couldn't make it happen. Instead, the Adrian put their hand on Victoria's head gently, setting James down on the floor next to her without speaking and walked toward the kitchen. The lock on the kitchen door clicked and the door swung open. They turned to Victoria behind them. "Don't worry, darlin'. Ev'r'thang'll be alright now," the Jamie said, a sense of peace translating itself to him from the Adrian, telling him that it was in his hands now as they walked through the door into the backyard.

■

Bethea Walton looked at her daughter, then her son-in-law, saw the seriousness in their eyes and took her attitude down a notch. "The legend of Willow's Weep. Lord, have mercy. It was so long ago since I've thought of it. It was just one of those tales children tell each other around the campfire. Now let me think for a minute," she said pondering. "I know it comes from the original settlers of Sayreville and the area east of town. They were pilgrims from England, Puritans or Quakers something like that, kinda like the ones in New England, but stricter."

Josiah's mind traveled back to the last time he had been at the house, remembering that feeling, that image with the cold, dead black eyes and those words, *Nigger slave*, then remembered the way he felt when he saw that oatmeal box. *Can't be*, he thought to himself, *"jus' can't be...or can it?*

"It sounded so romantic when I was a girl, like our own Romeo and Juliet story," Bethea went on. "Willow was the daughter of one of the area founders, a powerful land owner and the parish minister," she waxed nostalgically, her eyes wearing the gaze of the young girl she once was, then came back to the table.

"Well, anyway, as the legend goes, she fell in love with a boy from the other side of the township, a farmer's boy and a Catholic, from what used to be the French side. That's why all the streets over there have French names. Well, of course, her strict father forbid the relationship. As the tale goes, the boy was supposed to come and get her one night to elope, but he never came. Maybe her father bought him off or scared him off, but nonetheless, he never showed up. Broke the poor child's heart. She waited for days and when he still didn't come, she went up on the hill behind the house, took poison, laid under the tree there and died. Since then, they've called it *'Willow's Weep.'*

As the old woman spoke, Josiah thought about what Bethea was saying about the girl taking poison and dying on the hill and the feeling of sadness that overwhelmed him when he was up there, then her story about the soldier killing himself in the lake and Michael coming to him to ask about the suicide in his pantry, *"A suicide's house,"* was what Michael had called it. All of it came rushing in a flood through Josiah's brain, images and feelings coming together in an overwhelming sense of urgency. *Oh, dear Lord, Michael!* his mind screamed and he got up from the table and rushed to the phone in the hall.

His arthritic old fingers fumbled with the little desk top phone diary, trying to find Michael's number and dropping it on the floor. He heard light footsteps behind him. "Help me, Ella, please!"

Ella Willis bent down, retrieving the little book from under the table and taking the phone from his hand. "I'll do it," she said, seeing her husband's hands shaking.

"Hurry, Ella, please. I can't explain it right now, but Michael's in touble. There's been three suicides connected to that house…that we know of, then Jane and the way Michael was talkin' when I saw him. . .there's somethin' in that house making 'em do it. Ella, lock me away if I'm wrong but, I think I saw it, out back of the house. It was a man, the oatman and he called me a…nigger." Ella Willis not once ever in forty years of marriage doubted her husband and she wasn't about to start then. His eyes were as sincere as they were the day she met him and she dialed the phone. It was busy.

Josiah Willis had always driven like an old man, even before he was old, but this time was different. He was on a mission, to save a life, to save a friend. *What an odd pair they were; big, rough ol' white Michael and little old black Josiah,* he thought as he hit the gas, tearing down the road toward the Grange, his Bible by his side. *I'm comin', Michael. I'm comin'.*

■

Mike looked out over the valley, holding the gun close to his chest under his coat, pointed at his heart, tears pouring from his eyes as he looked out over the horizon for the last time, his finger tight against the trigger.

Adrian and Jamie walked slowly towards the hill, their eyes fixed on Mike's lonely, solitary figure standing next to the tree. Adrian called out, *"Please, Willow, don't. I'm here now."* Mike's figure turned toward them, but Mike was not all they saw. They saw a small, frail figure, a girl, a young girl in a plain black frock with a square white pilgrim collar, her hair covered by a plain white bonnet tied under her chin. She looked at them, her large, dark eyes burning with anger; the grief of abandonment in her plain, un-pretty face. Jamie and Adrian walked closer.

From the edge of the lake, another voice came. Ted Barker called out to the hill, grim, pale and still dressed in his army uniform; a large red stain where his heart had been. *"Leave him alone. You have what you want now."*

Then Jamie saw the outline of the gun under Mike's coat. His heart ripped into beating wildly. "Please, Adrian, don't let her hurt 'im, please," Jamie begged the Adrian inside him. *"Willow, stop, you don't' have to do this anymore. I'm here,"* Adrian said through Jamie's lips. Willow's eyes grew darker, pitch black as they came closer, bitter tears flowing from her eyes, down her cheeks. *"You left me,"* the Willow in Mike said, *"You said you loved me...and you left me alone...because I'm...ugly."*

Then another voice came. The figure of Graham Stanhope, gaunt and pale, short brown hair, graying at the sides and full reddish beard, appeared in his work overalls standing to the left of the back door to the house, nearest the mud room; a large red stain where his heart had been. *"Don't hurt him, Willow. He's a good man."* Then another, a man dressed in an early 18th century waistcoat, riding pants and boots with long wavy brown hair was standing by the fire pit; the same look, the same hole in his heart, *"How many, Willow? How many?"*

∎

He'd left his house so quickly that it never occurred to Josiah Willis what he would do when he got to Mike's. What would he say? *Michael, there's something bad goin' on here and you gotta get out? That an oatman is after him?* Then he thought about what Bethea had said, *A parish minister? And a man of God? How could that be? What man of God could countenance such human suffering?* and he remembered those cold, black dead eyes and those disgusting words. *Well, we'll jus' see about that, who the real man of God is in Sayreville. I ain't afraid of you, oatman.* And he drove like the wind down the winding curves and twisiting bends that led him closer to Fairfax Grange. *Jus' hold on, son. I'm almost there.*

He'd just turned off the main hillside road onto the road that led to the Grange, running it all through his head, what Bethea had said, a boy, a girl and her father; the oldest story in the book. He saw something moving on the side of the road. He was on them before he knew it and hit the brakes. His tires squealed like a four alarm fire, but he was too late. He swerved to avoid hitting them before he knew what they were, running off the road into the field; *ducks.*

■

As they all looked into each others eyes, Adrian mixed with Jamie, mixed with Mike, mixed with Willow, ripples formed on the lake behind them; frenzied splashing, frantic movement, as ducks came swifty from every direction toward the water's edge, two then four, then more, eight, ten, and sounds, words, howling from the water's edge as they came on the land. *Idol worshipper! Fornicator,* the large one with the cold, dead black eyes cried out in a booming voice as it rushed toward them, leading the others behind it. *Blasphemer, sodomite!* another one cried out shrilly; a woman. Then another, deep male voice, *Papist! Devil! Hereitc!*

They all came shouting and rushing towards the hill in a flurry, the large one at the front, *Corruptor!* He seemed to direct his words toward Mike, then a booming, vibrating voice came echoing from the largest duck again, *Papist whore, my daughter, willful child, ugly girl. Shame on our house and thy father.* Then another voice, mutton chop whiskers dressed in a Union soldier's uniform from the Civil War, standing at the bottom of the hill at the far end of the yard, *No more, Willow. Let him go.*

She saw them all through Mikes's true blues, then looked toward the largest duck and the flock behind him. No longer merely ducks, figures stood above each one, men dressed in long black frock coats, and white shirts with flat black hats, women dressed plainly as she was, unadorned in nothing else but black and white, their heads covered with white bonnets, all with cold, dead black eyes; the congregation.

Jamie held out his hands, exposing the bruised, bloody rings around Adrian's wrists to the Willow in Mike. "*I never left you. I've been here, with you, all the time,*" Jamie's lips said, sad streams of tears running from Adrian's eyes. "*I never left you. I love you, Willow.*"

Willow's eyes changed. No longer angry and bitter, they rounded into an expression of sadness, grief and longing. Mike held out her free hand to them. The Adrian in Jamie took the Willow in Mike in his arms, embracing them, "*I never left you.*" Willow put her head on Adrian's shoulder.

While they held each other, the Jamie slowly reached his hand in-between their chests, feeling for the gun. He found it gripped tightly in Mike's hand, pressed close to his heart. Jamie slowly wrapped his hand around the butt of the gun and could feel what Mike was feeling, so alone, unloved, abandoned.

He tried to work the gun gently away but Mike's hand resisted, his finger pulling more tightly around the trigger. Jamie raised his head, searching for the Willow in Mike. "Please, don't hurt him," Jamie pleaded, but Willow was gone, embraced with Adrian, lost within the two of them. They were Mike's own true blues he saw. "Please, don't, Michael," Jamie said. "Give it ta me," he pleaded.

"I can't," Mike said sobbing hopelessly, holding firm to the grip of the gun. "I don't want to be alone anymore. You'll all leave me and…I'll be alone," Mike's trembling voice came back, his face awash with an unending flow.

Seeing the vision from the mud room, Michael's true blues, dead and staring at the ceiling, Jamie let his mind roam. He was a young boy again, he and Jane standing next to each other in the bathroom mirror, staring at each others faces; the line between who was who blurring before their eyes. He let himself go, reaching inside himself to let the line blur even further, until the line no longer existed.

The lead box encased in concrete that he'd lived with so long and that had been cracking little by little, more and more since he had come to Fairfax Grange suddenly exploded, rocking his insides with elemental force, erupting and splitting itself wide open, the *Danger. Contents Unknown* sign ripped in half. He looked back into Mike's eyes with theirs. "Please, Michael…for me," he begged. Jamie saw Mike's eyes widen and fill with an unmistakable look. "Is that you?" Mike asked, his fingers loosening their grip on the gun. "I've missed you so much." Mike opened his mouth again. "I…I…" he started but couldn't get the words out.

The ducks came closer, the figures floating above them as if gliding on mist, chanting and chiding, led by the largest, the Minister, cold, dead black eyes glaring at them, moving up the side of the hill. "*Fornicators! The wages of sin is death,*" the Minister shouted, pointing at the Adrian in Jamie, then directly at the Jamie, "*Incest! Incest…Man shall not draw near to any flesh of his flesh. So sayeth the Lord,*" the Minister's voice boomed. "*Blasphemers! Sodomites! Fornicators! The wages of sin is death!*" The congregation shrieked, chanting wildly from behind him, pointing accusingly at both the Adrian in Jamie and the Willow in Mike.

Holding Mike where he was for as long as he could, Jamie carefully slid Mike's finger from around the trigger and felt the gun give way. Once he had it safely in his own hand, Jamie grabbed hold of Mike's jacket and with a quick jerk pushed hard, forcing him back to arm's length with a single shove, and in one swift, split second movement, whipped the gun around and let her rip. *Pow! Pow! Pow!* Shots rang out in rapid succession as he picked off one duck at a time starting with the largest. Blood curdling screams and cries of pain filled the air. *Pow! Pow! Pow!* One after another, they leapt into the air with the force of the hits, then dropped to the ground, blood spurts mixed with feathers and duck shit flying through the air as he blasted away until the barrell clicked to empty and the yard was quiet.

When the ring of shots faded, Jamie looked back into Mike's eyes, but saw Willow and felt himself drifting back into a small corner of himself, letting Adrian come through. Adrian took Willow by the hand. He and Mike both gasped at the same time as Adrian and Willow lifted out of them and walked by themselves to the edge of the hill, fading into the mists rising from the lake, disappearing into the colors of the sunset as the sun descended into the horizon.

The silence was deafening as Jamie looked back at Mike, into his very, very true blues, and knew he'd fallen off the edge, never to return, and he ran. He turned and ran, dropping the gun on the lawn as he ran back to the house, leaving Mike alone, alone again on the top of the hill.

A minute later the back door opened again and Victoria came running out. "Daaaddddy! Daaadddy!" she cried out breathlessly. James toddled behind her as she ran, tripping over his own feet and falling more than once, then getting back up and running again, determined not to be left behind. "Oh, Daddy! Oh, Daddy. Please don't go away!" Victoria cried as she leapt into his arms.

■

Mike went upstairs to his library, trying to get his head around what had just happened. *Was it real? Did it really happen?* he asked himself as he bent down to take the gun box from under his chair to put the gun back. *What was I thinking, to bring a gun into the house with Victoria and James?* he scolded himself bitterly for being so foolish, and his feelings, they weren't his own, or were they? Was there something in him, deep inside him that the girl, Willow, saw, recognized in him, and that poor, sad boy, beaten, tortured and murdered, all because he loved a plain girl. Mike's heart broke for them. They were just children, lonely unloved children.

Did that boy, Adrian, see himself in *his* Jamie? It was the first time he had called him that, even in his own mind, and he thought it again, *my Jamie*. He took a pill from the bottle he got from the doctor at the hospital and unconsciously started taking off his clothes as his thoughts whirled around in his head. *And all for what?* He thought about the ducks and what he'd seen, a congregation of what? God's people? A God that let them hate…and hurt their children. Anger welled up in his guts as he stepped into the shower.

He let the hot water run over his shaved head as he thought about the girl, plain of face, like him, unloved in her parents' house, like him, abandoned and hurt, angry, like him. He thought about the images of the men with their hearts blown out; all of them plain, ordinary, special to no one, left alone with no one to love.

He ran the soap over his body thinking about how they had taken his side, not wanting him to suffer like they had, dying alone and unloved. *"I'll make it up to you, all of you. You will all live here in my house with me and my family. You'll never have to be alone again. I promise. I know your hearts and your names, Graham Stanhope, the carpenter, Ted Barker, Horatio Redmon the soldiers and Jeffrey Forrest, the horseman, I know you. Be my friends. Stay with me. Guard my children from all the things that can happen to them when they're away from me. Live in my heart and in my house with us as long as I have breath in my body."*

He stepped out of the shower and toweled off, looking down at the partially healed split in his toe and thought about Jamie. *What are you feeling right now? Are you still afraid?*

When he'd got back to the house with the kids, Jamie was already in his room with the door closed. *What are you thinking? Do you feel free because this monster was not your monster? Will you let me protect you from your monster now? Do you feel safe in my house?*

His mind went back to the morning when he'd come downstairs and Jamie had just met Victoria and James. *"Daddy did you know Jamie has tattoos on his arms and that he talks funny because his neck is red?"* then the way he misspelled his name on the plaque and in the letter. *"You are not ugly, Micheal…"* He got a most peculiar feeling in his chest. His heart had been ripped apart so randomly, so violently, torn to shreds by a vengeful god that was not his own, strewn in pieces on the floor of his soul, scattered around him.

It started at the very bottom, working itself upward, a gentle hand picking up the pieces and pulling them together, holding them lovingly as they worked carefully, one stitch at a time, Victoria, James, Willow, Adrian, the men, Jamie and…Jane. *Is that you?*

He put on his most comfortable pair of jeans, white tee and an old flannel shirt Jane had picked up at some flea market because it was already broken in and she knew he liked that. He was just about to put on some soft clean socks when he heard Victoria downstairs.

"Daaaadddddyyyy!" she cried out running around the first floor as he ran down the stairs. She was frantic. She grabbed his hand, tugging hard, pulling him back toward the front door. "What's is it, sweetheart?"

"It's Jamie. He's going away. Hurry!" she cried, dragging him with the full weight of her little body. "He's got his bags. Do something, Daddy!" Mike looked out the front door and saw Jamie's black leather-clad back heading down the walk toward the drive, the American flag print bandana on his head, his saddle bag over on shoulder, his khaki-green duffle bag in the other hand. Mike panicked and flung the door open, dashing out onto the front porch.

"What the hell're you doing? Where are you going?" he shouted at Jamie's back. Jamie stopped in his tracks at the sound of Mike's voice, shoulders slumped, and set his duffle bag on the ground, not turning to face him. Mike, still in only his bare feet, stayed on the porch. "Answer me?" he shouted.

"I hafta go, Michael," Jamie said, flatly without turning around to face him.

"What the hell does that mean? How can you do this, and without a word? Just run away? What the hell is wrong with you? I thought we finished this. The monster is gone. You don't have to be afraid anymore, run away anymore. I don't understand," Mike's booming voice shouted, shuffling back and forth on his cold feet, rubbing his shaved head. Jamie stayed motionless, silent. "How can you just run out on us like this, and without telling me why? Please, Jamie, just talk to me," Mike begged.

"I cain't, Michael," Jamie said and picked his duffle bag back up, taking a step. "I don't wanna but I…hafta."

"Wait!" Mike cried, his mind reeling, not understanding, scrambling for what to say, what to do. "Is it me? Did I do something? Even if I did, how can you leave them?" Mike called out, desperate to keep him from taking another step and pointing at the window where Victoria was watching, tears running down her little face. Mike looked over to her, a second later a little blonde head popped up next to her. Jamie stopped and dropped the bag again, looking up to the sky, long streams of tears running down his own face.

Don't look, Jamie, don't look or you'll nev'r be able ta do it.

Mike's true blues began to well too, feeling so helpless, abandoned…again. "Why are you doing this? I don't understand. Have I failed you so badly? And now after…Didn't that mean anything to you? How can you do this? Is it me?"

"Ya jes' don't git it do ya, Michael? That is why."

"Get what?"

"It is you, Michael. It is *you!* It's always come down to *you,* fer her…and now me. Da ya git it *now*, Michael? We're twins, *identical*, like the freaks ya hear 'bout on the TV," Jamie said, turning his face in profile, wiping his eyes with his hand, struggling not to look back. "Whin she burnt 'er hand bakin', I got a mark," and Jamie raised his hand over his head without turning. "Whin I skinned my knee playin' ball, she got the bruise." Mike just stood there with his mouth open, hands on his hips, shuffling in the cold trying to understand. "Whin ya loved 'er, my addiction went away and whin Victoria and James were born, I was thar, too."

Mike's eyes went wide as the dawn of what he was saying washed over him like a tidal wave. "I still have the bruise on my chest from whar the steerin' wheel hit 'er. D'ya git it now, Michael? I let it git away from me, let it go too far. It's my fault, but I jes'...couldn't help it. I had ta...fer you. Thar ain't nothin' I wouldn't do fer ya, and now it's too late to go back. That's why I hafta go. If you knew whut's happened, you'd want me ta go. Please, don't make me say it, Michael."

"Say what? Goddamn it! Just fucking say it," Mike shouted, stomping his bare foot on the cold wooden step, wiping angry tears from his own eyes. Mike saw Jamie's back rise and fall with a deep breath then let his head hang down.

"How kin I look at ya ev'r'day and not see all the wonderful thangs she ever loved 'bout ya...the way she did. The way ya opened yer heart to us so we could see whut it's like ta be...loved. I cain't...look at ya and not see. I cain't. I jes' cain't," Jamie said, lost in his own confusion, no longer having his little lead box to contain him as he struggled to keep himself from completely giving up to it. Nothing left to protect him, he felt like he just wanted to crawl inside himself, run away from the gaze of those sincere, honest, very true blues, *Danger. Contents Unknown*, but there was nowhere to go. "Do ya understand now, Michael?" he said angrily, wiping his face on his sleeve and picking his bag up again. He took another step.

Mike's gait widened as he paced back and forth, panic ripping through him, rubbing his head. *Do something! You can't let her go again, can't let him go, can't let them go. Do something, Michael! Nothing else matters, not ever again.* Chaos, confusion whirled wildly around his brain, synapses snapping like an overloaded electric socket, sparking, blinding white heat, making it impossible for him to think clearly; the image of those quiet, shy hazel eyes, the way they looked at him making him feel so special, like he was the only man in the world, and that glorious overbite that he loved so much, smiling at him, making him feel that the love he had to give mattered to them, gone forever away from him, everything that ever made him feel special in the world gone forever. He felt the tension of his new stitches as they pulled against his heart, beating out of control in his big chest.

Nothing else matters, Michael, nothing! his mind screamed at him, ranting and raving, desperate, then it blew, an explosion so intense his body rocked with it, shattering everything he ever thought he was or knew, or felt, or thought was true in his world, nothing else mattered. Smoke and sirens swept through his entire being, then stopped, replaced by a quiet calm; the answer.

It was so simple, so easy. He should have seen it before, but in that moment it all came rushing back to him, the sandwich, mushrooms not anchovies, the books, the way he could make Jamie calm the way he did with Jane, and the letter. *"I feel afraid like we used to. Is that you?...I send you my heart, Can you feel it? Identical! Identical!"* kept shouting itself in his head. If it worked for her it would work for him. And Michael Golden splintered for the last time in his life, knowing what he had to do and nothing in the world was going to stop him. He was going to do whatever he had to, whatever it took, to finish his house and make him feel whole again.

He stopped pacing and stood at the edge of the porch, shivering with cold. His lips started to move, his lower lip trembling as he tried to form the words, spoken so long ago, his big chest heaving, a flood of tears running down his face, his hands reaching out as he began to speak.

"I...I...I sometimes have a queer feeling with regard to you—especially when you are near me, as now: it is as if I had a string somewhere under my left ribs, tightly and inextricably knotted to a similar string situated in the corresponding quarter of your little frame..." His big calloused hands moved poignantly as the words came out, touching his chest then reaching out again. *"And if that boisterous channel, and two hundred miles or so of land come broad between us, I am afraid that cord of communion will be snapt; and then I've a nervous notion I should take to bleeding inwardly. As for you—you'd forget me...* I built a good life for us once and I can do it again, if you'll let me. If you'll—" and he held his hands out, palms up, blisters almost completely healed.

Chapter Fifteen

Broken Boxes

R abbi Judah Abramow hunched his shoulders, pulling up the collar of his long, black overcoat against the freezing December wind with one hand and holding his little black yarmulke tight to his head with the other as he hurried for the door of Temple Beth Israel synagogue, fumbling with the keys in his stiffening hand. As he slammed the door behind him, shivering in the foyer, brushing the snowflakes off of his shoulders and shaking them out of his beard, he heard a rattling noise coming from the main room telling him he wasn't alone in the building.

He slowly opened the door a crack, careful not to draw any attention to himself, worried that he might be in for another desecration like the fire six months earlier that destroyed so much of the main room. He peeked through the cracked door and breathed a sigh of relief, smiling when he saw the shaved head and the shape of the large back in a plaid flannel shirt with the sleeves torn off that the young men call *wife beaters* of all things, kneeling over by the new carved wall cabinet. "Michael, what are you doing here? It's Christmas Eve. You should be home with your family." Mike Golden startled and turned to face him, not getting up, then smiled himself.

"It's not Christmas Eve in here for you, Rabbi. It's almost done anyway. Just a little more and it'll be finished. I'm really sorry for the delay, but the carvings on the new doors took a little longer than expected. Once I finish installing the locks and hinges, it'll be done and I'll go home," Mike said. Rabbi Abramow walked over to him, looking up at the new carved doors depicting the exodus of the Israelites out of Egypt on one door and Moses' descent from the mount to deliver the Ten Commandments on the other. He gasped. The carving took his breath away. The faces on the participants held such emotion, joy, freedom; the fine polishing making them seem to glow with a sense of humanity.

"Oh, Michael, it's beautiful. That out of the ashes of a crime should come such faith-affirming beauty," the Rabbi said and put his hand on Mike's bent shoulder as he carefully screwed in the lowest of the ornate brass hinges by hand. "We rejoice in that my friend Josiah sent you to us when we needed you," the Rabbi said backing up to get a fuller view of the tableau in the yellow light from overhead. "But I'm glad to see you anyway. Don't go anywhere," and he rushed away, back to the door that led to the offices.

He was back a moment later, keeping one hand behind his back, smiling sheepishly, his dark brown eyes giving away an impish twinkle as he came closer to Mike. "If anyone knew," the Rabbi said quietly blushing, "I'd be drummed out of the corps," and he handed Mike a small, flat package wrapped in Christmas paper with Santa Clauses all over it and a red bow. Mike sat back on his heels and opened the package to find a book, *My Name is Ascher Lev*. Mike looked up at the Rabbi, his true blues misting, the holidays always made him as sensitive as a child.

"I don't know what to say," Mike choked.

"It's a modern story of my people and the conflict of a young boy between his talent for art and his responsibilities to his faith," the Rabbi said, nodding proudly. Mike smiled back, knowing Reverend Willis must have had a hand in this, too.

"I won't tell anyone if you don't, Rabbi," Mike laughed and put the book in his tool bag, wrapping and all. The Rabbi laughed with him and reached out to take his hand to help him up.

The edge of Mike's wife beater hiked up and the Rabbi saw the shiney colored image on the ball of his shoulder, an angel with blonde hair, in flight; white gossamer wings, a golden sash and flowing pale blue robes.

"What a beautiful tattoo, Michael," he said, looking closer, admiring the delicacy of the lines. "It looks new."

"Yessir, fresh from this morning. My Christmas present to myself," Mike said smiling proudly.

"I've always admired the compelling work the artists are doing these days. You must be blessed to have an angel on your shoulder as you go through life," the Rabbi said looking deep into Mike's true blues.

"It's even better than that," Mike said as he stood to face the Rabbi, exposing his other shoulder. "I have two," he beamed revealing another, *identical* angel tattooed on his opposite shoulder.

■

The snow was beginning to come down heavy around Fairfax Grange, the lights from the Christmas tree twinkling through the large front window, the smell of baking wafting through the half opened window in the back to let out some of the heat.

Inside Jamie Arnette was wiping the sweat from his face. He'd been baking since early morning and was feeling as hot as Texas asphalt in July. After the last batch of biscuits was finally in the oven, he turned around to find little James staring at him from his chair, just waking up from an afternoon cat nap and rubbing his eyes sleepily. James held his arms out in the familiar motion. "Up," he asked. Jamie went to him and took him out of the chair and onto his hip where he belonged. Just then Victoria came through the doorway, looking at Jamie, frustrated, her eyebrows furrowed above her true blues, so much like Michael.

"Jamie! We have to hurry and wrap Daddy's presents before he comes home," she whined, almost stomping her foot, again so much like her father that Jamie couldn't help but smile and give in to whatever she wanted. He had gotten so involved with the holiday baking he'd almost forgotten about the wrapping. He looked at the clock. It was after three P.M.

"Dayum!…okay, let's rock, little girl," he said following her back into the living room where she already had the paper, tape and bows laid out. He put James down on the floor and went to his room, coming back a minute later with three large bags labelled, "Sayreville Sportsman," and put them in the middle of the floor.

Jamie opened the first bag and took out a big black and white buffalo plaid flannel shirt. He quickly unrolled a tube of bright red paper with green holly all over it, then sat next to Victoria on the couch and they began to wrap. He gave her the pen and told her what to write, *For Daddy, Love Victoria.* She stuck it on the present, then got up and put it under the tree.

Jamie opened the next bag and pulled out a big shoe box, opening the lid to show James. "New lumberjack boots from you, my little man." James ignored him, completely enamored by the bright scraps of paper left over from wrapping the shirt and the opened bag of multi colored bows. Victora just waved her hand at him as if to say, *'Oh forget about him, I'll do it'* and unrolled another tube. This one was blue metallic paper with big white snowflakes.

Once the boots were wrapped, Victoria filled out the card, *For Daddy, Love James.*

Jamie opened the third bag and pulled out a big roll up straw cowboy hat with a beaded leather band around the crown. They wrapped that one in green paper with golden silhouttes of the nativity on it. When Jamie gave her another label, she looked at him quizically. "Make this one to Daddy from Santa," Jamie said, smiling to himself. Victoria did as she was told and put the hat under the tree, then looked at

Jamie with her true blues, innocent and questioning. "What about you, Jamie? Did you forget Daddy?" Jamie laughed out loud, then looked at her sincerely, smiling from ear to ear. "Believe me, little darlin', I would nev'r, ev'r fergit yer daddy. I got 'im somethin' real special, somethin' that I know he wants really, really, really bad."

■

"Pleeeaaase honey," Carly Acton whined to her huband, Jesse, as they drove slowly down the snowy road through Sayreville on their way to her parents in Scranton. "Every year you get me something I love. We're doing really well this year. I got a nice raise and you got a promotion. Isn't there something I can get you that you want? We've been married ten years now and you're gonna hit the big four oh next month." She took his free hand and squeezed it. "And you've been the best husband a girl could want, or this girl anyway. How about a trip, like a second honeymoon? Mexico? Aruba? You name it, anything you want you can have, honey."

Jesse was just about to tell her that there was nothing in particular that he wanted, and that maybe he would get a new truck in the spring when they passed a long snow covered driveway with "Fairfax Grange" carved on a wooden sign at the entrance. On the other side of the driveway entrance Jesse saw another sign, three feet high and four feet wide, painted white with big black letters and a bright red bow on top. Jesse Acton's eyes went wide, twinkling with excitement and he smiled, raising his eyebrows with an evil grin. "You did say '*anything*' didn't you, honey?" He pulled over and took out his pen.

4 SALE

VINTAG 1977

HARLEY

CHERRY MINT COND.

CALL (732) 462-4068 OR STOP BYE

■

Jamie had just gotten out of the shower and redressed in his *angel* clothes for the night, white tee shirt, faded blue jeans with the knees blown out and no shoes, waiting for Michael to come home. The house was clean, the baking was finished, the bookkeeping was done, the kids were clean, the presents were wrapped, dinner was in the oven and now it was time for him to relax with a Captain tea and breathe for awhile.

He'd no sooner sat down when he started to worry about Michael driving in the big snow storm that was coming, making the winding roads in the area dangerous. He turned the radio on in the kitchen to listen for the weather and for some Chirstmas music for the kids. Victoria was just taking the last batch of cookies off the baking sheet with the spatula when Jamie heard the tinkling of the tamboreen and the dum de dum de dum that signaled Mariah Carey's Christmas song. He had never cared much for Mariah Carey, but that one song got to him every time.

> *I don't want a lot for Christmas*
> *There's just one thing I need*
> *I don't care about the presents*
> *Underneath the Christmas tree*
> *I just want you for my own*
> *More than you could ever know*
> *Make my wish come true*
> *All I want for Christmas is...*
> *You*

Jamie picked James up and started to spin around the kitchen floor and sing with Mariah in his whiskey-voiced cowboy twang. Victoria jumped up and down with them.

> *I don't want a lot fer Christmas*
> *Thar's jes' one thang I need*

I don't care 'bout the presents
Underneath the Christmas tree
I don't need ta hang my stockin'
Thar up on the fireplace
Santa Claus won't make me happy
With a toy on Christmas day
I jes' want you fer my own
More than you could ev'r know
Make my wish come true
All I want fer Christmas is you
You, baby

"Weeeeeeeeee! Victoria squealed as they all danced around in a circle, James giggling as Jamie bounced him on his hip, the snow outside coming down in large, heavy flakes, faster and faster. Jamie bent down and picked Victoria up with his other arm, kissed her and sang to her, waltzing around the kitchen floor surrounded by the smell of baking.

I won't ask fer much this Christmas
I don't ev'n wish fer snow
I'm jes' gonna keep on waitin'
Underneath the mistletoe
I won't make a list and send it
To the North Pole fer Saint Nick
I won't ev'n stay awake ta
Hear those magic reindeers click
'Cause I jes' want ya here tonight
Holdin' on ta me so tight
Whut more can I do
Baby all I want fer Christmas is you
Ooh baby
All the lights are shinin'
So brightly ev'r'whar
And the sounda children's
Laughter fills the air
And eve'r'one is sangin'

I hear those sleigh bells rangin'
Santa won't ya brang me the one I really need
Won't ya please brang my baby ta me...

As they danced and sang and loved and laughed, Victoria heard the phone ring. It was her special ring and she knew she had to answer it. She wriggled herself down from Jamie's arm, jumped around in a circle, then backed away slowly toward the doorway so he wouldn't notice and went to the phone table. Jamie twirled around still singing to James, then slowed down to look at the blizzard brewing outside of their bay window. "Look, James, snow!" he jiggled and pointed for little James so he could watch.

"Snnnooooow!" little James mimicked laughing. Jamie saw his reflection in the glass and stopped to look at himself, the music fading behind him.

Oh I don't want a lot for Christmas
This is all I'm asking for
I just want to see my baby
Standing right outside my door
Oh I just want you for my own
More than you could ever know
Make my wish come true
Baby all I want for Christmas is...
You

He stared at himself in the glass, remembering again what it was like to have Jane standing next to him when they were young, in their bathroom mirror back in Pittsburgh. For a second he thought he could see her again, standing right there next to him, just like they did then, reflected in the glass, then fade into him.

Who am I? So much inside him had changed. He no longer felt ashamed, no longer dirty and used. All that seemed swept away, replaced by a warm glowing light radiating from the center of his broken box, shards of his old life and everything connected with it strewn on the ground around him like so much rubble, letting him feel in ways he'd never known but somehow knew he'd missed all his life. It took his breath away and he gasped at its power.

He suddenly felt the urge to turn around. Someone was behind him. *Victoria? Whar's Victoria?* He walked to the doorway. Victoria was standing at the phone table with her back to him. Funny, he hadn't heard the phone ring. "Victoria, sweetheart, who is it?" She turned around, the receiver still to her ear, her true blues wide, innocently caught off guard.

"Yes, he's here. It's okay now?" she asked into the receiver, never taking her eyes away from Jamie's. "Okay. I will. Merry Christmas. I love you, too. Good-bye," and she put the receiver back on its cradle.

"Victoria? Who was it, sweetheart?"

"It was Mommy. She said to tell you that she loves her new job. She has a beautiful office and she's doing very important work with a doctor who helps children. She said you'd know what that means. She said to tell you that you're doing fine right here, Scout, and that she loves you very much."

■

The windshield wipers could hardly keep up with the increasing snow fall as the Willises headed back towards the Calvary Road Baptist Church for the afternoon Christmas Eve service. The unveiling of the new altar top at the morning service had been such a resounding success. It was the finest piece of workmanship anyone had ever seen, so full of life and hope. It made him expect a much larger turn out in the afternoon and evening with the word having spread, making everyone want to come out and see it.

"Slowly, Josiah, slowly," Ella Willis cautioned her husband. "If you have another accident, they'll take your license away or drop your insurance or somethin', ol' man.

Then what'll we do?" Bing Crosby's voice came through the radio singing *White Christmas* and she slid over the seat to get closer to him and took her husband by the arm. He looked over and smiled. "Do you remember when we first heard this together?" she asked him, smiling back.

"I sure do, my wife. Dancing at the Christmas Ball in Baltimore, 1965. You wore an emerald green ball gown that showed off your hourglass figure and you had gardenias in your hair like Billie Holiday. Oh, I was the envy of every man there. So proud to be with you, Ella. Ugly, black African me with beautiful, sweet cocoa you. How I managed that I'll never know. I guess I had God on my side even then," Josiah said, remembering how shy he had been around girls back then, never any girl's first pick for anything, just a poor ghetto boy who loved God and wanted to feel equal to something just once in his life. She did that for him.

Her love made him more than equal. It made him a giant in his heart, strong and fearless to try and change the world he lived in, spreading the Word of God to his people so they wouldn't feel so alone. Hell, he even put up with her dang blasted dragon of a Mama just to be with her. Ella squeezed his arm.

"My husband, when I looked in your eyes that very first time when you were waiting for Betty Savage in our dorm, and the things you said to me, I knew I could never do better than to have your heart, black African that you are. And nothing was gonna get in my way, not even my Mama," and she laughed, squeezing his arm tighter. "And I have never once regretted one single minute of it, not one."

"You've made me the man I am, my wife," Josiah said, his eyes getting misty.

"And you have made me the woman I am, my husband," Ella said and started to hum the last strains of *White Christmas* as they drove through the snow.

Almost at the church by then, *White Christmas* ended and the radio announcer's voice came on. "*Next up on our Christmas Eve 'Call In' night, we have a very special request from a*

*young lady to her husband, any version of 'I'll Be Home for Christmas,'
and given the choice, I've got a notion to go with one with a little country
flair for a change, so here we go, folks, Vince Gill's 'I'll Be Home for
Christmas,' from Jane to her husband Michael with love. Merry
Christmas, Michael, wherever you are."* Ella looked at Josiah and
he at her as the music played.

> *I'll be home for Christmas*
> *You can count on me*
> *Please have snow and mistletoe*
> *And presents on the tree*
> *Christmas Eve will find me*
> *Where the love light gleams*
> *I'll be home for Christmas*
> *If only in my dreams*
> *Christmas Eve will find me*
> *Where the love light gleams*
> *I'll be home for Christmas*
> *If only in my dreams*
> *If only in my dreams...*

"The Lord works in mysterious ways, my husband," Ella
Willis said.

"Praise the Lord, my wife," Josiah Willis responded.

■

Carol Arbach was running late and was just about to close the
office at half day for the holiday after she finished going
through the day's mail. She heard the door to Dr. Walsh's
door open and his voice. "Carol, go home already. Whatever
it is can wait until after the holiday. Some things are more
important than work, even ours," he said and pointed to the
picture of a chubby little boy with curly brown hair and dark
brown eyes about eight years old that Carol always kept on
her desk. "Yes, you're right. I know," she said turning to

smile at him. "The man of my house," she said picking up the picture, looking at it adoringly, then setting it back down.

She picked up the next envelope in the pile and saw the return address. She opened it and pulled out a card. "Dr. Walsh!" she called out. A moment later he came back with his coat over his arm. "I think you should see this," she said, handing him the card.

Dr. William Walsh wanted to slap his own head, like he should have had a V-8. With all his training, experience and intuition, he should have seen it coming, but he hadn't. *"He heals me—Is that wrong?"* It had never even occurred to him…Radical Cognitive Bonding with Transference.

It was a photo Christmas card with the picture framed with holly leaf graphics. Michael Golden in his light blue V-necked sweater under a navy blue Carhartt jacket; the twinkle of love in his blue eyes concealing a lingering hint of sadness, his broad smile reading pure *Proud papa.* He was standing with a smiling, bright faced little girl on his hip with his black hair and blue eyes in a navy blue velvet dress with a square white collar. His other hand was on a black leather clad shoulder; James "Jamie" Arnette in his black leather biker jacket over a white tee shirt, the unmistakable sheen of happiness shining in his eyes and an easy sense of new found peace in his wide overbite smile. He was holding a little blonde boy in his lap wearing a straw cowboy hat and overalls and pointing to the camera as the little boy waved.

"Seasons Greetings From Our House To Yours"

The Goldens

On his way out, Dr. Walsh stopped to look at the pictures on his wall, examining them closely, his pale green eyes glistening as they went from face to face; the faces of the doctors, wise, compassionate…gentle, then the faces of the children, sick, injured, afraid, seeing in them the faces of Jamie and Jane Arnette as children, then as adults. He thought about what Michael Golden had said that day in his office about how much he was affected by those pictures. Yes, he was going to fight this monster with everything he had, filled with a renewed sense of determination, for the rest of his life, like a warrior with an angel on his shoulder, and he was going to win.

"I'm here, Doctor, ready to start my new job."

The End

So lately, I've been wonderin'
Who will be there to take my place
When I'm gone, you'll need love
To light the shadows on your face
If a great wave should fall
It would fall upon us all
And between the sand and stone
Could you make it on your own

If I could, then I would
I'll go wherever you will go
Way up high or down low
I'll go wherever you will go

And maybe, I'll find out
The way to make it back someday
To watch you, to guide you
Through the darkest of your days
If a great wave should fall
It would fall upon us all
Well I hope there's someone out there
Who can bring me back to you

Runaway with my heart
Runaway with my hope
Runaway with my love

I know now, just quite how
My life and love might still go on
In your heart and your mind
I'll stay with you for all of time

If I could turn back time
I'll go wherever you will go
If I could make you mine
I'll go wherever you will go

I'll Go Wherever You May Go,
The Calling

Mama, I found someone
Like you said would come along
He's a sight, so unlike
Any man I've known
I was afraid to let him in
'Cause I'm not the trustin kind
But now I'm convinced
That he's heaven sent
And must be out of his mind

Mama, he's crazy
Crazy over me
And in my life is where he says
He always wants to be
I've never been so loved
He beats all I've ever seen
Mama, he's crazy
He's crazy over me

And, Mama, you've always said,
"Better look before you leap"
Maybe so, but here I go
Lettin' my heart lead me.
He thinks I hung the moon and stars
I think he's a livin' dream
Well, there are men
But ones like him
Are few and far between

Mama, He's Crazy,
The Judds

TESTAMENT

■

"My twin bro and me have just turned 18 and people find it weird because he's a guy and I'm a girl and they are amazed at how close we are. When we were 9 years old my brother went to stay with my grandmother while we stayed in the city for a couple of months. One night my father told me that it was quiet, then suddenly I woke up and I wouldn't stop crying; it looked like I was choking but I wasn't. I wouldn't stop crying and I kept trying to reach over to my brother's cot, then my dad realized that something was up so he told my mum to ring up my grandmother to check on my brother. My mum didn't believe but she rang my grandmother and my gran found that my brother (who has asthma), was in his cot, almost choking to death. They rushed my brother to the hospital and he recovered. According to my father, it wasn't until my gran said the ambulance was there that I stopped crying. My brother and I have a bond so strong that nothing can break it. We know what each other is thinking and we know when the other is in trouble. I wouldn't give up being a twin for the world."

Kyle-Twin

■

"Growing up a twin was uncanny. There were times when my brother John seemed to know what I was thinking and he was always finishing my sentences for me. We still had our own lives though, and at 21 I left home and got married.

Three months later I was rushed into hospital to have my appendix removed. Next morning I was amazed at how little pain I'd felt. *'How are you?'* John asked when he visited. *'I'm fabulous,'* I said and then I peered at him. He looked pale and drawn. *'But you don't look so great. What's up?'*

'I had awful stomach cramps last night and kept vomiting,' he replied. *'They only lasted an hour and the doctor said there's nothing wrong. It's a complete mystery.'*

Suddenly a thought hit me. *'What time did you start feeling sick?'* I asked him. *'Nine o'clock,'* he said. *'But that's the exact time I started my operation,'* I cried. *'And it only lasted one hour.'* For a moment we were totally spooked. But we shrugged it off as a coincidence and forgot about it.

Then I became pregnant. I didn't suffer morning sickness and the labour was an easy one. John came to visit me in hospital. Again, he looked as sick as a dog and explained that earlier that morning, he'd been struck with terrible back and stomach pains. *'It was unbearable,'* John added. *'Then, when I found out you were in labor...'* I sat up. *'Are you saying that you suffered my labor pains?'* He nodded. *'Strange, isn't it?'*

After that, we read studies about twins and discovered it wasn't unheard of for one twin to feel the other's pain. *'Please don't have any more children,'* John begged me. *'I can't go through all that again!'*

'Sorry,' I told him as nature took its course and I fell pregnant twice more. I didn't know whether to feel pleased or sorry when, again, it was a breeze for me, but John suffered terribly.

Twenty years passed and I enjoyed excellent health - much to John's relief. Then, one day, he rang and asked if I was feeling ill. *'No,'* I replied. *'Why?'*

'*I've been experiencing hot flushes and nausea,*' he sighed. '*And I'm so moody all the time; I'm driving my mates crazy. The doctors are baffled. Are you sure there's nothing wrong with you?*' I burst out laughing. '*There's an easy explanation,*' I said. '*You're going through my menopause!*' I told him I'd been diagnosed with it the previous month and had been amazed when I'd had only minor symptoms.

For the next few months John's mates had to endure his moods and he had to put up with hot flushes. Fortunately, when I went on hormone replacement therapy, his symptoms eased. Today John lives in Tweed Heads, NSW. He's not married, which is a shame. What other man could understand so well what women have to suffer?"

Linda -Twin

■

"I remember being around 6 years old when a strange accident happened to my twin and me. I was playing softball at a family gathering, while my sister was playing inside with my other cousins. I was pitcher and I pitched the ball to my cousin. When he hit the ball I saw it come directly at my face but there was not time to react. The ball hit me in the nose and I fell to the ground clutching my nose, but felt no pain. Everyone surrounded me and then we heard my sister come crying from inside. Her head was tilted forwards and blood was dripping from her nose. It was like she had been standing in my place. No-one could explain the accident and since then we have had no other experiences similar to that one."

Sharon-Twin

■

"We can be away from each other for years and then we come together and we are still the same; I mean like our sayings, our gestures, laughs and how we speak – it's weird!"

Roman - Twin

■

"Do you find my twin attractive?

As the mother of twin teenage girls I have seen some ugly sights - where poor innocent teenage boys get stumped on the above question. It's a real Catch-22 - they are 'damned if they do and damned if they don't,' as the saying goes. You can see their brains ticking over as they run through the probable consequences of each answer '*No, you are the most beautiful girl in the world but your identical twin is only average,*' somehow lacks believability. On the other hand, saying '*Yes, I find her attractive, too*' leads to further awkward questions. Some brave boys have battled on, trying to be honest, and damn the consequences. They've found themselves forced to admit that if they had met the other twin first, they may well have become involved with her. The very boldest have conceded that yes, they would like to sleep with her sister as well as herself, and even better if it was both together (the ultimate male fantasy - a pair of beautiful young women devoting themselves to his pleasure!) If the tears and/or tantrums haven't started by now, they are sure to follow. Any devoted young man, trying to please his capricious girlfriend and not mortally offend her twin at the same time, learns to walk the minefield around questions like these, or hits the road. Here's a tip for answering that tricky question - try: '*I find your twin attractive because they remind me of you* <grin>'."

Anon

■

"I am a fraternal twin. My twin brother has sadly been gone since 1987. He was hit by a car at age nine and he later died in the hospital. Before he died, he told me that he wasn't going to make it. Ahhh, the twin connection. So when my family went to see him that night before he passed away, I said my goodbyes. I knew it was the end, and I knew I would never see him again.

After his funeral, he came to see me and told me that he was happy that I went to actually say goodbye to him. He does still come to see me once in awhile. At first it was all the time, and it would scare me.

Being nine years old, it would freak me out, anyone, to see someone floating over you when you wake up suddenly in the middle of the night. He occasionally pokes me to wake me. Just to say hi.

But even though he's been gone for nineteen years, we still have that twin connection. It's always been there, and I have a feeling it always will be.

No one knew he was in the womb with me until twelve minutes after I was born. So in a sense I hid him. He was the surprise package, you can say.

One night he broke his arm, just before our last birthday together, and I was at a friend's house and suddenly my arm starting hurting, and my friend asked me what was wrong and I told her that I thought my twin had just broke his arm. When I got home later that evening, I found out I was right."

Becky-Twin

■

"I am not a twin, but I do have a friend that is a twin of another. He and I, one of the twins I was with that I will call Mark, were in store, a video game store to be exact, well his brother who I will call Andy, had gotten in a car accident.

There was no phone call or anything but Mark had suddenly stopped talking in the middle of his sentence. I wasn't sure what was going on in his head, but he had this sudden urge to go to the hospital, saying his brother was hurt.

Well, on the way, I was driving; he just suddenly started to cry. When I asked what was wrong he said he could not *'feel'* his brother anymore. I didn't really understand what he was talking about until we got to the hospital and found out that his brother had died.

I just thought that I should share my experience with a twin before, I was really saddened by the loss of a very good and close friend, all three of use grew up together, but I thought it was amazing how far apart they were and he being able to tell what was going on with his brother.

I'm not sure how the connection between twins works all that well, but it is still amazing."

Christina

■

"My twin brother and I always went to school together from the time we were little. When we began high school we ended up going to different schools. One day as I was leaving school I started to get terrible pains in my nose, the back of my head, around my eyes, and in my ribs.

On my way home I received a phone call to get to the hospital as soon as I could because my brother had gotten beat up in school and the boys did very severe damage. When I arrived at the hospital they informed me that my brother had a shattered nose, broken eye sockets and cheek bones, a fractured skull, and possibly cracked ribs. I couldn't believe what I was hearing. I had felt pain in all the places that my brother did."

Kelly-Twin

∎

Our names are Jack and Jill, like the story book, and we were each other's best friends growing up. When we became teenagers we drifted our own ways. Jack went to the service and I got married. I moved to Okinawa, Japan for three years. Then I came home. Jack moved a 2 1/2 hour drive away from me and we just couldn't seem to get the old bond back.

Then one day I took my boys fishing. I had an extraordinary pain shoot through my left arm. Three places in my arm hurt very badly. I couldn't figure it out as I had done nothing to the arm to make it hurt so. As quickly as the pain came, it left and I forgot about it and just wrote it off as a fluke.

A couple of days later I was talking with my mother on the phone and she told me that Jack had fallen off scaffolding at work and had been injured. Without missing a beat I said, *'He broke his left arm in three places didn't he?*

She said, '*Yes, how did you know that?*' I told her of the incident with my arm a couple of days before and she said we always did have a connection.

Jill-Twin

■

"My twin brother Harry just passed away two weeks ago and I am devastated. We were also married to twin sisters so the bond and connections were extremely close. I loved this guy more than words. I am waiting for some sign he is okay. If anything like that is possible it would be with us because we were extremely close. We even thought alike. I don't think I will get over this."

Frank-Twin

■

"My twin daughters are identical, mirror-image twins. They have always had bodily connections. I used to think it was all a feeling until my husband slammed the eldest twin's poor fingers in the car door. She of course yelped right away and he felt terrible. Her sister yelped, too. We were used to that. What we were NOT expecting was that the younger twin would get a crease across her fingers! That's right: twin A slammed her fingers in the car door and twin B got the crease and the bruises! We have been scratching our heads on that one for years! And since they are mirror image, the twin who got the crease and bruises, got them on the OPPOSITE hand! Go figure!"

Carol

■

"My 4-year-old twin daughter, Lexie, fell off her scooter yesterday, and skinned her face on the sidewalk. Her left nostril was bleeding. She and I were sitting on the front step, while I held a tissue to her nose. My other twin, Bella, was standing in front of us, she said, *'Mom, I have a bloody nose!'* I looked up and her left nostril was bleeding too! I'm still in awe!"

Jenni

■

"At the moment of this writing, my twin brother lay in a hospital bed, diagnosed with severe brain damage and will be taken off life support day after tomorrow.

I have this hole in me I can't fill, but maybe I can share a story in his remembrance. I had a bad car accident back in February 1996 where my head hit the windshield. I was taken to the hospital, my head was stitched up and I sent home.

Later that evening I received a call from my twin brother who lives in another state. Before I had the opportunity to tell him about the accident, he told me he had the worst headache of his life.

I hope to see him on the other side; he will be the first to greet me.

For my twin brother Raymond…"

Richard-Twin

■

"I have a twin sister named Debbie and we are 41 years old. When I was in my twenties I got married and moved away to another state. I would call her on the phone and she would be fixing the exact same dinner I was fixing, right down to the very same time I was cooking.

We each sent our mother a Mother's Day card and it was an identical card. We lived two states away from each other.

Our husbands both have sisters with the same birthday. Our last names are also first names…"

Leanne-Twin

■

"My twin story begins 23 years ago with the birth of our son. My twin sister was unable to have a baby because of infertility problems. I had a difficult pregnancy with gall bladder problems, 3 false labors and giving birth 3 weeks before my due date.

My twin sister was hosting a surprise baby shower for me when I went into labor. She opened my baby gifts while I was on my way to the hospital.

The next day I was induced and my twin was by my side until I delivered and she could feel my pain because she experienced a migraine headache the whole time I was in labor, after the birth of our son, her headache was gone. Our son is very special to his aunt because we have shared him. He had 2 Moms while growing up."

Marcy-Twin

www.ingramcontent.com/pod-product-compliance
Lightning Source LLC
Chambersburg PA
CBHW051526260626
47170CB00003B/801